THE BOXER

By
Peter McInnes

Caestus Books
2001

THE BOXER

By Peter McInnes

PUBLISHED BY CAESTUS BOOKS

Typeset in England by Christine Titchen
and printed by
Antony Rowe Ltd.,
Bumpers Farm,
Chippenham,
Wiltshire,England

First Published 2001
Copyright Peter McInnes

Set in Arial Bold

A catalogue record for this book is available from
The British Library

ISBN 0 9525301 5 5

To

FREDDIE, JACK and GORDON,

**who fought the good fight
with all their might.**

I

London's underground District Line runs at ground level there. If that seems wrong, there are long sections of the underground on the outskirts of the Capital where it runs along on the surface and passengers can look out on the streets. After rain, you can see puddles of water glistening at the kerbs of flat, tarred roads and reflecting passers-by. You can see the flower-pots, too, on window-ledges and fire-escapes and, when it's windy, you can see the hustling folk easing their way along against the blasts, coat-collars up and hats pulled halfway down over their faces. Ladies in stiletto heels have to be way down the course on days like that.

When I alighted at the station carrying my briefcase up the steps to the street, there were cabs on the rank under the structure. The driver of the lead cab was looking at page three of a tabloid which he held against the steering-wheel in front of him. I opened the rear, nearside door and got in; I could see that the driver was perusing THE SUN. He had it folded to the 'page three girl' and the expression on his face smacked of drooling.

"Where to?" the man finally said, putting the paper down carefully and flicking down his charge-flag.

When I told him Denmark Hill he started the motor, eyebrows raised, shoved the gear lever in and made an acute right turn. Up through Vauxhall we went, past Kennington Oval and, soon, the Elephant, on through Camberwell Green and, finally, up the Hill.

Near the crest to our offside stood a big, laid-back house with a crazy-paved path leading to its front door and little stone gnomes on either side to mark the way.

"You know this house?" the driver said as I paid him off.

"No, I don't"

"Well, it's called 'Joggi Villa' and there's a top young fighter lives here; he's challenging for the middleweight title and he's certain to win it. A guy's doing alright lives in one of these houses", he added.

"Keep the change," I said, handing him a tenner.

"Thanks," he said knowingly, adding: "if you ever want to write a real story about a cabbie in your paper, just come and see me. I got plenty!"

1

Ringing the bell I waited until the door was held half ajar on a chain. "Oh," I said. "Mrs. Baker?"

She had one of those round, even, pretty faces and big brown eyes, the white showing very white around them and dark brown hair drawn back and held by I couldn't tell quite what.

"Yes?"

"I'm Frank Cutler," I said. "Teddy said to meet him here about 9.30am."

She was in her late twenties and was wearing a white-and-red-flowered quilted housecoat and red slippers. Her fingernails were painted in the same shade of red.

"Oh," she said, "I think he mentioned something about it." This as she pulled the door back and motioned me in. There was a grey-carpeted hall with carpeted stairs running up one side and the rest of the hall leading back to a kitchen. Off to the left was a square living-room, carpeted like the hall and, after I had put my briefcase down, she led me in there.

"You might as well sit down," she said. "Teddy just got up."

"I'm sorry; I'm early."

"It doesn't make any difference."

She had her hair pulled back in a pony-tail and it was held by a small ribbon of the same red as the housecoat and slippers. She took a cigarette out of a pocket of the housecoat and a lighter followed before I was able to get my own out. Then she sat down on the sofa and pulled the housecoat around her and I sat down in a chair opposite.

"You're the one who's going to write the magazine article about Teddy?"

Her face never moved though I knew it had to open for her to speak. Yet it never moved and she didn't look either at me or through me. It seemed as if she were looking at a pane of glass between us.

"Yes, I'm the one."

"What sort of article are you going to write?"

"Oh, I never know but it'll be a nice one."

"If it's about Teddy it'll have to be a nice one; he's a sweet guy. Please, just don't pull the trigger like some of them like to."

"I'm not a trigger man."

"Let's hope!"

What a placid face for all that suspicion, I thought. The room itself looked smart, with the grey carpeting, modern furniture and the precise folds of the drapes with the woodwork and ceiling a flat, clean white.

"You have a nice home here; it's very pleasant."

"I make it as nice as I can."

"Look," I said, "if it'll put your mind at ease, all I'm going to do is to be around Teddy for the final month and write a feature about how a fighter prepares for, and goes into, a championship fight."

"Oh?"

"I mean, I'm just going to watch Teddy and the people around him, see what he does and listen to what he says. I want to write copy that will give readers an understanding, or anyway a feeling, of what a fighter goes through."

"Do you think people will be interested in that?"

"All I know is that there's a magazine editor who is interested; it was his idea not mine, although I like it."

"Hello," Teddy said.

I had heard him coming downstairs. He was wearing light-grey flannel slacks, Lonsdale trainers and a light check shirt buttoned at the neck. They were tasteful clothes and he fitted into them perfectly. I put it thus because Teddy had a strong neck and shoulders and chest and a narrow waist and small hips. Without knowing him, a person would guess that he was an athlete and only his nose suggested the possibility of a fighting man. Perhaps the heaviness of his brows and one small scar above the left eye also gave a clue. His light brown hair was cropped short back and sides and he had light blue eyes and, when he smiled, they twinkled.

"I see you and Mary have already met," he said after we had shaken hands. "I'm sorry I'm late. How about some breakfast with me?"

"No thanks; I've eaten."

"Have a cup of coffee then while I'm eating. Mary will make coffee."

"It's made," she said.

There was a nook with a window at the table's end and you could see a garage and small yard enclosed by fencing and there was a swing and slide in the yard on which a young boy was playing. He was wearing blue jeans and brown rubber boots, the

3

same colour as his hooded jacket. He looked to be about five years old.

"Teddy junior?"

"That's him," Teddy said, "and he woke me at seven this morning."

"Me too," the wife said.

She was standing by the gas range and was boiling a couple of eggs in a saucepan.

"So I chased him out," Teddy said. "At half-past he was back so I chased him again. When he came back I called to Mary go get him out because I needed to sleep."

"You sleep plenty," the missus said.

"I wanted to slumber some more."

"You slept enough."

Teddy let it drop then, but I thought about it. The great thing he had to sell was his body, for a class fighter's body is one of the wonders of the world. Just think of the things it can do when the mind orders it and, because of these things, it bought the house, the furnishings in it, the clothes they were wearing and the food they were eating. A month from now this man will step into a roped square called a ring and put that body against another man's. Reams will be written and read about this and there will be multi-thousands of pounds involved. Throughout the land thousands of people will watch it in their homes or on big screens in pubs. The goggle-box of TV.

Then, after it's over they will read about it and, if it's a good fight, think about, talk about and argue about it with those who don't agree their opinion. And all of this, I mused, depends on his body so, if he wants to rest it now, for God's sake let him rest it.

"You take sugar and milk?" Teddy said.

I just couldn't fathom that Mary.

II

We drove down and across to Vauxhall Bridge, crossed it, up to Victoria, down the King's Road in Chelsea and along to Earls Court, the sun struggling to peer through the murk of a grey London day which was getting a little warmer. Teddy had a Fiat

Brava, white and three years old and he drove the busy streets as if it were his living.

"Ever been in an accident?" I said.

"What's the matter?" he said, laughing. "Do I make you nervous?"

"Just the opposite; I drive so much myself that I can't put up with most people behind the wheel, but I've learned that most fighters and clergymen are good drivers."

"But some fighters have accidents."

"Sure, old Jack Johnson got killed in one when he was travelling at breakneck speed and Tyson seems to be an absolute glutton for them. And, many years ago, I knew a young teenage welterweight named Johnny Ware who was crushed to death driving a lorry when a tank ran straight over it. But athletes generally have such great reflexes and clerics have such great faith that I feel safe with them."

"I had a bit of a bang a couple of years ago," Teddy said. "Some chap ran straight into the back of me when I was slowing down to stop at a red light for one-way road repairs. I had Mary and the boy with me, taking him to the zoo, and this other guy started yelling and cursing, trying to make out I'd stopped suddenly without warning."

"Did he ever find out who you are?"

"He said he wanted to hit me but, when I showed him my licence, he looked at it and he looked at me; then he said: 'What business are you in?' When I said boxing, he looked at me and said: 'Are you Teddy Baker, the fighter?' I nodded."

"What happened then?"

"Nothing much; he became almost apologetic."

"A good job, too. Our law says a fighter's fists are lethal weapons."

"I know but, in any case, what would I be trying to prove?"

"Nothing. The rest of us have something to achieve by standing up to some slob; a fighter doesn't have that urge because he gets rid of it through being in action That's why I say that, as regards manliness, fighters are just about the best adjusted males in the world."

"I don't know; any fighter is only as good as his last fight and, sometimes, I wish I could've been a P.E. teacher or something."

"You win this one, and you're the Middleweight Champion of the World."

Teddy threaded the car through heavy traffic west to East Sheen, where we stopped at the Derby Arms, landlord of which hostelry was, then, that great old scientific ringmaster Len Harvey, partnered as mine-hostess by his sweet wife, Florence.

It turned out that the ever-beneficent Len had arranged that Teddy should sign autographs on postcard-pictures for a club of handicapped children which the veteran maestro sponsored and, this duty done, we set off again, hitting the M.3 at Chiswick and heading south towards the Guildford exit.

Clearing the big smoke's outskirts and reaching the shimmering green, Teddy suddenly said: "This really is something, isn't it?"

The sun had driven away the haze almost completely and, from the top of the Hog's Back, you could see miles in almost any direction.

"It's a great view," I said.

"I just love it," Teddy said. "Doc brought me here to see it before we decided to set up camp at the Barley Mow and I knew right away it was the right place for me to get ready." Doc Eastlake was his manager.

Changing tack, I said: "What did your old man say when he heard that you wanted to be a fighter?"

"He'd be happy to watch me make a success of anything."

"What did he do for a living?"

"He was a painter and plasterer. But my dad wasn't well and I used to try to help him. Saturdays, and sometimes Sundays, and during school holidays, when I was about fourteen or fifteen. You stand on a scaffold and you plaster all day long and you gotta be strong. It's all about holding that stuff over your head. My father had terrific strong shoulders and arms but he had hardening of the arteries and he used to get dizzy."

"That's pretty awful in itself."

"He'd get so dizzy he'd have to grab out for the wall to keep from falling. Then he'd sit down just holding his head in his hands and I'd tell him to let me do it. So he let me do the rough coat on the walls, but often he'd get up and say that it was not good enough and take over again. Once I had to catch him when he was falling and I had to turn away when he sat down because I

6

was crying. I mean, I was fourteen or fifteen and I was crying like a baby, but I didn't want him to see me crying."

"He must have been a man of real courage, Teddy."

"Sometimes I hear people say that fighters have guts. After some fights I read in the papers about how brave a fighter has been. They've even written that about me. No one seems to understand, you see, and in a way that makes me kind of sad. Know what I mean? After all, what does a pug do that's so great? It's his chosen business and he doesn't even think of the punches coming at him; he doesn't even feel them."

I know, I know, I was thinking, but please don't say it that way. You are balancing the equation between fear and courage; telling me that you don't know the one, so you don't need the other. As I try to climb up to you, I find that, instead, it is to me that you are climbing down.

"What does a fighter do that matches my old man's life? Nobody ever told him that he had guts and no one ever paid much attention to him. Yet he was standing up there every day fighting that dizziness, and all the time he was dying."

He stopped talking and I said nothing. Because I couldn't think of anything to say.

"When I think of my Pa I think of his temper, too. He used to shout at my mother so bad that it made her cry. He used to shout at me and hit me when I was young. Sometimes, after he'd blown up, nobody dare talk in our house for a couple of days. I probably shouldn't say it now, but a lot of the time I used to hate him. We never really got along and I'm ashamed of it now."

"You shouldn't be; it's very understandable."

"Talk about courage," he said. "My Pa had courage."

We were up high now and Teddy said, thoughtfully: "I reckon I'd like to live up here, somewhere."

"You have a nice house," I said, "and what would you do up here?"

"I'm not sure, but I'd like it. Mary wouldn't though; she loves London."

"Where does she come from?"

"My old neighbourhood of Lambeth. We knew each other as kids and her old man still manages a pub around there as licensee."

"How long have you been married?"

"Oh, nearly seven years."

7

"Having seen your home now, I'd say she makes a good job of it."

"I'm not complaining. I've got it so much better than most people, but being married to a fighter is tough on her."

"It must be. What will she do now while you're away for a month training for the big one?"

"Her mother is going to come and stay with her in the house for a few days at a time. She takes care of the boy and that gives Mary a chance to get out and about. She sees some of her old girl friends and they go to a show, or go shopping or go for a meal. It makes a nice break for her, being free of the youngster."

"All youngsters are a problem."

"Our boy is a problem because we're not supposed to let him get too excited. He's a smart little chap and he's got a temper, too, but we're not supposed to slap him or even discipline him too much."

"Who says this?"

"The doctor."

"Oh, has he had medical trouble?"

"He has epilepsy."

"I'm very sorry to hear that."

"About a year ago we discovered it. I came home from the gym one evening and Mary was crying. The kid had had a tantrum or something, and then he fell down kicking and twitching right there on the kitchen floor. Mary called the doctor and he came and gave the little chap something. Then he had tests done which showed he is epileptic, so now we've got to take it very easy with him."

"I'm sure he'll be alright," I said, trying to think of the best way to put it. "Youngsters nearly always grow out if it and they can live a pretty normal life."

"That's exactly what our doctor said."

"I don't think you'll be old enough to remember Paddy Roche, the old Irish middleweight who fought the best in the world all over the place in the 'twenties, 'thirties and early 'forties?"

"No, but I've heard a lot about him and seen his record in the annuals."

"He was an epileptic."

"He really was?"

8

"Certainly; he was very severely struck in his early days. I don't think many folks knew about it and, certainly, the Board of Control never had wind of it. Their doctors never picked up traces of it through all his numerous medical examinations; in fact, before he quit fighting altogether when he was well over forty, he never suffered a single fit but, near the end, he managed to contract a dose of V.D."

"Is he still alive?"

"No, he died sometime in the 'seventies in a mental hospital, where he had been working for years as an assistant nurse since quitting the ring. He must have then been in his mid-seventies."

"I think I remember reading something about it now."

It's extraordinary how the mind works, but for no apparent reason my thoughts switched to the once-wonderful racing car driver Mike Hawthorne, whose father had owned a garage near the Guildford end of the Hog's Back. Mike had died instantly many, many years before when his MK.120 Jag was crushed to smithereens in a terrible accident when golden-locked Mike was having a friendly dice against a friend at breakneck speed. It must have been the place and the vintage air that brought it all back.

Then it came back to me that I had been in the Army and stationed not so far away, at Deepcut, near Aldershot, at the time. All in a flash the wonderful boxing team we had then came back to me: there were Henry Cooper and his brother, George, then there was Joe Erskine, Arthur Howard, Dennis Booty, Nicky Gargano, Derek Glanville and George Whelan among others. They were, of course, all national Service conscripts and so amateur at that time. But, on demob, with the exception of Gargano, they all turned pro', most of them becoming champions and at least two household names. Our 'Enry, in fact, was knighted in the Millennium New Year's Honours list, and thus became boxing's first 'Sir' and official 'Knight of the Roped Arenas.'

Teddy broke the chain of thought with a jolt. "So old Paddy Roche had that too," he said.

"Yes," I replied. "He did indeed."

III

Teddy felt better as soon as we reached the famous old Inn where was to be his training camp. The place is a cross

9

between a roadhouse and a pub; an unexpected setting for those who don't know the place because there are only a few scattered detached houses near it. There's a big lake on the south side and a lot of pine and hemlock way down on that side of the Hog. The hillside rolls right down to the lake, on the other side of which run mainline railway tracks. Most of the concentrated building has been to the west.

About ten years previous, visiting fighters from overseas, most of them imported by the star promoter, Jack Solomons, started using the hostelry's accommodation. The spacious function room was fitted out as a gymnasium, part paid for by the brewery and part by master showman Solomons. After which, during the autumn, winter and spring, name pugs shared the place with the bar trade, occasional diners and elderly men who wanted to get themselves into some sort of shape; usually by losing weight. In July and August, when boxing slows almost to a halt, it becomes a summer diner's resort with extensive three-sided lawn, smallish swimming-pool and kiddies play-area.

"Well, it still looks right," Teddy said as we drove into the spacious car-park in front of the building. "I really like it round here."

"Yes, it's fine," I said, though I was thinking that you had better like it here because you are going to be here for a whole solid month in strict training.

"We can take our bags in later," he said.

The building is painted white, with the windows and door trim coloured red. I suppose this is excusable because the owner's name is Rene Capini and he is Italian. His Irish wife wanted the place renamed 'The Irish Immigrant' but, when they took over the place, they compromised and left the name as it had always been. So it still says 'The Barley Mow' on the big sign at the head of the forecourt, and also big in red letters across the whole front of the building itself.

"Hey, what gives around here, my bon ami?" Teddy said as he spotted Capini in the small foyer. It was purely a gesture, though his pronunciation of French left much to be desired!

"Hello, Teddy," Capini said. "And Mr. Cutler."

It is a small, square lobby with speckled linoleum on the floor and a couple of plastic-covered occasional chairs, a fold-up coffee table and an artificial palm tree. At the back there's a hotel desk with the key-rack behind it. The walls are panelled with doors to the bar and sitting-room on either side, the left one of which takes in the dining-room entrance also. And, immediately inside the front door, against the wall to either side of it, are two phone-booths.

When we entered Capini was leaning against one of the booths watching a telephone repair-man, who was on his knees by the open door of the other booth, putting some tools he had been using back into his bag.

"So what's new, bon ami?" Teddy said.

"He's fixing the phone," Capini said, nodding at the repair man.

"It's fixed," the fellow muttered, looking up," but I'm telling you, Rene, the very next time it happens, out it goes."

"What's the matter with it?" Teddy said.

"I'll tell you what's the matter with it," the workman said, looking round at Teddy. "Some wise guy's been trying to rig it again, thumping on it."

He rose to his feet and turned to Capini.

"I'm not kidding; I'm gonna tell the office. This is the third time and these things just aren't made to be banged around. Once more, and out it comes."

"It'll be the last time," Capini said, nodding.

"Who did it?" Teddy said sotto voce, when the telephone-man had gone and shut the door behind him.

"You guess," Capini answered, shaking his head. He is short and thin and probably in his sixties and, since he quit drinking, he always looks to be in mourning.

"I can't guess," Teddy said. "Who?"

"Your friend," Capini said; "Alf Penny."

"My friend?" Teddy said, smiling. "He's NOT my friend."

"That's a fighter?" Capini blurted, shaking his head again. "He found some way, last time he was here, to hit the coinbox of the phone with something; I don't know what it was but it caused it to make a noise like a twenty-p. was being inserted. I heard him telling a couple of the other fighters how to do it once and I told him to stop it."

"He's cracked," Teddy said, smiling.

"What sort of a fighter can he be?" Capini said sadly. "All the time he is trying to be funny and playing tricks on people. How can a man like that be a fighter?"

11

At least when Capini was drinking he was a champ in a bracket of his own. For a small person he was phenomenal and then, well lubricated, nothing bothered him, not even fighters like Alf Penny. I thought that some doctor must have put the fear of death into him and how too bad that was. Now he is just sad and lonely.

"So you've put me in the Royal suite?" Teddy was saying.

"For a nice fellow like you, anything I have is yours." Capini said. "I mean that, Teddy."

"Thanks. I'm flattered."

"And you too, Mr. Cutler."

"Thank you, Rene."

"Who's here?" Teddy asked. "I mean, besides Penny."

"That heavyweight from Bournemouth who eats like a horse. Killer Cassidy; all he seems to do is eat."

"I expect he's trying to build up his strength," I said, grinning. For some strange reason I find doleful people like Capini amusing and I get an urge to egg them on.

"Yes, strength," Capini said. "soon he'll be so strong that, when he gets knocked cold, it'll take a tractor to haul him back to his corner."

"Who else is here?" Teddy said.

"Strength," Capini was muttering, still thinking about it and shaking his head.

"Is Ceroni here?"

"Yes, he is here."

"Of course he would be, because he fights the week before I do."

"And Harry McCormick; that is all."

"Let's go to the gym," Teddy said to me.

"You don't want to bring your things in now?" Capini said.

"We'll bring everything in later."

"You have the corner room over there, on the pool side," Capini said, pointing upstairs. "And you are across the hall, Mr. Cutler."

"Many thanks."

"When Nat Waller comes, he will use the other bed in your room, Teddy. Is that OK?"

"Of course."

Nat Waller was Teddy's trainer; at least, that was his title. Actually, Doc Eastlake trained Teddy as well as managed him and

12

Waller was the conditioner and rubber and the hand-up pail man in the corner at fights.

"That Capini isn't a bad kind of guy," Teddy said when we walked into the sitting-room. "I can't help but like him."

"But he has his troubles," I said.

At the back of the sitting-room a stairway leads to the upstairs. An old rug covered most of the floor area, and a television set stood facing outwards from the far corner opposite the stairs. Most of the furniture in the room--an old maroon plush sofa and three armchairs with soiled head covers on them plus a couple of wooden folding chairs--was grouped in a sort of semi-circle, facing the television. With the room devoid of humanity, I got the impression that the sofa and chairs had cornered the TV set and were about to spring on it and stifle it in repayment for all the indignities it had heaped upon them in a long, long chain of events long past.

The gym is beyond the sitting-room. It was added to the main building like some afterthought as a flat-roofed dancehall; in fact, it still is a dancehall on Saturday nights during the summer. For the rest of the year, however, it makes an excellent gym, even with a bar there and the tired and dusty gaudy streamers still looped from the ceiling.

As one comes through the doorway the bar is on the left, stripped now of bottles and glassware but used by managers to rest their private flasks and drinking vessels and by trainers to fill their water-bottles. The floor ring stands a few feet away and slightly off right, with two rows of folding chairs on its door side and there is a speedball platform off left with a heavy bag chained from a steelbar roof-hook about ten feet from that. In the far left hand corner, two curtained partitions make a tiny dressing-room and the adjacent loo contains a simple shower unit.

"From Walsall, Staffs!" Teddy said, raising his voice as he approached the ring, "Alf Penny."

Penny was in the ring with Harry McCormick. They were just moving around gently during a break between rounds, just loosening and shadow-boxing, and when Penny heard Teddy he stopped, turned round and smiled. With the thumb of his right glove he hooked his gumshield out.

"Thankew, thankew!" he said, raising his two gloves above his head in the prizefighter's salute. "How are you, Teddy?"

"Time!" yelled a stentorian voice.

13

It was old Sid Brown, standing and leaning over the top ring rope. Sid was an old negro fighter, turned Jehovah Witness. I don't know how old he was then because everyone just called him Sidney. But I remember him fighting thirty years before and it seemed he'd been around forever. I remember his younger brother, Manley, stopping Joe Bugner on the latter's pro' debut as a sixteen yearold, and that was back in the year dot.

He never stopped quoting the old ring maestros, like Len Harvey, Nel Tarleton and Tommy Farr--they did it this way, or that or what they said was.....But no one resented it in the arguments, the way you get to resent old-timers, because he knew as much about boxing as any man alive---even if he was only ever a reasonable eight-rounder himself. He really did, and for years he had been bringing kids up out of the amateurs and then losing them to big-name managers who offered huge signing-on fees. I could name a half-dozen class fighters that he made, in the sense that he was the one who started to draw out the best in them, but some right jerk always managed to move him out. Someone would always get to the kid, and the kid would listen to the con, then look at old Sidney and be gone. They would pay the old 'un a few hundred, maybe, and some of the kids got good purses after that, but they were never the class-draw they should have been because, after they left Brown, they never improved, and I often wonder just how good they might have been.

I used to get very sore about this, and one night I watched a youngster go in a featherweight eliminator and get clobbered by a man he shouldn't have been facing at all at that stage of his career. Walking out of the Albert Hall I saw old Sid standing among the crowd in the main entrance, wearing a dark blue beret rather in the style of the first-ever black British champion, Dick Turpin.

"It's just too bad, Sidney!" I said.

He just shrugged his shoulders and shook his head so I walked on and then, sooner than soon, he had another one. Now he had Harry McCormick.

McCormick was a light-welterweight and one of those light-tan coloured fighters, trading on his reflexes like Ali in his younger day and flash, too.

Now McCormick was stalking Penny, always walking forward, feinting, flicking out left hands, face never changing but always trying to corner Penny by cutting off the ring area. Penny

14

was moving himself, awkward, too tall and gangling for a lightweight; too loose and without real purpose other than to protect himself and punch when he thought he saw a chance. They were both sweating and Penny's had spotted through his T-shirt while Harry's had soaked his tight against that coffee torso. We watched them for a couple of minutes, McCormick stalking and Penny skating.

"I might as well bring my foot-locker in, " Teddy said.

"I'll give you a hand," I replied.

We walked out to the car and Teddy opened the boot. He heaved the heavy black locker out, put it down on the gravel then reached and put his hand on the handle of my suitcase.

"We can take the bags in now, or fetch them later."

"Why don't we shift the locker first?" I said.

"OK."

"What ever made Alf Penny decide to be a fighter?"

"I wish I knew."

"He doesn't look right in the part."

"He's a little better fighter than he looks."

"Even so, he's got no chance."

"I know."

He slammed the boot shut and checked the self-locking. Then we picked up the locker, he at one end and me holding the strap handle at the other, and so we walked to the front door, negotiated our way through it to the gym, across it and into the dressing-room.

Joe Ceroni was in there alone and he was just finishing dressing. He was a good looker, handsome, dark-eyed and dark-haired and with almost classic features. The first time that I saw him fight, I knew that was sure to be his trouble.

"Hello, Joe," Teddy said.

"Hi," Ceroni said, looking at us.

"You know Frank Cutler?"

"I've heard of him," Ceroni said, nodding to me, and then he picked a towel up off one of the benches, put it round his neck and went out.

"Not much of a talker," I said.

"He never says much," Teddy said, looking out of the window at the pool. "Penny calls him Silent Ceroni."

"His face is his problem."

15

"You're telling me. Do you notice how he often pulls his head away when he's in close?"

"I know; he should make up his mind whether he wants to be a fighter or some kind of TV star."

"I reckon you're right."

There is just enough space in that dressing-room for the rubbing table, a couple of benches and a pair of those folding wooden chairs. There are hooks in the partitions for clothes and there's a door leading into the loo. That was there first, of course, so over that door there is one of those rectangular frosted-glass lights with a silhouette on it of a man in top hat and tails, looking as though he might be the brother of that Johnny Walker in the whisky ads. When the place became something of a fight camp and the extension was added, the loo was enlarged just enough to hold a shower.

"Greetings!" a voice said, and it was Jakie Turner. He was a pretty helpless, sallow-skinned raw-boned ex-fighter from Manchester who managed Killer Cassidy. I had seen the two of them, Killer Paul punching the heavy bag and Jakie watching, when we first came into the gym and now he was holding the door open for the Killer who came through it, red-faced and too fleshy and sweating profusely inside a white robe.

"Hiya, Jakie, Paul," Teddy said. "You know Frank Cutler?"

"I know Jake," I said, shaking hands with him, "but I've never met Killer."

"Hello," Cassidy said, extending me a big paw with the bandages and tape still on it, then sitting down on one of the chairs which creaked ominously, sweating and spreading his legs. "God, I'm tired."

"That's what I'm always telling you," Jakie said, working with the scissors to cut the tape on his man's right hand so he could unwind the dirty gym bandages. "You stay in shape, and you won't get so tired."

Cassidy looked up at Teddy, his face red and wet from exertion, and winked.

"He thinks I'm kidding," Turner said pathetically, turning and protesting to me, as if I were the one who was about to solve the problem for him.

"When are you fighting?" Teddy said.

"Oh, in a couple of weeks."

"He's meeting that Scotsman, Ben Shaw, at York Hall."

16

"Are you a manager or something?" Cassidy said, looking up at me puzzled.

"No," I said smiling, "I'm a magazine and newspaper feature writer."

"Oh," he said and then, after a pause: "That's a pretty good job, ain't it?"

"At times; you see, I'm a freelance."

"What you gonna write about up here?"

"Teddy, and how things go as he approaches the big fight."

"Yeah?" he said, and then he glanced across at Teddy. "That's good."

"You're going to write a magazine article about Teddy?" Turner said.

"That's right."

"What are you going to write?" Cassidy said thoughtfully.

"I don't know; I just got here, Killer."

"How would he know what he's going to write?" Jakie Turner said to Cassidy. "How on earth would he know that when he's just got here? Why don't you get undressed and take your shower?"

"Just let me sit awhile, will you Jake?" Cassidy said.

What a pair of fight fraternity, I thought.

IV

Fighters and their entourage eat together at one long table. It is just inside the doorway from the bar and it's also close to the kitchen. There are a few smaller tables spaced around the room, most of them by windows that look out on to green. In the far corners of the room are artificial palm trees, light-faded and dust-greyed, standing in soil-filled wooden casks.

"Is the steak good, Teddy?" Ivy said.

Ivy is Capini's wife. She is a sad-faced, undernourished looking woman, taller than Rene but much less robust. She does the cooking and, with the aid of two or three women who live quite nearby, just about everything else that needs doing: room-cleaning, washing-up and washing clothes; the lot. Capini does the ordering, keeps the books and tends bar.

"It's good," Killer Cassidy said. "I could eat another one."

17

"You could eat anything," Penny said. "Besides, who's asking you?"

"Dunno," Cassidy said with his mouth full of food.

"It's a good steak, Ivy," Teddy said, smiling at her. "Very good."

"For the new champion, Teddy," Ivy said, smiling with him and went back into the kitchen.

Teddy was sitting at the head of the table with Penny on his left and myself on his right. Next sat Cassidy and his manager, and then Harry McCormick and Joe Ceroni with Sid Brown at the bottom end of the table.

"You remember that steak we had in Soho that afternoon, Jakie?" Cassidy said.

"Who'd you ever box in Soho?" Penny queried.

"Can't remember," Cassidy replied and he glanced at his manager. "Who'd I fight?"

"Now, ain't that something?" Turner said, putting his knife and fork down and glancing at me. "He don't remember the guy he fought, but he remembers the steak he ate."

"Well, it was a great steak," Cassidy said, "and I remember that the fight was one of them late night affairs at the Queensberry Club, in Old Compton Street."

"Whatta you want now; good looking?" Penny said.

"Throw me some of that toast, will you?" Ceroni answered.

"Well!" Penny said, tossing a slice of toast. "He talks; the silent one has spoken, Noisy Ceroni."

Sid Brown and McCormick had not been saying much, either. Once in a while Sidney would say something to his man in a low voice, and Harry would apparently answer in a word or two and then they would go back to eating.

"Well," I said. "Old Dumb Dan Morgan used to preach that a heavyweight needs to have only four moves. He has to be able to walk to a table, sit down, pull up his chair and get eating with both hands."

"And he was right," Penny said. "Look at Killer and you're seein' the next heavyweight champion of the world."

"Oh yeah," Turner said, looking at me again. "Morgan thought that was funny, but he didn't handle this guy. This fat slob's eaten a great big hole in my pocket and then some."

18

"Tell him about the great hotel fire, too." Penny said, highly amused.

"So you think that's funny, too," Turner said, looking hard at him. "Some comedian; some Ronnie Corbett."

"Whatever happened?" Teddy said. "What fire."

"This idiot almost burned the place down," Jakie said.

"Who-me?" Penny queried, scratching his jaw. "I was the hero."

"You're a goon," Turner said, then: "You know what he did?"

"Not me," Penny insisted.

"Will somebody please tell us what happened?" Teddy asked, enjoying the whole scene.

"Well, this chump," Turner said nodding towards Penny, "he started a fire in the wastepaper basket in our room-one of those metal waste-bins."

"Me?" Penny said.

"Paul is up there taking a sleep before his workout yesterday."

"That was a workout?" Penny interrupted sarcastically.

"So this birk gets a lot of paper and rubbish in the bin and he sets fire to it. Then he nearly knocks the door down yelling: 'Fire! Fire!' "

"I'm a hero."

"Then, when Paul wakes up and tries to get up, this mutt has tied his shoelaces together. So he can't move his feet."

"And then, gentlemen of the press," Penny said, "I heard these horrible screams so, not even thinking of my own safety, I rushed into the flames, picked up the burning basket and ran out with it. I put it in the shower and I came back and rescued the baby and I returned it to its mother's loving arms."

"Remind me to sleep with my clothes on to-night," I said.

"Right enough," Teddy said, laughing through it.

"This place is all wood," Turner said. "It would go up like nobody's business."

"Just relax," Penny said, "now I've had that practice I'll be on hand to save all you dopes."

"Oh yes," Cassidy said, eating, "you did it alright."

"I did it? Here's a guy wants to take my medal away. Why, I'm the man who saved your appetite for the world. If I hadn't saved you, Killer, you would never eat again. Just think of that."

"But you still did it," said Cassidy, still munching away merrily.

"And they would have buried you six feet under and the worms would have eaten you. What a feast! Boy, what a feast them worms would have had to look forward to."

"This boy's insane," Turner said, nodding towards Penny but talking to me once more. "Believe me, he's not all there at all."

"Our room still smells from that smoke," Cassidy remarked.

"Capini gave him hell," Jakie said. "What'd he tell you?"

"He said that I'm a hero for saving his place," Penny answered. "He told me I'll always be first with him around here, from now on."

After dinner Sid Brown and Harry McCormick went for a walk while Turner, Cassidy and Ceroni went into the sitting-room. When I looked in, they were sitting in front of the television set, watching some news programme. Teddy and Alf Penny were in the bar playing the pinball machine, one of those electrified quadrupeds with lights that flash on and off, a harsh sounding buzzer and a silly voice that tells you exactly what to press next if you want to win. You do it and don't. So great is the variety of these seemingly endless machines, that I never play them because it would be like learning a foreign language and not worth the effort.

"Now strike for here," Penny was saying while Teddy was working it, lights blinking and buzzer sounding. "Let it down here."

"What do you win if you beat this octopus?" I said.

"A big well done from Rene Capini," Penny replied, nodding towards the maestro who was standing behind the bar.

"IF you're drinking," Teddy said, "you get a free shot of whatever you're having. Chumps like us get a few token coins so we can play the thing some more."

"So that proves Capini serves two-bit whisky," Penny said brightly. "Don't it prove that?"

I looked at our host, who shook his head in despair.

"Let's go to a film," Teddy said, watching the last ball roll down and disappear when the racket inside the machine stopped. "What's on?"

"I've seen it," Penny said. "It's called 'This Gun for Hire' and the lead girl in it is terrific."

"That's where that nice vocal number came from, isn't it?" Teddy asked.

" 'Have Gun Will Travel' " Penny said, raising his voice well out of tune and waving his arms about," 'A Knight Without Armour In A Savage Land'."

"Would you like to go?" Teddy asked me.

"Anything you want to do, I'm with you."

"You want to see it again, Alf?"

"I've got nothing else to do, so I'll give you a break."

"Be my guest," Teddy said. "We'll walk."

"You mean you wanna walk?"

"It's only a mile and a half," Teddy said. "I like walking."

"Not me; I'm sorry," Penny said.

"You win," Teddy said. "So to-night I drive, but after this we always walk."

I hadn't seen a film, other than on TV, in years, but this one was a stinker and well fitted its billing of 'Golden Oldie'. It wasn't even in technicolour, but when we came in the girl, Sally Gray, was emitting beauty and elegance while her man, Alan Ladd, had both rugged good looks and character. They were standing in a bedroom with small-flowered wallpaper against pink and fluffy curtains. It evolved that the place was a sort of railway hotel back in the days of steam, and she was saying that suddenly it made her feel all unclean and it wasn't supposed to be that way because it was supposed to be a beautiful romance. That made him angry; he shouted at her and she began to cry.

Needless to say, they made up right there and it gradually became clear that she was married and he was not. He was a transatlantic airline pilot, but she had a young daughter at boarding-school, plus a husband who was older and a Piccadilly department-store head, well-known and often busy outside working-hours heading charity fund-raising drives and hoping some day to be decorated.

It went on and on and, finally, there was Flight 1202. Her husband had to go to Paris on business and she knew her pilot was also flying 1202 and so did not want to go to the airport. She could see, however, that her husband wanted her to see him off and so, while a chauffeur drove them, he suggested that she was a bit run down, dear, and that she should visit her sister in Worcester while he was away.

21

At the terminal at Heathrow the loud-speaker was calling Flight 1202 passengers. Her husband was chattering away and her pilot walked by in his uniform, cap and trench coat carrying a briefcase. He looked at her and she looked at him and her husband went on talking about what he was going to accomplish in Paris. Finally, he kissed her and went through the departure gate.

Next morning she was having coffee and toast when the house-phone went and a voice told her that there was someone to see her from the airline. It took some acting, then, when the visitor told her that the plane had crashed and that her husband had been killed. Tragically there were no survivors, he told her.

When the airline man left, he met a colleague who had been waiting in the lobby, and he remarked how well she had taken the news and what a remarkable woman she was to have concern about the others on board at a time like this.

In the final scene she walked out on to a balcony and the sky was pure blue. Crossing it was a jet liner, silver in the sunlight. She looked up at it and the plane was the last thing you saw and the music swelled into that song number.

"Do you wanna see the beginning?" Penny said when the theatre's house lights came on. "I can tell you the beginning."

"Let's see it," Teddy said. "It can't be too long."

"You want to see it, Frank?"

"Sure, Teddy."

Certainly, I thought, I must see it. I must find out how these two met and why the film got its seemingly pointless title. Well, they met on a south-bound train journey from Durham, where she'd apparently been doing a highly-paid hit job for a person or persons unknown. Unfazed by this and with time on his hands before he was due at the airport, they'd spent the night together at a small hotel in Paddington and that was it. Love.

"That was alright," Teddy said, as the three of us walked up the small main street to his car. "I thought that was quite a good picture."

"How about that wench?" Penny said. "How about a classy piece like that?"

"Did you like the picture, Frank?"

"Sure, it wasn't bad at all."

"Our love is forever," Penny mimicked in rusty alto. "No flighty, transient thing."

Oh yes, probably as forever as the ocean, I thought, and the mountains and the sky have a small cry at no extra charge. That is the trouble with this writing business. I have a right to my ego, everybody has, but no, you must establish what those psychiatrists, psychologists and those social-services people call rapport. Teddy must be made to believe that you like what he likes and that you believe what he believes and then, without realising it, he will believe in you and, thus, you will be able to extract from him all that is within him and your editor won't know what it was like or that it was totally dishonest. He will think that you did it all with clever questions and the word processor or typewriter. Why, he will ask himself, aren't they all so clever?

"How about that apartment that dame lived in behind Park Lane?" Penny said as we drove back. "How would you like to shack up with her there?"

"Stop your silly dreaming," Teddy said.

"Have you ever been in a flat like that, Frank?"

"Yes, once. I had a relation who ran a West End Club with a beautiful flat adjacent to it."

"What was it like?" Penny asked.

Trying to get to sleep that night I lay there a long, long while, thinking what a strange world we live in....

V

His first two days in camp Teddy slept late and just took it easy. After breakfast we would take a walk as we would another after dinner in the evening. The rest of the time he spent playing cards with Jakie Turner, or playing the machines with anyone willing, watching any sport which happened to be showing on television or simply lying on his bed reading the newspapers or some magazine.

"I've found out this is the best way," he said the second afternoon, lying on the bed near the window while I stood looking out at the pool. "I know it's better if I come out two or three days early, get away from the wife and the boy and, you know, relax."

This is a sort of transition period, I was thinking, a kind of lull in which to get ready to prepare and it is, basically, a sound idea.

23

"You know," he said, "it means I can do exactly what I want to do."

"I understand. It's bound to be good for you."

"I couldn't do it before I started coming away to camp. I used to train like a madman every day at the 'Beckett. But now I'm getting older, I like it this way although it means leaving home."

He was only just twenty-nine.

"After a couple of weeks, though," he added, "I start thinking about getting home again."

"Does your wife ever visit you in camp?"

"She has a couple of times. Some friends of ours drove her out; they had a meal, looked around the place and went back home. I phone her two or three times a week. If she's not in, I talk to her mother and find out how the boy is doing."

"How do she and Doc get along?"

"They never meet up these days."

"Does she like Doc?"

"Well, Mary is kind of stand-offish. I mean, she doesn't take to everybody, and she doesn't understand or like the fight business."

"Very few women do."

"You're right of course," Teddy said thoughtfully.

About teatime the next afternoon I saw an old black 1100 in the car park and, when I went down to the bar a few minutes later, Nat Waller was there. He was a medium-sized man, with a craggy, battered face and slightly cauliflowered left ear--trademarks, both. He had boxed as a featherweight forty years before, and he had been Doc Eastlake's first fighting protégé. It said much for his loyalty that he had been with the Doc ever since.

"Hey, Frank Cutler!" he called to me when I came in and then, to the fat man standing at the bar with him: "This is that fellow I was telling you about, the writer."

"Hello, Nat."

"Hello, Frank; this is my friend Percy."

"How do, Percy."

"Nice to meet you, Frank."

"He drove me up here," the trainer remarked. "He's got his big car so he very kindly drove me up."

Percy was perspiring freely. It wasn't particularly warm in the bar but they were supping beer and Percy was just standing there, fat and red-faced and perspiring on his brow, under the eyes, on the end of his nose and in the crevice of his chin.

"What'll you have to drink?" Waller invited.

"Give me some of that Scotch in plain water, Rene."

""This guy is a great writer," Waller said, talking to Percy and to Capini, who was standing behind the bar pouring my drink.

"I know," Capini said, nodding and then putting my drink down in front of me.

"Thanks, Rene," I said, "you've just about saved my life."

"He don't knock people," Waller said to Percy. "He's not like them other writers, always at peoples' throats. He never knocks nobody."

"You mean hardly ever," I grinned.

"He writes for all the big magazines," he went on, still putting on a show for Percy. "All the really big ones."

"Oh yes?" Percy said, seemingly impressed.

"I remember him when he was on the newspaper," Waller said, and then to me : "Don't I remember?"

"Certainly."

"How many years have I known you?"

"I don't rightly know; but far too many."

"What, far too many? You're not so old."

"Well, since I can't seem to get any younger, I hope I get older."

"You think you're gettin' older; how old do you think I am?"

I know exactly, I said to myself. I happen to know that you're sixty-three.

"Oh, I don't know," I said. "I guess about fifty-eight."

"You see," he said excitedly, turning back to Percy. "I don't look it, but I'm sixty-three. He thinks I'm fifty-eight. You see?"

"Er--um," Percy murmured.

"I'm sixty-three," Waller said, turning back to me. " Feel my hard belly; go ahead."

"I believe you."

"Go ahead and feel it."

I felt under his ribs in the front and it was indeed hard.

"Like a rock," he quoth. "Hit me a punch there."

"No. Best have another beer."

25

"I'll have one, but please hit me there. Go ahead; hard."

I pushed a short right hand up into his belly, not hard, but harder than I would want anyone to hit me.

"Harder; go ahead, harder. That was nothin'."

"No, Nat--please."

"You see, though, I'm in good shape, eh? How many mugs my age are in that kind of condition? How many fighters, even, are in that kind of shape to-day?"

"Not too many."

"You see?" he boasted to Percy. "That's from a guy who knows his boxing. What'd I tell you on the way up? I mean about old-time fighters and the fighters about to-day?"

"That's right," Percy said, putting down his glass and wiping his mouth with the back of his hand, then nodding.

"Percy could tell you," Waller intoned to me. "I was tellin' him how we thought nothin' of runnin' ten miles and sparring twenty rounds in the gym."

"Fighters don't think much of that to-day, either," I said tongue in cheek.

"You think I'm kiddin', eh?" Waller enjoined.

""No, I don't."

"I'm not kiddin'. To-day, you tell a fighter to do half that stint and he looks at you like you're crazy. To-day...."

"I know."

""You want the same again, Mr. Cutler?" Capini said.

"Yes, and serve these gentlemen again, too, please."

"Do you know who's the best conditioned fighter in action to-day?" Waller queried.

"I can guess."

"Teddy Baker. Teddy is far and away the fittest fighter in the ring today. You write a story based on that, you'll have a good story because nobody ever wrote like that."

"Well, I'm not exactly here to write a story on conditioning."

"I know; don't I know? You'll get a good story because it'll be about Teddy Baker, the new Middleweight Champion of the World. Isn't that right, Percy?"

"That' right," Percy said, mopping his brow.

"I mean, you'll have an exclusive that will sell a whole lot of them magazines."

"I bet."

26

"Sure, why ever not? I'll tell everybody I know to buy the magazine. Percy'll tell everybody he knows. Right, Percy?"

"Sure. I'd like to read it," Percy agreed.

"See what I mean?" Waller said. "You gonna put me in that story, aren't you?"

""Undoubtedly. I'm going to write about what a boxer goes through going into a big fight and the people around him. You'll just have to be in there, Nat."

"Really?" I could tell you a whole lot of stories you could use. Do you know what I used to do before a fight?"

"No."

"Listen to this, Percy; you too, Rene."

"I've already heard it," Capini said.

He was standing behind the bar with his arms crossed, and when I caught his eye he slowly shook his head.

"Before a fight I used to eat garlic. You know why?"

"I don't have a clue."

"Well, I didn't like to fight at close quarters. You understand? I mean, I could in-fight well enough and I could punch to the stomach in close. But I preferred to move around and box at distance, you know? Everybody knew that; so they used to try to get in close, see? Then I got the idea, eat garlic."

"What gave you the idea?"

"I used to like it anyway; I'm from the East End and Jewish."

"I guessed that. By the way, what's your proper name?"

"You won't put that in the story?"

"I won't, but what is it?"

"Nathaniel. Nat Waller; put that in. Everybody knows me; Nat Waller."

"I've promised."

"So, I fought a man at the old 'Ring, Blackfriars.' You remember Jimmy Ramsey? For a featherweight he was a strong guy, liked to lay on when he had the inside position; I blew a little garlic at him and he pulled out fast. Boy, I had eaten so much garlic that, in the dressing-room, Doc wanted to die. He wouldn't stay with me; he went out into the fresh air then he walked round and round the hall. You ask him, he'll tell you.

"So, the fight finally starts and Ramsey moved inside and I blew a little at him and he pulled out. Later he came in again and I panted in his face again and you shoulda' seen the look he gave

27

me. He says: 'You filthy punk'; he didn't get close again and I beat him easily."

"I like that, Nat," I said, winking at Capini who shook his head more in sorrow than anger.

"I'm not kiddin'. I did that for several fights, maybe six or seven and then, one night in the same hall, I'm in with another guy but somebody must have warned him. I'm loaded knowing he likes to fight inside and he comes tearing in, so I let him have a whole blast but nothing happens. What I don't know, because I can't smell it through eating it myself, is that he is loaded too. The referee steps in to break us and I thought he was going to pass out. He didn't even dare come near us again, and this bum lays all over me. It's a rotten fight and the crowd start booin' and hollerin' for us both to be thrown out."

"If I'm permitted a pun," I said, "you guys really stunk the joint out."

"You're right, but just listen to what happened. The referee complained to the Boxing Board and they stopped me doing it. Said they would take away my licence if I did it again. You wanna use that in your article?"

"Well, I never know exactly what's going in until I settle down to write it, but I appreciate the story."

"I got plenty more, like how I used to tread on a guy's toes when we were inside to bring his head down, then-wham!-a right uppercut would lift him clean off his feet."

"Percy," I said, "how long did it take you to drive down here from the 'big smoke?' "

"How long did it take us?" Waller repeated. "It took us almost two hours; the traffic getting out of town was awful and it's nose to tail on the dual-carriage ways now as well. Every day of the week and Sundays as well. Right, Percy?"

Percy nodded.

"It won't be long before nobody can move anywhere for cars and lorries so you know what they're doin'? You know what they're workin' on now?"

"No, Nat, what?"

"They're workin' on some way man can move in the air."

"I thought the aeroplane was invented some years ago."

"I don't mean like an aeroplane or helicopter. I mean without wings or motors or jet engines. Just walking through the air; you don't think it's possible?"

28

"Anything is possible these days. What about men walking on the moon?"

"I heard about it someplace. They're workin' on some way so that a man's not held to the earth, so he can just walk through the air. I think I read it."

"You mean that they're trying to overcome gravity?"

"Whatever it is, it's supposed to be top secret, but some of the old-timers could do the trick. You know that, don't you?"

"No."

""I mean the real old-timers, like Jesus. Jesus could walk on air, couldn't He?"

"It was written that He walked on the water."

""Water, air. One is as hard as the other, ain't it?"

"O.K., if you say so."

""The thing is, He knew the secret, but He didn't tell no one. Now they're tryin' to find the secret and, when they do, everybody'll be able to go any place. There'll be plenty of room around for everybody, the whole sky and everything."

Poor Capini was shaking his head sadly again.

"Make me another, will you, Rene?" I said.

"Where you goin', Percy?" Waller said.

"I'll back in a minute," Percy said.

"He's a hell of a guy, don't you think?" Nat enthused.

"I expect so, but he talks too much."

"What? He don't talk that much, but he's a hell of a guy, eh? He's got a real good job, too. Did you know that?"

"What does he do?"

"I don't rightly know what he does, but he works for the Electrical Union. It's one of them real good jobs. I've known him for maybe fifteen years and he's never been out of work. He knows some of the high-ups, too. Every year he gets a month's vacation with pay, and him and his wife go off to some place like Majorca or Tenerife, where the weather is always so beautiful. But once, he was tellin' me, he and his wife took their vacation down in Bournemouth."

"Attention, everybody!" Penny said.

He was walking in with Teddy. They shook hands with Waller and Penny asked Capini for a glass of water and the maitre d'hotel handed it to him.

"How do you feel?" Waller asked Teddy.

"Fine."

29

"You'll get into wonderful shape, You'll be in the finest condition of your life and, as I was tellin' Cutler here, he'll have the first exclusive story about the new Middleweight Champion of the World."

"That's great," Teddy said, smiling and winking at me.

"Did you bring any skirt down for us?" Penny said.

"Certainly," Nat replied. "I've got three of them waiting out in the car."

"Our love is forever," Penny sang, throwing his arms about, "no flighty, transient thing."

"Hey, Percy," the trainer said, seeing Percy back supping his beer. "This is Teddy; come and shake hands with Teddy."

"Hi Percy," Teddy greeted him.

"I'm pleased to meet you," Percy said, shaking Teddy's hand limply.

"And this is Alf Penny," Waller went on.

"The uncrowned Lightweight Champion of the World," Penny announced, shaking hands vehemently with Percy.

"I'll crown you!" Teddy commented sarcastically.

"Lookit!" Penny said, letting go of Percy's hand and measuring him up with his eyes. "Take a look at this guy; here's a fellow built like my Killer. How'd you like to spar a couple of rounds with a heavyweight who's down here, Killer Cassidy, no less?"

"No thanks," Percy replied quickly, shaking his head. "Not me."

"Is Cassidy down here?" Waller queried.

"Sure," Teddy said.

"Good. The first few days you can use him as a sparrin' partner."

"I bet this guy can out-eat Cassidy, though," Penny opined, still looking at Percy. How about matching him eating against Cassidy? You like to eat?"

"I love to eat," Percy said.

"Percy wants your autograph," Waller said to Teddy. "Rene, give us one of them cards you've got."

Capini reached behind some glasses to the rear of the bar and handed over a postcard. One side was a photograph of the inn, taken from the pool side.

"Write 'To my friend, Percy,' " Waller said to Teddy. "Then sign it 'Teddy Baker'."

30

"Certainly," Teddy said, putting an arm around Nat's shoulder. "Who's got a pen?"

Without saying anything, Capini handed a pen over to Teddy, who put the card down on the bar and wrote on it, finally waving it to dry the ink.

"You write on it, too," Percy said to Penny.

"Me? Sure I will," Penny purred, and he took the card and began to write on it. 'The uncrowned Lightweight Champion of the World, Alf Penny'. "Don't you ever lose this."

"You put your name on it too," Percy said to me. "Please do."

"Why me? I'm not a fighter."

""Put it on," Waller ordered, "when your story appears in the magazine Percy'll have your signature too. He will be able to show it to people."

"Well, you asked for it," I said.

"Thanks," Percy said when I handed the card back to him. "I'll be right back."

"Where's he goin' now?" Penny said.

"Out with our signatures to forge our names on three cheques," I suggested.

"What him? No way," Nat said. "He's gonna call his wife to tell her he'll be late home."

"What a build the man's got," Penny offered. "He works for the Union."

"Percy's a hell of a guy," Waller said. "You wait 'til Killer sees him; he'll be jealous as sin."

"Wait 'til Cassidy sees him," Penny said. "I'll tell him: 'In ten years you'll look like that'. He'll likely be proud of it. I'll tell Jakie that he should manage this guy too. He'd have the greatest stable of eaters in the world."

"I'll tell you something about that garlic," Waller said confidentially to me. "The night after them fights I couldn't get a bit of skirt, you know? No dame would stay with me, and that's good. A fighter shouldn't go skirting right away after a fight. A fighter gets all wound up; he should unwind easy like. A couple of nights later and it's alright, but not straight after a ring battle."

"You're plumb crazy," Penny said.

31

VI

The morning after Nat Waller arrived, Teddy did his first roadwork. When I was younger and working for the newspaper, I would occasionally go out on the road with fighters. I don't mean that I would try to keep up with them or, necessarily, go all the way with them but, at least now and then, I would rise from my couch when they did and jog maybe a mile or two. Then I would about turn and start walking back until they caught me up on their way back, and I would try to stay with them until we got back to camp.

It used to make me feel as though there were two little men inside my guts, having a tug-of-war with my intestines. Yet I always felt glad after I did it, because it was a way of getting close to the fighters. They would kid me about it and it often became the camp's standard joke and lasted right up to the day of the fight.

"Wake me when you wake Teddy, will you, Nat?" I said to Waller before going to bed.

"Whatever for?"

"I want to get up when he does."

"Hell, I'm gonna get up at six-thirty," Teddy said.

We had been watching TV and already it was ten o'clock. Teddy was standing and stretching while Waller was still seated in one of those old, overstuffed chairs watching a commercial for an electric mixer, though I simply couldn't visualise him ever baking a cake.

"What on earth do you want to get up for?" Waller said, standing up himself when the commercial had finished. "Relax; get a good rest while you're down here. Just sleep and eat and breathe this wonderful air. Make the most of it."

"I haven't anything else to do. I just want to get up when Teddy does, watch him go out and be around when he comes back. That's all."

"Okay, I'll wake you; I wouldn't get up though, if it was me. I'd have a lie in."

"I understand, Frank," Teddy said. "I'll see you in the morning."

When Waller thumped on my door I got up, dressed and went into their room where Waller was mooching around, looking for something on the top of the cluttered dressing-table and on the card table where he had his gauze bandage and tape and two or three bottles, one of which I noticed was Adrenalin. Teddy was sitting on his bed, seemingly oblivious of it all. He had on long woollen underwear and tracksuit trousers, and he was pulling on a pair of heavy army-issue boots though he still looked half asleep.

"Now I bet you wish you had stayed in bed," Waller said, eyeing me.

"Don't worry; I'll feel fine later. How are you, Teddy?"

"I'll let you know later, too," he grinned.

"Let's get a move on," Waller said. He seemed to have found whatever it was he was looking for and he was watching Teddy lacing his boots. He was clad in old chocolate brown trousers, worn shiny at the rear, and a black and orange striped shirt plus, over that, a dark navy-blue zippered jacket with the knitted collar and cuffs showing distinct signs of wear. On his head was perched a blue cap with its peak wrong-way round to the rear and carrying a white C.

"Where'd you get that Chelsea cap?" I asked.

"This?" he said, taking it off and admiring it. "One of them football writers got it for me; I've always followed Chelsea since I was a boy and I used to go to Stamford Bridge a lot. Now I wear it for luck."

"Get off," Teddy said. "You wear it to keep your bald head from showing."

"Yeh, yeh. Let's get goin'."

It was a fine, clean morning. The rising sun had already become almost semi-circular in the east and it was the kind of morning that makes you regret not getting up early more often. When we got outside and I breathed in the clear, still, night-chilled air, it somehow made me think of a drink of mountain spring water.

"As we walked across the forecourt, Teddy was pulling on a heavy old polar-necked sweater over his woollen top and we could see old Sid, Harry McCormick, Ceroni and Penny waiting at the roadside. Sidney was saying something to McCormick and Penny was shying stones across the road and into the hillside while Ceroni was just standing muffled up and with his hands in his trouser pockets.

"I'm ready and willing," Teddy said. " Who's goin' to lead?"

33

"I'll lead," Penny said. "I'll lead us to a nice soft spot where we can all lay down."

"You lead," old Sid said to Teddy.

"Not to-day; this is my first day on the road."

"Then you lead," Brown said to Harry McCormick.

McCormick said nothing, but he walked across the road with Teddy, Penny and Ceroni following him and that was the way they started out. They jogged in a line at an easy pace-- McCormick, Teddy, Penny and Ceroni, at the side of the road running northwards and against oncoming traffic--a golden rule, this last, for safety purposes. They jogged in step, arms moving and bodies swaying together rhythmically. We watched them moving like that, growing ever smaller until they reached the top of the rise and then they disappeared over it.

"They'll be back in forty-five minutes, maybe an hour," Waller said.

"More likely an hour," old Sid said, "the way they jog, walk and sprint".

"It's like I said," Waller said. "In the old days we used to think nothing of goin' ten miles. I was tellin' Frank, here, that."

""They run far enough," Sidney said, "if they run. That Penny, he don't like to run. He likes to walk and talk."

""Teddy'll make 'em run," Waller said. "In a few days Teddy'll get his sea legs and they'll have to run like hell to keep up with him."

"Teddy's a good boy," old Sid averred.

"People think a fight is won in the ring," Waller remarked to me. "You know where a fight is won? Right here, right here on the road and in the gym."

"Yes, I know."

""Not much use talkin' about it," Sidney offered.

"Shush!" Waller said, stopping and pointing. "What's that?"

We had started back to the house but we stopped. What Nat was pointing towards was a small olive-green bird with white-marked brownish wings. It had fluttered to a halt on the top of a rhododendron bush. It was about twenty feet from us, the bird riding up and down on the swaying leaves.

"It might be a goldfinch," I said, "but it isn't."

"It looks a bit like a canary," Waller queried. "Is it a canary?"

34

"See that reddish cap? It's possibly a ruby-crowned kinglet."

"Really?" Waller said

As soon as I offered that, the bird was gone. It took off, the yellow-green of its belly showing when it spread its wings in flight.

"It was a ruby-crowned kinglet. The reason its head was red is that it's either courting or it's got some dispute on with another male."

"So you know about birds?" Waller said, "How do you know that?"

"I don't really know much about birds; I just saw it all in a book by the late Henry Whitng."

"Henry Whiting? You mean the man who used to be a sportswriter?"

"That's right. He used to write a sports column in the old Evening Star."

"I remember the bloke well; he used to cover a lot of boxing years ago."

"That's right. He used to be on a weekly radio programme. You know the one I mean?"

"Sports Scene on Saturday evenings."

"That's the one. One section of it was a panel who answered listeners' questions, and he was red hot as a member of that."

"Was he as good as they made him out to be? I mean, they called him the 'Memory Man' and made him out to be unbeatable."

"Well, Nat, nobody goes around fixing TV or Radio quiz programmes."

"And he knew about birds too, eh? Certain sure, I remember him well."

"Here comes Cassidy now," old Sidney said.

Cassidy and Turner were coming out of the hotel building, Killer had on a grey flannel sweatsuit, the legs held tight elastically around the tops of his shoes. He had a towel around his neck tucked into the partly unzipped neck of his sweatsuit, and Jakie Turner looked small and slim beside him.

"Where is everybody?" Cassidy said when they reached us.

35

"Gone," Waller replied. "They must have gone off five minutes or more. Where have you been?"

"Where's he been?" Jakie said, looking disgusted. "In bed. I woke him at a quarter-past-six. Ten minutes later I come back out of the bathroom and he's fast asleep again."

"I slept well."

"You always sleep good," Turner said.

"If you were to hurry, you might just about catch them guys even now," Waller said. "Teddy ain't gonna take it too hard this his first day."

"Can you really imagine him catchin' them?" Turner said sarcastically.

"Supposin' I don't run today, Jakie? I'll work twice as hard in the gym and run harder tomorrow."

"No chance; you run today."

"I wanted to hit the road with the others; it's not the same runnin' alone."

"Get going. You run. Maybe tomorrow you'll get up when I tell you."

They began walking towards the entrance. We stood there and watched them for a moment, the big heavyweight depressed now and the small-time manager disgusted.

"See what fighters are like today?" Waller said.

"But that ain't a fighter," old Sidney mocked.

"He calls himself a fighter, don't he?" Waller insisted. "I mean he goes into the ring and he gets paid. He pretends he's a fighter, don't he?"

"No use talkin' about him," the old negro yawned.

I went back in, took a shower and shaved. About forty minutes after the runners had set off I looked for Waller and found him in the kitchen, talking to Capini's wife who was busy working and only half-listening. We walked back across the forecourt, where old Sid was waiting by the road. After a little while we saw Harry McCormick come trotting down the slope on our side of the road. Teddy was about a hundred yards behind him with Ceroni right behind Teddy. By the time that pair reached me Penny was just coming into sight.

"You made it too hard on our first day," Waller said. "You'll be stiff."

"Not too bad," Teddy said, taking deep breaths and sweating. "God, Nat, it's less than a month since I fought and I'm in pretty good shape already."

"Well, I think you took it too hard. Wanna bet me?"

In their room the trainer helped Teddy out of his sweater and tossed him a towel. While Teddy sat on his bed, wiping his face and neck, Waller knelt down and took Teddy's heavy boots off. Then Teddy swung his legs up on to the bed and lay back on the pillow.

"Now just take it easy and cool out," Waller said.

"I know, Nat," Teddy acknowledged.

"Well, it doesn't hurt to remind you."

"Who put this here?" Teddy asked.

There was a small white plastic radio on the grey-painted bedside table behind the two beds.

"Rene lent it to you," Waller said. "His wife gave it to me this morning. She says Capini wants you to have it while you're here."

"That's kind," Teddy said, motioning for me to look at the radio. "I was meaning to get one before I came down here, but then got all bogged down with things the last couple of days."

"So Rene likes you," Waller suggested.

"He's a nice guy, isn't he?" Teddy said switching on the radio. "I must remember to thank him; he's alright."

"And you're alright with him, too," Waller said. "You don't give him any trouble and he badly wants you to win this fight."

"And so say all of us," Teddy agreed.

Teddy turned the radio on to a station where the announcer was just finishing reading the news and then a disc-jockey took over playing record requests. While Teddy lay there relaxing and cooling off, Waller went downstairs and in about five minutes he came back, carrying a cup of steaming hot tea with lemon but no milk in it. Teddy sipped away at that slowly, and then he waited some ten further minutes before he doffed his road clothes and took a shower.

"How frequently do you shave when you're in training?" I said when he came back.

"Every other day," he replied, "then I prefer to shave at night just before I go to bed. I mean, on the days I shave, of course."

"That's so his face won't get sore if he boxes that next day," Waller reasoned. "You understand, in strict training you've got to do everything with a reason. You don't just do things, you have to have a real reason."

"I understand, Nat," I said.

We went down to the dining-room, where the fighters and Turner and old Sid were having breakfast at the long table The room was bright now, with the sun pouring through the window on to the white tablecloths.

"Seems Paul made it," Teddy said, looking at Cassidy and winking at Jakie.

"Are you surprised?" Turner said. "He makes all the meals; never been known to miss."

"What?" Cassidy said, loading his spoon in his second soft-boiled egg.

"Nothing," Penny murmured. "don't let nothing bother you. Just eat."

"Pass me that sugar-bowl, will you, Alf?" Teddy said.

After his near-pint of orange juice, Teddy downed a bowl of dry cereal with half a banana and cream on it. Then he had two soft-boiled eggs with toast and a cup of milkless tea. When he had finished we walked out through the bar into the lobby, where Capini was standing behind the high hotel reception desk, leaning on it and reading a morning tabloid.

"Rene," Teddy called.

"Yes, Teddy, what is it?"

"I want to thank you, bon ami, for lending me that little radio."

"Pleased to do so."

"Yes, but I appreciate it."

"It's only for you I'd do it. Those other fighters I wouldn't do anything for."

"Thanks anyway."

"I mean it, Teddy," Capini insisted, and then he shrugged his shoulders and I could see that he was embarrassed. "I've got the morning papers here, if you'd like to read them."

"Thanks", Teddy said. "I was going to drive into town for them."

That afternoon Teddy used the gym. With Waller hovering around him with a towel over his shoulder and talking at him the

38

while, he exercised on the mat, skipped rope and shadow-boxed four rounds.

VII

"Who fancies an outing to the flicks?" Penny suggested.

We were finishing dinner. Teddy, Cassidy and Ceroni were still downing their stewed fruit while we had been listening to Waller. He had been telling us about a friend who had bought a chicken farm down in Hampshire, and the way Nat told it, the place was a paradise in which only the chickens worked.

"What's on?" Teddy wondered.

" 'Eight Belles' " Penny replied. "It's supposed to be good; it's about the Navy and it's one of them musicals."

I had noticed a big review of it in one of the Sunday papers and it seemed to be about as much about the Navy as 'Lady Chatterley's Lover' was like the 'Bells of St. Mary's'.

"I'll go," Cassidy said.

"How about you, Jakie?"

"If he goes I've gotta go."

"Don't you trust him, then?"

"Oh, I trust him. I trust him to call in at MacDonald's later, eat three or four beefburgers and drink two or three cokes."

"Do you want to go?" Waller asked Teddy.

"No thanks."

"What's the matter?"

"Nothing. I just want to have a good walk and then go to bed early."

"Then I won't go," Waller said.

"Go ahead, Nat," I said. "I'll walk with Teddy."

"I don't know."

"Go ahead," Teddy said. "It'll be nice to have Frank walk with me."

"I'd like to see it," Waller said pensively. "I was in the Navy myself."

"It's not that kind of a Navy," I said.

"You were in the Navy?" Penny said askance. "What Navy?"

"Whatta you mean, what Navy?"

"What war?"

"The World War."

"It must have been some war!"

"We won it, didn't we? I could tell you some things about life in the Navy; but you just wouldn't understand."

"Did you kill any Germans, Nat? Or were you just floppin' around on board some man o'war with some of those pretty WRENS?"

""He was in the Portsmouth Navy Yard," Teddy said. "Right, Nat?"

""He sure was some admiral," Penny interrupted.

"Do you want to go?" Waller said to Ceroni.

"I'm not sure."

"Come on, Joe," Penny urged. "Let's live it up."

"All right," Ceroni agreed.

"You had it pretty good, eh, Nat?" Penny said. "You worked in the Portsmouth Navy Yard and lived nearby going, no doubt, up to London every weekend. Did you get any medals?"

"I lived in Brixton then," Waller offered.

"You lived in Brixton?" Penny said.

I looked at old Sidney and McCormick at the end of the table. Sid had already stood up and Harry was getting up, but it was near impossible to tell how much of the table talk either of them followed anyway.

"Sure," Waller said. "It was still mostly white in them days. There weren't many coloured folk in Brixton."

"Get off," Penny said.

"Ain't that right?" Waller said, turning for confirmation to the old coloured ex-fighter.

"What?" Sid said, for they had started to walk away from the table.

"I was sayin' that, when I used to live in Brixton years ago, it was nearly all white folk lived there. Ain't that right?"

"That's right," Sidney said, nodding once.

"Is that right?" Penny accepted. "I never knew that."

"There's a lot of things you don't know," Waller said. "I could tell you a lot of things you don't know."

"Don't bother yourself," Penny said.

Teddy and Penny played a couple of games on the pin-ball machine and, when the others were ready to leave, Teddy herded them out to the lobby. He handed the car keys to Penny, but

Waller positively grabbed them out of Penny's hand and gave them to Turner. Thus they left, arguing.

Together, Teddy and I went upstairs and I got a jacket and went into Teddy's room where he was in the process of donning a new light-tan windbreaker. I think if he had worn a straight-jacket he would have looked good in it, but perhaps that is merely the way that Teddy seemed to me. I mean, the perfect proportions of his body and the skills trained into it would still, in my mind's eye, have been present underneath anything, in the way the art of one or two great writers I have idolised has made even what were called their weakest efforts seem, to me, for that same precise reason, excellent.

"We'll walk about a mile," Teddy said, "and then turn around and head back. Alright with you?"

"That's fine with me."

It had been a beautiful sunny day, but now the sky was clouding over and a faint mist was intruding. We walked across the road and started toward Guildford, walking side by side until a car would come bearing down on us. Then we would press on single file as the vehicle sprayed the bushes, the road and then us with its lights and its noise as it rushed by.

"When I used to walk with Downes," I remarked, "he used to challenge the cars."

"He used to what?"

"He'd stop in the road and spread his feet and shake his fist at cars, cursing them to force them to steer around him. It used to scare the hell out of me."

"He'd never let them hit him, surely?"

"Of course not, but it used to worry me anyway. It would be before some big fight with thousands of pounds in the till from ticket sales already, not to mention TV and Radio fees already contracted. I used to think how the promoters would die if they could see it; some nameless guy in the dusk bearing down on the great Terry at breakneck speed, unknowingly heading towards possible infamy."

"Terry was a character. Why do you think he did it?"

"I don't know. Maybe because he just had to be the one in command in all circumstances. Maybe in revolt against training or, yet again, maybe he just resented someone driving along in comfort, whereas he had to sweat his guts out, even though he

41

would shortly be paid some six-figure sum in purse money for one evening's work."

"Maybe, but he always was a real character."

"Do you mind the roadwork and the walking, such as this?"

"No, not any more. I used to, but I really quite enjoy it now."

"Do you know what it was that changed your mind?"

"When I turned pro' I was a real eager kid. Good fighters were my heroes then and I did everything Doc told me. Then, after a while, it got to be, you know, routine."

"After you won a few fights?"

"That's right. I don't mean that I got cocky, but you know how it is, don't you?"

"Doc would never allow you to get cocky!"

"You can say that again."

"So what made you accept the training?"

"That's a good way of putting it--accept. That's exactly what you have to do. You have a few tough fights where you don't think you will be able to rise from your stool after eight rounds. I think that does something to the way you look at it all."

"It doesn't do that for some fighters."

"Well, it did for me. Maybe you remember that, at one time, Doc fed me couple of those tough ones right in a row That did it; at least, I think that's what did it. It gets stuck in your mind."

"What made you decide to be a fighter?"

"Mostly the idea of getting big money, I suppose, the sort I could never hope to see any other way. But I always liked to fight. Ours was a pretty tough neighbourhood across the water in the east, and we used to have street fights. We had a gang, and there was this kid, Ray. He was a bit older and kind of the leader and he and I used to control everybody. I don't quite know why, but we just did and I just liked it."

"Did you have a temper then?"

"Sure, like my pa. As I told you, he used to get real mad at me, and at my mother and make her cry. I'm not saying that he was a bad man and, afterwards, I could see it made him feel pretty lousy himself. He just had a hot temper, and even before he died I had made up my mind I wasn't going to get that way. Then I started boxing."

"How did you actually come to start?"

"Mind, here comes a car."

We stepped off the ashfelt road and waited this time. The car was probably doing fifty but, standing as close to the road as we were, with me feeling naked in its lights and resenting it, it seemed to be going much faster as it sped by.

"Whush," Teddy imitated its speeding sound.

"How'd you begin fighting?"

"In the Boys' Club, then in ABA clubs' tournaments. Like I told you, there was this geezer who, sort of unofficially, led our gang, Ray. You'll meet him; he always comes up for a day when I'm training away here. Now he runs half the newspaper stands around St. Paul's and Lambeth. He's a good guy but he's as wide as the Thames. He used to train me in the gym and handle me at shows Then, when we decided that I should turn pro', he still handled me. Doc bought him out.

""What'd he pay him--do you remember?"

"A lot of lolly; he gave him five hundred in notes. They came to the agreement on a street corner in Shaftesbury Avenue opposite the bottom end of Great Windmill Street, where Solomons had his gym. There had been a big-fight weigh-in at Solomons place about an hour earlier which explains the meeting-place."

"That must have seemed a lot of money then."

"It sure was and it was a big break for me. I'd had four bouts and got thirty quid each for the first three; for the fourth it was forty-five. That fourth one was out at Watford Town Hall. Doc was there and he must have seen something about me that he liked. I don't know what it was."

"It was what you are now, and he spotted it way back then."

"I reckon that's right."

"I don't suppose Ray knew much about training or managing?"

"Ray? No, he's just a great guy. Besides, after Doc took me over, he had me in the gym for nine months. I mean, before he let me have another fight. I know he turned down a lot of offers of work but, believe me, in those nine months I found out how little I knew about fighting."

"I can believe that."

43

"Any pro' who thinks he knows how to box should spend half-an-hour in the gym with Doc. He'd soon bring the boy to his senses."

"There's nobody else like him."

"The man's a genius. I was scared of him, too. I was just a kid and the night he came to our flat to pay Ray, meet my mother and sign contracts we were all sitting at the kitchen table. He said to me; 'Look, if I take you I'm the boss.' I said: 'Yes, sir' and he said: 'I mean that. If you don't like the idea, say so and I'll get out right now. Otherwise, you do what I tell you the way I tell you. You can ask questions, but when I give you the answers, that's it. I don't like arguments. I'll tell you when you're fightin', who you're fightin' and where you're fightin'. You just do the trainin' and the fightin'; I'll do the rest.' Then he said: 'That is after you learn how to fight.'

"I thought I knew something about fighting. I figured that I'd show this chap. I must have been very cocky but, for nine months, he had me in the gym without a single fight. 'Step here move there, the foot nearer the place you want to go goes first, always the same distance between feet to give stable balance. Elbows in, chin down, always work for the inside position when in close. Stop! What are you tryin' to do, make me out a liar?' That's always his great saying when you don't do something his way. He looks you right in the eye and kind of snarls it at you and he makes you feel ever so small and useless."

"What were you doing for money without any fights?"

"He was giving me twenty-five quid a week, most of it for my mother and I always ate my main meal with him so he could keep an eye on what I ate and talk boxing to me, too. He really filled me full of boxing."

"A lot of people don't realise that about a good manager All they know is that he's taking 25% out of the purses which can be a lot of money if the fighter makes it."

"Yeah, but suppose I quit? Where would he be then for the five hundred and the twenty-five quid a week and the expenses? Many's the time I've thought about quitting, too."

"Seriously?"

"To be honest, I don't really know. I'd finish working in the gym some days and I'd begin thinking about giving it all up. I mean, probably Doc would have been at me and at me. I couldn't seem to get things right and I was hating him and the very sight of the gym."

"I can believe it."

"But what else cold I do?"

"That's what makes top fighters. The ones who can do something else easier and better do it--or should do it."

"What could I do? I quit school as soon as I could and I didn't want that plastering, like my old man did it. You look at the boys from my neighbourhood; good blokes but what kind of future did they have? If they were lucky, working a betting-shop, cleaning the streets, working on a dustcart, tending bar, porter in an hotel but, most likely of all, drawing dole money and turning to thieving. So what could I do? I certainly don't want any of those things."

"Oh, I don't know. I think there must be any number of things a personable young man like you could do."

"Maybe. If I win the title I can always trade on that. There's Public Relations, being a brewery representative and starring on TV advertising is well on its way in now. If I make real money with the title, I might invest in property. Look at Henry Cooper; he's a big noise with Lloyd's on the Stock Exchange now, and he never won a world title. What could I do, though, when I was just a kid starting out?"

"Not much, I'll admit."

"There's nothing else for you, so you don't pack it all in."

"When did you stop thinking about giving up?"

"All of a sudden things start to come right for you," he said, stopping and gesturing with his hands. "Doc keeps telling you: 'Do this, do that. Throw the hook like this with your elbow raised, throw the combinations I've shown you, then cut off the ring for the opponent like this.' It doesn't really mean much to you because you don't really understand it. So he gets you a few fights and you try your best and you win yet you still don't feel good. You'd rather fight your own way. Then, all of a sudden--I remember the particular fight--you try something and it works, so you try something else and that works, too. It's like pieces of a jigsaw puzzle and, all of a sudden, everything fits into place. For I don't know what reason a door swings open and you see the meaning of everything."

"I know what you mean; it's the same with a lot of things. Jim Laker, who used to bowl marvellous spin for Surrey and

England, once told me about learning to bowl his kind of stuff, flight and pace variation and all that, and what a great feeling it was when it all came to him. That was the year he routed the Australians in the final Test at the Oval.

"The feeling is extraordinary. In a moment or two the mist disappears and all become clear. Your mind tells you what to do and when that happens it's the most wonderful feeling. I can't explain it, but really it's something I think I'll only feel that once."

"I know. Yet I think, Teddy, that everyone, no matter what he or she does, has felt that way at sometime. Perhaps it's why we all go on."

"Then Doc takes you down," he said, laughing. "He gives you that sourpuss look, shakes his head and goes at you again."

"But he knew it, also, the moment you found it. He enjoyed it as much as you did."

"Mebbe, but he'd never let me know. Two days later in the gym he's showing you something else, just as tough to master, but now you go along with it without question."

"As you said, a great man."

"You wouldn't believe it, but I think I want to win the title as much for him as for myself."

"I can believe it. At his age he won't be up there again. He won't have another contender like you. If he doesn't make it now, he never will."

"He'll make it this time," Teddy said. "I'm sure I can beat this guy, just as certain a we're walking here."

VIII

Two days later, shortly before midday, Doc Eastlake arrived, cantankerous, vehement and vindictive, with every reason to be all of these things, and the best man to handle a fighter that I have ever known. I have known many who led their fighters to titles, for all these accolades mean nowadays, and some who took them right to the end of the rainbow. I have learned, however, that Destiny distributes the passes to these places and I keep telling myself, trying to believe it, that really it is not important how far you go but how you make the trip. Doc always paid his own passage.

46

"So you really think so, do you?" Doc was saying to Rene Capini when I walked into the lobby.

He was white-haired and bespectacled now, tall and thin, neatly dressed in a dark blue suit and, somehow, emitting an intimation of another time and of matters legal rather than fistic. He was standing at the desk while Capini stood behind it, and off to one side, standing next to an old black suitcase, Mickey Evans was waiting. He was a six-rounder, who, in a dozen or so years in which he must have lost by far the best part of his eighty or ninety fights, had appeared in most of the towns in England which still purveyed small-time boxing. Winning or losing, he never failed to give a good show and he was what, in trade parlance, is known as a 'journeyman'.

"I don't know," Capini was saying and he shrugged his shoulders. "Teddy is a good fighter and such a nice boy. He never causes no trouble. He has manners."

"Isn't that nice?" Doc said, nodding. "What do you think this is, a popularity contest where the judges give four points for neatness and four more for being kind to his mother? Ah Rene, you stick to your maitre d'-ing."

"I still don't know," Capini hedged.

"Hello Doctor," I greeted.

"Hello Frank," he replied, turning and shaking my hand. "How long have you been here?"

"Seems like all my life. Almost a week."

"I warned you."

"I already knew."

"You know Mickey Evans?"

"Hello Mick," I said and we shook hands. He was a stocky, short-armed welterweight with the story of his ring wars written over his eyes and under them and across his flattened nose.

"Glad to know you," he said.

"Capini, tell him where he sleeps," Doc said, and then to Evans: "You can take the bag up; Nat Waller's around somewhere."

"O.K."

"You have room four," Capini said. "You go to the top of the stairs, then turn right."

Evans went into the sitting-room, carrying his case.

"He's going to work with Teddy?" I said.

47

"Aah," Doc said. "What can you do? You go to the Beckett and there's nothing there. He'll have to do for a while."

"At least it's a living."

"Isn't that dreadful? There's a fella should have been talked out of it after a year. Instead, he goes all over the place getting his brains scrambled. Dreadful; he's just an opponent for the big noises who have proteges to feed. At least he won't get hurt sparring down here."

"What do you pay him, if I may ask?"

"Fifteen quid a day plus his keep. For him it's a break. Next week I've got Lefty 'Satan' Flynn coming down. You know Lefty?"

"I certainly do."

"Well, he's well over the hill but he's still got the brain. Rene?"

"Yes, Mister Doc?"

"Come in and give us some lubrication will you?"

It was too early in the day for me, and I don't think Doc really wanted to drink, either. I think he just wanted to talk.

"How'd you get here?" I wondered.

"My nephew. Thirty years old with a college degree, a wife and two kids and a good job in a chemical factory. Now he says he wants to manage a fighter."

"That's your fault".

"My fault? It's my fault I put him through college."

Doc had an academic year at Magdalene, Cambridge, himself before he quit book learning. That's why the fight fraternity gave him the Honorary Degree of Doctor.

"When did he catch fight fever?"

"He was just a kid, running round the streets of Walworth. I had Dave McCleave then. You remember him?"

"You know that."

"I'm getting old."

"What about Dave McCleave?"

"He used to train in Joe Bloom's academy off the Charing Cross Road."

"I remember it all so well."

"I used to take the kid there every day for three weeks to watch him work and see that wonderful left hand. Great idea; he shadowed McCleave like a dog might. Dave made a mascot of him, let him walk with him, shape up with him, even bought him

48

ice-cream. He bought the youngster a pair of fight gloves and he never got over it."

"I can understand that."

"So, he wanted to be a fighter; that's why I pulled strings to get him to college. I said: 'I'm promising you, Billy, if I hear of you pulling on a pair of boxing gloves I'll hit you on the head with a cricket bat and I'm not kidding.' I'd have done it, too."

"I don't doubt it, but there was always that tiny chance he could have made it."

"Oh, if he could have been a good fighter I'd have let him. Don't you realise that? But he couldn't have made it and this is the worst business in the world for amateurs; they're liable to get killed. How many fighters do you think I've refused to handle in forty years?"

"Probably dozens."

"Dozens? I'll bet I've turned down a hundred. I say: 'Look, son, you can't make it. Be a mediocre plumber and you won't get hurt and, what's more, you'll make a living. Be a mediocre fighter and you may get permanently injured or even killed.' So the kid goes away hating me and he goes to somebody else. Possibly he's a better fighter because he hates me. He's gonna show that Doc Eastlake, but that doesn't make him a fighter. Nothing on God's earth can make him a fighter. The kid goes to one of those rich slobs who gets one of those amateurs with a towel over his shoulder to train him. He gets his brains scrambled. There's maybe fifteen thousand professional boxers in the world today. You know how many of them really belong in it?"

"You tell me."

"About two hundred; maybe less than two hundred."

"It's that way in most walks of life."

"Hiya, Doc!" It was Jakie Turner. He walked straight up to Doc and pumped his hand, smiling for the first time since I had been there.

"Hello, Jake," Doc answered the greeting. "How are you?"

"Alright. I'm glad to see you; you're going to win the undisputed title, eh?"

"How's your fighter?"

"My fellow?" he said quietly. "You tell me; he don't want to train; he don't want to do nothin' he should do. The way the heavyweight division is today I tell him: 'Look, you're in with a

49

chance. Do what I tell you to do. Please do me a favour, will you?'
But it's useless; all he wants to do is eat and sleep."

"Dear me," Doc said.

"Teddy can work with him, if you want it. I mean, my guy's
big enough. He'll just move around and Teddy can throw them in
there, if you want it."

"Thanks, Jakie, I'll let you know."

"Anything I can do, Doc. You just tell me what I can do
with my fighter. What the hell can I do with him?"

"I understand, Jakie."

"I'll see you later."

"What can he do with him?" Doc cracked when Turner had
left and then he mimicked him. " 'Please do me a favour; do what I
ask you.' Can you imagine asking a fighter to do you a favour? Do
what he asks him? Ask a fighter nothing; tell him. You know what
he should do with that Cassidy?"

"I could make several suggestions."

"That's no fighter and that's no manager, either. Dreadful."

He had a way of sliding the word out, as if it were a
product of pain. His face would narrow and his eyes would grow
smaller and sharper and he would slowly spit out the word.

"How ever did he get in the business?" I said.

"I don't know He couldn't manage a public loo, but they all
think they can manage a fighter. The Board doesn't care how he
got in, so nor do I."

"You should and I do."

"How do they all get in? A kid is a street fighter and he's
got a pal. The kid boxes in the amateurs and his pal goes into the
corner with him. The kid wins a dozen fights and wants, naturally,
to turn pro' and make money through his fists. So he brings his
pal along and his pal's gonna train him, maybe even manage him.
They're old friends and it's a beautiful thing. The kid has a half-a-
dozen fights and gets flattened. He quits; but does his pal quit?
Oh no, of course not. He's a trainer now and he's up in the gym.
He's got a towel over his shoulder and he's licensed so he's in for
life. Some innocent-looking youngster comes walking in and
wants to be a fighter. Now he's got another fighter. Now he's got
another fighter and he's gonna be a big cheese."

"You make it sound real."

"Do you really think that I'm making this up? Most trainers
know nothing about training; they're rubbers, valets. They've got

a towel, a bucket and a lot of gall. Dreadful." Only this time he spat the word out letter by letter.

"What can you do about it?"

"Do? Nothing. All you need to be a trainer or manager is the gift of the gab so you can impress an Area Council and the money to pay for a licence. This entitles some bum to ruin a boy's life, maybe even end it. You know this Alf Penny who's down here?"

"I can hardly help but know him."

"Do you know who manages him?"

"No."

"A man called Burt from Hertford."

"I don't know him."

"Of course not. Guess what he does for a living?"

"I should think he's probably some kind of bookmaker."

"Wrong."

"Alright, he's probably one of the big men in the microchip racket."

"He's a manufacturer and he's worth millions. Wherever he goes, though, somebody says: 'Who's that?' Somebody else says: 'Burt and he's got real money.' The first guy says: 'What's he do?' The other mug says: 'He makes falsies.' He could make ten million and they'd still goggle. So poor Burt is gonna manage a few good fighters now. Then they'll say: 'There goes Burt who manages fighters.' Isn't that something?"

"It has never even occurred to me to wonder who it is that manufactures falsies."

"Try and figure what he's doing in boxing."

"I pass."

"He's still sending out falsies into the pits of punishment, as the newspapers dub a boxing ring."

"It's both pathetic and tragic. There are a couple of people down here, Rene, and Jakie, who would prefer Burt's product to his pugilist."

"They're right, but Burt is staking him. Puts him up here, pays his bills. Lets him work with old Sidney's fighter and gets him a fight when he can. Buys a hundred ringside tickets and gives them to his friends."

"And teaches him nothing."

51

"They ought to teach him to throw his protector, his ring boots, his shorts and his gumshield into the dustbin and thumb a lift home."

"Speaking of lifts, where's that nephew who brought you down? Talking with Teddy?"

"He should be almost home by now."

"Are you kidding?"

"I didn't even let him get out of the car. I gave him two ringside briefs to the fight and I said: 'Turn this machine around and start heading for home.' "

"You're a hard man, Doc."

"I told him once; 'Look at yourself and look at me.' He put in four years in that lab and now they've got him in the front office. I said: 'In ten years, with your ability, you can own a piece of that place. What have I got? Forty-three years in the fight business and what have I got? Let's say I started out selling cars. By now I'd have a Ford agency or somesuch. I'd have a manager and I'd have salesmen, mechanics as well. I'd sit back and, in the winter, I'd fly off to Bermuda for a month. In the summer I'd settle for Europe.' And he wants to manage a fighter."

"I wouldn't mind managing a fighter like Teddy Baker myself."

"Not to-day. With television you've got no chance. You're not a manager, you're an agent. They dictate who you have to fight, where you're gonna fight and when you have to fight."

Doc had a name for Teddy. Person to person he called him Edward, but to others he always referred to him as the pro.

"Suppose the pro gets licked," he said. "In the old days you could get him bouts all over the country and gradually bring him back. People out in the sticks never saw him before. To-day, if an up-and-comer gets licked, he gets licked in front of the whole country, millions of folk drooling in front of their goggle-boxes. So, where are you gonna take him? They'll all say: 'But we watched him get licked in his last fight on TV.' D'you fancy another drink?"

"I'll have one more, if we can find Capini."

Doc walked out to the lobby and came back with our host, who mixed the drinks and stood listening now.

"Television, uh!" Doc said. "Four weeks ago my pro is in Harringay. Twelve million people see it, and we get decently paid for that but only ten-percent of a very poor gate. In the old days we'd have packed that huge hall and come away with twenty-five percent plus a guaranteed minimum at least. You put nine years of your life into a fighter and the payoff is you're a showcase to the nation, and perhaps most of the world, for salted peanuts."

"That's what people call progress."

"Progress? Did you read that story in the morning papers after the fight, about the man who lives off the King's Road, in Chelsea?"

"Which man do you mean?"

""Some big business man. My pro is fighting here in town, so this guy has to be big. He and his wife invite half-a-dozen friends to view the action on TV. In the old days, a businessman wanting to look important would buy, say eight ringside tickets. To-day what do we get out of him? Nothing. He pours out large doses of whisky for his wife and friends, and that's all it costs him."

"I remember now. Yes, I read the story. Somebody went through his luxury flat and got away with around twenty-thousand nicker."

"Well, that's what the papers said but it'll probably reduce to fifteen or even less. They're in there watching the fight and somebody comes up the fire-escape, gets into a bedroom and lifts the three fur coats and the wife's jewels."

"I refuse to celebrate the triumphs of the forces of evil."

"But I celebrated because it served him right. I read it in the paper next day and I rang the man up. I said: 'My name is Doc Eastlake and I manage Teddy Baker who fought on TV last night. It serves you right.' He said: 'What does?' I said: 'If you'd brought your friends to the fight this wouldn't have happened. Let that be a lesson to you.' He said: ' What? Who is this?' and I finished: 'Doc Eastlake and I manage Teddy Baker. It serves you right.' And then I hung up."

"The poor fellow probably thought it was all part of the plot."

"Poor? Like I'm rich, but you're right. He thinks I nursed my pro' along and eventually got him that fight just to set up the lift."

"I'm surprised you didn't have plain clothes visitors from the Old Bill."

"Police? The jolly old 'boys in blue' can't find anything. They can't even find their socks and shoes in the morning."

"I thought they slept with them on."

"I had a brother who was a bobby and my mother thought it was great. One of London's finest, no doubt. I was just a young fella, and living at home then. My brother and I slept in the same room and he was a great cop. Handsome and upright. A great beat-walker and with a twelve-inch eye. You know about twelve-inch eyes?"

"No, they're new to me."

"He could walk along a footpath and tell whether a car was parked just too far from the kerb and give him a ticket, same if it had wheels just fractionally over double yellow lines. That takes talent. One night I got him feeling just a little inebriated and he's in kip, getting his good nine hours, and he's got his uniform and everything laid neatly out for the morning. I took his shoes and socks, tied them together and hung them on the light shade in the middle of the ceiling.

"When I wake up it's just about getting light and he's making a vile racket, moving things all over the room. He's on his hands and knees, looking under the bed and he's in and out of the closet. I said: 'What are you doing, Sherlock?' He says: 'I can't find my shoes and socks; I put them right under that chair.' By now mother's there too, looking.

"I'm lying in bed and I said: 'Don't panic; remember what they taught you. Make a systematic search.' He groused: 'I did. I always leave them under that chair. I've looked everywhere they could be.' I said: 'That's the trouble with you people; you can't cope with the unexpected. Look somewhere they shouldn't be. Look up there on the ceiling because maybe they're hangin' from the light. Just look.' He looked up there and, sure enough, there they were. Ma went absolutely berserk."

"No doubt through that lesson he made a great detective."

"He died a detective. In an Acton back street in the middle of the night, with a .22 bullet in his guts."

"Your brother was murdered?" Capini deduced.

"Sure," Doc said, sipping his drink thoughtfully. "That was his son drove me down here today."

Rene Capini just shook his head.

"Speaking of law and order," I remarked after a while. "A couple of months ago I read that an old friend of yours died."

"Who was that?"

"Flicker Beale."

54

"Yes indeed," Doc said.
"I suppose you sent flowers."
"You want to know the truth?"
"Naturally."
"Indeed I did."
"I'm not surprised."
"I sent him a wreath marked 'Safe and Happy Journey'. I'm not kidding, it cost me twenty."
"I like that for a send-off."
"Do you remember that night?"
"How could I ever forget it?" I said.

IX

I shall remember it s long as I live. I was young then and I had been on the paper in Fleet Street about three yeas. They had me teething on boxing and I was getting on well with Doc. He had a good-looking white heavyweight at the time, fair of hair and complexion, out of a small village near Northampton and named Dick Kelly.

Kelly's father, believe it or not, had been both a useful fighter and a Roman Catholic priest, and the latter was a natural for Doc. The big kid was devout enough anyway, but Doc had him wear dark suits, sombre ties and carry a prayer-book into the dressing-room. He dubbed him Brother Kelly. It was an era when you sold a fighter to the public in every way that you could.

This was soon after Marciano retired undefeated with the title and there was some confusion in the heavyweight ranks. Archie Moore and Patterson stood out, but both were really only lightheavies and Moore was well into his forties. Brother Kelly was white, British, good-looking, very big and he could fight a bit as well. On top of all that he was managed by Doc.

Now, when a youngster starts out to become a fighter and, somewhere, walks into a gym bag in hand, he is like a rough-cut block of marble emerged from the quarry that is the mass of man. In any block a stonemason can see many things, yet a master sculptor can see but one. In his eyes, no two blocks of marble are alike and the thing he sees is the thing for which the block was created.

That is the way it always was, too, with Doc. In the boxing business, as in any business, there are numerous masons but only a handful of master sculptors, and the best of these was Doc. I studied him for years, with a dozen fighters, working carefully with reason and inspiration, shaping slowly, then stepping back and examining what he had done, containing his excitement and his fear, also, behind that cynical front.

Until Teddy Baker came along, Brother Kelly, more than any of the others, was the one. The greatest sculptor in the world, working in marble, cannot add a thing. If it is not there it is not there. No man makes it because no man is truly creative, but by subtraction from the whole he reveals. That is the nearest any man can come to creation and that is why the great live in fear. Only they can see all of it and they are afraid that, in their process of subtraction, they will not reveal the all of it and what is hidden will remain hidden forever. They are even more afraid that, in the process, they will cut too far and destroy that much of it forever. It is that way in the making of all things, including the making of a fighter.

At that time Doc had Brother Kelly living in a boarding-house on the far side of Dog Kennel Hill, S.E.5, while Doc and I happened to be living in the same hotel. It was in Gloucester Road but it is not there any more, which is just as well because it was not much of an hotel.

It was autumn and at about ten-thirty that night the 'phone in my room rang. It was Doc. He asked me to go down to his room and, when I got there, the door was open so I walked in. He emerged from the bathroom, pressing a strip of adhesive tape over a wide strip of gauze on his right cheek.

"Whatever happened to you?" I said.

"I've just had a visit from the Almighty," he replied.

"Who?"

"Flicker Fred Beale," he told me.

It was no misnomer because he operated with a flick-knife and he honed the blade until it was as sharp as a razor. He was liable to slit a body from cheekbone to jaw if he was crossed or if he was working on a commission. It was always the right cheek because he was left-handed. He was a professional enforcer.

"What happened?" I asked him.

"The Syndicate is trying to buy exclusive rights to my fighter's services."

56

"What did they offer?"

"What difference does it make what was offered? They offered a hell of a lot of money but I told Jarvis' man: 'Look, I put too much into a fighter to have him tied up to one promotional outfit. I've got to have a completely free hand with any fighter I manage, and that goes for Brother'."

"What did he say?"

"What did he say? They're not debaters; they're effing thugs. It was friendly enough at the time, but I knew the repercussions would come."

"What happened with Flicker?"

"I heard this knock on the door so I opened it and he was standing there. I held out my hand and he went for my cheek. I got my hand up but took it right there. It's not too bad at all. I hit him in the belly with a hook as hard as I could, and when he dropped his hands, I hit him on the chin with a right-hand."

Doc had wanted to be a fighter when he was a kid but he had been much too frail for it. His body could not take it but, knowing it and teaching it as he could, he could punch well above his weight.

"Did you knock him out?"

"No, but the hook in the belly made him feel bloody awful. I'm lucky it's warm out so he didn't have a top coat on. He'd have cut me for sure if the belly punch hadn't folded him/"

"Then what?"

"I picked up his hat, helped him up and led him to the lift."

"Very noble. What did he say?"

"Neither of us said a damn word from the moment he knocked on the door. I just realised that now you ask."

"I believe that."

"What were we going to talk about?" Doc said, and he tossed something on the bed in front of me. "Here."

It was a small gold flick-knife with the gold loop at one end to be attached to a watch-chain. It was still open, the blade, as I've said, like a razor.

"Am I to have this?" I asked him.

"No, let me have it again."

I handed it back to him. He was standing by the bathroom door and he pressed the tip of the blade against the door trim.

"Look out," I warned. "When that blade breaks it may fly."

It snapped almost as I spoke. I caught a glimpse of it glitter in the light and then it fell to the floor.

"You'll enjoy stepping on that in your bare feet," I joked.

"That would be the coup-de-grace," Doc muttered, looking for it now. "There it is, right by the leg of the bed."

Doc picked it up. He went into the bathroom and I heard the toilet flushing as he came out.

"I flushed it down the loo," he said.

"Good riddance."

"Before I called you," he said, "I called Joe Bromide."

Joe was still writing a sports column even then. He had never made an enemy in his life and he knew Doc and respected him and Jarvis Burns knew Joe and respected him.

"I told him the whole story," Doc said. I told him what I told you. Now I'm going over to see Burns and I want you to come along."

"I'll go," I said. "I haven't heard that he's trying to buy into typewriters."

"I'll be honest with you," Doc confessed. "I want Joe and you for protection. These people aren't afraid of the Old Bill but they respect the power of the pen in newspapers."

Burns had a cellar bar round the back of Chandos Place. The eye on the door knew Doc and, after he let us in he disappeared briefly, then came back and led us to a small table at the back of the tiny dance floor where Burns was sitting with one of his henchmen.

It was a small place with a three-piece band, a comedian whose material was filth personified, a gigantic talking parrot and half-a-dozen girls with the shortest of short transparent skirts. Jarvis Burns was a suave one though well on the way to becoming a complete crook. He did not achieve the entirety until two years later, when they found him dead in the gutter outside the block of luxury flats where he lived in Park Lane. The lead they found inside him told its own story. He died like he lived. Fast.

"Hello, Doc," he greeted, not bothering to get up. "Sit down."

"This is Frank Cutler, the boxing writer," Doc said.

"I always read your stories," said Burns.

"I'm flattered."

There were two empty chairs at the table and we sat down.

"You write well," Burns said to me, "you write like Joe Bromide."

"I try not to," I said, "but he's so bloody good and I can't help myself."

"He writes good stuff because he's a good guy," Burns continued.

"I just had Joe on the phone," Doc said.

"Really?" Burns said. "I never see him, except at fights; he never comes in here. He's what is called a family man. He's alright, is he?"

"He's fine," Doc said. "I told him you were interested in buying into Brother; then I told him I just had a visit from Flicker Beale. I told him I still don't want to sell."

"Oh yes," Burns said. "You could be right. I don't want to buy no more, either."

"Good," Doc said, "and you better give this back to Flicker."

He tossed the knife onto the table. Burns shoved it over to his sidekick who picked it up, looked at it, closed the broken blade and put the knife in his pocket.

"Care for a drink?" Burns asked.

"You want a drink?" Doc said to me.

"I'll have one."

In fact, we stayed for two drinks and we didn't talk boxing. Jarvis wanted to talk football with me; he was an Arsenal fan. Two weeks later they got to Brother Kelly and he found a soft spot in the ring at Harringay and lay down on it until he was counted out. I was at that fight and I was in Doc's room in the hotel later that night when he paid Kelly off.

"I still have two years left on your contract," he said with the big fair kid sitting on the bed, still frightened and staring at the floor. "I don't want to know anything about it and I don't even want to see you any more. You're through."

That was the last time I ever saw him and I last saw Flicker Beale on a hot summer afternoon about two years before Doc and I stood at Capini's bar. There was a red-haired fledgling from some magazine who had an assignment to shoot some pictures to go with a piece of mine. He could not have been more than twenty-four or five and he knew nothing about boxing. I took him up to the gym and introduced him to Solomons' right-hand man, Bobby Broadribb. Bobby winked at me and abused him to see how he would shape up. When he made it, Bobby gave him the run of the place.

He must have shot fifty pictures and, when he was done, I was going over to complain about life to my agent and we walked down Windmill Street and turned right towards Piccadilly Circus. I spotted Flicker by the Underground subway outside Ward's Irish House and he looked as though he was about to die right there.

He was never robust but now his hair was absolutely white and his face was grey and drawn. In all that heat he had on a heavy, brown herring-bone worsted suit and he was even wearing a waistcoat with a thin, gold watch-chain looped across it. It was obvious that he was in trouble and I walked up to him with the red-haired young photographer following me.

"Howdee, Flicker," I said. "I'm Frank Cutler."

"Hello," he said putting out his hand but breathing in gasps. He had asthma and a bad heart and he was sixty-five at the time.

"Are you alright?"

"Yes," he said, gasping. "I'll be alright."

I introduced him to the red-haired youngster and he gave him his hand. He was still propping up Ward's emporium.

"Let's go inside where it's cooler," I suggested.

"I'm okay."

"Come on," I persisted, because I was afraid he was going to collapse right there.

I took him by the arm; the photographer held the door open and we went to the first table. I sat Flicker down and then we both sat down with him.

"Let me get you an iced drink," I offered.

"Please don't bother; I'll be fine."

"I'll get it," The photographer volunteered.

He went to the bar and came back with a glass of iced water, which he put down on the table in front of Flicker.

"Thank you, young man," Flicker said, still breathing hard and in gasps.

"You're very welcome."

"Go ahead and drink it," I urged him.

Flicker picked up the glass and his hand was shaking. He held it with both hands, took a couple of sips and set it down again. As hot as the day was, though, and with that heavy suit and waistcoat on he wasn't sweating.

"Can I give you a lift somewhere?" I said.

"No thanks, I'm just going home."

"Let me take you."

"No, I'll be okay now."

"I'll call you a cab."

"No, I'll just rest here awhile. Really, I'll be alright."

"Drink some more of that water."

We sat with him for a few more minutes then I stood up and the young photographer stood up.

"If I can't take you home, Flick, or get you a cab, we'll be going. Rest here now, won't you?"

"Yes I will," he said, "and thank you very much."

He raised his hand slowly and I took it. Sitting there, he turned a little then and gave the photographer the same hand.

"And thank you very much, young man," he finished, "for the water,"

"You're welcome," the kid said.

We walked out on to the pavement in the heat and the last I saw of Flicker he was still sitting at that table, white-haired and grey-skinned, wearing that heavy suit but not sweating a bit and looking at that glass of water in front of him.

"Who is he?" the young photographer asked.

"Oh, he's been around for years and years."

"Will he be alright? I feel sorry for him."

"I hope so."

"What does he do?"

"Nowadays I don't know, but he used to have some kind of job in Madame Tussaud's 'Chamber of Horrors.' "

"Good grief," the young man said, "he looks as if he's some kind of cleric. He's so polite. I thought perhaps he was some kind of Jehovah's Witness or something."

No, son, I thought, you have the wrong man. Brother Kelly's father was a Roman Catholic priest.

"He used to be around the fight game many years ago," I informed him.

"Him?" he answered, "I can't believe he was in a tough game like boxing."

"It is strange," I said.

I was thinking of Doc and then I thought of the old Blackfriars Ring. I remember him when he had a stable of fighters based in a basement gym, always spotlessly clean, in one of the narrow back streets which abounded in the old Covent Garden market area. He looks very distinguished nowadays, dinner-jacketed at the fights where he's not working a corner with some fighter, the more so with that scar on his right cheek. You've read about him, sonny I was thinking, but he didn't get that scar at a church Garden Fete. If I told you where he got it, young fellow, it would stand that red hair of yours right on its ends. But I won't tell you because you haven't lived long enough around this business to understand.

"This is where I'm going," I said. "If you need any more help with pictures any time, give me a ring."

"That's great," The photographer said. "I'd like to do some more things with you."

He was a really nice young chap and he gave me his card.

"I remember it very clearly," I said now to Doc, standing there at the bar at Capini's. "Whatever became of Brother Kelly?"

"He's an instructor at one of the best health clubs in the country. It's up near Tring, in Herts."

"Are you serious about that?"

"He's been there for years. He handles a lot of those obese businessmen, gives them exercises and, if they want it, teaches them how to hold up their hands in fighting pose. They send their sons to him sometimes, too. They seem to think he's the cat's whiskers."

"And I can just hear them telling him that he was right to get out of boxing, that it is a racket and that he's far too good for it."

"You can bet on that," Doc said.

X

Teddy Baker was the fighter that Doc Eastlake had originally wanted to be. To this union the one gave his youth and its riches and the other his years and his genius and now, as they approached together their moment I felt, as I had known I would, the growing weight of my own involvement.

It is something that happens to only a few of us scribblers, the few that live, eat and sleep boxing. I have known it happen also over a footballer and even a racehorse and I have felt its beginnings within myself in as insignificant a thing as a mere gesture. Kenneth Wolstenhome, the former wonderful BBC soccer commentator, was a football fanatic, while Peter O'Sullivan, also of BBC TV fame as commentator, race-reader and form guide, knew near everything about every racehorse that ever lived.

Those few of us attempt to avoid this personal involvement in our business but it is a losing struggle. Total impartiality is, or would be, the key. We should maintain our poise and what we would wish to be our objectivity, but what we fight is the admission of our own defeat in the willingness with which we ascribe so quickly to another the remnants of what we once believed to be our own potential for success, perhaps even greatness.

I can only vaguely recall my first meeting with Doc Eastlake. He was sitting ringside at the Aldershot Military Boxing Centre nearly fifty years ago as, a bundle of nerves, I made my way towards the ring to contest a heat of the Army Championships. There was a lot of top amateur talent on show that night (it was, of course, back in the days of conscription) and Doc wanted to see the best of it in action with an eye to possible signings in the future. He had a few words with me in the bar after the tournament ended, giving me his card.

The night I first saw Teddy Baker was at an open-air show at the old Clapton Greyhound Stadium. It had been hot and terribly humid for days that July. About mid-afternoon the storm had come, darkening the daylight over the city, but cutting the air open with the flashing strokes of a huge cleaver. Now it was twilight and the storm had gone. The stadium was sodden but the show had to go on and, as I left the Underground and walked over to the arena, I could feel the air on my hands and face and in my lungs. You could see it, after several almost breathless days, bring life back again into the people on the street with me. It revived their eyes and brought back the will to walk freely once more.

At ringside I sat watching the preliminary bouts, not expecting much and so not asking much, and in the intervals between rounds and the longer ones, between bouts, I listened to the crowd-sound and felt the night come. I tried to find the stars which I knew were there above the ring lights and above the thin, grey pall of smoke that hovered, translucent, over and around us. Then the chief supporting bout came into the ring and there was

63

Doc, climbing through he ropes, then holding them open for a fair-haired kid in a green-and-white silken dressing-gown.

He was not more than twenty-feet from me and he and his assistant second were busy ensuring that their man's ring shoes were thoroughly rubbed in the resin box and generally fussing around him. And then Doc leant back against the ropes, arms spread wide along the top rope, squinting across at the other corner where the opponent was just coming in. Then he straightened up and I saw him looking round the working press, nodding here and there, older than when I had last seen him and thin and narrow-shouldered in his white coat sweater with pockets. He spotted me looking at him and he opened his mouth and threw his head back in evident surprise. He pointed towards me, formed some words with his mouth and I nodded to let him know that I would wait there for him later.

"And from Denmark Hill," the Master of Ceremonies said through his microphone, at ten stone twelve pounds, Teddy Baker!"

There was a splattering of applause that comes from the polite irregulars and I saw the kid, preoccupied, stand up, nod in acknowledgement and Doc take his robe. The boy had a fine body, perhaps a little short in the arms, and I followed his gaze to the opponent and saw that the rival was some two inches taller and had the reach to match.

When the opening bell clanged I watched Doc's man walk out slowly and then start to circle, hands low, looking out of the tops of his eyes and there was no question about it; he was the Doc's fighting product. This is what a painter does in his masterpieces so that you would recognise them, even without his signature. And the writer in his writings, if he is enough of a scribbler, so that you know that no one in the world but he could have penned that epic.

For five rounds it was nothing much to write home about, two earnest kids trying, the one patternless but inventive, desperately improvising as he boxed along, and Doc's boy always knowing what he wanted to do, but still a little confused, making the opponent miss and then not quite being able to bring off the counter. Yet in the sixth round it happened. Doc's Teddy Baker, working underneath, missed a right hand but slid his right foot forward with it and, rising with the punch, brought the left hand up and over to the other man's jaw.

It was one of those flashing picture punches. It snapped the other fellow's head back and he went down, first on his rump and then he rolled around on to his back. But this was a game 'un and at 'nine' he was just up shaking his head, trying to clear the haze while the referee wiped his gloves. At the command 'Box On' Doc's protégé was on him again like a tiger, throwing both hands to the head until the third man stopped it.

In the main event two colossal heavyweight maulers disqualified each other as serious contenders and, when it was over, I waited while the crowd thinned towards the exits and then I watched the newspapermen working ringside under the glare of the ring lights and I envied them. I knew many of them and realised that what I envied was the assurance in the clicking of their typewrites and their power of concentration. Above them, in the centre of the ring, a loud-mouthed Irish foreman was abusing an ageing, grumbling workman in overalls who was one of the crew starting to roll up the ring canvas. But still the clicking of the typewriters and the ringing of the press men's telephones went on ceaselessly.

In a little while I saw Doc approaching, with the fighter following him carrying his bag. Doc was trying to pick a path towards me through the tree-stump disarray of the forest of wooden folding chairs. I signalled to him to wait there and, when I found my way through to them, I shook hands with Doc and he introduced me to Teddy.

"Congratulations," I said, shaking the fighter's hand.

"Thanks a lot," he replied. His light-brown hair was crew cut and he had young, clear blue eyes.

"You have a live one," I said to Doc, motioning with my head towards Baker.

"Who can tell?"

"You can."

"Yep," Doc affirmed, putting on his sour expression. "Trouble is, at my age you hate to start at the beginning again with another one."

"Where are you going?"

"I want to take him out and get him something to eat."

Outside the stadium we finally flagged a cab and went to a small restaurant where the fighter had a steak, followed by stewed prunes and a coup of hot tea and lemon. He was a quiet youngster, and Doc and I had a drink and talked about people we hadn't seen in years. Then the three of us took another cab back to the hotel and went up to the room Doc and his fighter were sharing.

"You go in and take a hot tub," he told his kid.

"I already had a shower at the stadium," Teddy reminded.

"I know that," Doc said, "Now take a tub; put some of those Epsom Salts in it and soak for about fifteen minutes."

"Okay."

Doc pulled the eiderdown back off one of the twin beds and folded it at the foot. Then he pulled the covers back.

"Feel like going out somewhere?" I asked him.

"Not for me. I saw too many people for one night already. I've got a bottle of Scotch here, hardly touched. Let's go to your room and let this kid try to sleep."

"Fine with me."

Doc opened the bathroom door and said something to his fighter above the sound of the running water, then he went to the cupboard and got the bottle. We went up to my room and Doc called room service and, in a little while, a pageboy arrived with a bucket of ice, a large bottle of club soda and two glasses.

"What kind of stuff is that?" Doc queried, looking at the bottle of soda.

"It's very good," the page said, "everybody uses it."

"I never even heard of it," Doc said.

"It's alright with me," I said, signing the tab. "I don't use any anyway."

"You've got nothing else?" Doc persisted.

"Everybody drinks this," the bellboy said.

"Alright," Doc said, and then he tipped the boy a two pound coin and the boy, surprised, thanked him before going out and closing the door.

"All you need is a bath with running water and a tank of bottled gas and you're in the soda-water business," Doc opined, showing me the bottle with the strange label. "I should have thought of something as easy as this."

"That's not a bad-looking fighter you've got," I said.

"Maybe," Doc said, pouring the Scotch. "He's only a beginner."

He handed me mine with the ice in it and I went into the bathroom and added a little water. When I returned, Doc was sitting on one of the beds, his drink in his hand.

66

"I know he's a beginner," I said. "They all are at one time."

"He's green," Doc reiterated. "Got an awful lot to learn."

"Sure," I agreed, "but I watched him carefully tonight. I could see the Doc Eastlake in him."

"You could, could you?"

"Very much so."

"He executes pretty well at that, doesn't he, for a boy with less than two dozen fights under his belt?"

"That's what I mean."

"That wasn't a bad sequence he dumped the other guy with, eh?"

"I thought it was great."

"You liked it, eh?"

"I did."

"You know that he missed that right hand on purpose?"

"I was hoping you'd tell me he did."

"Sure; that's that shift to southpaw. The other guy is still congratulating himself about the right hand that missed him when the hook unloads itself on him."

"It's a thrilling thing to see."

"Name me the other fighters could do that."

"Robinson."

"Right. Another."

"Ali".

"Another."

"I pass."

"Armstrong, and that's about all in the last half-century."

"Why don't you stop kidding to me?"

"What? You're really excited about this kid."

"He should have had that other fellow out of there in three."

"Perhaps."

"Perhaps? Absolutely. Definitely. From the second round on I was telling him: 'Now go out there and throw that shift into this bum and he won't know what hit him' Do you think he'd do it? No. He's out there paddling around like a guy lost in a swamp. Coming back to the corner, I finally said to him: 'Look, what are you tryin' to do, make me out a liar? You're disgracing me here in front of a lot of people and some of them are my friends. You throw that shift into him this round or when you come back next time I won't be here.' "

"I rather care for that!"

"So he finally threw it," Doc said, nodding. "Have another drink."

"I'll help myself."

"You know why he finally threw it?"

"Why?"

"Because he was more afraid of coming back to the corner and finding me gone than he was of throwing it. Isn't that dreadful?"

He got up, mixed himself another drink and sat down again on the bed.

"I can understand it, though," I said.

"Understand what?"

"Your kid, Until he tried it he couldn't believe in it."

"Uh! For three months we worked on it in the gym between fights. He's got it down now perfect."

"I know, but a fight is quite another thing; it is for real. You believe in it because of Robinson and Ali and Armstrong and a lifetime in the business. What has the kid got; two years and your word?"

"Did I ever lie to him?"

"Of course not, but a man has to find out for himself."

"They're not believers, none of them. I could name a half-dozen--you can remember them--that could have been something if they just believed in it."

"I know and I do remember."

"You don't just tell them; you show them. The only thing any real man's afraid of is the unknown. So you try to show them and then there'll be no unknown. When a boy starts to fight he's like a new-born kitten. He can't see. All he has in there is gloves. The air is full of them, until he learns he can ignore most of them. Then the mystery starts to disappear and you can really get to work on his own punching. You build up a combination and he won't throw the big one. It's the unknown again; he's afraid of what might happen if he commits himself. But what can happen if he'll just believe? Does he think I want to get his head knocked off? So you have to scare him into it. Understand?"

"Surely. You're using fear to fight fear and that's basic."

"That's right, but isn't it dreadful?"

"But the price is right. Now he knows and now that's his move. As long as he's a fighter he'll have it and believe in it."

"You should have seen him when we got back to the dressing-room. He was like a dog with two tails. He said: 'It worked, it worked! Did you see that?' So I said: 'Of course it worked but you should have thrown it in the third round.' He said: 'I know, I know and I'll do it the next time.' I said: 'You should have done it this time; remember the punches you took from the third round on.' He said: 'I didn't take many.' I said: 'Of course not because I taught you not to, but when you go to bed tonight just lie there still and try to remember the punches you took from the third round 'til the sixth. Try to count them and consider that you wouldn't have had to take even one if you'd gotten that guy out of there when you should have.'

"And I told him something else, too. I said: 'When that bloke got up, why didn't you hit him one shot at least in the belly?' He said: 'I know that was wrong; I just got excited.' I looked at him and I said: 'Excitement is for amateurs. You're supposed to be a pro.' "

"You haven't changed, Doc," I said and I was enjoying it.

"So Edward is taking his shower and I walked out and bumped into one of those con-men that have the opponent. He says: 'My boy wasn't right tonight.' I said: 'He looked alright to me.' He says: 'That kid of yours misses that right hand and gets lucky with the left.' I just said: 'Oh yes' and I walked away. Isn't that dreadful?"

He had stood up and he walked to the drinks cupboard and was mixing himself another drink.

"Lucky," he said, voice full of sarcasm. "For months we worked on that--left foot, right foot, right hand, shift, spacing, leverage--and this bum calls it luck."

"Ignore him. You've already called him a con-man so what can you expect from him?"

"Nothing. I used to ignore them."

He was beginning to feel the drinks a little now.

"I used to ignore them," he recollected. "Ignore them; all my life I ignored them, but can you imagine that?"

"What?"

"That sob; can you imagine? 'You were lucky,' he says."

"Forget him; he just isn't worth getting steamed up about."

"That's what I used to think, but how the hell are you going to be able to ignore them?"

69

"Why not?"

"There's too many of 'em. You can't ignore them; they outnumber people like us a thousand to one. You know that, don't you?"

"Sure I do, but it's nothing new. They were always a thousand to one."

"Amateurs. A really good fighter can't win because, if he stops an opponent early, the boo boys say the opponent's a bum steer and swallower. If the really good prospect is given a hard fight, the boo boys say he himself is a bum. How many people in the stadium tonight could read what my man was doing up there in the ring?"

"I don't know but very, very few."

"Just three or four?"

"Maybe."

"Isn't that dreadful?"

"But it doesn't really make any difference."

"That's exactly what I used to think and say. I used to say: 'It's Doc Eastlake and this is the way you do it.' To hell with the rest of them, I used to think. I'll show them before their very eyes and they won't be able to miss it; I'll walk right through them. And where the hell am I?"

"You're in a quiet but comfortable London hotel right now."

"I'm sixty-eight years old in overnight hotel digs with another green fighter. That's where I am. I've got nowhere very, very slowly."

"Oh, come off it. Shamateurs have always crowded the highways to every and anywhere, so it's never been easy for the pros' to get through. Now you've got a willing, good-looking kid who looked good tonight. If I was a fight manager I'd wish I had him."

"You liked him, eh?"

"I think he's got a lot of potential and he'll listen."

It seemed to pick him up.

"He can be a real good boy," he said.

"A hell of a one. You're just too nervous to let yourself enthuse."

"I've had too many goddam disappointments."

"Haven't we all? But this is a new deal."

"He likes to fight, too. You know?"

"I could see that very clearly."

"He got the other man hurt and he wanted to kill him."

"I saw it. So you bawl him out, telling him that excitement is for amateurs."

"You know what I meant."

"Of course I know."

"A fighter's got to feel excitement or he's nothing."

"Otherwise he'd just be a guy going through the motions."

"But he's got to learn to control it and let it go at the right time and in the right place."

"Certainly."

"I wanted him to put that excitement into one good shot to the body."

"I know."

"That's the hardest thing in the world to do, people don't understand that. It's the hardest thing in the world to teach a fighter to control that excitement without stifling and killing it."

"It's the secret of everything from painting to, hell's bells, loving."

"It's the hardest thing in the world to teach."

"Or to do."

"Do? If I can teach it he should be able to do it."

"Yes."

"This one might, too, This boy's a learner. I abuse hell out of him but he's a good kid."

"I can see that."

"You have to abuse them because you can't afford to let 'em think it's easy. This boy has never had an easy fight and, what's more, he never will. I won't let him. I get him opponents he can lick, but men who look to knock his block off. I get him guys like that one tonight, that he can learn on and from, but no tankers. This it the toughest business in the world and one easy win could ruin him."

"You worry too much because you wouldn't let it ruin him. You'd find some way to bring him back to size."

"You can't always do that. Nowadays the clever dicks worry about bringing a prospect back if he gets licked. Hell, that's not a problem. You match him right and he loses a tough fight, so he either comes back or he doesn't. If he don't, he's not enough fighter and you can forget him."

"I suppose so."

"It's the other ones. I've lost fighters the other way and you know that's true because you've seen it."

"I have indeed."

"You put a boy in with some guy you figure to be tough and something happens. Maybe your boy gets lucky or the other fellow is off his feed, takes a couple of good punches and resigns. Then you look at your kid and you can see it in his face. 'Oh boy!' he's thinking, 'This is for me.' "

He was room-pacing now glass in hand, and he stopped at the foot of my bed and looked down at me sitting there and watching him.

"He's gone," he said. "You're looking at a fighter who just left. Gone."

I know, I was thinking. I've seen it happen to fighters and I could tell you about some writers, too.

"I lie awake sometimes over this boy. Every fight I accept for him I worry. Half the time when I'm in the corner I'm hoping the other guy will nail him with a couple of blockbusters; It's just that I want to be certain he's not chinny. Isn't that dreadful?"

"It's the way it should be."

"It's hard as sin to make matches for a prospect like this."

"It's like Peter O'Sullivan used to say about horse-racing. There's a slight element of chance involved."

"Can you imagine?"

"What?"

"He wants to get married."

"They very often do."

"Youngsters; they can't understand. They've got one chance in life and they've got perhaps ten years to take it with both hands. They make it in ten years or they don't. So they want to get married."

He had finished his drink and he stood up, walked over to the drinks cupboard and put the glass down on it.

"Doc, you're trying to go against the laws of nature and civilisation. It's quite normal for a human being to want to get hitched up. Why not just be pleased he wants to get married rather than simply live in sin with some wench?"

"Fighters aren't normal human beings." He said, staring down at me through those rimless glasses and raising his voice to me. "Get that out of your head. You should understand that a fighter is a freak. He's got ten years in the toughest business in

72

the world, a business that calls for every ounce of his strength and every second of his life. There isn't a goddam thing he does that doesn't affect his business. He's not a copper, a lawyer or a writer. He won't be able to spread it over thirty or forty working years; he's got to live it all now, or never."

You have always asked too much, I was thinking. There have been many of us who have asked that of ourselves or others at one time or another, but we have deserted in compromise and now you are the only one I know who, after all this time, still carries on that lonesome crusade against reality.

"Blasted women," he said. "What do they want?"

"They only want what everyone else wants, and they're bound by the same laws, into the bargain."

"What does she want with a fighter?"

"Maybe she doesn't want anything with a fighter. Maybe she just wants a nice young chap named Teddy Baker, who happens to be a fighter."

"Not this one; I've met her."

"And didn't like her."

"Of course not. She's a good-looking girl with big brown eyes and a nice figure. I can read her like a book."

"I suppose so."

"She wants Teddy Baker, the fighter. He's the best grab she knows because he's a fighter and it's glamorous. He's starting to get his name in the papers and he might even become the world champion. 'There's Teddy Baker's wife,' people will say. She'll have a mink coat and they'll go to night-clubs, The Head Waiter'll know them and it'll be a ball. The hell it will!"

"You're imagining all this."

"Like hell I am. I met her and she's got a head of her own. That's the trouble. If she was some cow-eyed little thing I'd say maybe this'll work, as long as she keeps looking up at him that way. But not this one. This one has a mind but she don't know she'll be marrying a freak.

"What can it be? For God's sake, he'll be home for two weeks and gone for three. What kind of marriage can that be? He's a long shot to make it at best, right? Now let's say he doesn't make it. Twenty years from now he's still trying to figure out why. There he sits at night, a working man just trying to meet expenses, his dreams all gone, and hers also. Then he looks across at her. She's put on a lot of weight and she's sitting there in some old house-dress and he says to himself: 'Maybe if I hadn't married her I'd have made it!' They do that, you know The ones that don't make it are always grabbing at something. Wouldn't that be a wonderful marriage?" He picked up the bottle and there was still some Scotch in it.

"I'll leave it here," he said, "and you can finish it."

"I'm not a lone drinker, either."

"Blast the whole thing!"

"When are you leaving?" he said as I walked him to the door and we shook hands.

"Oh, I may stay on here two or three more days."

"We're motoring back mid-morning."

"I'll see you around, then, before too long."

He walked out into the hall and turned back towards me.

"Can you just imagine that?" he said.

"What?"

"That lunatic says: 'Well, you were lucky tonight.' Can you imagine? Amateurs!"

I watched him start across the hall and then he was gone.

XI

Somewhere seven years had gone, somewhere between an open-air fight night in East London and an afternoon in the small dressing-room at the countryfied Barley Mow in the greenery of Surrey. What the years take from the old they give to the young and so, in seventy fights in seven years, Teddy Baker had become many fighters I had known. 'If Youth Only Knew and if Age Only Could.'

Any form of art is ritualistic and I had observed this one so many times. It is the way a man, preoccupied, prepares his paints or inserts two sheets of blank paper, with a carbon between them, into a typewriter or strips out of his street clothes and puts his body into the trappings of the ring. For another man this would be an awkward act, embarrassing in its gladiatorial fraudulence, but for this particular man it has become the most natural of rites.

Teddy had hung his jacket over the back of the chair and then he sat down and took off his slip-ons and his socks. Nat handed him a clean pair of white woollen socks; he put those on and then he put on his ring boots. Resting first one foot and then the other against the edge of the rubbing-table, he laced the boots in silence. Now he stood up and pulled his white T-shirt over his head and tossed it on the chair. Next, he started to doff his grey-flannel slacks.

"Where are you supposed to hang things around here?" Waller said, looking at the array of hooks with clothes draped all over them.

He had been mothering bandages and jars at one end of the bench. At the other end, Mickey Evans was already in his ring clothes and had wrapped his hands in grey-soiled bandages before taping them. Now he was simply sitting on the bench and waiting.

"Where did you put your stuff?" Nat said to him.

"Me?" Evans said, surprised. "Here."

He reached over, putting his hand on his slacks, pants, T-shirt and sweater hanging from one of the hooks.

"D'ye want me to take them off?" he asked.

"No," Teddy said, looking across. "Leave them where they are."

"The sparring partner got a place to hang his clothes," Waller said. "The fighter got nowhere."

Evans looked at me and shrugged his shoulders.

"Just forget it," Teddy said. He was folding his slacks and placed them over the top of the jacket on the back of the chair.

"Somebody's got to take charge around here," Waller said. "I bet that Rene never comes in here. What kind of a place is he runnin'? Who's fightin' for the title anyway? You're the most important guy he's got here."

"Hand me the gauze, will you Nat?" Teddy said.

Waller handed Teddy the first roll and I watched him bandage his right hand, around the wrist and then down and around over the body of the hand, between the fingers and back over the body, flexing the hand now and then, the white bandage building like a cast. Nat handed him a strip of the wide tape and he wrapped it over the bandage at the wrist. Then the trainer handed him, one at a time, the narrow strips and he took each one and pinched it in the middle, then stuck it on the back of the hand, brought it over between the two fingers and stuck the other end to the gauze covering the palm.

75

"Do you always bandage your own hands?" I asked, when he had started on the left hand.

"Always," he answered, wrapping the tape.

"Since he first came to me," Waller said, standing there and watching, waiting with a small strip. "Not for fights, though; Doc always bandages him for fights. But Doc and me taught him to do his own hands as soon as he put him with me. While he's doin' it, a fighter can tell himself how it feels. Get me?"

"No matter how often I watch fighters do it," I said to Teddy, "I still marvel at the sureness and neatness of it."

"Hands are a fighter's tools," Waller said. "He's got to take care of his tools. A fighter damages his hands and he's nothin'. I've known many a good fighter have to quit with bad hands. You remember Danny Hurley?"

"Yes," I said.

Waller was talking about Danny Hurley and I was watching Teddy. He was oblivious to the chatter and, knowing that kind, I never press them at such a time. Often the newspapermen will descend on them like a pack of hounds and flush them out, but it really isn't any good.

"First he couldn't do the right hand properly," Nat was saying, talking about Teddy again now. "You know what I mean, tryin' to work with the left hand? So we told him always to do that hand first. Now he does one as good as the other. Right, Teddy?"

"True," Teddy said, taking the tape from the conditioner.

When he had finished the hand he pulled on a pair of brief, tight, white woollen trunks and a white T-shirt. Then he picked up the use-hardened brown leather harness of his cup. Nat Waller collected the jar with Teddy's mouthpiece in it, a jar of vaseline and a towel. Then, with Mickey Evans following us carrying his own mouthpiece, jar, towel and protective cup, we walked out.

It is the fighter's place. The ring, the gym and the dressing-room are his kingdom and, in their environment, the good fighter is supreme. He breathes, walks and talks in many places but this is where he belongs. He himself is not aware of it and never will be until years after it is all over. Then, maybe, it will come to disturb him that something has gone out of his life forever, not just the ring battles, but something else. That something else is all of it.

Teddy walked through the gym, one of all the other fighters and yet apart from them, as they were one with, yet apart from, him. In the ring Cassidy was mauling with a young heavyweight who came up from Guildford each afternoon with two other fighters and Charlie Mahoney, who managed them and managed Ceroni, plus Charlie's son, who helped train them. At the heavy bag, Harry McCormick was shouldering it and throwing hooks and short right hands into it and, at the speedball, Ceroni stood, blank-faced and sweating profusely, rhythm-punching the ball over his head, louder and louder, first one knee and then the other coming up, the two like pistons in perfect synchronisation. Near the corner, formed by the dressing-room and the outside wall, Mahoney's two other fighters,, a middleweight and a welterweight, did sit-ups on the mat, their hands locked behind their heads. In the pen space near the bar Alf Penny was alone, rope-skipping in place, sweating too and the only one unwatched.

Jakie Turner leaned on the top rope of the ring, watching Cassidy and shouting to him. Ten feet from him, Mahoney's son leaned, watching the other heavyweight. By the heavy bag old Sid, poker-faced, watched McCormick. Mahoney stood between the speedball and the mat talking to Doc but watching Joe Ceroni, the current hope of the stable, but at the same time stressing his presence to the two others on the mat.

When Teddy walked through, with Waller and Mickey Evans following him, he moved to the open floor by the bar. Alf Penny stopped rope-skipping to say something to him, and then he continued with the rope and Teddy moved around, rotating his arms and shoulders, stopping to bend over, feet spread to touch his toes, stopping again to do a deep knee bend, straightening and walking again, rotating arms and shoulders as before, with trainer Waller leaning on the bar and watching him and Evans moving around and doing the same, but always with an eye on Teddy and being careful to keep out of his way.

"Hey Frank!"

It was Charlie Mahoney and I walked over to where he and Doc were standing and we shook hands. Mahoney had his stable in Bournemouth because he lived there, but he worked mostly out of London where he had started in the game and where he was regarded as just about the most affluent of all of them. He looked it. He was a semi-short, pink-faced immaculate man who bought his clothes at Robert Old's and ate his steaks in Farthing's when in the seaside town, and at the Savoy when in London. I can recall an occasion when he explained to me, unabashed and for no

77

particular reason, how important it is that a man have friends in the right places. He tried hard, always, to say the right thing and never to fall out with anybody.

"Doc tells me you're going to write a story about Teddy," he said, and he had to raise his voice to be heard above the noise of the speedball.

I nodded midst the noise and he turned and took a couple of steps before putting his hand on Ceroni's shoulder. Joe stopped the ball with his hands and turned.

"That's enough," Charlie commanded. "Cool off and take your shower."

Ceroni nodded and, without a word, walked over to the ring, pulling off his ball-punching gloves. He then picked his towel off the top rope and wiped his face and neck.

"You can both go in now, as well," Mahoney said to the two on the mat.

He was in his sixties and had been at it for thirty years and was a great merchandiser. He was occasionally referred to by the boxing writers as being an astute student of styles and abilities, but really his business acumen lay in buying and selling. One of his best fighters had been structured by old Sid, another had been self-taught and the truth was that Mahoney knew no more about fighters than most of the football results tipsters know about footballers, or than most of the newspaper racing experts know about racehorses.

"Teddy's a good boy," he now offered.

"I like him, but I can't stand his manager," I replied. I was trying to bring Doc into it because, in the presence of business success and affluence, I was attempting to let both of them know that my man was still Doc.

"You want me?" Doc said, turning from us.

Cassidy and Mahoney's heavyweight were finished in the ring and Jakie Turner had walked over. He had been standing there listening and eyeing Doc.

"How about my Killer working with Teddy?"

"With Teddy? No thanks."

"I thought you wanted him. I mean, Nat said you might use him. You remember I mentioned it?"

"He's too big, Jake."

"They could just move around."

"I've got Mickey Evans," Doc said. "Charlie'll let me use that middleweight of his if I need him. I've got Lefty Flynn coming down. Thanks anyway, Jakie."

"Whatever you say," Turner said, shrugging, but clearly waiting for Doc or someone to say something else.

"Thanks again," Doc said.

"I've got to look after my man" Turner said and, the towel over his shoulder, he walked over to where Cassidy was thumping the big bag.

"Can you imagine?" Doc burst out. "Can you imagine my pro, Edward, pushing that hunk of lard around?"

Well, he was only trying to be helpful," I said.

"Shamateurs!" Doc exploded.

He saw Nat coming out of the dressing-room now carrying the headguards for Teddy and Evans and he walked across to him and took Teddy's. While Mahoney and I watched, the two fighters climbed into the ring. Teddy stepped into his cup and adjusted it over the white woollen tights, and Evans climbed into the sweat-blackened leather carcass of his.

"How do you like my feller?" Mahoney said to me.

Evans was fitting on his own headguard, but Doc was leaning over the ropes and fastening the strap on Teddy's. Waller was standing near the edge of the ring canvas with Doc, holding Teddy's gloves, ready to give them to Doc.

"Ceroni?"

"He's gonna be a good fighter."

"He's got talent."

"You keep an eye on him," Mahoney said. "Remember I told you."

That's the least of my concerns, I thought. I am involved here in a crisis and you want to show me conjuring tricks.

"You fancy Teddy in this fight, eh?" Mahoney said, looking at me out of the sides of his eyes.

"Yes."

"The other man's a good champion; you know that."

"And Teddy's a worthy challenger."

"That's right and old Doc is due a break."

"Yes," I said. "But just don't tell him that."

"He's a very odd guy."

"He just doesn't expect to get the breaks. He never has and I don't think he ever will."

79

"In this racket you have to."

"You can apply that to any business," I said.

No use talking about it, I thought. The play for a lucky break, the dependence on it has come to be regarded as almost a mathematical factor but to a few, even in the winning, it is an admission of defeat.

"Time!"

It was Waller, standing on the ring-apron with Doc, looking up from the three-minute timing clock and yelling to Teddy and Evans. When he called it, the two fighters turned to face each other, a little top-heavy in their headguards, Teddy with hands held low, looking out of the tops of his eyes, and Evans sticking out the big sixteen-ounce pillow on his left hand.

"I have to go and pick up my crew and get back," Mahoney said. "I'll see you tomorrow."

"Fine."

"Remember what I told you about Joe. If you ever want to do a story about him just let me know. He's yours."

"Sure I will, Charlie."

"Always glad to help," he said.

I watched Teddy and Evans spar three rounds, the gym quiet now except for the shuffle of their ring shoes on the canvas, the thud-slap of their punches and the low, short rushing of their breathing through their noses. Teddy was holding himself back all the time, never wasting a move. When it was over he worked a couple of rounds on the heavy bag and two more on the light bag, after which I followed them into the dressing-room.

"Close the door, will you Frank?" Doc said.

"Sure."

Only Alf Penny was still there, in an old pair of green-grey slacks and white T-shirt; over it he sported a soiled brown suede unbuttoned jacket. He was sitting on the bench, long black hair still wet from the shower and still sweating a little just below the hairline in front. He pulled his legs in underneath him to let the others pass by.

"Now I'm gonna tell you this once and for all," Doc said.

Teddy had his white terry-cloth robe on, pulled up close under his chin. The perspiration was beaded on his forehead and he sat down on the chair and extended his legs out forward.

"I know," he half remonstrated.

"Don't tell me you know," Doc said, standing in front of him and squinting down at him. "The only way to tell me anything is to show me."

"Alright," Teddy said, looking up at him.

"Now I don't want to see you take one single step back in this camp. Not even one. Understand?"

"I understand."

"I don't care what this other feller does."

He motioned back with one arm towards Evans, who was sitting on the bench next to Penny and sweating in a soiled dark-blue robe and starting to peel the bandage-wrappings off one hand.

"I don't care how this feller or anybody else down here moves to you. I want them to move on you, but don't let me catch you taking one step back."

"I know," Teddy said, nodding and looking down along his legs.

"Give him that towel."

"Here it is," Waller said, serious-faced and handing Teddy the towel. Doc waited while Teddy wiped himself over, face, neck, chest and under the armpits.

"Move to this side, move to that. Circle him but don't ever give him his angle and don't ever step back."

"I know," Teddy said, wiping now his crutch. "I mean, I understand."

"Look at me."

"Yes," Teddy agreed looking up at him, his hands with the towel held in front of him.

"People who are supposed to know think the other guy can fight. But he can only fight if you let him. Anybody can fight if you let them, but you never should let them. What they don't know, but you and I know, is that any opponent can't do anything with you if you don't give him the room he needs, and he'll be absolutely nothing if you back him up."

"I understand, Doc."

"Get him his hot tea, Nat."

"I thought he'd have it when he comes out of his shower," Waller said.

"But I want him to have it now,; I want him to keep that sweat longer."

"Whatever you say, Doc."

81

He was cutting open the bandages on Teddy's hands and, when he finished, he put the scissors down on the bench next to his jars and went out.

"That was alright today, Mickey," Doc said to Evans.

"Thanks."

When Doc made an exit I sat down on the other chair and watched Teddy sweat. On ordinary mortals sweat is the visible, often repulsive, evidence of our lack of condition, but on the trained athlete it is the finely balanced weighing of the water content and the exact equating of the chemical formula, and so it belongs.

"That's not a bad head of steam," I said to him.

"Yep," he said, wiping his hands now with the towel. "Just what I needed today. I haven't felt quite right; not properly loose, you know. I think a good sweat like this will get me going right."

"You're welcome to it," Penny said.

"You were sweatin' good today yourself," Teddy said.

"Who wants it?" queried Penny. "There's only one thing I ever wanna get up a sweat doing."

"Just forget it," Teddy said.

"Who can forget it?"

"Hey, Alf," Evans said, "why don't you get a good short back-and-sides haircut?"

"A what?"

"He's right," Waller interjected. He had come in carrying the tea, a cup on a saucer in each hand, with a slice of lemon floating in each. He kicked the door shut behind him and handed one steaming cup to Teddy and the other to Evans.

"He's right, what?"

"Get one of them crew haircuts like Teddy's got."

"Why?"

"Because then it don't look so bad when you get hit a punch. You get hit a head punch now and your hair flies up. It makes the punch look like it's good."

"Are you kiddin'?"

"No; the way you've got your hair long now, it could lose you a close fight."

"You're crazy!"

"No he's not," said Evans, sipping his tea.

"It's a fact," Waller said. "You see some man's long hair fly when he gets hit, and everybody in the crowd lets out a shout.

Referees and judges have got ears, even if some of them are caulied."

"Maybe, but you two chumps ain't got no hair; you're just jealous. Don't try to con me. Nobody's cuttin' my hair short."

"Just what are you tryin' to be?" Waller said, "a fighter or a sheik?"

"A sheik!" Penny said, laughing and turning to Teddy. "You hear that? You get that? Here's a guy getting mixed up with what happens to you when you've been on the hard booze too much and for too long. Where'd you get that word; you got any more words like that?"

"Like what?"

"I'll bet you had some sheiks, hey? I'll bet you hit the hard stuff good and long."

"I've never been drunk in my life."

"You've always been a good boy, hey? Tell us about it, Nat."

"I'll see you gentlemen later," I said.

"Okay Frank," Teddy said.

I walked out through the gym and, when I got to the lobby, I saw Doc sitting in the porch in one of the red-painted metal tubular chairs. It was the warmest afternoon we had had; the sun had passed overhead and Doc was sitting there, looking across the parking forecourt towards the road.

"You're right about not backing up with that other guy," I said, sitting down.

"Of course I'm right."

"The moment you said it I could see his fights and I knew you were right."

"You want to know something?"

"Yes."

"This champion's made for Teddy."

"It'll be great if it turns out that way."

"If? It has to. People have the idea the other guy's a great fighter. That's a bit of a joke."

"He's a pretty good one, Doc. Let's give him that."

"He has to be. He's champion of the world, and the undisputed one at that. And he's the only one that all the sanctioning bodies agree about."

"That's what I mean."

83

"But still not a great fighter; let's not get confused about that. He's faster than the rest so he covers better. He looks so good in the ring but he's not quite what he looks. You've got to see through all that."

"I can see it now that you say it."

I meant it. I could picture that lithe brown body and the fast hands and all the natural grace, but I could also see now that always, without it being a conscious thought, there had been an impression lying dormant within me that something was missing. In a similar way, a passage of music can lift you and then leave you up there alone, feeling yet not quite knowing that something is missing and wondering what is wrong.

"Window-dressing," Doc said.

"Yes, it's pretty to behold."

"Made for my pro, Edward. For nine years I've fed him everybody I could find who'd come to him. That's why I've made every one of my tigers a counter-puncher. It's the only way you can con the other guy into thinking you're fighting his fight. When he finds out that you're not, it's too late. Surprise, surprise. Christmas is over and the ante is up. It'll be the same with this great champion."

"But somewhat tougher."

"Naturally. That's the way it's supposed to be, isn't it?"

"Sure."

"Listen. After forty-three years I've got a boy who's learned everything I could teach him. He's even learned how to walk out there and make it look tough. He makes it look like it's close but it isn't. He's just inside those punches or outside them. The ones he's taking, he's taking where it doesn't matter. He's even kept the secret. That's the great talent, because nobody knows this except the blokes who've fought him. I could name you a handful who came to Teddy after he beat them and told him they had never had it done to them before. They still aren't sure what happened, but whatever it was they never thought that anybody could do it to them. I'll list them for you, if you want their names."

"You know me for a believer."

"Who are those wenches; do you know them?"

I had seen them as soon as I had stepped on to the porch, but I had had it on my mind then to talk to Doc and, partly turned away from them, I had forgotten all about them. They were sitting

84

in a red drophead somewhat ancient Alvis, the top down, taking in the last spread of sun in the parking space and about sixty feet from us.

"What are they doing here?" Doc wanted to know.

The one at the wheel was a blonde, and about thirty years old, and she seemed to be reading a book The other was a brunette, older but only they knew by how much. She was smoking and occasionally, without turning her head, saying something to the blonde, who would then raise her eyes, looking straight ahead and then return to the book.

"Who are they?" Doc said.

"Mama mia!" Penny said.

He had come through the doorway behind us and he was now standing between Doc and me.

"Mama mia!" he said, "how do you like that?"

"I asked you who they are," Doc said.

"Top Secret. This information is classified. Ain't that what they do in the War Office?"

"Who are they, curse you?"

"I ain't allowed to give out this information. You screws can put me in solitary and torture me if you want, but I ain't gonna sing. I'll give you just one clue."

"What is it?"

"Ask Ceroni."

"Joe Ceroni knows them?" Doc spluttered.

"Knows them? And how!"

"How do you know that?"

"Oh, no you don't. You know who that dark-haired one is?"

"Who?"

"She's the blonde's mother."

"Isn't that dreadful?" Doc said, glancing at me.

"I told that Ceroni to just put me down for that mother. That's all. I never had a mother like that. Two nice-looking bits of skirt, ain't they?"

Why, she's got to be old enough to be your own mother," Doc said.

"My mother was never like that. Every day could be Mother's Day. Savvy?"

"Joe Ceroni!" Doc said, disgusted.

85

"They must have some interesting conversations," I said. "I mean, discussing things like the lasting evidence of the transcendentalist influence in modern literature."

"What?"" Penny said. "What?"

"What exactly do you believe in, Alf?"

"I believe in that," Penny said, still looking at the two women.

Harry McCormick had come out of the door behind us and he walked down the two front steps. He was carrying a sweat-suit and a pair of white woollen socks, presumably taking them from his room to hang them out and, without so much as glancing at the female element, he walked by the car and round the corner of the building. As he went by, the brunette glanced at him and then leaned forward and, apparently, stubbed her cigarette out in the ash-tray on the dashboard.

"A vintage old car too, eh?" Penny commented.

"If it's a fighter they want," I said to Doc, "they just saw one. Harry McCormick."

"That's right."

"I should tell them," I said. "I should say: 'Look, if you're specialising in fighters, that was Harry McCormick. One of these days, in a year of so, he's going to be in the ring with your boy. Meet Harry McCormick.' "

"The dirty bitches that can't keep their hands off fighters," Doc said vehemently. "Why, that Ceroni's no more than a kid."

"Come on," Penny said. "Just 'cos you mugs can't do it, don't knock it."

We were playing them so hard, sitting there on the porch with our eyes and all our thoughts on them, that I somehow knew that they knew it. You could tell it, really, through the way they just sat there, each holed up behind her own indifference.

"Who on earth are they?" Capini said, walking out on to the porch.

"There," Doc half-explained.

Ceroni had come out of the gym door and walked up to the car on the brunette's side. He couldn't have said more than three words, but the blonde turned towards him and, leaning over a little, said something to him across the other woman, and then the other said something and smiled. Ceroni turned and, without looking at us, went back into the gym. When he did, the blonde started the car and the back wheels ground into the gravel and they went by us, across the car park and towards the road, looking straight ahead.

"Mama mia!" Penny intoned for the third time.

"So that's who they are, is it?" Capini said. "They should be arrested."

"Get on," Penny said. "What do you want to do, play jailer?"

"That new fellow who has those cabins down the road," Capini remarked to Doc and me, "he called me last week. He said: 'You know one of your fighters comes here.' He told me what he looked like. I knew who it was and I said to him: 'You shouldn't allow that; that's against the law.' He said to me: 'I have to make a living.' I think I'll tell Mr. Charlie Mahoney about it."

"You tell him nothing," Doc commanded.

"Mr. Charlie Mahoney has money invested in that boy He sends him down here to get in condition and he has a fight coming up. That's not right to Mr. Charlie Mahoney and I should tell him."

"Tell him nothing," Doc said. "Let him find out for himself."

"I don't know," Capini said, shaking his head. "I think it's terrible."

"You're just jealous," Penny said. "I know about you foreign ginks."

"I know your type, too," Capini said.

He walked back into the lobby and Penny followed him, talking not to, but at, him.

"What's it going to be like between that mother and daughter in a few years?" Doc said. "I mean, when the mother can't perform any more? Won't that be dreadful?"

"I'm thinking of Mahoney," I said. "I like what you told Capini."

"Charlie Mahoney'll find out for himself."

"Yes, but he's so saturated with his own success. The great Mr. Mahoney knows everybody and knows everything. I just can't wait to see him tomorrow, knowing that everybody else knows that his fighter is playing around and Charlie doesn't know it himself. I'm enjoying this and you should be, also."

"I don't give a damn about flaming Mahoney," Doc said.

XII

Teddy had returned after roadwork with the others and had had his breakfast. I had left him lying on his bed reading the morning papers and listening to the radio while Waller sat at the table writing postcards. After three lovely fine days, it had come on to rain hard and I was standing in the porch, looking out, when I heard the bus stop on the road. Then I heard it backfire and start away again, after which Lefty Flynn came walking across the car park through the rain.

He was as black as the ace of spades and he was wearing an old dark grey sharkskin suit and he was bare-headed. He was carrying an Army kitbag slung over his left shoulder and, under his right arm, a small and battered old brown suitcase tied with thick string. I watched him walking through the rain eyeing the hotel and then, as he got closer, looking at me.

"Hello, Lefty," I said when he came up the two steps. "My name's Frank Cutler."

"Why sure," he said, putting the suitcase down and shaking my hand, the while smiling and showing his so-white teeth. "I remember you, Mr. Cutler."

"Thank you."

The rain had soaked the tight curls of his hair, wet his face and darkened the shoulders of his jacket but he seemed not to notice it.

"Yes, I remember. Once you wrote a story about me in the paper. That was quite a time ago, but do you remember that?"

"I remember it well."

"It was a good story and I've got it at home still. My wife likes it, too, and she's put it in the scrapbook she's got full of my cuttings."

"I'm pleased to hear that but I don't like the weather you brought with you."

"You wanna know somethin' about this weather?"

"What?"

"I used to say what you just said. When it rained I liked to say it was bad and miserable, but then I figured that, when it's stormy weather for some people, it's got to be fine weather for others. It all depends."

You're so right, Satan."

"Since then I read a newspaper story about Houston, in Texas, where there was a drought because it didn't rain for a very long time. I boxed in that part of America, you know?"

"I know you did."

"Even then it didn't look too good to me. I mean, you see all that country out there and it ain't like here, green the way we get it, and I notice the people didn't look happy to me, even then. I reckoned they don't get enough rain, so I reckon you've got to have rain to be happy. And that's why I never call it bad weather no more."

"Right again, Satan."

"I never expected to meet you down here, Mr. Cutler."

"I'm going to write a magazine story about Teddy."

"That's good. I'm glad to hear that because Teddy's a good fighter."

"He's lucky to get you to work with him, Lefty."

I don't know. I just hope to stay in there with him. I hope I don't disappoint Mister Doc Eastlake."

"You won't. Do you want to go in?"

"I suppose I should sometime."

He was about the right size for a welter-cum-middleweight, about five feet nine inches and solid as a tank. There was never any fat on him, even at his age. He was a black with a face, widespread by nature, that neither gave him away as a fighter nor denied it, and that was truly amazing. It was as rare to find such life still playing in the face of a fighter going nowhere after nearly two hundred fights as it is to find it in the look of a very old man.

"Let me carry that."

"No thanks; I manage it fine."

I held the door open for him and walked up to the desk with him. Capini, needless to say, was behind it, heavily engaged as usual with a pencil and a sheaf of papers.

"You know Lefty 'Satan' Flynn, Rene."

"I know you, Mr. Capini; I've been here before."

"Lefty Flynn," Capini said, looking at him askance. "You've come today."

"That's right," I said. "You see it for yourself."

"They told me he's coming tomorrow," Capini grumbled, talking to me.

"Mister Doc Eastlake told me to come down today," Flynn said, "so I come today."

"I don't know," Capini said, spreading his hands and shrugging his shoulders to me.

"Where does he stay, Rene?"

"How do they expect me to run a place like this if they don't tell me when this one or that one is coming?"

"I don't mean to cause no trouble, Mr. Capini."

"You're not causing any trouble, Lefty, " I said. "Capini's got room for you."

"He'll have to treble up with old Sid and that Harry McCormick."

"That'll be fine with me."

"Now I must go up to the attic and bring down a divan."

"I'll bring it down, Mr. Rene. You show me where and I'll bring it down."

"I'll have to show you later."

"Come on, Lefty," I said. "I'll show you where their room is."

"Thank you, Mr. Cutler."

He picked up his things and Capini went back to his papers while I led Flynn up the stairs. At the top I pointed to the room where old Sid and McCormick were staying. When he made for it I turned the other way, looked into Teddy's room and went in.

Teddy was lying on the bed, his eyes closed but the radio still playing. Waller was still sitting at the table, still writing postcards, and Penny was sitting near the window reading a morning paper.

"I'm writing a few cards," Nat said, looking up at me.

"A few dozen," Penny said sarcastically.

"Did you get my Christmas card?"

"Sure I did. Thanks, Nat. I thought I had thanked you."

"Did he get your what?" Penny chipped in.

"My Christmas card."

"And months later you're askin' him did he get your Christmas card?"

"And why not?"

"Boy, you're nutty; a real rich fruit-cake."

"What time is it?" Teddy wondered, still lying there but stretching now.

90

"Did you sleep?" Waller said.

"I'm not sure. What time is it?"

"It's a quarter past one."

"Then I must have dropped off for half-an-hour or so."

"It's rainin'," Penny said. "Lousy rain."

"Lefty 'Satan' Flynn is here," I said.

"He is?" Teddy said, sitting up and swinging his feet to the floor. "That's good. When did he arrive?"

"Just now."

"Where is he?" Waller said. "I gotta see him."

"He's rooming with old Sid and McCormick."

"Three spades," Penny said.

"He was a great fighter," Teddy said.

"That's too right," Waller agreed.

"What?" Penny said. "Who?"

"Lefty Flynn," Waller said. "He was some fighter."

"Are you kiddin?"

"That's the truth," Teddy said, looking at Penny. "When I first started fighting he was a great fighter."

"How come in those days I never even heard of him, then?"

"I'm telling you," Teddy said, "when he used to box at Solomons' place everything stopped. I mean, the other fighters used to stop whatever training they were doing and just watch him. Is that right, Frank?"

"Absolutely right. The managers even stopped arguing and haggling."

"I used to watch him," Teddy said, "when I was just beginning. Doc never liked to have me watch other fighters. When he'd catch me watching in the gym he'd make me do something else, but one day he saw me watching the Satan and he said: 'That's alright. You can watch this guy and learn.' I remember the day well."

"How come he never won a title then?" Penny demanded.

"Pardon?"

"If he was such a great fighter, how come he never won any title?"

"What's that got to do with it?" Waller said.

"Fellow, you're rocky; what's it got to do with it? If you're a great fighter you surely win some title, don't you?"

I looked at Teddy and Teddy looked at me and shrugged. "Not always," he said.

"Why not?"

"Lefty never got the breaks because he didn't have the right connections"

"So, if he's a great fighter, he makes his own breaks."

"It's not that easy; it's very complicated, Alf."

"What's so complicated?"

"Let Frank here explain it to you."

"Why me?" I wondered.

"Okay, I'll explain it to you," Teddy offered.

"No thanks," Penny said. "I want to believe this."

"Then go ahead, Frank," Teddy said.

"Well, in the first place Lefty was never a sensational fighter. He was never a crowd-pleaser simply because he knew too much and never went out to put on a show. He went out to get a job done, but for the people who hung around Solomons' he was a real pro'. The ordinary people who go to the fights can't tell a pro' from an amateur."

"I still don't get it."

"You're in the entertainment business, Alf."

"I am, am I?"

"All of you are. Why do you think it's taken Teddy so long to get a shot at the title? He's too solid and competent to be a 'you-hit-me-and-I'll-hit-you' crowd pleaser. The crowd want to see plenty of blood and guts stuff; fighters who put their life on the line every time the bell rings. Lefty might spend eight rounds just lousing the other fellow up, if that was the best way to fight that particular man on that particular night."

"I don't know. You mugs still ain't convicin' me. I still think that, if he was such a great fighter, he'd have won a title."

"Alright; he's also coloured."

"What's that got to do with it? For a long time now, almost every world champion has been black."

"For one thing, we're going back years and years, Alf. We're talking about a coloured fighter nobody wants to fight because he isn't colourful. Besides, he's far too good and you can't do anything with him."

"You ought to have seen the way he could mess you about with his gloves, arms and shoulders," Teddy said.

92

"Also, he was mishandled. He had several managers who should have been selling insurance or driving a bus or something, and who had no idea what a class performer they had. No white guys would meet him unless he carried them--and he did that, as well. None of the top half-dozen welters or middleweights would box him at any price, so he had to go in with people who outweighed him by up to twenty pounds. Look at his record. He boxed all over the world and met all the tough ones."

"Did he ever get knocked out or stopped?"

"Five or six times."

"Properly, or did he take dives?"

"I've never asked him. Why don't you?"

"No thanks, not me."

"Are you convinced now?" Waller said.

"Maybe, but I ain't lettin' on."

"Listen," Waller said. "I can name a lot of good fighters who never made it to a big title. How about Ginger Sadd and Dave Finn for starters? From way back I could name you...."

"Oh, I know you could. Some of them sheiks, eh?"

"Sheiks," Penny said, turning to Teddy. "Yesterday he dumps that on me, the great Nat. He says: 'What you wanna be, a fighter or a sheik?' Can you imagine, me a sheik? Why don't you lay down, Nat, you and our sheiks. Here's a bum who don't know he's dead."

"Listen...."

"I'm not listenin'," Penny said, and he got up and walked out.

"He really is crazy." Waller said.

"He's just a silly kid," Teddy said. "He's not really a bad guy."

"You know something?" Teddy said to me.

"No, what?"

"It really is a crime he never won a title."

"Who?" Waller said.

"Lefty Flynn. You know, everything you told Alf was the truth, but I still don't understand it myself."

"You don't understand what?" Waller said.

"I just don't understand it; a fighter like Lefty Flynn. He never made a bad move. I used to get a kick just watching him pick off punches in mid-air. You never saw anybody else could do that as well as him."

93

"I knew some others," Waller said, " years ago we had fighters about could do that.

"I don't get it. What do the fans want? Why couldn't they see how good Lefty was?"

"It's too intricate an art, Teddy."

"How do you mean?"

"It's too much an art for the average person, fight fan or not, to understand; all they see is the result. If it's a bloody war in there, that's great. If one of them gets knocked out, even greater. That's all they've got the brains to understand."

"But there's some fiddlers nobody can knock out. There's guys nobody can look good in there with. You know that."

"Certainly."

"It can't be right. Maybe you box the toughest guy in the world for you because of his style. So you manage to lick him and people don't like it. Is that right?"

"No, but that's because the fighter, as a practitioner of what was once called 'The Noble Art of Self-defence,' is in the most peculiar and unfortunate position."

"What do you mean by that?"

"Because each and every fight is in front of an excited and bloodthirsty audience. You know well enough that a painter doesn't have to perform that way."

"I hadn't thought of that."

"A painter sets to work on a tough task and, if it doesn't go well, he maybe hides it. It never gets shown so nobody looks at it and says: 'He's a bum; he couldn't paint a brick wall.' Great painters have their attics full of work they never show. Maybe some of that work they liked better than anything they're famous for, because they completed a tough task in a way nobody else ever did it. It doesn't show as a real triumph, though, because it never could, but they don't have to display it in front of an audience of amateurs who couldn't understand anyway. You folk have to show every time out and a fighter is only as good as his last fight."

"I never thought of it that way."

"I'm gonna see Lefty," Waller said, and he went out and closed the door behind him.

"I feel really sorry for Lefty," Teddy mused.

"What about yourself?"

"Well, I've made good money."

94

"Stop kidding to me."

"What?"

I've got to get you to talk to me now, I was thinking.

"Stop trying to have me over," I said.

"I'm not having you on."

"Look, I'm your friend and I like you. I'm Doc's friend, too, I've known him for more years than I care to remember. He's the best in the business and you're the best fighter, pound for pound and punch for punch, in the ring today. People don't know that. They won't even find it in the newspapers. Don't tell me you've made good money; you should have made ten times as much and you should now be champion of the world."

"I know that."

"You've got to be sore about it."

"I keep reading in the papers what a great champion this man is."

"Everyone reads that."

"It's like a poker game. You've got to be lucky."

"You're wrong."

"How do you mean?"

"You've got to be lucky, but only in the deal. After forty-five years in the business, Doc finally got dealt a fighter who could learn and do all the things Doc has been trying to teach all those years. Where were you dealt in? You were dealt the body, the mind and the reflexes to be that fighter; now you two gentlemen are holding the winning cards. You've just got to play them right."

"We'll play them right."

"I know you will."

"Everybody always talks and writes about this super champion. They say he's a great fighter and sometimes that makes me a little sore."

"So it should."

"He's not a great fighter; he's a real showboat. D'ye want to know the truth?"

"Certainly I do."

"The other fellow's made for me."

"I know he is."

"Doc and I know exactly how to nail him. They say he's a banger but he can't punch with me. I'll back him off in any

95

exchange; you watch who backs off in the very first exchange."

"I'll be watching."

"That'll show you and everyone how great a champion he is. I'm tired of hearing that and I just want to show people."

"Well, you will."

"By all that's holy, I will."

"You see? Finally you're very lucky. You've got the chance now and the cards to do it. Many people go through life without ever getting that chance."

"I'm sure that's right."

The door opened and Penny came in.

"Hey!" he said to Teddy. "Big news."

"What is it?"

"Your wife and your boy and your brother-in-law are here."

"You're not joking?" Teddy said. "Let's go down, Frank."

"I need a good wash first," I said.

XIII

I reckon they had been talking ten minutes or so when I went into the dining-room. They were sitting at a table for four by a window that looks on to the pool, and the boy was running back and forth among the other tables, from one end of the room to the other.

"Come and join us, Frank," Teddy invited.

Seems they had exhausted whatever it was they had been talking about, because Mary and her brother were just sitting there with their drinks in front of them and Teddy was scribbling lines on the plastic table-cloth with the tip of one of the table-knives.

"You know Mary and this is her brother, Ken."

"Hello, Mary."

"Hello again," she said, nodding.

"Pleased to meet you," I said to her brother, and he half rose to shake hands.

He appeared to be about thirty-five and about a head taller than Mary. Although he wasn't thin, there was a drawn look to his face and he was balding. He had on a Lonsdale cotton-flannel sports shirt and, clipped to the breast pocket, were a ball-point

96

pen and a silver automatic pencil. Shoved into the pocket behind them was a small black leather note-book. On his feet he wore white Lonsdale trainers.

"Was the driving difficult in the rain?" I asked.

"It wasn't any fun," Ken said.

He's got to be some kind of supply clerk, I was thinking, or I can't place people in their slots any more.

"What will you drink, Frank?" Teddy said.

"I'll get them," I said. "What's yours, Mary?"

"Scotch and soda, if I may."

"You, sir?"

"No thanks," Ken declined, "not for me."

Capini poured some Martell over some ice for me, then mixed Mary's drink and I brought them back. Through the window behind Ken I could see that it was still raining hard.

"My God," Teddy said, "can't you make him stop?"

The boy was still running up and down as hard as he could go, and now he was stamping his feet with each step, on the bare wooden floor.

"What can I do?" Mary said.

"Psst, Tiger!" Teddy said, calling the child.

The boy, running, heard him but paid no attention. On the next trip past us, though, he ran close to our table and, as he was about to dive out again, Teddy reached out and caught him around the waist.

"C'mon," he said, pulling the youngster to him with the boy wriggling to get loose, "I want you to meet Mr. Cutler."

"Hiya," I said.

"I wanna run," was the reply.

"How about us having a party?" Teddy said in desperation. "We'll have a party right here and you can have ice-cream. How would you like some ice-cream?"

The kid was short and wiry with short brown hair and he had brown eyes like his mother. He had on new brown shoes and a grey flannel suit with short pants. I realised that he and his mother were dressed as a pair, for she had on a grey flannel suit and a red blouse. There was a red ribbon holding the pony tail at the back of her head.

"I don't want ice-cream," he grumbled, squirming to get away from Teddy.

"C'mon, I'll get you some ice-cream."

"Okay," the child said and, taking him by the hand, Teddy led him out to the kitchen.

"Can you recall, Mary, when you first met Teddy?" I said after a while.

"When I first met him?"

"Yes."

"Who knows?" she said.

"We all lived in the same flats," Ken said.

"I know that."

"She always knew him. They were playmates."

"What's the first thing you can remember about Teddy? I mean, going back in your mind, what do you recall about him? Maybe it's something he said to you or you said to him, or maybe something that you saw him do?"

"All the kids were together," Ken said. "She wouldn't remember things like that."

Big brother has got to be a supply clerk, I was thinking, when Teddy came back, still holding his son's hand and, with his other hand, carrying a dish of ice-cream and a spoon.

"Now," he said, putting the dish on the table and pulling another chair up for the boy, "this'll taste good."

"I was asking Mary," I said to Teddy when he sat down, "what she first remembers about you."

"What do you mean?"

"Oh, like when she and you first became aware of each other."

"I can tell you when I first paid any attention to her," he said, smiling and looking at her.

The boy was kicking on one of the legs of the table, and Teddy became aware of it at the same moment as I did.

"C'mon," he said. "Eat some more of your ice-cream."

"I don't want it."

"What's wrong with it? You love ice-cream."

"I don't want it."

"When did he stop liking ice-cream?" Teddy said to Mary.

"I don't know; he always has liked it before."

"Alright, but just don't kick the table."

"You were just saying," I said, "that you remember when you first noticed Mary."

98

"That's right," Teddy agreed. "We were playing a kind of rounders and somebody--I don't remember who--made a terrific hit and up the street where there was this car parked."

The boy was kicking the table again.

"Look, Tiger," Teddy said to him, "do you want me to belt you?"

"Don't talk to him like that," Mary said.

"Alright; then you tell him to stop because he shouldn't be kicking the table."

"Then guess," the boy said.

"Guess? Guess what?"

"Billy's cousin's name."

"What's he mean by that?"

"Billy Delaney's cousin," Mary explained. "He was playing with Billy Daleney the other day and his cousin was there."

"Guess," the boy insisted, kicking the table leg again.

"Alright, but just stop that kicking. Is it a girl or a boy?"

"I don't know."

"You don't know? You were playing with him or her, whichever Billy Delaney's cousin is, weren't you?"

"It's a girl," Mary clarified. "He knows full well it's a girl."

"It's a girl?" Teddy said to his young son.

"Guess her name," came the demand.

"Betty," Teddy said.

"Nope," the boy said, drawing it out lengthily, smiling and shaking his head slowly.

"Alice?" Negative headshake.

"Helen?" Similar reaction.

"I can't even think of any more girls' names," Teddy said to the rest of us.

"Ruth," Ken suggested.

"Nope. Guess again."

"Florence," Teddy said.

"Ha-ha. Nope."

"Grace," Ken offered.

"No-o."

"For God's sake, what's the girl's name?" Teddy said to Mary.

"I don't know; I never even saw her. He just came home and said he had been playing with Billy Delaney's cousin."

"Keep guessing."

"And he didn't tell you the name?"

"I already told you he didn't."

"Guess on," the boy said, starting to kick the table leg again. "Just guess."

"Let's see," Teddy said. "Frances."

"No way. Guess some more."

"This is silly," Teddy said, "we could guess all day. What was it you were asking me, Frank?"

"You were telling me about the game of rounders."

"Guess."

"That's right. Somebody hit the ball right up the street and it hit the back of this car that was parked there and..."

"C'mon, guess."

"...where the back sloped up to the back window, it hit there and bounced up in the air, over the top of the car..."

"Guess. You guess," the boy was saying, keeping time with his shoe on the table-leg now. "Guess. Guess."

"Oh, Alice."

"No fear."

"You guessed that one before," I said.

"I don't know any more."

"Guess."

"Why don't you guess?" Teddy said to Mary.

"I don't know the name; I've told you I don't know."

"But I don't know it either. He's the only one that knows."

"Guess, go on and guess," the boy said, still kicking in time.

"I don't know, Jane?"

"Nope," and, blessedly the table-kicking stopped.

"Judy?"

"Nope."

"Janet?"

"Nope."

"Jean?"

"Nope."

"How the hell are we going to guess it?" Teddy said to the rest of us.

"Try taking it alphabetically," Ken suggested helpfully. "That's the only way to do it."

"Guess."

"Even I'm getting interested now," I said.

100

"Guess."

"Abbey," Ken offered.

"Aachen," came from me.

"What?" Ken said.

"It's the name of a town in Germany."

"Guess."

"Barbara," Teddy said.

"Nope."

"This is impossible," Teddy said.

"Not blooming likely."

"I like that one," I said. "Impossible Murphy."

"Tee-hee-hee," the tormentor said.

"Adele," Ken voiced."

"You've got to be kiddin," the boy said.

"We've got to think of something else to get his mind off it," Teddy said.

"Keep guessing."

"Well, if anybody knows the phone number," I said, "I'll gladly call Mrs. Murphy and ask her."

"Guess. Guess."

"Look," Teddy said to him, exasperated. "We're not going to guess any more. The game's over."

"Just keep guessing."

"We did and we can't guess any more. You'll have to tell us."

"Nope."

"I'd like to know" I said to him. "Won't you tell me?"

"Nope."

"Look here!" Teddy said, raising his voice. "Tell him."

"Nope," came from the boy, and then he dropped his head and started to cry.

"Now look what you've done," Mary said

"Look what I've done?" Teddy blurted out. "What did I do? He's got us all going crazy here trying to guess the name of some child we don't even know, and now he starts to cry. I didn't make him cry."

"And I certainly didn't," Mary retorted.

"Come on," Teddy said and he picked his son up. The boy was still crying sitting on Teddy's lap, the fighter trying to rock him soothingly. "Just stop crying; what are you crying about?"

"I don't know," the little fellow said between the sobs that were shaking him. "I don't know."

"You don't know? You don't know what?"

"I don't know the name," the child was sobbing. "I don't know the girl's name. I don't know the girl's name."

"How about that?" Teddy gasped, looking at Mary. "He drives us all potty trying to guess a name he doesn't even know himself."

"That's the way he is," Mary said.

"We don't care what the name is," Teddy said to his boy, rocking him while the boy went on sobbing. "We don't care; who cares about that silly old name?"

""You know, you should never have started that guessing business with him," Ken said knowingly.

"You're right, you know," I said to him, trying to make my face express serious awe. "You're absolutely right."

"Of course I'm right."

"Do you have any children of your own?"

"You don't need to have children. All you need to have is common sense."

"I know what we'll do," Teddy said, bending over and trying to peer into the child's face. "I know what we'll do. We'll play the Bagatelle machine. Would you like to play the pinball game?"

"I don't know," the boy said, still crying.

"Come on, son," Teddy said.

He stood up and whipped the kid up on his shoulder and carried him off towards the bar, the boy still sobbing.

"It's never easy," I said to Mary. "I expect that it was never supposed to be."

"You're telling me!"

"If you just use common sense," Ken chipped in, "you won't have any trouble."

"No trouble at all?" I said.

"Well, you know what I mean."

"What was Teddy trying to tell me about the game of rounders?" I said to Mary.

"I've no idea."

"You don't recall that particular game with which, apparently, you had something to do?"

102

"There were lots of ball games played on our patch," Ken said.

"I remember them playing rounders," Mary said. "They used to play it all summer."

"What' so important about a game of rounders?" Ken queried.

"I don't know; I haven't heard Teddy's story yet."

"But what difference would it make. Teddy's a fighter now and that's what you're writing about, isn't it?"

"That's right."

"I don't understand how you writers work."

"So I would imagine," I said and then to Mary: "Can I get you another drink?"

"You might just as well."

"And for you?" I said to Ken.

"No thanks." He said, and then thinking: "Well, alright. I'll have rye and ginger."

I returned with the drinks and sat down. Mary was lighting another cigarette, deftly and behind that pane of clear glass that I had seen at the house.

"Do you enjoy watching the fights?" I said to her.

She inhaled deeply from the cigarette and then exhaled the smoke slowly. It is, I believe, a device many of those glaziers use.

"To be honest with you, I can take them or leave them."

"Do you go to Teddy's fights in London?"

"I have been to some."

"How many have you watched?"

"Oh, only three or four."

"Are you planning to write about Mary?" Ken said.

"To some extent, yes."

"Why do you have to bring her into it?"

"Because she's Teddy's wife."

"There's a lot of fighters who aren't even married."

"What was the first fight you ever saw Teddy box?" I said to Mary. "Was it before you were married?"

"Yes, it was at a baths place in Bethnal Green."

"What do you remember about it?"

"Well, his opponent was coloured."

"Arnold Sheppard." Ken said. "Teddy knocked him out in the fifth round."

103

"Tell me about it," I said to Mary. "How did you come to go to the fight and who did you go with? What sort of night was it? You weren't yet married to Teddy and you may just remember the dress you decided to wear. You'd never been to the fights before, so it was either the way you expected it to be or it wasn't. How was it?"

"I went with a girl friend because Teddy had given me two tickets."

"What kind of an evening was it?"

"It was in the summer. I don't particularly recall what kind of a night it was."

"Is that really important?" Ken said, "the kind of a night it was?"

"It might be."

"Why?"

"Because this was the start of Mary becoming a part of Teddy's way of making a living, his career."

"But Teddy's a fighter."

"What difference does that make? Teddy leaves home, has a pair of gloves laced on his hands and fights. Somebody else picks up a brief-case, kisses his wife goodbye and sets off for the office. They're both in the same tournament but each man doing his own thing. I'm merely trying to reconstruct the beginnings of the relationship that grew to involve Mary and the fights."

"What magazine did you say this story is for?"

"I didn't say."

"Well, what magazine is it for."

"The Brewers' Gazette."

"What?"

"You're afraid of this story, aren't you?" I said to Mary.

"Why do you say that?" she replied.

"Because I can feel it; I'd have to be pretty thick not to."

"She's got a right to be," Ken said.

"Why?"

"The things they write about boxing and boxers," Mary said.

"All those videos and movies they make," Ken said. "Teddy was never in a fixed fight."

"Of course not," I said, "not one fighter in a thousand ever is."

"Then why do they write such things?" Mary demanded.

"To make a living."

"People don't know what it's like, being married to a fighter."

"I'm sure of that."

"He's away half the time and, when he's home, he's not like other men."

"Naturally, he's a fighter."

"There's a lot of things we don't do and there's a lot of places we don't go."

"Believe me, Mary doesn't have an easy time of it," Ken commented.

"I never suspected that she did."

"Then the awful things they're always writing about boxing," Mary complained. "At least if Teddy were in some other business he would be respected."

"When he wins the title he'll be respected. Millions of people all over the world will watch it on TV and, in spite of what they may have heard and read about boxing, they'll respect and look up to him."

"I'm not so sure," she said.

"Maybe, if he could win the title," Ken said. "Then he could commercialise his name, but the champion's a great fighter. Don't forget that."

I didn't have to answer. Teddy was walking back towards us, holding his son by the hand.

"Some Bagatelle player," he said when he reached us. "He's a champ."

"I wanna play some more," the boy said, tugging at Teddy's hand.

"I have to go in and workout," Teddy said. "I'll take him in with me and he can watch everything. He'll like that."

"Nothing doing," Mary interrupted.

"I wanna play some more."

"Why? What's the matter? He'll like it."

"I know he'll like it. Do you think I want him watching his father punching other people?"

"Why not?"

"What does he know about boxing? All he'll see is his father hitting other people. Then he'll start doing it himself in the playgrounds."

105

"No, he won't."

"Listen, I know him better than you do. I'm the one who will have to put up with him and it's bad enough as it is."

"I wanna play some more."

"Okay," Teddy said shrugging. "I'll see you later."

"I wanna play more, more, more..."

"Your mother'll play with you," Teddy said over his shoulder and walked out.

"Alright, alright," Mary said, "I'll play with you."

"Well, I'm glad to have seen you again," I said to her.

"Thank you."

"And you, too," I said, nodding to Ken.

"Wait. I'm going in to watch Teddy box."

I walked into the gym with Ken following me. Ceroni was in the ring, boxing with Mahoney's other welterweight and Doc was standing alone near the chairs, watching.

"Did you rest?" I said.

"Sort of. I lay down for a while."

"Do you know Teddy's brother-in-law?"

"I've met him," Doc said, nodding to Ken.

"Tell me," Ken said, "what kind of shape is Teddy in?"

"What kind of shape?" Doc ejaculated, looking straight at him.

"That's right."

"Lousy shape," Doc quipped.

"What?"

"He's getting into great condition," I said.

"He'd better be," Ken retorted.

"Had he?" Doc countered, giving Ken that look.

"Sure, he'll need to be because he's meeting a tough fighter. The other fellow is some champion."

"You really think so?" Doc said.

"I certainly do."

"What line of country did you once tell me you're in?" Doc said, giving him that look again.

"Wholesale hardware. Why?"

"Good," Doc said as he turned and walked away. I followed him.

"Thanks," I said.

"For what?"

"Big brother."

"Isn't that dreadful? Doc concluded.

When Teddy came out, Evans and Lefty Flynn were with him and they loosened up for some little time with Waller fussing around Teddy. Then, in the ring, Teddy sparred the first round with Mahoney's middleweight, just hounding him, after which he worked two with Evans, starting to sweat nicely. When Evans finished and Flynn climbed in, I moved to near the ropes and stood next to Doc.

"Mind if I join you on the bridge?"

"Be my guest," Doc said, and then: "Lefty!"

Waller had finished fingering the vaseline on Flynn's face and then he put the gumshield in. Teddy was circling the ring, walking around loose-armed, breathing in through his nose and out through his mouth, and Flynn came over to where Doc and I were standing.

"Teddy'll let you set your own pace," Doc said to him. "Don't kill yourself the first day."

Flynn nodded and then hooked his white rubber mouthpiece out with the thumb of his left glove.

"Don't you worry 'bout me, Mister Doc." He said. "I keep in shape. I'll just keep him sweating real good."

"Alright," Doc said to Waller.

"Time!" the conditioner yelled.

Flynn put the gumshield back in, he and Teddy both turned and they boxed the three minutes. Lefty set the pace, not fast but even, moving in and out with that left firing at Teddy, but he making his own moves off it and Lefty catching almost all of them on the elbows or forearms or on one of the big, sixteen-ounce training gloves.

"Who are you looking for?" Doc said to me.

"Alf Penny."

I could see Mahoney watching with Ceroni, Sid Brown and McCormick bunched together also watching, and Teddy's brother-in-law sitting in the front row of chairs, staring hard at the pair in the ring. I reckoned that Penny had gone in for his shower.

"What do you want him for?"

"We were trying to convince him that Lefty knows something about fighting. With the big gloves on Flynn, even Penny should be able to see it."

"Time!" Waller shouted.

107

Teddy came over, mouthpiece in his left glove, and Doc took a towel off the top rope and wiped the sweat off his charge's face. Waller did similarly for Lefty and, with Teddy pacing the ring again, Lefty 'Satan' came over to us.

"Mister Doc?"

"Yes?"

"I believe I can hit him with a straight right hand."

"Why don't you, then?"

"You want me to try it, then?"

"What do you think I brought you down here for?"

"Yes sir," Lefty said, nodding and putting the gumsheid back in.

"Time!"

"Just watch this," Doc said to me.

"He's giving a great imitation of the respected champion," I said, watching intently.

And Flynn was doing just that. He was jabbing, then doubling the jab, head-feinting and picking off Teddy's jabs with the right glove.

"Lefty can imitate any well-known fighter of the last fifteen years," Doc enthused. "You name him and 'Satan' can ape him."

As he said it, Flynn let the right hand go. He leaned his upper body a little to the left and let it go straight from the shoulder. When he did, Teddy turned his head so that it just grazed the left side of his headguard and, pivoting back, he drove his own right hand hard, under the heart."

"Stop boxing!" Doc hollered.

The punch had driven Flynn against the ropes and the follow-up hook caught him flush on the cheekbone as his head dropped and Doc shouted. Teddy immediately grabbed Lefty under the armpits and the coloured fighter held on to Teddy for dear life and straightened up.

"Now let's take it easy," Doc said, calling to the pair.

"How'd you like that?" Waller said, moving across to us.

"Fine," I said.

"Teddy'll do something like that to the champion, too. They'll all see who's a great champion. Teddy is liable to kill him."

"Watch the time," Doc said, "how's the time?"

"Time!" Waller said, yelling it.

"Are you alright?" Doc said to Flynn.

108

"I'm okay," Lefty said, breathing hard and about to crawl through the ropes, but stopping now and straightening up. "He sure put one on me, Mister Doc. He's real sharp."

"He'll be sharper yet."

"Nobody even tries to counter my straight right these days. They reckon to slip it or block it nowadays, but not counter it. Truly, nobody ever did that."

"Alright, Lefty, and thanks."

Teddy worked only one round on the heavy bag, one on the speed-ball and then went in to cool out. Doc and I had started out towards the kitchen to avoid Teddy's brother-in-law, when Penny came after me."

"Hey Frank," he said. "Teddy wants you; he's in the dressing-room."

"Where were you when Lefty was boxing?"

"Right underneath a good old shower."

"I'll see you later," I said to Doc. "Why don't you buy Ken a drink?"

"I'll buy him a strychnine and soda."

When I got into the dressing-room, Teddy, Lefty and Evans were having their hot tea. Waller was making a great show of clearing up around the room.

"Whose towel is this?" he was demanding to know, holding up said towel.

"That's mine," Mickey Evans confessed.

"How about that punch?" Nat said to me.

"Good."

"How about it, Lefty?" Waller persisted.

"Knock it off," Teddy said.

"You wanted me?" I said to him.

"Yep. I want to finish telling you about that game of rounders."

"Fine; I'm listening."

"We played the ball game a lot and this one bloke could hit the ball miles. I think it was him who struck it this day and it hit the back of this parked car where the back end slopes up by the rear window. It was a hard rubber ball--you know the kind?--and it went right up into the air. Well, Mary and this other girl--I think her name was Alice--were walking along the pavement and we shouted a warning. They looked up in the air and they saw the ball starting to come down. The other girl put her arms over her

109

head, like frightened girls do, but I remember that Mary just stood there looking up and waiting for the ball. When it came down, she just cupped her hands and caught it, just as easy as anything."

"How come you're telling him that?" Waller wanted to know.

"Because he asked me if I could remember the first time I ever noticed Mary. That was the first time, when she caught that ball. I remember how all the kids cheered!"

"Thanks, Teddy," I said.

"Does that help you? I mean, can you use that?"

"I might. Do you, by any chance, recall what Mary was wearing?"

"It was summer-time and I think she had on a light blue dress."

"Thanks again."

"Just trying to be helpful," he said.

XIV

The slow turning of the door knob awoke me. It was deep dusk in the room with the green shades drawn and I was conscious of rain dripping somewhere outside and then of the light from the bulb in the hall reaching into the room and the silhouette of Waller standing in it and straining to see me.

"Are you awake?"

"Yes, Nat."

"It's still rainin'."

"So I hear."

"It's now seven-thirty."

"Oh?"

"We didn't go on the road, but we're goin' down to the gym. Teddy is gonna loosen up."

"Good, I'll be down."

"He's not gonna do anything much, just loosen up and skip rope, but you said you wanted to be around whatever we do."

"That's right, Nat."

"If I was you I'd sleep on."

"I'll be down, Nat, and thanks."

110

"Okay, but I'll close this door and maybe you'll go back to sleep."

When he shut the door and the room was darkened again, I lay just listening to the rain. I had left the window open about six inches at its bottom and the rain dripping on the sill sounded as if it was falling right in the room.

I wanted to lie there and idly listen to it and then, perhaps, fall asleep again but, after a couple of minutes, I got up, found the door and opened it half-way, so that the light from the hall would come in, but not too bright, because I didn't want to raise the blind to see the rain. Then I put on underpants and trousers, took towel and soap and went down the passage to the bathroom, washed and came back and finished dressing.

In the gym Teddy was skipping rope, wearing a grey sweatsuit and ring shoes. The ceiling lights were on, up among the red, white and blue paper streamers and Waller was leaning against the bar, towel over shoulder. Doc was sitting on one of the wooden folding chairs near the ring, the two of them watching Teddy.

"What the hell are you doing here?" Doc said when I walked up to him.

He had on a pair of dark blue trousers and a light blue V-necked sweater and he needed a shave. Sitting there, in the pale mixture of the yellow light from above and the grey light coming through the windows, he looked very old.

"Don't you remember me? I'm a member of the club, too."

"You really work at this, don't you?"

"Not any harder than you do."

"I don't want him to break the schedule." Doc said. "I let him sleep an hour longer but, if he doesn't do something in place of the roadwork and sleeps all morning it'll throw him all off course."

"Let's hope we don't get three or four days of this rain."

"It's raining for the other fella, too."

There is always the other fellow. You don't just turn in your corner and walk out and meet a stranger. Even if you never saw him before the weigh-in, you have known him and he has known you for all of this long while, so I watched Teddy and listened to the tick of the rope and the pat of his feet in the big, quiet room. Then, in the rhythm of it, my mind moved away from me and I saw the place as from a high, far rafter and, in that gym, the three of us focused upon the one; the one spring-footed and loose-wristed, sweating in his cage of rope and staring, darkly, out through it.

"Alright, that's enough for now," Doc called to him. "Knock it off."

Teddy gave the rope a few final double-timed twirls and, on the last one, turned towards the bar passing the rope into his right hand and, whirling it a half-turn, flung it in an arc towards Waller. Raising both hands, Waller got one hand into it as it reached him and the wooden handles hit the floor.

"What are you tryin' to do, kill me?"

"That's it," Doc said. "Now walk round awhile."

I watched Teddy as he walked, sweating, rotating his shoulders, making a tour around the chairs in front of the ring, then starting the circuit again. When a man runs or walks on the road it is conceivable that he is seeking a world bigger than his home or room but, when he walks in a place like a gymnasium, it is for only one reason and I tried to picture the champion in his own place but in this same moment of cooling off.

On such a morning of rain and greyness there, in one of London's poshest West End hotels as a celebrity American visitor, I wondered if he lay luxuriant in bed before he, too, walked his gym after training, for it is important. When a match is finalised, what each man does with the same moment is a part of it, just as every act a man has ever performed, every thought that he ever possessed and what made him as he now stands, become moves in it, for time now reveals that this is a part of man's eternal struggle for superiority against man.

"Okay," Doc said. "That'll do."

"Right," said Teddy, walking over to us. And then: "Hello, Frank."

"G'morning."

"Do you want your tea in your room or down here?" Waller asked.

"In the room," Teddy said, "my clothes are up there."

He was sitting on the bed now, with just the white terry-cloth gown on and a towel round his neck, the hot teacup cradled in both hands, blowing across the top of it to cool it and slowly sipping from it.

"What do you think of my bother-in-law?" he wanted to know.

"He's quite a brain," I said.

"What did you say?"

"He has what they call a good head on his shoulders."

"Are you kidding?"

"Yes."

"Who?" Waller said. He was sorting his rolls of gauze and tape again on the table.

"My brother-in-law."

"What's the matter with him?"

"You tell me."

"When he was here yesterday," Waller said, "he was asking me how many rounds you worked every day since you got here. He wrote it down in a notebook; how far you run on the road, as well. What's he want all that for?"

"Don't ask me," Teddy said. "You should have asked him."

"I've got it now," I said. "He's not in wholesale hardware; that's just a front. He's a bookie, and he's getting ready to lay his odds on all the possible results of the fight."

"I can just see that," Teddy said, "a jerk like him."

Waller got in with: "He asked me 'how does he sleep, on his back or on his side?' I don't know and then he says: 'I mean, does he sleep well all night long?' So I said: 'Certainly he sleeps well.' What does he think I do, sit up all night and watch you sleep?"

"It reminds me of the second Mills-Lesnevich fight," I said.

"What about it?" Teddy enquired.

"The Board sent a psychiatrist to both camps to analyse the two fighters. Lesnevich's people didn't want to let him talk to Gus, so he started on manager Joe Vella. When the tradepaper's Jack Wilson and I got there Vella was blowing his top. He steamed: 'You know what the looney asks me? He asked me how many times a day Lensevich goes to the bathroom. What does the jerk think I do here to earn my percentage?' "

"What happened then?" Teddy wanted to know.

"The last we saw of the psychiatrist, he was drinking whisky in Solomons' office, interviewing old Dinny Powell, who was one of the American's sparring-partners."

"What could he get from him?" Waller wondered.

"Yesterday," Teddy said, "we're sitting there talking, Mary and Ken and me, and he says: 'Now, if you win, you should make one or two defences and then retire.' I said: 'If I win? Watta you

113

mean IF I win?' He says: 'Well, you know what I mean. The other fellow is a good fighter and accidents can happen.' I said: 'Stop it, will you?' "

"So Mary says: 'Don't get sore' and I retorted: 'Who's sore?' Then she says: 'Well, the other fighter feels the same as you do. He's just as sure he's going to win as you are.' I said: 'What? What's that got to do with it?' "

"Best finish your tea," Waller said.

"What do you think of that?" Teddy said, looking at me.

"I mustn't."

"Why do they act that way?"

"Well, I can't speak for your brother-in-law."

"Believe me, nobody can."

"I prefer to believe, though, that your wife is just instinctively preparing herself--and you, too--for the possibility that exists in her mind that the other fellow, who has a chance to win, just might. That's all it is."

"When you're a fighter you never think of that. Believe me, I never once think that anybody I fight can lick me, and especially not this man in this fight."

"But your wife isn't a fighter and, if something should go wrong, she doesn't want her whole world, and yours, to collapse."

"Nothing's going wrong."

"Of course not, but you asked a question."

He quaffed the last of the tea and put the cup down next to the radio on the bedside table. "Many's the time," he said thoughtfully, "I've wished I was in some other business for just that reason. I mean, when other chaps get home from work they can talk about it with their wives and their wives understand what they go through."

"Don't you be so sure."

"You don't think so?"

"How can they understand? I don't care what the business is, unless they're in it themselves they can't properly understand what it's like."

"So Ken says: 'If you win, have a fight or two and retire.' Right now I'm boxing better than ever before. If I win the title, I'm on top. Why retire? I like the game; I spent nine years learning the business and he wants me to retire. What else could I do as well as I can fight?"

"I agree," I said, "but what intrigues me is the thought that probably not one person in the millions, with TV, who watch a fight even thinks that a fighter can have a brother-in-law."

"I suppose they think that you just go in and fight."

"That's right."

We could hear a pounding on a door or a wall somewhere and some muffled shouts.

"What's that?" Waller said, looking around.

"Lord knows," Teddy said. "Let's find out."

When we got out into the hall Doc, in a flannel robe, was opening his door and Flynn, McCormick and old Sid were coming out of their room. We were all looking at the door to the room where Jakie Turner and Cassidy slept and, wedged across it was a piece of rope with one end sharpened to a point. Wrapped around it and around the door-knob with a glob of glue or somesuch, was part of a twisted clothes-line.

"What's goin' on?" Waller said.

"Somebody's in there," Lefty said above the pounding.

"Oiy, let us out!" Jakie's voice came through the door.

"Go and get your scissors," Doc said to Waller.

"How about that?" Teddy said to me, laughing.

When Waller came back with the scissors, Penny appeared in the hall with Mickey Evans. As Waller made for the door Penny, shirtless but wearing a pair of slacks, grabbed the scissors from him.

"Here, let me do it," he insisted.

"Come off it," Waller said, trying to get the scissors back again.

"Let us out!" Turner's voice came through the door and now the pounding started again.

"No you don't," Penny said, holding the scissors well away from Waller. "Those are my pals in there and I'm the guy who lets 'em out."

"You're the bum who did it," Waller said.

"Come on, for chrisesake come on!" Turner was yelling. "Let us out!"

"Relax, relax," Penny said, shouting it at the door. "I'll rescue you."

"I'll get you for this, Alf," Jakie Turner's voice shouted back. "Open it, I say."

"What's the matter? What on earth is the matter?" Capini said, coming around the corner from the stairs.

"Let us out, you bleeder, LET US OUT!"

"I'll handle it, Rene," Penny said. "I got friends in there."

"We're no friends of yours," Turner's irate tones came back. "Open it, I say!"

"Look at this," Penny said, pointing with the scissors to the rope. "Some genius must have done this; he soaked the rope so it would shrink and get tight. The nut had to be a great brain."

In front of the door on the floor there was a small puddle of water.

"Open this door or I'll murder you!" Jakie Turner was cursing, pounding again.

"Open it, Alf," Doc said quietly.

"Sure, Doc," Penny said slowly, looking at Doc. "I'll open it."

"Open this f-----g door!"

"It'll take a little time," Penny said, sawing at the rope and calling through the door. "Just relax, friends. Alf Penny's got everything in hand."

"You bloody well open it!" Turner said, pounding on the door some more.

"Please, you'll make me nervous," Penny said as he continued sawing. "There."

When he cut the rope the contraption fell to pieces and Penny turned the knob and pushed the door open. As he did so Turner, in a pair of striped and badly rumpled pyjamas, came through it and Penny, backing off, held the scissors in front of himself and pointing at Turner. "Wait a minute, friend, I rescued you."

"If you didn't have those scissors," Jakie said, still moving toward Penny, "I'd kill you."

"Why me?" Penny said querulously, circling a little now, the scissors in front of him as Turner still moved on him.

"Jakie, back off," Doc commanded. "Nat, take those scissors."

"Here, I'll take them," Teddy said. He walked between the two and took the scissors from Penny, holding Turner off with the other hand.

"I oughta give you a right hand," Turner said to Penny.

116

"No thanks at all; no thanks do I get," Penny said, addressing the rest of us but still eyeing Jakie Turner cautiously.

"I'll give you some thanks," Jakie said, pressing against Teddy's arm.

"Whatta you so sore about?" Penny wanted to know. "I didn't do it. Besides, you weren't gonna get up to run, anyway."

"You did it alright," Cassidy's voice boomed out of the room. He was still lying on one of the beds. "We know you did it."

"Me?"

"Yes, you." Jakie said, a little calmer now. "Suppose the place had caught fire and we were trapped in there. Did you ever think of that?"

"You and your fires. I rescued you from one, didn't I? I'd rescue you again, but in case I died trying you could jump out of the window. What is there to worry about?"

"Oh yeah?" Jakie said. "You can get killed jumping from this high."

"Who gets killed? Let Cassidy jump first and then you jump on top of him. He's as soft as sin."

"I ain't so soft," the Killer said from the bed.

"Do you hear that?" Penny said, addressing the rest of us again.

Doc had gone back into his room and shut the door while old Sid had disappeared from the other doorway, although Lefty and McCormick still stood there watching the action. Jakie turned to me.

"I'm glad we're leavin' tomorrow," he said. "I've had enough of that lunatic."

"You're really going tomorrow?" I said.

"We certainly are. Who's there to work with here apart from that one heavyweight Mahoney brings down? The fight's next Thursday, so we'll go into Toby's Gym for a couple of days. What my man needs is a lot of work."

"Is that what he needs?" Penny said, his voice full of sarcasm.

"Why don't you shut it?" Turner said.

"Yes, why don't you, Penny?" Waller said.

"Take your shower," Doc told Teddy and he was standing in his doorway again. "Don't hang around out there."

"That's best, you take your shower," Waller said to Teddy.

117

XV

The next morning Teddy, Lefty and I walked out to the road with Jakie and Cassidy to see them off on the nine-thirty coach. After a day and a half of rain the world--or where we were--seemed to have been washed clean. The sky was a spotless blue, but there was a cool, steady breeze blowing across us to mean that, at least by noon, we would be getting those high-piled banks of swift white clouds.

To anyone seeing but not knowing us we would have appeared a curious group. Jakie, worried less they missed the coach, led us carrying his suitcase. Teddy strolled with his hands in the pockets of his pants, his jacket zipped up to the neck. Lefty, walking behind Teddy and me, carried the smaller of Cassidy's two suitcases, and he himself trailed us carrying the big one loaded with his gear.

"Maybe it's already gone by and we've missed it," Jakie said.

"No," Teddy said, looking at his wrist-watch. "They run the same as trains; nearly always late but never early."

"Here it comes now," Left said.

We saw it coming, shining in the sunlight, down the rise of the road to the south.

"Be lucky," Teddy said, shaking Cassidy's hand. "You can lick this guy you're meeting."

"Thanks Teddy," Cassidy replied.

"He'd better lick him," Jakie said, "the money it's cost me down here."

"Good luck, Paul," I said, shaking his hand and then Lefty hugged him goodbye and I could see that Cassidy was pleased that we had walked across to see him off, but that he was struggling to cover his embarrassment like a big child. Then we all shook hands with Jakie and he remembered to wish Teddy the best. And that was the way we bundled them off, with the manager in the almost threadbare topcoat and battered trilby and his big heavyweight in a new grey tweed overcoat and bareheaded following him down the aisle of the half-filled coach, the two of them lurching as they heaved their bags on to the luggage-racks when the coach started off.

"Well, that's that," Teddy remarked as we watched the back of the coach getting ever-smaller, the blue-grey exhaust fumes swirling back from the flatulent bursts.

"That's it," Lefty said, "you're so right."

We walked back across the car park and I noticed then, consciously for the first time, blossom beginning to burst through on the adjacent bushes and that the rhododendrons had suddenly come into glorious red and violet bloom. Beyond and above the roofline of the building the long, thin, crowded branches of the big willow by the pool hung in yellow fronds so that the whole, moving in the breeze and the bright sun, seemed a golden fountain.

"You've just lost two clients," Teddy said to Capini when we got to the porch.

I had just seen the latter come out on to the porch and then just stand there, arms folded across the front of his butcher's apron, watching us amble across the car park towards him.

"Yes," he said. "And some customers."

"What was the matter with them?" Teddy wondered.

"The matter with them?" Capini said, outraged. "When it came to paying their bill this morning, that Turner says: 'I'm sorry, but I don't have the money now. I'll pay you after Killer fights on Thursday.'"

"So he'll pay you then," Teddy said.

"So he'll pay me then. When my meat man comes today I suppose I am to say to him: 'Don't worry; I'll pay you after Cassidy fights someplace on Thursday.'"

"In York Hall," Teddy said.

"Yes. My butcher would be pleased to hear that. York Hall."

"Ah, Rene," I said, "you are indeed one of the world's privileged minority."

"I'm privileged?"

"Certainly. You are one of that small but all-powerful group of holders who control the destinies of the rest of us. By exacting the privilege of extending credit to Jakie you will, on Thursday, without lacing on a glove, throwing a punch or selling a ticket, become a party to the profits of a prizefight. Cassidy will now be fighting for you, too, and it's in exactly that fashion that all of the world's greatest fortunes have been amassed."

119

"Really," Capini said, disgusted.

"From Cassidy you may branch out into railways or munitions or whatever. You've got to decide what you're going to do with all your money."

"That's right, bon ami," Teddy enjoined. "Whatever will you do with all your money."

"Money? You think I make anything from that Cassidy?"

"Sure," Teddy said. "Why ever not?"

"The way he eats? How can anybody make any money?"

"Now you're trying deception," I broke in. "You know you're flattered."

"I'm flattered?"

"Absolutely. Every time you see Cassidy eat you know he is paying his most sincere compliments to the wonders of your wife's cooking."

"Compliments! With him that's no compliment; Cassidy would eat anything."

"Let's go round and sit in the sun," Teddy suggested.

"Fine," I agreed. "Lefty?"

"Thank you, I'd like that."

"I would like it too," Capini grumbled, "but I have to work."

"But remember you're a creditor," I said. "We're not."

On the hotel side of the pool there was an unpainted single-plank bench and we sat there, sheltered from the wind by the building and warm in the sun.

"York Hall," Teddy mused. "I fought there four times."

"How many times did you fight there, Lefty?" I asked.

"Oh, seven or eight times, I think. I don't remember exactly."

"How many fights have you had, anyway?" Teddy wanted to know.

"Somewhere around a hundred and fifty-six. But I had a lot that are not in the record books. I fought on unlicensed shows and had a lot of bouts in Australia, more than it shows in any book, so I never did figure out how many times I went to the post."

"How come you went all the way to Australia?"

"I just couldn't get no fights here, so my manager at that time got me a couple of outings across the pond in San Francisco and, after I knocked those two boys out, there wasn't anybody would meet me around there either. So I sent what money I had home to my wife and found myself a job as a mess-boy on a freighter ship which was due to sail for Australia."

"Who managed you there?"

"I manage myself. There was a gentleman working on the ship, way below in the engine-room, and he was a fight fan and had been to Australia before so, when we got to Melbourne he took me to a gym which he'd visited before, and I found the local promoter and told him I was a fighter. He said to me: 'Just comin' off that ship, can you box six rounds the day after tomorrow?' I said: 'Mister, I can fight six rounds right now.'

"When I told my friend from the ship, I said: 'How about you getting one of them other gentlemen from that engine-room and you two be my seconds?' And he said: 'Me? I just like to watch the fights. I don't know what you're supposed to do in the corner.' I said: 'You just get another gentleman and I'll tell you what to do. It's dead easy.'

"Then, the night of the fight, there must have come, I reckon, more than a dozen gentlemen from the ship to the fight club. When it came about time to go down to the ring my friend he was scared. He had this other gentleman from the ship with him and they're in the dressing-room with me. I said: 'What make you worried? There's nothin' to be scared about.' So he said: 'But we don't know what we're supposed to do.' I said: 'I'll tell you what you do. You gentlemen just follow me down to the ring carryin' that pail there with that bottle in it and with the sponge and my mouthpiece and the towel. Then I'll tell you what to do as the fight goes along.' Then he said; 'But supposin' you get cut and I don't know what to do?' I said: "Get cut? Gentlemen, I ain't never been cut in my whole life and I ain't gonna start getting cut tonight. You got nothin' to worry about.' That was the truth, too."

"How was the fight?" Teddy wanted to know. "What happened?"

"They had me in against some red-headed boy that, maybe, hadn't had more than ten or twelve fights. By now I'd only been in Australia a couple of days, yet I kinda liked it already. The people seemed nice to me so I had it in my mind that I'd like to stay there for a while. Then I figured that, if I was going to stay there and get work, I'd better be careful in this fight. I mean, this had better look like it's a good fight--you know what I mean--and that I better not hurt this red-headed boy too much because he was almost like a child, when you come to think about it."

121

"So what did you do?" came Teddy's next question.

"I make it a real good fight. This red-headed boy, he was a professional fighter over there, but he was like what we call a novice here."

"Just imagine," Teddy said to me, "Lefty in with a novice."

"I wish I'd seen it," I said. "What about the fight itself, Lefty?"

"Well, that kid was game. When the bell rang he come out punchin' and lookin' to knock me out. The people liked that right from the start. They was on their feet cheering and I figure that, if they like this, I best go along with it, too. I let him come to me; but you know how you do it. You make it look like a war, but those punches he was throwin' they only look good to the crowd. Yourself, you're catchin' most of them on the arms, shoulders or with the inside of the glove, and once in a while I would let one catch me to see how hard this boy could hit. You know how you do it."

"I know," Teddy said grinning. "Nobody could do it better than you, Lefty."

"The crowd loved it but, when I got back to my corner after each round, I wanted to laugh. I would take my gumshield out myself and just sit there holding it in my gloves until it was time to put it back in. My friend from the engine-room would say: 'What do we do now? What are we supposed to do now?' I'd say: 'One of you gentlemen give me the bottle to rinse my mouth, and the other sponge my face a little, if you don't mind.' Then I recall my friend looking at me all scared like and he said: 'But are you alright? Don't get hurt now, will you? The other fella's tough.'

"They were so scared that I wanted to laugh. I said: 'Now don't you worry; I'll be fine.' So, at the end of the fourth round, I reckoned I'd better do somethin'. By now I've made that red-headed kid look so good that, to win, I've got to knock him out. But I've got to be careful how I do that if I'm gonna stay here in Australia. I mean, you can't offend people, can you?"

"No, Lefty," I said, "you can't."

"That's so, and also I don't want to hurt that red-headed boy none. Seems he's a nice boy, so I start pressin' him a little more in the fifth round. The crowd are goin' crazy and stamping their feet, so I stepped inside him and I hit him a right hand in the body as solid and hard as I could. Well, his hands came down and he just started to fall forward and then, to show good, I hit him with a hook to the chin, but not too hard, because the body punch had already finished him, and he went down on his face while the referee counted him out."

"How did it go down?"

"Fine. I mean, the fight was so close in the eyes of the fans they liked it even if their boy didn't win. In Australia they're nice people and they stood up and cheered me."

"How about your friends from the ship?"

"They were shakin' hands with each other in the corner and jumpin' up and down with excitement. After the fight, I guess there was a dozen of those gentlemen from the ship there and it seems they had a bet on me, 'cos they took me out to dinner in a restaurant and they had a real time of it. They wanted that I should stay with the ship, and they had it all worked out that every time we'd reach some port I'd fix myself some fight and they'd all go to it and bet on me like they did that night. They really wanted me to do that."

"I'll bet they did," I said. "They had it all arranged that, in time, they could sack every seaport in the free world."

"They were even gonna speak to the captain and they were gonna find me a place to train on the ship. They thought that the captain would like that, too, and I sure was sorry, after they treated me like that, to have to disappoint those gentlemen on that ship."

"Did you tell them you wouldn't do it?" Teddy said.

"I explained to those gentlemen that I couldn't train on no ship and that I was really a professional fighter. I just had to stay some place and fight, and I made up my mind that I was gonna stay in Australia."

"How long were you there?"

"I think almost two years. As for the people, they were real nice to me."

"And how many fights did you have there?"

"I don't know for sure, but I reckon about twenty or twenty-five."

"Did you play ping-pong with all of them, like with the red-haired kid?"

"No sir, though I did with most of them. I made them into real good fights, right up until I stopped the middleweight champion of Australia. Then I fought their lightheavyweight champion and I outpointed him. And then I was matched to fight the heavyweight champion. He didn't know too much about the game but he was big. He had nearly two stones advantage on me and he kept hittin' me on the arms until I could hardly lift 'em, just blocking his punches and he was given the decision after fifteen rounds. Then I came home because I wanted to see my wife and my daughter and, anyway, there wasn't nobody else for me to fight down there neither."

"How long have you been married, Lefty?" I asked.

"Oh, fifteen years or so. My wife she works in a laundry."

"How old is your daughter?"

"I can hardly believe it, but she's twelve years old already. At her school they say she's smart, too."

"What's she going to do when she finishes school?"

"She says she's gonna be a nurse and I like that."

"I like it too. That's fine."

"Would you excuse me now?"

"Of course, Lefty."

"Speakin' of the laundry reminds me I gotta get my own."

Flynn left us then, and I asked Teddy what he had meant about the laundry.

"He does his own laundry every day down here. You know?"

"No, I don't know."

"Well, the only clothes he brought, besides what he wears on the road mornings, is the grey suit he's got and that sweater he had on today. Also he's got a change of shorts and socks and two T-shirts and, I suppose, some handkerchiefs. Each day, after the workout, he washes out his shorts, socks, jockstrap, T-shirt and a handkerchief. He hangs them out in the furnace room off the kitchen and then, daily after he takes a shower, he has clean clothes to put on."

"He's a truly wonderful bloke."

"He should have been champion and made some money. Of course, the 'colour bar' was still on in Britain which made a crack at Ernie Roderick's British title out of the question, and there was no chance of getting an American over here to defend the world crown in those days."

"I know, and one of the most amazing things to me about him and his type is that they never seem to resent us whites. We're the ones who did it to him and his like, you know."

"I suppose so."

124

"We surely are."

"I noticed today that he looks a bit like that old jazz trumpeter and vocalist, Louis Armstrong."

"If he could have played a trumpet like he used to fight he'd have been even greater than Louis Armstrong."

"That's true."

I wanted to ask Teddy how, believing as he did about Flynn, he felt about using him as a sparring-partner and banging him around. However, I could not find the right way to express it and then he stood up and I shelved it.

"Doc's got him a six-rounder on the bill," he said. "Lefty'll make himself a few hundred plus what he's getting up here. At least it's something."

"Yes, it is."

We walked around beneath the sweep of the willow, moving about in the wind like some giant sweeper-upper, round the south end of the building and started across the parking space to the front door. A new light-blue Ford Escort had apparently just driven in and a petite got out, shut the driver's door and walked towards us.

"Excuse me," she said, "but can you tell me where I can find Teddy Baker?"

"I'm Teddy Baker."

"Oh good. I'm Cindy Burton from ITV's Len Johnstone show."

"The what?" Teddy said, shaking hands with her.

"The Len Johnstone show on television. Don't you know about it?"

"Oh yes; Doc did speak to me. This is Frank Cutler, Miss---"

"Cindy Burton. I'm glad to meet you, Frank."

"I'm gratified."

"I assume you'll be with us on Monday," she said to Teddy, "so I thought I'd just run down here and ask you a few questions about your background and---"

"Hold on," Teddy said. "I don't really know."

"But, as we understand it, you're going to be in London on Monday, aren't you?"

"Yes, we are. We have to go to the Boxing Board offices for the preliminary medical, but I don't know about your show. You'll have to talk to Doc about that."

"Doc? I don't think I know anybody called Doc."

"He's my manager," Teddy said, smiling, "and I hate to tell you this, but he's against television."

She was a dainty little thing, about twenty-five with a nice face, which required little make-up, and rimless glasses, but the way she looked at that moment you might have thought that Teddy had said that his manager, Doc, was against God.

"You're not serious?"

"You'd better talk to Doc. I don't know anything about TV. Frank here is a magazine writer, so probably he knows more about it than either Doc or I do."

"Frank Cutler?" she said. "You write for magazines?"

"I confess."

"I know your name and I'm sure I've seen your articles."

"I'm pleased and thank you."

She could be testing the water, I thought, but for some reason I'm much more inclined to believe them when they're plain or homely. Why, I was wondering, do I invariably believe this kind and suspect the fancy frauleins?"

"Why don't we go in and find Doc?" Teddy said.

"Fine," she agreed, "although I must confess that I'm a little nervous about meeting this ogre."

"Don't be," Teddy assured her. "Doc's okay; he's a wonderful person."

"Lead on," came the reply.

She had on a dark-green tweed suit that probably came out of Shaftesbury Avenue, and a pair of flat-heeled, brown shoes with fringed flap-over tongues for her day out in the country. Over one shoulder was slung a huge, saddle-leather bag and she walked with a good stride for such a small woman.

When we had ushered her into the hallway, Teddy went upstairs to find Doc while I took her into the dining-room and sat her down at a table by the window. She refused a drink and asked me a few questions about the place and who ran it and then Doc came in, peering at her. Teddy introduced them and we all sat down.

"And now what do you want from me?" Doc said quizzically.

"Really!" she said, looking at Teddy and me. "Now I am scared."

"Easy, Doc," I said.

126

"I hate television."

"So I've been told," she said, "although I find it almost impossible to believe."

"You can believe anything I tell you, lady, even though most of the things you hear in boxing are lies."

"But, really, you can't hate television. What's there to hate? What did it ever do to you except provide good publicity?"

"Everything, to both questions. Your business eats mine. After your business started showing my business, nearly all the small fight halls in the land folded because even fools won't pay for something that somebody else is giving away for free. Why do I hate it?"

"But I can't see what earthly difference that makes to you. After all, Teddy Baker doesn't box in those small halls you're speaking of."

"But where do you think he learned how to fight? Do you realise that you may be sitting at this table right now with the last of the real professional fighters? My business isn't like your business, where they tear a piece of bark off a tree and the first creature that crawls out they build into a--what do you call it?"

"I've absolutely no idea what you mean."

"I think a television personality is what you mean," I said.

"That's it," Doc said. "The first thing that crawls out they make into a television personality. Have a good look at me."

"I'm doing just that," she said.

"You're looking at a man who's got a fighter and the sports pages and that's all I ever had for around fifty years. I'm not married because I never wanted to be, and for the last donkeys' years I've been living in the same hotel. I must know almost every cabbie who works in and around the West End, both day and night. I know their troubles and how many kids they've got, but one night, when your business was just starting to take hold, I got in a cab. Are you listening?"

"I most certainly am."

She certainly was, too, because she couldn't understand Doc at all.

"So I sit back and the cabbie says: 'Say, Doc, how about that Patsy Haygate?' I say to myself that he's not a fighter. 'Patsy Haygate?' I said, 'isn't he an Irish tenor?' He starts to laugh; for the first time in my life a cabbie laughs at me. He says: 'Doc, are you joking?' So I said; 'No, who is he?' He says: 'Who is Patsy

Haygate? He's famous. He's the guy who announces the fights on all the big TV shows. He's great.' I told him to stop the cab and he wanted to know why 'cos we hadn't got there yet. I said: 'Yes, we are. We just passed where I want to go.' Then I got out and slammed the door and walked the rest of the way in the rain. Television? What do you want from me?"

"For a start, we need Teddy Baker on the Len Johnstone show on Monday. Teddy has confirmed what Mr. Solomons' secretary told us, that he has to be in London on Monday anyway."

"We shouldn't even be going into town for the medical," Doc said turning to me. "I told them: 'Send your doctor down here.' But they said: 'We want Teddy and the champion together for the photographers. If you both come to town Solomons' publicity men can stick dynamite underneath the late ticket sales.' Now we have to go on television, too."

"It was Solomons' people that suggested it," she said. "They called us and said they'd agreed it with you."

"Why don't you get the other man? He's the great champion and since when is television interested in being second?"

"The people in Windmill Street suggested Teddy. The young lady there who handles the publicity explained that Teddy is intelligent and makes a good appearance; now that I've met him I'm convinced that he's just what we want."

"Thanks very much," Teddy said.

"Oh, come on now. Be frank with me," Doc broke in.

"What do you mean?"

"You know you don't want the other man because he's coloured. Admit it."

"That's just not so; we've had lots of black people on the show."

"What kind of a show is this, anyway?"

"It's a half-hour show from five to five-thirty each day Monday through Friday. Len's a fine person, he's an old-stager and he does a wonderful job. It's basically an interview show and we have two guests for interview each day. We may have someone who's just written a book or is appearing in a new show; or it may be someone who's in the news or a sports, stage or film star. We've had a footballer, a cricketer, a rugby player and a tennis star as regards sport."

128

"Is it aimed at women?"

"No, it has general appeal but you'd be surprised at the number of women who have become interested in what used to be just men's things. Since boxing has been shown on television, you'd be amazed at the number of women who enjoy it now."

"I wouldn't be surprised at anything," Doc said. "What time does Teddy have to be there?"

"We'd like him to get there between two and two-thirty, to meet Len and to see the set-up and get the idea of what we'll ask him to do. They we'll run through it with a quick rehearsal, but really all he'll have to do will be to walk in and sit down so that Len can chat with him about his career and what lies ahead. We're honestly excited about having a top boxer on the show."

"Righto," Doc said, "we'll be there."

"Thanks a million. You had me getting scared but you're not so bad after all. Your bark's worse than your bite."

"Don't you believe it."

"Are you married?" she asked Teddy.

"Yes, I am."

"Boy, there's an idea. Could we get your wife on with you."

"I don't know," Teddy pondered.

"But I know," Doc said. "No, and a thousand times no."

"Really? It would be terrific on the show. Whyever not?"

"Because he's a fighter in training."

"I don't understand."

No, I thought, looking at her, I can believe that. I'm quite certain you don't.

"You don't?" Doc said. "Well, let's just put it this way. He doesn't look at his wife from now until after the fight. Quite clear?"

"Yes, if that's your rule."

"I'd like to ask you a few questions," she said to Teddy, "if I may."

"Certainly," Teddy said. "Go right ahead."

She reached into the shoulder-bag and brought out a packet of cigarettes, took one and I lit it for her. Then she produced a shorthand notebook, flipped it open professionally and sat forward with a small gold pencil poised.

"First of all, how old are you?"

"Twenty-seven."

"How many professional fights have you had?"

"Ninety-odd."

"How many have you won?"

"All but three."

"How did you come to be a fighter?"

Teddy told her about the boys' club and the amateurs and how Doc discovered him. She was asking Doc details of this when we heard the shout and turned.

"Ahoy, where's the next champion of the world?"

"Hullo, Raymond!" Teddy said, his face breaking into a big grin and then he stood up. "Come on over here!"

He was a little guy, dark-haired and wearing a dark-blue suit, with the open collar of his white sports-shirt folded down outside the collar of his jacket. Behind him were four others, all in their late twenties or early thirties and all of them with wide grins on their faces. They stood there while Ray came over to us.

"This was my first manager," Teddy said, after he and Ray had shaken hands and hugged each other. "Ray is the one I was telling you about, had me in the amateurs. All the others are from my old neighbourhood patch."

Ray shook hands with Doc and then Teddy introduced him formally to Miss Burton and to me.

"Look," Teddy said to him, "I'm tied up for the next few minutes so take the guys into the bar. Take Frank with you, too. Tell him about life underneath the arches. I'll be in shortly."

"Sure," Ray said, smiling at Teddy. "Of course I will."

"Fine," I said. "I'm glad to have met you, Miss Burton."

XVI

"So you're all from Teddy's old stamping-ground," I said.

"Correct," Ray confirmed.

"And the best place in the world," the one called Freddie said. "We're serious; it really was the greatest. The best neighbourhood in the world."

"It used to be when we were kids," the big husky one called Petey said. "But it ain't the same no more."

"Tell me something that is," Freddie suggested, "but it still ain't bad."

130

We were spread out along the bar while Capini served us. Petey and his brother had asked for beer, but Ray and Freddie and a quiet good-looking one, dressed in brown sports clothes and wearing a tie who was named Harry, had ordered whisky.

"Cheers, and here's to Teddy Baker, the next Middleweight Champion of the World," Ray toasted.

"Absolutely," Freddie said, and we all drank to Teddy.

"These blokes you're looking at here now," Ray announced, "we're all Teddy's gang. Since we were kids, we've all been the same gang."

"All except Dominic who ain't here," Freddie said. "Dom had to work today."

"What does Dom do?"

"He's got an important post with Inland Revenue," Freddie said, and the others all laughed.

"But a real good lad," Ray said.

"The very best," the one named Petey said. "He wanted to come down too. He so wanted to see Teddy."

"It's too bad," Freddie thought out loud.

"So what do the rest of you do for a living?"

"Me, I've got a share in a snooker hall," Ray said. "Freddie here works in a petrol-filling station, Petey drives for a brewery, Harry's a fireman while Anton's a barman at the London Palladium."

"That's a wonderful old theatre," I said; "I've seen some superb artistes perform there over the years, though I haven't been in recently."

"Why not drop in sometime and ask for me. I'm always there nights."

"I'll try to do that."

"But Teddy's the one," Freddie said; "Teddy's our boy."

"We go to all of Teddy's fights," Ray said proudly, "except the ones way out of London. I mean, we couldn't go to Bristol, Glasgow and Birmingham, but it all began with his first fight when I put Teddy in his first four-rounder at the Café Royale. All of us went and we've never missed any fight of Teddy's we could get to. We drove up to Watford the times he fought there and then we'd drive home through the night."

"How's about the first fight Teddy had in Watford, Harry?" Freddie said.

"Oh yeah," Harry said.

131

"What about it?" Ray asked.

"There was this bum wanted to bet us," Harry said.

"Wanted to bet us?" Freddie said. "He didn't want to bet us, you mean."

"That's right," Petey said. "He didn't want to but he did."

"Some guy sittin' right behind us," Freddie said to me. "A loud mouth who's rootin' for Teddy's opponent. You've seen Teddy fight, right?"

"Correct."

"He don't look to put the other guy away in the first round or two; I mean, usually he don't. He usually tries to figure the other man out first."

"Doc taught him that right from the start, how to measure up his man," Ray said. "Doc really is some manager."

"He's the best," Freddie said, "but this loudmouth is rootin' for the other man. He's hollerin': 'Kill him! Knock him out! He's from south of the water so he can't fight. Knock that bum out!' This keeps up all the first round and, when he starts it again in the second, I turned round to him and I said: 'Look, Mac, why don't you turn that volume down?' He says: 'Waddya mean?' and I said: 'You're disturbin' people; the fighter can't hear you anyway.' Then he says: 'He can hear me alright and he'll knock that bum right back to Lambeth and you know what you can do.'

"Now I'm quite a big guy, see, but this bloke don't realise we're all together. So, when he says that, Ray is sitting next to me and he ain't very big, but Anton leans over behind Ray and he puts that big paw of his on the mug's shoulder and he pushes him right back in his seat. Ain't that right, Ants?"

"Yeah, that's right."

"So Anton says: 'He don't know what he can do, Mister, but you know what you can do?' The feller says: 'Waddya mean?' and Anton says: 'Put up or shut up.' The idiot says: 'Alright, if you wanna bet.'

"I ask him how much and he says: 'I'll bet ten pound. Are you kiddin'?' I said. 'All that noise you're makin' and you're gonna bet a lousy ten. I'll bet you fifty, even.' The guy says: 'I ain't got that much with me.' I said: 'Whatta you got?' He says: 'I'll bet twenty' and I said: 'You're on.' "

"So what happened?"

"What happened was that Teddy knocked the other man out in the fifth round."

"Good punches," Ray said and the others nodded. "Teddy kept hittin' him in the guts and, in the fourth round, he switched upstairs and hit him on the chin with a hook and I said: 'Oh boy, here it comes.' He let him off the hook then but, in the fifth round, he caught the man with another hook to the head and the fellow's head finished right under the bottom rope when he went down. What a punch it was!"

"Yep," Freddie said. "I took the mug's twenty and he turned out to be not such a bad guy at all."

"No," I pondered, "not after he was leaned on a bit."

"We bet on all of Teddy's fights, We always place some before the fight and then we find some sucker at the fight makin' a noise or somethin', so we oblige him. You know?"

"Except in Reading," Petey said.

"Bejeez," Anton ejaculated. "That wasn't right at all."

"I believe that was a very bad decision," I said.

"A very bad decision?" Freddie said. "Is that what you call it?"

"It was about the worst decision there ever was," Ray said. "The referee gave it to the other guy when, believe me, Teddy won at least eight of the ten rounds. Absolutely diabolical, it was."

"How about Harry that night?" Freddie said, looking at him.

"Don't embarrass him," Ray said.

I looked at Harry and Harry looked at me, shrugged his shoulders and looked away.

"After the fight we're comin' out to catch the train back to Paddington and we look and we don't see no sign of Harry."

"I had to go and spend a penny," Harry explained, looking at me and shrugging again.

"So Ray and I go lookin' for him and we find him in the gents. Tell the man, Ray."

"Let's forget it."

"No; we find him in the loo and he's the only person there by now and do you know what he's doin'?"

"No."

"He's cryin'. Harry had tears in his eyes."

"And he's the only one of us don't bet," Ray said. "He didn't even have a bet on the fight."

133

I looked at Harry who was facing the bar. He had his head down a little and he was sipping his drink.

"Well," I said, "that just shows how much Teddy means to Harry and to all of you."

"Right," Freddie enthused. "Teddy is the greatest and after he becomes champion and people get to know it they'll see. How come them sports writers don't write about Teddy better?"

"They don't tear him to pieces or even knock him."

"I know, but they write about what a wonderful fighter the other bloke is. Teddy'll knock him out; why don't they write that about Teddy?"

"Well, the other man is champion and he's had most of his fights on the big London shows. Doc has moved Teddy all over the country and brought him along slowly. They won't have seen Teddy in too many of his fights and they haven't seen him in his best ones."

"They'll see him," Freddie said. "He'll show 'em; he'll show all those wise guys."

"Tell me about Teddy when all you gang were growing up."

"How do you mean?" Ray asked.

"Was he a tough youngster?"

"We didn't live in no Park Lane," Freddie said.

"Teddy could always fight," Ray said. "He liked to fight; I mean, he didn't go looking for trouble but he had what you might call a temper."

"Cripes, you remember what a temper he had?" Freddie said. "Wow! And now he don't have it no more; you ever notice that?"

"Now he's a real pro," I said.

"He had a temper alright," Ray agreed, "but he used it right. He wasn't a mean chap; if some nut did somethin' wrong, then Teddy would blow his top. He licked a lot of guys that way, especially in some of them fights we had with kids from other neighbourhoods."

"Was Teddy the toughest kid on your patch, then?"

"Teddy?" Freddie said. "No, Tony was. He was a couple of years older than Teddy and our kid was never crazy like Tony."

"Who was Tony?"

"Tony Marino," Ray told me. "Dom, the other one that couldn't be here today--the guy that works in the Tax Office--was Tony's younger brother. Tony was the toughest."

"I remember now," I said, "Teddy has mentioned Tony."

"The roughest that ever was," Freddie opined. "There was simply nobody as tough."

"Except another brother," Petey contradicted, "Angelo."

"Get off," Freddie said, "Angelo wasn't tough. Guys that carry guns ain't really tough. Tony was ten times tougher with just his fists."

"Angelo was two years older than Tony," Ray said to me. "He's in Rampton now."

"A life sentence, recommended twenty," Freddie informed. "He killed some poor slob who ran a sweet-shop. They shoulda' hanged him but they could only give him life."

"Tell me more about Tony."

"He was the leader," Ray said, laughing.

"What a mucker!" Freddie said. "You remember that day we're all up on that roof and the law comes down the street lookin' for us?"

"I sure do," Anton said.

"It's walking along sniffing around and we're all lookin' down. Tony, like Ray's told yer, he was the leader, says: ' Watch me drop this on his potata.' Know what he's done?"

"I just can't wait to know."

"There was a brick up there; he dropped it right on him."

"Did it hit him?"

"On the shoulder. Lucky for us he didn't hit him on the head. Might've killed him if he'd hit him on the head."

"And did we run," Ray said.

"Right over the roofs. We come down where Harry lived."

"Were you in on this?" I asked Harry.

"Not on that day."

"He was probably readin', " Ray said, "Harry used to read a lot."

"I'm all for readers."

"I still like to read," Harry said.

"The bluebottle knew who done it," Freddie said. "About a week later he sees us on the street and he grabbed Tony. Remember?"

"Sure I do."

"He made a pass at him with his truncheon and Tony ducked under it and gave the law the knee. He gave him the knee as hard as he could and the copper turned white. He grabbed himself, doubled right over and went into a shop. He went into the Frog's; remember how we all run?"

"I remember," Harry said, "and I told Tony the bluebottle'd have him for this and he'd get arrested. Tony just said: 'Take me in? If I'm taken in it'll be a joke in the nick. They'll laugh at him, that a kid like me give it to him; he won't dare take me in.' "

"And he was right," Ray said.

"Tony was always right," Freddie said. "He had brains and what a fighter he could have made. He could punch like Turpin; he'd have beaten the world."

"What happened to him?"

"He's dead," Ray said. "He got killed in the Korean War."

"Yes, Tony was there," Freddie said. "He was a hero. Can you imagine that? Tony was a hero."

"I can believe it."

"He was a sergeant," Freddie said. "A lad who came back safely told us. At night he used to go around where they had men posted to make sure they were alright. Everything was dark and silent and, we were told, the enemy used to creep out of some caves or something, so one night Tony sees this Jap sneakin' up on one of his sentries. Tony didn't want to make no noise because he didn't know how many Japs there were about, so he just sprung on this one and, the bloke told us, he choked him to death with his bare hands. What a fighter Tony was!"

"That's not how he got killed, though," Harry said.

"He got killed helpin' a mate. This guy was wounded and layin' out in the open when Tony run out and picked him up and started to bring his back to safety. Them Japs opened up with a machine-gun and killed Tony."

"It's a strange thing," Ray said. "A lot of people thought Tony was no good because of Angelo and the way Tony acted wild; I mean the old people who lived on the patch."

"I saw his mother a couple of weeks back," Harry said. "One Sunday afternoon my mother said to me: 'Why don't you go and see old Mrs. Marino? Since Dom got married she lives alone and she's not so well.' So I went up to her flat and she's just sitting there in her rocking-chair. She's got Tony's picture there on the table, in his uniform, and by the side of the picture she's got the Korean Medal and the Citation that they sent her."

"Yep," Freddie said, "Tony got the Korean Medal."

"What's the matter with the drinks?" Capini said.

"Anton and me reckon this beer's flat," Petey replied.

"Rene's making another round now," I said. "Come on, tell me about Mary."

"Teddy's wife, Mary. She lived on the patch."

"You ever met Mary?" Ray wanted to know.

"Yes."

"Well?"

"Tell the truth," Freddie said, "I was surprised when Teddy started goin' with Mary. Teddy never paid too much attention to girls."

"Not like you." Petey interjected.

"Mary never paid too much attention to Teddy, either," Ray joined in, "until he became a fighter. Then he became somebody in our neighbourhood."

"Her old lady didn't think so," Petey recalled.

"Ray was best man when Teddy got married," Freddie said. "Right, Ray?"

"Where did they get married?" I said.

"In the City Hall," Freddie answered.

"No," Ray said. "It was in the Municipal Building."

"How come they got married there?"

"They were gonna' get hitched in the Register Office," Ray informed. "Mary's old lady wasn't set on the idea of Mary marryin' Teddy, so Mary had the idea they should go down to Winchester and get spliced by some Justice of the Peace. Romantic like, you know?"

"Oh yes," Freddie said.

"So Teddy had this old Ford and, one morning in the summer, he got the car out, picked me up and then he picked up Mary. The had their Birth Certificates and everything and we drove down to Winchester.

"It's a nice old city but we don't know exactly where to go. Ahead there's an Eldorado ice-cream man got his car parked in some square and Mary says: 'Stop and ask him; he'll know where there's a Justice of the Peace'.

"Teddy stops the car and the ice-cream feller comes over and stands there. I'm sittin' by the car window nearest the man and I'm waitin' for Teddy to say something. The guy says: 'What'll you have, folks?' So Helen says to Teddy: 'Go ahead, ask him.' "

"Wait 'til you hear this," Freddie said to me. "This is Teddy for you."

"Teddy says: 'What flavours you got?' I'd like to die."

"What do you think of that?" Freddie said to me.

"So the ice-creamer reels off a whole list of flavours and Teddy says to Mary: 'Which'll you have?' Mary says: 'Nothing' and was she steamin'. So Teddy says to me: 'How about you, Ray?' I said: 'No thanks' and Teddy says to the guy: 'I'll have a toasted almond.'

"While the guy went to fix it, I reckoned I'd better do something. Teddy and Mary are just sittin' there sayin' nothing and I feel sorry for Teddy. When the ice-creamer comes back and gives Teddy his ice-cream I said to the man: 'Can you tell us where the Register Office is around here?' The bum says: 'I don't know because I don't live here; I just work here and I never saw a Register Office.'

"So we drove back home, nobody saying a word and they dropped me off at my place. Next day Teddy came round and picked me up and we picked up Mary. Then we went down to the Municipal Building and some fellow married them in the Register place. Then they went to Brighton for a few days."

"When they got back Mary's old man had a blow-out in his bar," Frankie said. "We all went and it was a pretty good party."

"Teddy's got his own home on Denmark Hill now," Petey said. "You ever been there?"

"Yes, I met him there the day we came down here," I told him.

"It's a real nice place, ain't it?" Freddie said.

"Yes, it is. Do you blokes visit him up there?"

"We've been there once," Ray said.

"Teddy called us on the phone one night," Freddie said. "Mary was going out so he rang us and we all went up. It's a nice place."

"Give us another round, will you Rene?" Ray called.

"What are you guys talking about anyway?" Teddy said, walking up to us.

"Who's that bit of skirt you've been sittin' with?" Freddie said. "You can do better than that."

"Television," Teddy told him. "She's from television."

"You're gonna be on television?"

"Early on Monday evening."

"What time?"

"Five o'clock. It's the Len Johnstone show."

"I've heard talk about that show." Freddie said.

"We'll all get away from work and watch it," Ray said.

"Listen!" Freddie said to me. "You'll have to come down our way right after the fight. When Teddy wins the crown we're gonna have a real knees-up blow-out that night. Be sure you're there."

"It will be a real blow-out, too," Teddy said to me.

"Where will you have it; at Mary's father's bar?"

"Hell no," Freddie said. "We've got another place. It's called the White Lion and it's on the Albert Embankment at the Vauxhall Bridge end."

"You can ride down with me, Frank," Teddy said. "You'll see Lambeth and these guys as they really are."

"I'll be there. We'll meet after the fight."

"How come you blokes came down here today?" Teddy said.

"It's Saturday, ain't it?" Ray said.

"So it is," Teddy said. "Just shows you. Down here I lose track of the days because every day is the same."

XVII

By Monday it was raining again. It was just a fine drizzle when Nat woke me up and Teddy went out on the road with the others but, by the time they had all come back and Teddy had cooled off and we had all had breakfast, it had turned into a steady spring deluge.

We left around ten o'clock in Teddy's car. Doc sat in front riding shotgun with the fighter and I sat in the back with Waller. The change of routine and scenery seemed to spark Waller and he talked almost incessantly: about a car he once owned until the finance company claimed it, about his trip down to the Barley Mow with his friend Percy, about the kind of hotel he would run if he were Capini and, when we came off the M3, about the whole of England's motorway system and about the hazards of highway construction. Now and then, while Waller was talking, Doc would say something to Teddy and he'd nod and say something to Doc in reply. I doubt if they heard much of what Nat was saying.

When we got to the West End, Teddy put the car in a new underground park near Piccadilly. It was a quarter before midday and, in the miserable rain, we did well to hail a cab to take us up Regent Street and into Hill's Place which lies just off the Oxford Street crossover.

The Board Offices in Ramillies Buildings were far too luxurious for some of its dodgy tenants, Waller was saying as the four of us rode up to the third floor in the lift.

"I remember once----" he started to say.

The lift stopped and we followed Doc out. The Board's Chief Inspector, Andy Cunningham, was standing in the entrance to the Board's suite of offices and, when he saw us stepping out, he smiled and shook hands all the way round.

"I'm very glad to see you," he said to Doc.

"Oho, what were you worried about? You thought we wouldn't show?"

"No, but Teddy's gonna be on that television show late this afternoon, right?"

"No," Doc said, "he's not."

"What? He's not gonna be on? I was just talking this morning to some young gal from ITV who said it was all set. She said she'd been down to see you."

"Relax, fella," Teddy said.

"Then you'll be on?"

"Course I will."

"What are you trying to do, kid me?" Cunningham said to Doc.

"Kid you? The smartest guy in boxing? Whyever would I want to try to kid you?"

"We might as well go in; the doctor's in there."

There were several photographers sitting on the big settee inside, their cameras in their laps, and two of them got up and shook hands with Teddy and with Doc. Doctor Phil Kaplin, the Board's senior medical Officer was sitting on the corner of a desk, talking to a big, florid-faced man; this was E.J. Waltham, their General Secretary and formerly a top-class referee. When he finished talking, Kaplin walked over to us and shook hands.

"You're looking good," he said to Teddy.

"Thanks. So are you."

140

"He should," Doc said. "He dyes his hair but he's as old as I am."

"But I'm in shape," Kaplin said.

"His name's not Kaplin, either. He's a Jewish immigrant but he won't admit it."

"Who won't admit anything? Listen, I saved a few of your fighters."

"I know you did," Doc said smiling. "You're alright."

"Let's go in."

"Where's the other fellow?" Doc demanded.

"He's not here yet. I'll look at Teddy and get it over with."

He led us through the outer office and into a medium-sized room. There were scales there, a desk and a couple of chairs. Teddy sat down and the medico, using his pocket flashlight, peered into his eyes and then down his throat and into his ears. Teddy then stripped to the waist and the doctor put his stethoscope on first his chest and then his back. When that was done, he wrapped the blood pressure cuff around Teddy's left upper arm, squeezed on the bulb and read the dial.

"All great," he said, "and the brain scan is back and it's perfect. Now strip right off and I'll weigh you."

"As you were, Edward," Doc said. "Nix on that."

"What?" Kaplin said. "What's the matter?"

"He's not going to weigh, He'll make the weight a week on Friday."

"He's got to weigh; it's a title fight."

"Not today it isn't. The fight's a week from Friday. What difference does it make what he weighs today? Are you afraid my man won't make the weight or do so only after starving himself?"

"Of course not."

"He'll make one sixty a week from Friday and he'll do it perfect. In fact, I'll tell you exactly. He'll come in at a hundred and fifty-nine."

"The Rules say that, for a title fight, both contestants must weigh at the preliminary examination. He doesn't have to scale one-sixty today, but I just have to have a record of his weight."

"Now the Stewards are writing Rules that make work for doctors, too," Doc said to me and then to Kaplin: "They used to write Rules to make work for themselves, so how come now they're cutting the doctors in as well?"

"The Board has to protect the public who are paying a lot of money buying tickets to watch a world title fight. And the Board has to have some proof that both contestants, on the date of examination, are within comfortable reach of the middleweight limit."

"Don't give me all that about the Board and the public. As soon as you challenge for a title the Board want to manage your fighter. Why do you think I never took my boys into the top ten as contenders before? I've been bringing fighters in at their best weight for over forty years. When I bring a fighter in on the day of a fight at a stipulated weight, all he has to do is spit once then step on the scales and he makes exactly what I wanted him to make the day we signed for the fight. You don't imagine that I'm going to blow this one, do you?"

"I know you're not, I just have to have the respective weights in my report. What have you got against that?"

"Plenty. I manage my own fighter. The Board doesn't manage him and the newspapermen don't manage him. I don't want it in the papers what Teddy Baker weighs today."

"It's not going to be in the papers. This is for our own information and records."

"You might just as well have it published in Peter Wilson's column or on the front page of the 'Evening News'! There are more leaks in these offices than there were in the 'Titanic' when she went down. Edward doesn't weigh."

"Then what do you expect me to put down for the record?"

"Put down eleven seven and a half."

"I can't possibly do that."

"How long have you known me?"

"I don't know, but it must be well over thirty years."

"Did I ever lie to you in all that time?"

"No."

"Teddy Baker scaled eleven-seven and a half pounds yesterday afternoon. Put it down."

"You're a tough man, Doc," Kaplin said, looking Teddy over and then feeling him around the stomach and hips. "I'll do it for you, but don't say anything."

"You're okay, doctor," Doc said and then to Teddy: "Put your shirt and clothes on."

"Gentleman, Gentleman, please, make way for the champion!"

He came through the door with three others from his camp and Solomons' minder-man, Sailor. There was a big smile on his face and a day's growth of beard. He was wearing road clothes--heavy shoes and khaki trousers, a grey woollen shirt and dark green zipper jacket. He was, perhaps, an inch taller than Teddy with a good slim build that showed in spite of the clothes and, on his head, was a red woollen toque.

"There's my man," he said, walking over to Teddy with that smile still on and his hand held out. "How are you, Teddy?"

"I'm fine, You?"

"My, but you look good."

"You're late," Kaplin said to him.

"Hello, Doctor," he said in greeting, shaking Kaplin's hand. "Man, I've had people to see and things to do. You can't expect a guy like me to always be on time."

"When in Rome, you should do as the Romans do."

"C'mon," Doc said, motioning with his hand to Teddy.

"Hiya, Mr. Eastlake."

"Hello, champ."

We walked through to the outer office where the photographers plus some journalists were still waiting. Teddy tightened the knot in his tie and put his jacket back on. Waller was talking with the pressmen.

"What did he really weigh yesterday?" I asked Doc.

"Eleven-seven and a half. Kaplin's alright. He knows what's the truth."

"I just wondered."

"I'll wager that champion has to weigh-in there," Doc said, nodding back towards the other room. "You know that, don't you?"

"How about that big greeting I got?" Teddy said.

"That was phoney as sin," Doc said. "Dreadful."

"Who does he think he's impressing, showing up in those clothes? Maybe he'll think that you'll think he's having trouble doing the weight."

"Dreadful."

In about ten minutes Sailor re-emerged, leading the champion with his entourage in tow.

143

"Now, what have you got in mind?" one of the photographers said as they all stood up. "What do you want us to do?"

"Just relax," Sailor said. "You know I get paid for thinking, too."

"We've all got deadlines for the pictures," the same photographer said. "Let's get on with it."

Seemingly from nowhere, Sailor suddenly produced a gilt-painted cardboard crown, on the front of which was painted in black letters: CHAMP. He took the red toque off the champion's head and replaced it with the crown.

"Man, dig that crazy hat," one of the champion's team said.

"How about this?" the champion himself said, grinning broadly.

"Will you two guys look towards my camera, please?" one photographer said.

"No, we need them over here," another said. "We don't want the light of the window in the background."

"Have it your way then," the first agreed.

The pair of them were soon posed, Teddy with his left hand cocked and reaching for the crown on the champion's head with his right hand, the champion blocking the right with his left and about to throw his own right.

"Isn't that dreadful?" Doc said to me as we stood there, the flash-bulbs going and the photographers jostling.

"Go on, you've seen far worse than that."

"Thirty years ago. Don't they ever come up with anything new?"

"What's the matter?" Sailor asked.

"Nothing," Doc said. "It's great."

"It'll certainly make all the papers."

"Now what do you want next?" the first photographer said to him.

"Doctor Kaplin!"

"Hello there."

"Lend us that stethoscope a minute, will you?"

They had the champion discard the cardboard crown, take off his jacket and open his shirt while they posed the two of them with Teddy, neat in his light grey sports jacket, dark slacks blue shirt and grey tie, using the stethoscope on the champion's chest. Then they posed the doctor using the stethoscope on the champion, with Teddy looking over the doctor's shoulder.

"Now what?" a photographer asked his journalist colleague.

"Now go back to your offices," Sailor said.

"That's all?"

"What did you expect, Page Three Girls?"

"It's up to you."

"I'll be seein' you," the champion said to Teddy, smiling as ever and shaking his hand.

"That's right, we'll be getting' together soon," Teddy said.

When we got outside the rain had stopped, so we walked down Regent Street to Piccadilly and then up to the little Kosher place in Windmill Street, which serves wonderful boiled beef with the etceteras. We took the first booth on the right and Doc and I ordered a boiled beef sandwich and a drink apiece, while Teddy had a cup of tea and dry toast and Nat ordered boiled beef with dumpling and a poached egg on it.

"What time is it?" Doc asked as we were finishing.

"One-twenty," I told him.

"Far too early to go to that studio," Teddy said. "Let's take in a News Theatre first"

When we emerged from the hotch-potch of news and cartoons it was four o'clock, Teddy having slept through most of the programme.

We took a cab to Holborn, and when we alighted there and I looked at the place I decided that it must be either a remodelled old store or, possibly, formerly a hotel. The front had been re-done in new red brick, with plate-glass door and aluminium trim. There was a semicircular lobby with the walls painted light green and with a cork-tiled floor and we walked up to a very young man who was seated at the reception desk, talking into one of three telephones thereon.

"Can I help you?" he said, taking the phone away from his mouth and ear, but ready to go back to it.

"What's that woman's name?" Doc said to me.

"Cindy Burton."

"Will you take a seat?" the young man offered.

We spread ourselves along a long, curved, tan plastic-covered sectional sofa that fitted the curve of the wall. The receptionist youngster put the phone back in its cradle, waited, picked it up again, listened and dialled.

"So this is what these places are like," Nat Waller said.

"No," I said, "it's just what this place is like."

"How do you mean?"

"TV is ever-developing so that nothing is like anything else."

Cindy Burton came out of a passage to the rear of the desk. She was wearing a dark blue suit and a light blue mannish shirt with a round silver clip at the neck.

"So you're here," she said, shaking hands with Teddy and then Doc. "Good!"

"Is it?" Doc said. "The only reason we're doing this is that I'm a kindly old man and I felt sorry for a young lady like you."

"Let's go back; Len is looking forward to meeting you."

"Len and Cindy," Doc said to me. "Dames and boxing; whatever's our business coming to?"

"You don't want to go back to fighting with barefists on barges, do you?"

"Yes I do."

It was a huge room, probably an old storage-place, with a frightening air now of calculated disarray. Deep into the room and slightly off to our left, a group of parochial schoolgirls, not yet in their teens and dressed in navy-blue skirts and white blouses, sat on a three-level wooden structure flooded by lights. At either end of the top row of girls a nun sat and, in the front of the group, a guitar-player in a black cowboy costume stood, his back to them and facing a TV camera. He was playing and singing and smiling at the camera and, to the right, off camera, a piano-player and a bass-fiddle man, also in cowboy costumes, were accompanying him.

"Just wait here," Cindy Burton said to Teddy. "I'll find Len."

"Who's that cowboy singing?" Waller said to me. "I'm sure I've seen him somewhere."

"I've absolutely no idea," I said.

"Get on," Waller said, "I bet I know that guy."

Off into the vast room there was a kitchen set and, at another angle, a study or office set. To the right of that there was what appeared to be the corner of a living room, with two brown upholstered armchairs with a varnished corner table with a

146

modern, chartreuse lamp on it. Across the floor stretched the heavy black cables to the cameras and the stand-up flood-lamps and, moving around and stepping carefully over the cables, were several people, men and women, all of them young, a couple of the men with headsets on and one or two of the women carrying clipboards. All of them gave the appearance of being studiously harassed.

"This has got to be a madhouse," Doc said.

"What's Teddy's mother doing here?" Waller asked, half of himself.

"Where?"

"Right there."

Teddy had moved about fifteen feet from us and was talking to a small, grey-haired women wearing a black cloth coat and a small, black felt hat. She was fingering a black leather handbag and seemed worried, and Teddy was doing the talking, shrugging and explaining something.

"Tell them to come over here," Doc said to Waller. "What's going on here, anyway?"

Waller went over and shook hands with Teddy's mother and then brought them across to us. Doc shook hands with her and then Teddy introduced her to me

"We didn't know you were going to be here, Mrs. Baker," Doc said.

"She didn't know either," Teddy said. "That Cindy--Miss. Burton--called her on Saturday night. Then she called her this morning and told her to come along."

"I don't know," Mrs. Baker said shrugging. "She told me that she had seen Teddy and that I should come here."

"She didn't tell me she was going to ring up my mother," Teddy said to Doc. "You were there."

"Well, you're here," Doc said resignedly.

"But I don't know what to do."

We stood in awkward silence, watching the guitar-player in the cowboy clothes finish his number.

"And now," he said, smiling sweetly into the camera, "I hope you'll all join in a song with me called 'Morning Town Ride'. I'm sure you all know it as well, and like it as much, as I do. Isn't that right?"

"Yes," several of them murmured, most of the others nodding.

147

"Then let's all sing it together. Dick!"

He signalled to the piano-player, who led into it with the bass man, the guitar-player picking it up and then he started to sing.

Behind him the lips moved and the young voices sounded small and far away. I looked at the two nun sisters flanking the top row, and their lips were moving, too. My mind moved ahead to the next line but my eyes stayed on them.

'Maybe it is raining, where our train will ride, but all the little travellers are warm and snug inside...'

"My God," Doc said, nudging me. "Did you just see what I saw?"

"The sisters singing it?"

"Let's get out of here. What is this?"

"This is the brave new world."

"Dreadful."

"Lenny will be right here," Cindy Burton said. "Are you people enjoying watching this show?"

"This is Mrs. Praeger; I mean, Mrs. Baker," Doc said.

"Yes, I know. She got here before you did."

"Why didn't you tell us she was coming?"

"To tell you the truth I didn't know myself, not until this morning."

Doc had made his bloomer like the very best of us do.

"Mrs. Praeger?" I said. "Why Mrs. Praeger?"

"Teddy's old man came from Germany and his name isn't really Baker, but for God's sake keep that under your hat. I got him to change his name when he first turned pro' because it was quite soon after the war. Wearing the moniker Praeger wouldn't have helped him on his way at that time, any more than it would now, for that matter," Doc confessed.

"Oh, Charley!" Cindy Burton called.

A young man, wearing a white shirt and a black knitted tie and charcoal-grey trousers, turned and walked towards us. He had a sheaf of papers in one hand and was marking them with a pencil.

"This is Charley Adams, our Assistant Director. This is Teddy Baker, his mother and his manager, Mr. Eastlake."

"How d'you do," Charley Adams said, nodding a couple of times and then he turned and walked away, studying his sheaf of papers again.

148

"Here comes Lenny now," Cindy said.

He came, stepping over the cables, towards us, about six feet one and silver-haired, wearing a white suit (God only knows how he managed to keep it clean), with a white matching shirt and a red bow tie.

"Kenny, darling," Cindy Burton said, "meet Mrs. Praeger, Teddy Baker, Mr. Eastlake and----"

"Nat Waller," the conditioner said, introducing himself. "Hello."

"Nat Waller and Frank Cutler."

"How do you do?" Johnstone said. "All of you."

He had on pancake make-up which gave him an orange look, but he had a pointed nose and blue eyes and seemed to be in his early forties.

"Exactly who's going on, anyway," he said, looking at Cindy Burton and then at some papers she was carrying. "Not all of them?"

"Oh no," Cindy said. "It's all there; first Mrs. Praeger and then Teddy. The rest of them will just be watching."

"Good," Johnstone said, and then to Teddy and his mother: "I'll see you on, then."

"Wait a minute," Doc said. "What are they going to do?"

"Why, I'm sure Cindy's explained that; haven't you explained that?"

"No, but I'm going to now."

"Fine, then it's nice to have met the rest of you."

He turned and walked back across the floor to where the young man named Charley Adams and professionally identified, it transpired, as the A.D. was waiting for him. In front of the camera the guitar-player in the cowboy clothes was sitting on the bottom level of the wooden structure, smiling and nodding and talking with two of the parochial schoolgirls.

"What about this?" Doc said, affronted.

"It's very simple," Cindy Burton said. "There's nothing at all to worry about. Len's very, very good at this and he'll lead them."

"Lead them where?"

"Well, they're on the second segment. Kenny has a Formula I driver on the first half; he's over there getting ready now. In the second half, after the commercials, the announcer will

149

take Teddy's mother in. Perhaps you'd better leave your coat and handbag here, Mrs. Baker. Here, let me take them."

"I don't know," Teddy's mother said. "Is my dress alright?"

"Oh, it'll be fine; really, it's just fine."

It was a black dress, plain except for a small white-lace collar. With her coat off, Teddy's mother was smoothing the dress, the front then the sleeves.

"I don't know," she said again.

"Then what?" Doc said. "This lady doesn't know what she's supposed to do."

"She'll sit down with Kenny over there and Kenny will simply ask her some questions."

"About what?"

"About Teddy, naturally. About his boyhood days. That's why we wanted her on the show. After all, no one knows about Teddy's boyhood better than she does, and this is a homely show. I mean, it has a very big mixed-sex audience, and they'll just love this."

"I'll bet," Doc said.

"And what do I do?" Teddy said.

"Yeah," Waller said. "What does Teddy do?"

"You'll be told when to walk in. All you do is walk in and sit down and Lenny will talk to you. Haven't you ever been on TV before?"

"Several of my fights have been televised, but nothing like this."

"I'm quite sure you'll be splendid and you don't have to worry about a thing."

"I should have my head examined," Doc said aside to me.

"We'd better go over there now," Cindy Burton said, taking Mrs.Praeger-Baker by the arm and Teddy following. The guitar-player in the cowboy clothes was smiling his sign-off tune into the camera and, when he finished and the parochial-schoolgirls started to file off the wooden structure, Doc and Waller and I went to where we could see and hear an announcer introducing the Len Johnstone show.

"...and here's Len himself!" he said. "Len?"

"Thank you Don and hi!" Len said, smiling into the camera. "It's a damp spring day here in London but we're here

150

with a super programme to help you spend the next half-hour, wherever you may be in the United Kingdom...."

The first half of the show was motor-racing, then more commercials, and then...

"Now," he said, "we're going to meet a very special kind of guest, Mrs. Augusta Praeger, the mother of Teddy Baker. Just in case there be a single soul who doesn't already know about him, Teddy Baker is a prizefighter who, a week from Friday night, will challenge for the Middleweight Championship of the World. We thought that, because so many of you, thanks to television, have become interested in boxing and have probably thought about it and wondered about the make-up of a top prizefighter, we would invite you to meet a fighter's mother."

Then, turning from the camera, he walked to the corner setting where Mrs. Praeger was sitting, turning a white handkerchief round and round in her hands nervously. At some signal Len Johnstone, smiling and hand extended, walked into the set.

"Mrs. Praeger," he said, shaking hands and sitting down beside Teddy's mother, "we're so happy to have you with us."

"Thank you," Teddy's mother said, nodding. She looked scared.

"We'd like you to tell us all about Teddy. We've never met the mother of a leading boxer before, and so we'd like to hear how he became a fighter, whether or not you go to his fights and a whole lot of other things. Just how long has he been a fighter?"

"How long? I don't know exactly, but for years. Teddy could tell you."

"Then could you tell us how and why he became a fighter; how did it happen?"

"He just liked to fight, I think. He always seemed to like to fight."

"You mean as a boy? That he fought with the other boys in, perhaps, south-east London where you lived?"

"That's right. They were wild boys but that's where we had to live."

"That was here in London?"

"Yes, across the water in Lambeth."

"But did you try to stop him fighting with the other boys?"

"I tried to stop him. I told him it was no good, fighting, but he had a temper. Like his father, he had a temper."

151

She kept twisting the handkerchief in her hands.

"Tell me, Mrs. Praeger, what did your husband do? What was his business or occupation?"

"He was a plasterer but he died."

"Well, plastering is a good trade. I'm sure, too, that he was a good man."

"Yes, he was a very good man."

"When Teddy wanted to become a professional boxer, did you try to stop him?"

"I couldn't stop him. He had set his mind on it and he was a grown-up then."

"Have you ever gone to any of Teddy's fights?"

"Me go to see him fight? No."

"Do you watch on television when he fights?"

"I still don't have a television."

"Do you listen on the radio?"

"Sometimes. Once or twice I have tried to listen."

"You say you tried. You didn't enjoy it?"

"I turned it off."

"Are you afraid that your son may get hurt?"

"Yes, always; he could be hurt."

"Tell me this. You gave birth to a son and watched him grow and you must have had certain dreams for him; all mothers do. What did you hope that your son might become?"

"I don't know about dreams because I never had dreams. I just thought he would get some kind of job."

"What kind of job?"

"I don't really know but he was learning to be a plasterer. My husband was teaching him. My husband was not well and Teddy helped him. Teddy is a good boy."

"I'm quite sure he is, Mrs. Praeger. So you hoped that he might become a plasterer like his father?"

"Yes, it's a good job. Today they get well paid, plasterers."

"Indeed they do, Mrs. Praeger, and I want to thank you. Now, if you'll just wait here we have a surprise for you."

He turned, then, into camera, got up and hurried over towards it and stood, waiting and smiling.

"Why, he's a dirty son of a bitch," Doc said to me. "What is he trying to do, make him out a criminal?"

"That seems to be the general idea."

"Teddy's not going on. I'm pulling him out."

152

"Wait a minute, Doc," I said, putting my hands on his shoulder. "You can't do that now."

"Why can't I?"

"It's too late. He's already there."

"Where?"

I pointed to one of the floor monitors that showed Teddy standing there, waiting to walk on.

Johnstone was still waffling on, but at some signal he began a new spiel.

"And now, Mrs. Praeger," he said, "here comes the surprise. Here, with us today, to tell us himself what it's like to be a star prizefighter, is your son Teddy Baker."

Teddy walked in. He shook hands with Johnstone and then walked over to his mother, kissed her on the cheek, and sat down beside her. Len Johnstone had seated himself on the other seat and was leaning forward, smiling at the other two.

"This is a nice surprise, isn't it, Mrs. Praeger?"

"Oh yes," Teddy's mother said, nodding.

"How long has it been since you last saw your son?"

"I'm not sure, but about three weeks, I'd say."

"You've been away in training camp, haven't you?" he said to Teddy. "Training to challenge for the middleweight championship on Friday week?"

"That's right," Teddy replied, looking rather bored.

"And you're going to win?"

"Well, I certainly hope and think so."

"But in your profession you can never be certain; is that right?"

"I suppose so, but then, we can't be certain that tomorrow will come, can we?"

"It is a precarious business, though, isn't it?" Len said smiling.

"I reckon you're right."

"How long have you been preparing for this fight?"

"I always keep in light training, but I've been away in camp in strict training just over two weeks."

"I've been talking here with your mother, Teddy, about your boyhood and what made you decide to become a fighter. Your mother isn't quite sure. Can you yourself tell us now why you became a fighter?"

"Oh, I just enjoyed fighting and I suppose that's why."

"Didn't you ever want to become anything other than a fighter?"

"How do you mean?"

"Well, did you ever think about being a lawyer or policeman or a train-driver, or any of the other things that most small boys want to do when they grow up?"

"I couldn't be a lawyer. I didn't like school much and I had to leave when my father died. I didn't want to join the police; is that what you mean?"

"Uh-huh, but did you ever want to be, say, a footballer?"

"Oh yes, when I was very young."

"Why didn't you, I mean, become a footballer?"

"Where we lived there wasn't anywhere to practise football except in the street and, if they spotted you, the police would chase you off doing that. We used to play rounders with a soft ball and a stick in the street, but that's nothing like the same thing. I never even owned a pair of football boots so I couldn't try to be a footballer."

"Tell us, and that means the millions of people watching us on their TV, how many fights have you had?"

"Professional? Ninety."

"How many have you won?"

"All but three. I've lost three decisions."

"Have you never been knocked out?"

"No, never."

"Do you ever think that, one day, you might get knocked out?"

"No, I don't believe I ever could."

"Your mother, here, worries about you when you fight. She worries about your possibly getting hurt or knocked out."

"I suppose that she does."

"Now, I'm keen to get to the heart of this, Teddy, if you don't mind."

"It's okay with me."

"Do you really mean that you never even consider getting knocked out?"

"That's right. I've got a good chin; that's what it's called in the fight game. I just don't think I could be knocked out, so I never worry about it at all."

"But you've knocked out plenty of others. Your opponents?"

154

"That's quite true."

"About how many opponents have you knocked out or stopped?"

"Well, let's see. I think it's forty-eight or nine"

"Tell us, how do you feel when you knock an opponent out?"

"I don't know. I don't really want to hurt him but a fight in the ring is man-to-man and it's him or me."

"But that's what you try to do, to hurt him, isn't it? You try to beat him any way you can; isn't that right?"

Johnstone was questioning with a smile. It was a small, humourless smile, set to imply sympathy.

"If you put it that way, there's nothing I can say."

"So, what do you feel when you see your man lying there on the ring floor after you've knocked him out? Do you feel relieved, or glad, or sad or what?"

"You feel excited. After all, you've both been trying to knock each other out and you've won. Your moves and your punches did it so it makes you feel good."

"Exactly."

"It isn't that you want to hurt him. You're trying to beat him through your skill. That is boxing."

"But you know that it's dangerous. You know, for example, that several fighters lost their lives through ring fights last year."

"Accidents will happen, but the safety regulations are much better now. We have to have regular medical checks, brain scans and lord knows what else; the rings have been made much safer, the rules altered to make for more safety......"

Johnstone interrupted with: "Now, Teddy Baker, you're married, aren't you?"

"Yes, I am."

"Do you have any children?"

"We have a boy."

"How old is he?"

"Five."

"Do you hope that he'll be a fighter when he grows up?"

"He couldn't be."

"He couldn't? Why not?"

"He's not well enough. He'll alright, but he couldn't be a fighter."

"I didn't know that. What's wrong with him?"

"We discovered that he has epilepsy. He's quite alright, but he has that."

"I'm sorry to hear that. I really am and I'm sure that all our viewers are, too."

"Thank you, but he'll be okay."

"But, if he were perfectly healthy, would you want him to be a fighter?"

"I don't know. It's impossible to say."

"Is it impossible to say? Don't you really mean that you have your doubts and, having them, you wouldn't want him to be a fighter? Isn't that right?"

"Maybe. Probably my wife and I couldn't take it."

"Precisely. You're a fighter and you know the strength of it and this is it. You wouldn't want you son to follow in his father's footsteps."

"Honestly, I don't really know."

"Ah well, unfortunately I see that our time on air is now up. I want to thank you, though, Teddy Baker, for being our guest and we want to wish you luck. You've chosen your profession, fighting, and I know we all hope that you make the very best of it when you fight for the Middleweight Championship of the World and whatever lies ahead after that."

"Thanks a lot."

He, Teddy and his mother stood up.

"And to you, Mrs. Praeger, you're a wonderful little lady and our hearts go out to you. And now....."

He sidled off, talking, in front of another camera, and Teddy and his mother came off towards us.

"And now what do you suggest?" Doc said to me.

"Getting very drunk. The whole thing was inevitable."

"But why did I have to be a bloody fool and be a part of it?"

"I did the best I could," a downcast Teddy said.

"It's not your fault, Edward," Doc said. "I was the idiot falling for it."

"But what was he trying to put over anyway?" Waller cut in. "After all, boxing helps him earn his living."

Cindy Burton came up to us, all smiles and in a hurry.

"You were fine, Mrs. Praeger," she said, putting her arm around Teddy's mother.

"I don't know," the widowed lady replied. "I didn't know what to do."

"Listen," Doc said. "Get that man over here."

"Who?"

"Len-whatever-his-name-is. Get him over here."

"I'm sorry," Cindy Burton said. "He's got a meeting with the programme controller in fifteen minutes and has to get across there. I'm sure he'd have liked to say goodbye to all of you, but he's a terribly busy person."

"See what I mean?" Doc said to me.

"Best forget it."

"Listen," Doc said to Cindy Burton. "I'm not blaming you; I just feel sorry for you."

"For me? Honestly, I don't understand. I thought it was a great show."

"The sooner we get out of here the better, " Doc said.

"Please. You'd be surprised at the impact this could have throughout the country. This is a very popular show, and after this I'm sure there will be many more people who'll be interested in Teddy Baker and the coming big fight."

"And stay at home and watch it on TV for free," Doc said. "Please, just don't tell me the tale any more. I'll repeat myself; I just feel sorry for you."

We left Cindy Burton standing there and walked out, down the hall and on to the pavement. It was getting misty again, so Doc hailed a cab and he and Teddy helped Mrs. Praeger into it.

"You'll be careful?" she said to Teddy, when he bent down to kiss her on the cheek.

"I promise, Mum, and don't worry. I'll be down to see you the day after the fight."

"He'll be the champion then, Mrs. Praeger," Waller said.

"We can't be certain sure," she almost whispered in reply.

We flagged down another cab, got in and headed for the car park.

"I should have known better," Doc said on the way. "All my life I've had a rule; when they send a bit of skirt or a cripple to ask you to do something, walk away from it."

"That's sound."

"Walk away from it. All my life I've followed that, so now I fall right into it, hook, line and sinker."

157

"There's one thing that Len Johnstone said that was the truth," I said.

"What's that?"

"If the viewers could really be made to believe that boxing is as bad and dangerous as that, they'd walk through hell to get to the fight."

"But isn't that dreadful?" Doc said.

"Speaking of sadistic impulses, Mr. Johnstone doesn't even need to climb into a ring."

"Dreadful. Holds you, thumbs you, knees you, butts you, elbows you. It's all my fault."

On the way back to the Barley Mow even Waller was morose. By the time we got in, what with the rush-hour traffic it was after seven. Teddy and Waller ate their evening meal with the others, but Doc and I stood at the bar for a long time so that Doc could let off steam.

"You know that several fighters were killed in boxing last year?" he said, mimicking the Johnstone voice. "What does he know about it, except through being a self-appointed no-nothing expert?"

"Have another drink."

"I will, but I just wish I'd been on that television with Teddy."

"You'd have had no chance."

"I wouldn't? Not with that microphonic gate-crasher?"

"Of course not; not even you. They're pros' at that racket and you're not. They inflate their egos by talking with amateurs who find themselves in a strange, synthetic setting. They write their own rules. He could do the same sort of thing in there with you or me or any one of us."

"You know that fighters were killed in the ring last year? But how many jockeys were killed in horse racing, how many riders in eventing, how many in football, bob-sleighing, skiing, motor-racing, drunken driving, crossing the road and God knows what else?"

"How about that drink?"

"What's the matter with you blokes?" Waller said, walking up to us. "We've finished eating already and you haven't even started. Ain't you gonna eat?"

"Is it still raining outside?" Doc wanted to know.

"I don't know," Nat said.

158

"Do me a favour and go and see, will you?"

At nine o'clock we went into the kitchen. Capini's wife had just finished washing-up, but she made us a ham sandwich apiece and coffee. Then we went back to the bar, and about ten o'clock Teddy and Waller and Penny came by. They had been watching TV and were on their way to bed.

"Are you two old boozers still at it?" Waller remarked

"Is it still raining?" Doc repeated to him.

"I told you before. It's stopped and I think it's gonna be nice tomorrow."

"Good. Then we can celebrate that, too. The good old weather and the good old Len Johnstone show."

"Some wench, eh, that Cindy?" Penny said to me "I watched the show and I'd like to get on it myself."

"Freddie called me," Teddy said. "He watched it, too, and he didn't think it was bad at all."

"See if it's raining outside, will you?" Doc said to Waller.

"Sure," Nat answered and then to me: "You don't want me to wake you tomorrow, do you?"

"If you don't I'll get you excommunicated."

"What's that?"

"I'll leave you out of the story. So help me, I will."

"You want to get waked, then I'll wake you. It's up to you."

XVIII

Next morning I felt the hand on my shoulder. I felt it and then I felt it again, this time shaking me and then, finally, I made out a figure bending over me and I knew then where I was.

"Frank?"

"Yes. Waller?"

"No, it's Teddy."

"Oh, I thought you were Nat."

"Doc wants you."

"Who?"

"Doc."

"Okay. What's the matter with him? Is he alright?"

But Teddy was gone, the door open and the light from the hall coming in. I got up and put on my dressing-gown and slippers. Doc was standing in the doorway of Teddy and Waller's

159

room, with his blue-flannel gown over his pyjamas and he looked terrible. His hair had not been combed and he needed a shave, his baggy eyes and face were almost as white as his hair and he looked about a hundred years old.

"Are you alright?" I said to him. "What's the matter?"

"It's Nat," he said. "Come in here."

"What's the matter with him?"

"He's dead."

"He's what?"

The overhead light was on in the room and it shone bright. I looked at Waller's bed against the wall and he was lying there, with the khaki blanket up to his chin and the white sheet folded down over the edge of the blanket. Only his face was showing, eyes closed, his head on the pillow, all of it, Waller and the bed, in that corner against the wall.

"He's dead?" I said. "How do you know he's dead?"

"He's dead right enough," Doc said.

"But why is he dead? How could he have died?"

"A heart attack," Doc said. "A heart attack, I reckon."

"A heart attack? Did he have a dodgy heart, then?"

"Maybe. Two years ago he had an attack of some kind."

"I didn't know that. Nobody ever told me."

Doc was sitting on the straight-backed chair near the table with Waller's tape and bandages and bottles on it. Teddy was sitting on the edge of his bed, his gown over his pyjamas, staring at the floor. They said nothing.

"I never knew that," I said. "What do you want me to do?"

"He told me that the doctor had said he should take it easy," Doc explained. "I told him to heed the doctor. I always brought another man into the corner to do all the carrying. Perhaps he should never even have been here at all?"

"Where else would he want to be? This would have happened wherever he was."

"Teddy woke me. He said: 'You better get up; there's something the matter with Nat.' "

"I didn't know what it was," Teddy said. "The alarm clock went off and Nat always gets up. He didn't today so I got up and shut it off. Then I tried to wake him up. How was I to know he was dead?"

"C'mon, my men!" Penny said. "Hit the road."

160

He was standing in the doorway dressed in his road clothes. It must have been obvious that something was wrong because he came into the room.

"What gives?"

"Nat's dead," Teddy said.

"What are you talking about?"

The others were in the hall now, crowded in the doorway and looking in--old Sid, Lefty, Harry McCormick, Mickey Evans and Ceroni, all of them heavily clad in their road clothes.

"Waller's dead," Penny said to them. "Teddy says Nat's dead."

"He's what?" old Sid, in the beret, said bemused.

They followed on into the room, then, cautiously. They seemed almost to fill it and they looked down at Waller. I looked at him again, too, at the shape under the khaki blanket and at the head on the pillow, balding, with that bashed, broken nose and that cauliflowered left ear. Now that I knew he was dead he seemed a yellow, curious figure out of a wax museum. He was so still and, somehow, shrunken. Move, Nat, I was thinking, all you have to do is move.

"Whatever happened to him?" Mickey Evans, incredulous, asked.

"He had a heart attack," I said.

"Why don't we all get out of here?" Lefty Flynn said

"Good idea," Doc agreed.

"You goin' on the road?" Penny said to Teddy.

"No."

"Yes you are," Doc said.

"I don't want to go. I feel out of sorts now."

"You're going," Doc said. "You had yesterday off and it's best."

"That's right," I said. "Doc's quite right. You're in training here and the sooner you get back into it the better."

"But I'm not even dressed."

"We'll wait," said old Sid, in the doorway. "We'll wait downstairs."

"Of course," Penny said, "we'll wait for you."

They left and Teddy shed his dressing-gown and pyjamas and dressed slowly. When he went out, Doc closed the door and sat down again.

"Now," I said, "what do you want me to do?"

161

"I don't really know. What do we do?"

"Is there any family? Did Nat have any relatives?"

"No. He used to have a sister, married, but she died a couple of years ago. There's her husband--if he's still alive, but he's old and wouldn't give a damn."

"Where did Nat live?"

"He had a room somewhere in Earls Court. I'll have to take care of that, too."

"Forget about that for now. I suppose we should get Capini. I'm sure he knows of an undertaker in Guildford."

"What time is it?"

"That clock says just after seven."

"We kept Rene up 'til one o'clock. He won't like this."

"He doesn't like anything. His missus will be in the kitchen by now. I'll tell her."

"I'll get dressed," Doc said.

When I told Capini's wife she threw up her hands and sat down. Then she began slapping her hands on her lap and shaking her head. I got her to go and wake her man in the adjacent cottage where they slept beyond the south end of the car park. Then I went upstairs and dressed quickly and went into Doc's room. He had barely finished dressing when Capini came up the stairs.

"How can he possibly be dead?" he said. "This is terrible; where is he?"

"In his bed," Doc said. "Go and see for yourself."

Capini crossed the hall and, in a moment, emerged from the room closing the door behind him and shaking his head.

"This is awful," he said. "Why did it have to happen here?"

"Do you know an undertaker in town?" I asked him.

"I only know one, though there must be plenty."

"One's enough," Doc said. "Give him a ring, will you?"

"I'll phone him," Capini said. "This is simply terrible."

Doc and I went to the kitchen and Capini's wife, Ivy, commiserated with Doc and made us coffee. We carried it out into the dining-room and sat at a table on the pool side with the new day's sunlight flooding the white table-cloth. When we had finished the coffee, Capini's wife came out and refilled the cups and, finally, we heard the fighters come back and we went out into the hall.

"Go up and use my room," Doc said to Teddy. "Cool off in my room."

162

"Alright," said Teddy, and he followed the others up the stairs.

"I'll go up with him," I said.

Doc went into the kitchen to get a hot cup of tea for Teddy and I followed the fighter into the room and closed the door. There was a wicker armchair with a large cushion on it by the window and Teddy, sweating freely, sat down in it.

"How was the roadwork?" I asked him.

"It was okay."

"Here, use Doc's towel."

"Thanks."

"Look, I know how you feel about Waller but you have to forget it. It may sound unfeeling, but the really important thing is the coming fight and you don't want to mess things up in your preparation."

"I'm not gonna blow the fight, but Nat was a nice guy. Why did it have to be him?"

"God alone knows that."

"He was with me for all my fights. From the time Doc took me on, Nat was with me for every fight except once in the early days when he had to go to his mother's funeral, way out somewhere in the sticks, and couldn't make it back in time."

"I know that."

"I was shaking him and saying: 'Nat, wake up--it's time to get up. You better hurry,' I didn't know he was dead."

"Of course you didn't."

Doc brought the tea in and gave it to Teddy. Then he went across the hall with Teddy's gown, shower clogs and another towel.

"After you've showered I'll get your clothes, he told Teddy.

We heard footsteps on the stairs and Capini entered with a man in a dark blue serge suit. He was short and stout and he looked to be in his early sixties. He had a round, pink face that was expressionless, as are so many undertakers' faces. His hair, grey now, was plastered back with a parting right down the middle.

"This is Mr. Edwards," Capini said, "the undertaker. This is Mr. Doc Eastlake, Teddy Baker and Mr. Cutler."

"May I extend my sympathy?" Mr. Edwards bleated.

"Thanks a lot," Doc replied.

163

"Tell me," Edwards said to Capini, "where is the deceased now?"

Doc pointed: "It's that room right there."

"I understand. Would you, uh, prefer to talk here or shall we go somewhere else?"

"If you're going across the hall we'll talk there," Doc said. "Teddy doesn't have to be a part of this."

"I understand and that's fine."

"Will you come with us, Frank?"

"If that's what you want."

We left Teddy, Capini went back downstairs and Doc led the way into the room. Mr.Edwards walked over to the bed, looked down at Waller and then turned back to us.

"As I understand it, there was no physician attending at the time of death?"

"That's right," Doc said. "He must have died in his sleep. Teddy-my fighter-found him just like that. I knew he'd had heart trouble."

"Well, I shall need a Certificate of Death. Is there a local doctor who was treating him?"

"Down here? No."

"Then I'll call the coroner."

"Why the coroner?"

"Because that's the law. It's just a matter or procedure that, in the absence of a doctor, the coroner must certify to the death."

"So notify him."

"Right, I'll do that. Have you informed the surviving relatives?"

"There aren't any. I'll handle everything."

"That's quite in order. Have you had a chance to think about the funeral and interment? Where will it be?"

"I don't know yet," Doc said. "This has only just happened."

"I suppose he should be buried near to where he lived," I said.

"There must be both a cemetery and a crematorium near Earls Court. How do I set that up and go about getting him there?" Doc said.

"I take it that Mr. Waller owned no plot?" Mr. Edwards said.

164

"No, I feel certain he didn't."

"In that case, I can arrange that for you. Will there be a church service?"

"No, he didn't go to church. Can't we use some funeral parlour around Earls Court?"

"Certainly. I'll make my call to the coroner now and then go back to my office. I have a burial later today, but I'll be back and I'll see to everything."

"Thanks," Doc said.

"I suggest that this room be locked. I imagine the coroner will want to see everything exactly as it is."

"Whatever you say," Doc agreed.

"But we should have Teddy's clothes moved out of here," I said.

"Clothes?"

"Yes, he did roadwork this morning and he's probably getting out of those clothes now. After he's taken a shower he needs to put on other clothes--slacks and a shirt and sweater. They're probably there in the wardrobe."

"Couldn't he wait? It probably won't be long."

"Wait?" Doc said, "wait for what? What difference does it make?"

"Well, it would be better to leave everything just as it is."

"Look," I said. "I'll pick out the clothes now, while you're here. Then well leave the room together and close the door."

"There aren't any keys for these doors anyway," Doc said.

That seemed to convince him so I went over to the wardrobe and opened it. I saw some of the things Teddy had been wearing. I took out a pair of slacks, a white shirt and light-blue sweater plus shoes with socks stuffed into them. There were a pair of shorts and a T-shirt on a hook and I took them also.

"That's all, " I said, showing the undertaker.

"Alright," he agreed, "you should understand that I just want to avoid any complications later."

We all left the room and Doc shut the door. Edwards went downstairs, after telling us again that he would handle everything, and Doc and I went into his room and I put the clothes down on the bed.

"Is everything alright?" Teddy wondered.

"What's this about the coroner and everything being left as it was?" Doc asked me.

"I don't know, but I imagine that it's just standard procedure."

"The law; it's always the law. The politicians and the lawyers haunt a man right to his grave. Can't they ever leave him alone in peace?"

After Teddy had finished showering and dressed we went down to the dining-room. The others were finishing breakfast and we sat by one of the windows again. Teddy didn't want cereal but had two soft-boiled eggs while Doc and I had coffee and toast.

"Anyway," I said, "the weather is nice. It's beautiful out."

"Yeah," Doc acknowledged.

"What are we going to do?" Teddy said.

"I'll have to go into town," Doc said. "Is there a bus this afternoon or tonight?"

"If you could drive," Teddy said, "you could take my car."

"Go in tomorrow morning," I said. "The funeral won't be until Thursday and tomorrow's only Wednesday. I'd drive you myself, but for the purpose of this piece I'm supposed to be doing here I should stay with Teddy."

"I want you with him anyway. Funeral; is there some way you can get out of having a funeral?"

"You could call it private and still have a burial or cremation."

"Private. It'll be private enough in any case."

"Mr. Edwards is here again," Capini said, walking over to us.

Edwards was waiting in the hallway with the coroner, who he introduced as Doctor Fisher. The man looked to be in his early forties, stern-faced and black-haired, wearing a dark grey suit and carrying a black medical bag and brown brief-case.

"You'll want to go upstairs?" Doc suggested.

"I've already seen the body," the doctor said. "There are some questions to be answered, so I'd like to find a place to sit down."

"Then you go upstairs," Doc said to Teddy. "Go to my room."

"I'll go with him," I offered.

"I'd rather have you here," Doc said. Teddy'll be alright."

We went back into the dining-room with the coroner and Mr. Edwards following us. We sat down at one end of the long table that had been cleared of the breakfast dishes and the

166

coroner took a printed form out of his brief-case, placed it on the table and took out a fountain pen.

"To begin with, the name of the deceased, please?"

"Nat Waller," Doc said.

"He'll want his legal name," I said.

"Yes, I must have his legal name."

"That's okay," Doc said, "Nathan Giordano."

"So he used an alias?"

"Not an alias," Doc said, "it was his fighting name."

"He was a fighter?"

"Years ago."

"Was he a good fighter and well-known?"

"Does that have to go down there, too? Do you mean to say that you've got a line on that form for that?"

"I'm merely asking."

"What else do you want to know?"

"Was there a middle initial?"

"Not that I know of."

The coroner filled in what looked like a couple of lines on his own.

"Was he married?"

"No."

"Ever?"

"No."

"Date of birth?"

"Fourteenth of July sixty-four years ago. You best work it out."

Doing the subtraction on a scrap of paper, the coroner wrote the year on the form.

"Place of birth; do you know that?"

"Stepney, I believe."

"Father's name?"

"I have absolutely no idea."

"Mother's maiden name?"

"God, how the hell would I know?"

"As I understand it, there are no relatives who would know?"

"Correct."

"Usual occupation?"

"Trainer of boxers."

"Kind of business or industry?"

167

"What? Prizefighting or boxing, I suppose. Make it boxing."

"Is there some difference?"

"Yes, as long as we're being so legal. Prizefighting is illegal, but boxing has been legalised."

"Was the deceased ever in one of Britain's Armed Forces?"

"No. He was exempted from National Service on medical grounds."

"Now, as to the cause of death."

"A heart attack."

"That's merely your supposition."

"Well, what else could it be?"

"It might be any number of things. We don't know."

"What do you mean?"

"It could have been a cerebral haemorrhage, a ruptured aneurism, an intestinal haemorrhage. It could have been many things."

"He had heart trouble."

"As a matter of fact, Mr. Eastlake, we don't know but that it could have been foul play."

"Foul play? You must be joking!"

"No. Until I've got evidence to the contrary, this man might have been poisoned for all I know. He might have died through strangulation or he might have been struck a blow on the head. There is no evidence at the moment, but it could be a fact."

"Did you ever hear anything like this?" Doc said to me.

"That's why I have to perform an autopsy."

"An autopsy? You mean you're going to cut the poor chap open?"

"You can be certain, Mr. Eastlake, that it doesn't make any difference to him."

"It does to me."

"I'm sorry, but that's my ruling. It has to be because it's the law."

"How long will it take?" I said.

"I'll do it this afternoon. Mr. Edwards will remove the body to his funeral home. The autopsy itself will only take about an hour and a half. I'll telephone with my findings, if all goes well."

"If all goes well?" Doc said "What exactly does that mean?"

168

"Take it easy," I said. "It's alright, Doc."

"Like hell it is," Doc said.

Doctor Fisher put his papers back in his brief-case and we walked out into the hallway. Doc was talking with the undertaker, making it clear that this should be a burial rather than cremation and that there should be a simple cemetery plot. The coroner motioned to me and I followed him out on to the porch.

"You do understand the necessity for this, don't you?" he said.

"Yes, I understand."

"After all, you recognise the circumstances which make it imperative that the cause of death be established. Besides, this Mr. Giordano, or Waller, was in the boxing business. Am I right?"

"What's that got to do with it."

"Are you in the fight business?"

"No."

"I didn't think you were, though you're familiar with the business. Probably you've read about it."

"About what?"

"About what kind of business it is, the types that are mixed up in it. How am I supposed to know who this man was or what went on here?"

"Alright, doctor. You'll phone us later?"

"I'm not over-keen about this myself. Performing an autopsy is no novelty to me and I was going to play golf this afternoon."

"I sympathise. We were going to have some gangsters up for tea."

"What?"

"Phone us when you're ready."

"Listen; there's a fellow in Guildford who used to be a fighter. You should see him."

"Why?"

"He's a drunk; a no-gooder."

"Is he the only drunk in the town?"

"No, but he's one of them. Boxing scrambled his brain and took away his self-respect."

When I went back into the hall Doc was still standing there, and Mr. Edwards was just coming out of one of the phone-booths.

169

"I've just called my son," he said. "He'll be straight over and we'll remove the body. I'd like to go upstairs now with you gentlemen and remove everything that may be on the body. I mean things like jewellery, watch, fountain-pen or whatever."

We went up to the room and the undertaker pulled the covers off Waller. I merely glanced at what he was doing, then looked at Doc, whose gaze was scanning round the room.

"There's nothing on the body," Edwards said, "except, of course, the pyjamas."

"That's fine," Doc said.

"My son will be here very shortly."

"Wait a minute," Doc interjected. "There should be a ring. Nat had a ring."

"There's no ring here," Edwards said. "There's nothing at all on either hand."

Doc and I walked over and we looked at both hands. There was no ring.

"There should be a ring," Doc insisted, "a ring with a ruby in it. He wore it on his left hand."

"It isn't here."

"I gave it to him myself about twenty years ago, on his birthday. He was born in July and that's the birthstone."

"Maybe he took it off," the undertaker suggested.

"He never took it off. Ever since I gave it to him he never took it off."

"You'll probably find it here somewhere," Edwards persisted.

"Maybe Teddy took it off, " I said.

"No," Doc said. "Why should he take it off? He wouldn't think of that."

I heard the front door slam and then we heard footsteps coming up the stairs.

"That's probably my son," Edwards said.

"Let's get out of here," I said to Doc. "We can look for the ring later."

We passed the young man carrying a stretcher in the hall and went into Doc's room. Teddy was lying on the bed looking at the ceiling.

"Is everything alright?" he said.

"Yes," Doc replied. "Did you see anything of Nat's ring?"

"His ring?"

170

"Yes, it's not on him."

"It's got to be 'cos he never took it off."

"Some shit must have taken it," Doc said. "Can you imagine that?"

"You can't be sure," I said. "When they leave we'll look around the room and through Nat's stuff. It may be there somewhere."

"But I never saw him take it off, ever, anywhere," Teddy said.

When we heard them leaving and going slowly down the stairs, Doc and I went back into the room. We searched all over the place, in all the drawers and in the pockets of Waller's clothes.

"Some shit's had it," Doc growled. " Can you take in a thing like that?"

"Who would take it?"

"Anybody. Who knows? This business is quite some racket."

"Well, not anybody. Who would steal a ring off a dead body? Not Capini or his wife. That's two out of the way"

"I don't know."

"Suppose we say nothing about it?"

"I don't care any more. I need a drink."

We went back to Doc's room and he told Teddy to keep quiet about the ring. We sat with Teddy for a few minutes and then Penny came in with the morning papers. Doc and I went downstairs, got Capini from behind his desk in the hall and we went into the bar.

"Mix us doubles," Doc said to Capini, "and that'll be all. Then you can get back to your work.

"Righto."

"I feel lousy," Doc said.

"So do I. After what we had last night we'd feel lousy under the best of circumstances."

"To Nat." Doc toasted, when Capini had left.

"The best to him."

"Nat and I went through a lot together; over forty years of grafting."

"I know and now I'm feeling a bit ashamed."

"Ashamed? Of what?"

"Of myself."

171

"Why? What's the matter?"

"Oh, about Waller. Nat was a nice little chap and I liked him, but I used to think how he pressurised everybody. And now I feel ashamed."

"God, how he liked to talk!"

"I probably shouldn't say this now, but I used to wonder, sometimes, how you put up with it."

"You want to know how?"

"Yes."

"Did you notice that broken and flattened nose? Or the cauliflowered left ear?"

"Of course I did."

"I put them there."

"You did?"

"Definitely. Nat was my first fighter."

"I know that."

"I learned on Waller. I was a green kid managing him. I put that busted nose there and that mangled ear. I learnt about the business with Nat. Many a time he used to get on my nerves too, but then I'd look at that nose and that ear, take in the scar tissue over his eyes and cheekbone and I'd say to myself: 'You're with me as long as you live. You're working with me.' "

"I should have worked that out for myself."

"It hit me, talking about it now. 'As long as you live', and that's the way it worked out."

"Yes. Suddenly today was the day."

"I should have been arrested, the fights I put him in. Some of those great old-timers they still like to write about; those great old managers like Ted Broadribb and Charlie Rose, what they pulled on me when I had Nat Waller. He might have been a contender."

"Really?"

"Not a champion but a real good fighter. I was real brave with Nat; I put him into wars. I'll tell you something--when he was finished, I was finished being a brave manager. I outgrew that with one fighter. Nat Waller."

"Most managers never do."

"I'll tell you something else. Every fighter I've had since Waller became a better fighter because of him, because of what I learned on Nat. Every one of them and that goes for Edward, too. I've told every one of them, though Waller never knew it, but

172

believe me I told them. I told Edward, my Pro, and he was very fond of Nat."

"I know. He used to go along with him the same as you did."

"A lot of mugs at Solomons' probably wondered why I kept Nat. He talked too much and he got excited in the corner. I could have hired ten better trainers but I didn't need a trainer because I do that. I needed a pick-up man for the towels and the pail and to give a rub-down. I didn't need a cutman either; I work the cuts."

"I know all the things you really do."

"I've thought a lot about Waller in the last few years. Did you ever ride in a train and see one of those scrap yards packed with old steam engines, rusting, all hooked up together in a long line?"

"Yes."

"I used to see those old engines and think of Waller. Each one of those old engines provides the guide to some part of every new diesel or electric locomotive on the rails today. Engineers learned on those old giants the way I learned on Waller. As long as I lived there could never be any scrap heap for Nat.

"Don't get me wrong. This was not charity. Nat did what he was supposed to do and he was loyal. There was no more loyal guy in the world."

"I know"

"Right after he had that first heart attack, a couple of years ago, I asked him about it and he said: 'The doctor says I should take it easy and that I shouldn't get excited.' Do you think I could keep him out of the corner?"

"No."

"About ten days later we're in Sheffield. Teddy got a bad decision--dreadful. He had the other fellow almost out at the finish and where's Waller? Jumping up and down and screaming at the referee--ten days after the doctor warned him he must take it easy."

"I can believe that"

"A loyal man who had nothing. Want to hear what was a big thing with him?"

"Yes, I'd like to know."

"Christmas cards. He sent Christmas cards to everybody."

"I might have guessed. He always sent me one; never missed."

"Most of the people never sent one back to him."

"I never did. You make me feel ashamed again."

"It made no difference. He got some and he used to hang them on a string in his room. There was an old, bricked-up fireplace there, and he'd hang the cards over that fireplace. He'd keep them there all the year round, until the next Christmas when the new ones came in. Then he'd save the old ones in boxes under his bed; over thirty years or so he had boxes full of them. That was his Christmas but I'll have to sling them all out now."

"Let it ride until after the fight."

"Yep, I'll have to. He had nothing and that's why, one birthday, I gave him that ring. At the time, I thought he was going to cry. Nobody ever gave him anything. Who the hell would take that ring?"

"I just don't know."

"But who would do a thing like that? Figure it out."

"Well, if you must go into it, you've got the fighters and old Sid Brown. One of them must have gone back into the room while we were in your room."

"Not old Sid."

"No."

"Penny?"

"I don't think so."

"Why not?"

"That wise-guy type wouldn't risk it."

"I think he's just the type."

"No, Doc. He's out in the open. Practical jokes and kidology, yes. But not taking a ring off a body. How about Mickey Evans? I don't know much about him."

"Mickey? Listen, he's so glad that I gave him a few weeks work he wouldn't take the chance. I know him."

"Not Lefty."

"Of course not."

"McCormick?"

"I don't know."

"A possibility, but my candidate is Ceroni."

"Ceroni? Why him?"

"I know Charlie Mahoney, his manager, and I know the way he treats his fighters, Doc. Ceroni's probably got nothing in

174

his pockets now--except, possibly, the ring and, when he's in Slough, I bet Mahoney gives him no more than a tenner a week. He has all his fighters eat with him, you know, so he can keep an eye on them."

"It's possible."

"Indeed. Ceroni's got those two women, or they've got him."

"Uh, he doesn't need cash for them; you can be sure they pick up all the bills. Maybe they're even paying him, for all I know."

"Nevertheless, picture the kid. He's got some pride and he'd like to make a show, to be able to flash some dough."

"That ring is worth around two hundred."

"I recall seeing it on Nat, now that it's being mentioned. Does Mahoney know about those wenches?"

"I don't know. My suspect is still Penny, in spite of what you say."

"You may be right but I doubt it. Too open. Not knowing anything about Harry McCormick, mine is Ceroni."

"In any event, we'll never see that ring again."

"I believe you're right."

We saw old Sid come through the door looking for someone, and then he saw us at the bar and walked over.

"Scuse me, Doc," he said.

"You're excused, Sid."

"You goin' up to town?"

"Yes, tonight or tomorrow morning."

"I'm sorry about Nat and I'll take care of Teddy while you're gone. I mean, I'll handle him in the gym, so don't worry about it while you're away."

"Thanks, Sid. Thanks a lot. I'll bring somebody back with me; Tim Holland if I can get him, but I'll get somebody. I appreciate it, Sid."

"Don't you worry about it. I'm glad to do it because Teddy's gonna be the new champion."

"Surely he is."

"I know I know the other boy and I've known him since he started. He ain't the fighter people think he is. He's got yellow in him but he ain't showed it to them yet. Teddy, he'll make him show it."

"He will, for sure."

175

"Nobody fought that other boy right yet. I been watchin' Teddy in the gym and the way he's boxin' is the way he's gonna lick him. You got that other boy just right."

"I know I have."

"You back him up and he can't fight you. The way Teddy counters and punches to the body he's gonna make it easy. I know the other feller and I been watchin' Teddy. What he knows and the way he punches he's too much for that champion, sure."

"Thanks, Sid."

"The people in our business, they don't know. They only think they know. I've known you for years, Doc. You've got a good'un now and he ain't gonna miss."

"Sensational, Sidney."

"I'll take care of him and it's a real pleasure."

Teddy went into the gym that afternoon stony-faced and Doc worked him harder than he had worked since we had come into camp. No one kidded around and it seemed to me that they were all working harder and that there was an air of resentment over it all. Mahoney said a few words to Doc about Waller and let it go at that. Teddy and Lefty were sparring the last round, with Doc and me standing together on the ring apron, when Capini tapped me on the shoulder and I turned round.

"Doctor Fisher is on the telephone in the booth."

"Cheers. I'll go and take it."

I went into the booth in the lobby, picked up the hanging receiver and identified myself.

"Hello Mr. Cutler," he said. "Just to let you know that I'm ascribing cause of death to coronary thrombosis with infarction--------"

"Hang on a minute; I'm trying to write this down. Did you say 'with infraction?' "

"No. Infarction." He spelt the word out. "That's an obstruction. With infarction due to arteriosclerotic heart disease. Have you got that?"

"In other words, he died of a heart attack."

"To all appearances."

"Wait a minute. What do you mean by 'to all appearances?' You performed an autopsy, didn't you?"

"Yes, of course."

176

"Then appearances have nothing to do with it. You were going on appearances before, but this is your professional finding, isn't it?"

"Yes."

"Good."

I hung up and, when I got back to the gym, Doc had Teddy banging away at the big bag. He was standing with his arms folded across his chest, watching.

"The coroner just phoned."

"Did he? What did he say?"

"That Nat died of a heart attack."

"Are you surprised?"

"Hardly. I really don't think that the doctor was, either."

"Political snob. He'd have liked to make a big thing out of it, wouldn't he? He might even have had his picture in the paper."

Doc took the coach to London that night. Teddy and I walked with him to the shelter to see him off, after which Teddy had a glass of warm milk in the kitchen and then went up to bed in Doc's room. In my own room, I lay awake in the darkness for a long while, thinking of Waller He'd wanted to be sure I'd include him in the story and then I remembered Nat's fat friend, Percy, and I felt sorry for Percy, too.

XIX

Next morning I slept late until I heard the fighters come back off the road, their heavy feet on the stairs. By the time I had showered, shaved and dressed, old Sid was coming up the stairs carrying a tray with steaming cups of tea on it. He took one in for Teddy and then went down the hall with the others.

I asked Teddy how he had slept. He was sitting in the wicker chair, holding his cup and saucer in both hands and blowing on the tea to cool it a little. Through the window I could see that it was another clear day.

"I don't know," he said. "It must have been midnight before I got to sleep and I didn't feel like getting up this morning. How about you?"

"The same, except that I didn't get up."

"Teddy Baker!" Capini's voice came up the stairs. "Telephone call for you!"

177

"All right, Rene, coming."

"You can't go down with that sweat on you. You'd better take that tea."

"Find out who it is, will you?"

I walked to the top of the stairs.

"Rene? Find out who it is."

"It's the telephone operator. She said that somebody has put in a 'personal' call to Teddy."

"Then tell her to ring back in half-an-hour."

I returned to the room.

"Maybe it's Doc," Teddy said.

"No, he wouldn't ring you at this time. He would know you just came off the road."

"This tea is almost too hot to drink."

"You remind me of Freddie Mills."

"Why?"

"He was in Solomons' one day training for Joey Maxim. He'd finished his work and we were back in one of those little dressing-rooms and Freddie was sitting on a stool. Dear old George Black of the Standard was bending over him and interviewing him; you probably remember the way George did. Alby Hollister came in carrying a cup of hot tea for Freddie in one hand. Alby was stripped to his undershirt and, just as he made to hand the tea to Freddie, George straightened up, and the cup and the tea shot up into the air. It did a complete loop and the tea spilled out and came down right inside the front of Hollister's undershirt, the slice of lemon and all.

"Alby jumped clean off the floor. He ripped off the shirt and the lemon fell to the floor. He's jumping around, screaming and grabbing a towel and Freddie is sitting there, clapping his hands and laughing fit to bust. He yelled: 'Stay in there, Alby! Stay in there, son, you gotta be able to take it!' "

"And Alby did?"

"That's right. You know how quiet he wasn't."

"Oh, I know that alright! So what happened?"

"Well, Hollister's drying himself off--his chest was all red from the scalding and Freddie is still laughing, roaring with his head back. Hollister says to him: 'What's the matter with you? Are you mad? What's so funny?' And Freddie said: 'You. You're always telling me that a man's gotta stay in there; how tough he's gotta be. So stay in there, Alby. Stay in there yourself. You see?' "

178

"He made real money, didn't he, with Maxim. Lesnevich and Woodcock?"

"Freddie? He was a good fighter and he was careful with his money."

"He certainly was tough."

"Alby was right. You've gotta stay in there, otherwise find another business."

"That's right. You'd be surprised, though, at the number of fighters who aren't that way at all. Pretty good fighters, as well. Anyway, people think they're good but they don't really want to know. How they get in the business I don't know."

"They have manual dexterity, fight on their reflexes, have fast hands and know how to cover up."

"That's true but it's not enough. Not if you're up against a real good fighter. He'll show you up for what you are."

"Indeed and that's the truth of it all. If it wasn't so, boxing wouldn't mean anything."

"This other guy isn't so tough. From the fights I've seen him in I know he's not tough enough. What's more, I'll prove it."

"Of course you will and you've got the equipment to do it."

"I wish the fight was this Friday. I'm getting sick of the routine down here."

"I can understand."

It wasn't half-an-hour. It was about twenty minutes after the first call that Capini shouted up the stairs again. Teddy had just come back from his shower and was finishing dressing. I walked downstairs with him and stood talking with Capini while Teddy went into the booth. He was in there for several minutes.

"That was Ernie Jarvis," he said when he came out. "He wants to write something about Waller for his paper. Says Doc rang him; I expect he called all the newspapermen."

"I hope he did. That's good."

"He wanted me to say something about Nat but I didn't know what to say."

"Very understandable."

"I just said that he was with me for all those fights and he was a great guy and I wish it hadn't happened. That sounds stupid now."

"What else could you say?"

"Do you know what he asked me then?"

"What?"

179

"He said: 'Just what does this mean to the fight?' And I said: 'What do you mean?' He said: 'How do you feel about the fight now?' And I said: 'Just the same. I'm gonna win it well, only more so now.' What else could I say?"

"Nothing at all. You did well. The bad thing is, when he writes his story he'll date-line himself as being down here in camp, and then he can collect expenses from his office."

"Is that right to do that?" Teddy said.

"He's still a good reporter for his paper." I said. "Why don't we have breakfast?"

After the meal I walked with Teddy. When we reached the road I suggested that we might walk into Guildford.

"No," he said. "If I'm going to walk, the hills around here are better."

"I just thought you might be bored with it. How many times do you see it, running around here every morning and walking twice a day?"

"I don't know, but I'm not here to have fun."

We walked to the top of the rise of road north of the hotel. I was trying to think of something to say to get Teddy out of it and, as we started down the gentle, curving-to-the-right slope of the other side, I looked at the vista, limited by pines on one side but open on the left, where two sloping fields lay bare in the sun. Once, in the deep past, they had been stripped of wood and growth and stone and now they lay bare, waiting for a planting, perhaps of corn. To me they seemed to be breathing the warm sun the way any man breathes the air after being under water at the end of a deep dive.

"Who do you think took Nat's ring?" Teddy said.

It was inevitable. When a man has just died he is suddenly, for a limited time, more alive than he ever was in his life.

"I wish I knew," I told him.

"Doc thinks it might have been Penny."

"I don't think so."

"He told me that but I don't think so either. Penny's not a bad bloke. Doc also said that you think Ceroni or Harry."

"There's simply no one else. I don't necessarily think one of them took it. It's just that I've eliminated the others

"How could anybody take a ring off somebody that just died?"

180

"I don't know. During the last war I saw rings, watches and good German binoculars on dead enemy soldiers. I couldn't take them off those bodies but some of our fellows could; the proper term for it is looting. I might just as well have taken them myself because someone was going to."

"I couldn't have done it, either."

"In the war, at least, I didn't resent the men who did it. In fact, I rather admired that ability."

"How do you mean?"

Here was a chance to take his mind of Waller.

"They were realists," I said, "and it was one of the things that made them good in combat. That type won the war for us and there's really no basic difference between men in war and men in peace. When a thing is done it's over. When a man is killed he's dead. If you can see things that way and accept them, you've got the attitude to go all the way in life."

"I still don't see it."

"You do in your own profession."

"How?"

"Take that man who interviewed you the other day on TV. To him it seems just as horrible for one man to punch another into insensibility as it seems now, to you and me, for someone to lift a ring off Waller's finger."

"But that's stealing."

"I know but that's not what gets to us. If that ring or some money or a watch had been stolen from Nat last week we wouldn't be anything like as upset. We accept that some people are crooks. What really rouses us is that the ring was removed from the hand of a man who had just died. Am I right?"

"Yes, I think you are."

"So, feeling as people do about death, we can't understand how anyone could do such a thing."

"I can't understand it at all."

"And that television man Johnstone, feeling as many people do about hurting other people physically, can't understand how you can punch another man until you knock him out or beat him some other way."

"It's not the same thing."

"Of course not because you have one attitude about the one, and a different one about the other. Suppose that TV interviewer had given you a chance to explain what it is you feel about boxing another man and hitting him. Suppose he had really been trying to find out the truth about you and about the fight game, instead of just trying to make his own points. If he had led you into expressing what you feel about hitting an opponent and hurting him, what would have had said?"

"I dunno."

"Okay. I'll put a question. You're Teddy Baker and on Friday week you're due to fight for the Middleweight Championship of the World. To win the fight you're going to have to beat the other man, maybe knock him out or, as likely as not, hurt him anyway. Do you enjoy hurting, or beating up, other people?"

"No, but I don't think of it that way."

"How do you think of it? What's in your mind when you try to punch another man as hard as you can?"

"I want to best him because he's trying to beat me under a regulated set of rules. That's what it's all about."

"Is that all? Don't you want to hurt him, to render his senseless?"

"I don't think of that. I think of getting the better of him, like you do in any other sport or game."

"If you knock him out how do you feel? He's lying there, counted out. Then how do you feel?"

"I feel great. A knockout is the best and surest way of winning."

"Going back to Terry Downes and the American champion, Paul Pender in the early 'sixties, if anyone saw their battles he saw a big part of the truth of fighting. After the second one--the one that Terry won--he was in the shower-room at Harringay. One eye was nearly closed and there was a metal clip holding the cut over the other one. Newspapermen were crowding around him asking him how he felt and he kept saying: 'I wanted to kill him. He's a good guy but I wanted to kill him' And that was all he could say."

"I know. I remember reading that when I was just starting to fight."

"Did you believe it? Did you believe that he could admire the other man and still want to kill him in there?"

"I don't know if I believed it then, but I believe it now. I've felt that way."

"You have?"

"It's just that you get so worked up in a fight. I mean, if it's a tough fight and the other guy is a good fighter and you're both trying to take one another out and end it. You like him for that, but the strange thing is it makes you want to win any way you can at the same time. It's him or you and it's a kind of desperate feeling."

"Terry liked Paul and Paul liked Terry. Three times they were ready to fight to the death, but do you know why they liked each other?"

"No. Why?"

"Because, in those three fights each man brought out the best in the other and gave him his greatest moment in both victory and defeat."

"I'd go along with that. I like the men that gave me my good fights. I think of them a lot and I'd even like to meet up with them again. I mean, just to sit around and talk about boxing and life generally."

"Freddie Mills once told me the same thing."

"He did?"

"He used to feel that way about Lesnevich, particularly about their Harringay fight, which Freddie lost. He told me once: 'It was my greatest fight and I couldn't have reached those heights without Gus. Though I took the championship off him two years later, I always liked and admired him for that first fight.' Both those great warriors are dead and gone long since, God bless them."

"I feel the same sort of way. I fought Al Morrow up in Leeds. In the first round he hit me a punch under the heart and I could feel it in my legs. We fought mostly toe-to-toe for ten rounds and never let up. When I got the decision guess what I wanted to do?"

"I can't."

"I wanted to kiss him. Now what the hell would that look like?"

"I've seen more than one fighter do it."

"I mean, for ten rounds I wanted to kill him and he fought as though he wanted to kill me, and then I wanted to kiss him. Explain that."

"Suppose you had killed him?"

"I don't know."

183

"Don't get me wrong. I understand this and I'm just trying to bring out the truth in you. This is what should have been done on that TV show."

"How come you like boxing so much?"

"Because I find so much in it; it's the whole epitome of life itself."

"How do you mean?"

"The basic law of man and the truth of life. It's man against man, and, if you're going to defeat another man, defeat him completely. Don't starve him to death, like they try to do in the fine, clean competitive world of commerce. Better to leave him lying there, senseless, on the floor."

"Maybe that's it but, honestly, I'm not sure."

"Listen, I'm not supporting this or trying to make out that it's good. I'm just saying it's there in man, in all men. I'm against violence and I hate arguments. I hope for a world where everything will be done through reason and with honesty and where force will be as nothing. Centuries ahead we may have this, but as of now there is still that remnant of wild animal in man and the law of life is still the law of the jungle--the survival of the fittest. As long as that be true, I find man revealing himself more completely in fighting than in any other form of expressive endeavour. It's a war all over again and yet they license it and sell tickets to see it which people grab like vultures because, without even realising it, they see this truth in it."

"I've never thought of it like that."

"Let's go back in time one last time. After England won the World Cup in soccer in 1966 we went to see Alf Ramsey and his players deep down in the bowels of Wembley. Now I was, and still am though he's no longer with us, all for Ramsey as a football manager. I think he represented the competitive essence of the game. Ramsey was a symbol of what football--or any game--is all about, the overwhelming desire to win. As we walked in he was standing in the middle of his players--Bobby Charlton, Geoff Hurst, Bobby Moore and the rest. Somebody said: 'Well, Alf, what about that?"

" 'What about it?' Ramsey said. Straightening up and looking straight at us. 'I'll tell you what about it; this team will beat them all 'til the cows come home!' So there stood us writers, taking it all down and, as I said, I'm not knocking football or Sir Alf (as he later became). This was a fine, aggressive quote-for

184

soccer--but, as I walked away, I was thinking of something else. Know what?"

"Something to do with boxing, I'll be bound."

"Spot on. Alf's men were going to beat them all 'til the cows came home and, some month before, I'd watched Ali and Henry Cooper, two men fighting for world dominance under the lights in Arsenal's Highbury Stadium, literally trying to take each other apart with that mass of mankind sitting in the darkness around them and screaming for blood. It was like two prehistoric monsters, knee deep in primeval ooze, ready to fight to the death and with the jungle all around them echoing to the noise and the bloody horror of it."

"Was it that good a fight?"

"Yes and it was the truth. When you want to beat another man, you try to beat him, literally. You don't foul him in the penalty area, or hook his feet from under him or sledge him with verbal abuse. Those are the refinements of civilisation."

"They're different things. A fighter is a fighter, a footballer a footballer and a cricketer is a cricketer."

"No, a footballer is a fighter, too. What does he do, when it comes down toe essentials? When it all becomes too much, they go at one another with their bare fists."

"You're right about that."

"It's the truth, but other games don't allow it and yours does. I like soccer, I like rugby and cricket. I like most of the refinements of civilisation, but I have to believe that of all sports--if that's what we can call them in today's lust for money--yours goes the deepest and thus goes the furthest towards the truth."

"I still envy those footballers, golfers and tennis players."

"I know, but do you still want to start all over again?"

"Point made, but nobody knocks their game. I wish you'd explain it to Mary sometime, the way you just explained it to me."

"I wasn't explaining it to you because it can't properly be explained to anyone. I was just talking."

"Mary's got a good head."

"I know she has."

"She seemed to like it at first because she went to three or four of my early fights."

"I dare say. But how can a woman--a wife--sitting outside a ring come away from a fight with the same feeling about it as you who were in there doing it?"

185

"I can see that. Many times I've thought that, if I was in some other business, she'd understand it."

"Not really, and I don't mean to apply that to just Mary."

"How do you mean?"

"Every man's in a fight, Teddy, no matter what line of country he's in. A woman can try to understand but she's really only a spectator."

"Then Mary reads all that twaddle they write about the fight game. If you read it and didn't know anything about it, you'd have to believe most of it. She'd like me to be in something everybody looks up to and respects."

"Everybody looks up to and respects the Champion of the World, in spite of what they read or think about the fight business."

"I know that's true, too."

At least his mind was off Nat Waller.

XX

That was Ceroni's last day of sparring and, after he had completed his three rounds, Teddy went in. Charlie Mahoney handled Lefty while Mickey Evans and old Sid handled Teddy. That night Mahoney stayed at the hotel. Teddy, the sparring partners, Penny and I watched a film on telly, something about an American G.I. who visited Britain in transit during the war and got involved with an English girl in a cellar and then had a fight with her English soldier boy-friend. It reminded me a bit of Rocky Marciano's experience when he came to Britain during the hostilities. When it finished, Teddy went straight to bed and I went into the bar.

Mahoney was there. He was talking with a middle-aged man and woman who, apparently, had just called in for a couple of drinks. When Charlie saw me he finished his conversation with them and, instead, sat down on the stool next to mine.

"How did my boy look today?" he said.

"Fine. He looked pretty sharp."

"He'll beat that other guy easy, no trouble at all."

"So he should."

"Why do you say that?"

"You know why perfectly well. The other guy is a short-armed middle-of-the-bill fighter who'll keep trying, but he'll never be able to reach Ceroni."

"I know and that's why I made the match."

"Naturally."

"See what Mr. Cutler will have, Rene."

"He knows," I said.

Capini set the drink down in front of me.

"That's why I picked him. It'll look good on TV and my boy will look great."

"Agreed."

"That's the way you've got to do it these days."

"Is it really?"

"Sure. What do the crowd know and, anyway, they'll see a good fight."

I started on my drink.

"You still fancy Teddy in this fight?" he said.

"I do."

"The American is being made favourite by the big punters."

"It'll come down. He opened seven to two down but he'll start near evens. The newspapermen will be down in a day or two to take a look at Teddy. He'll come out of his depression about Nat and they'll see him as he really is."

"The Yank will still close favourite. He'll be at least six to five."

"That's because he's the champion."

"And that's a good reason, isn't it?"

"Not necessarily."

"Listen, I like Teddy and I like Doc but look at their records."

"What does that prove? There's nothing wrong with Teddy's record, but you can't read a fighter in black and white, won, lost and drawn in a record book."

"But it's the class of the opposition. You remember that bout Teddy had in Norwich about a year ago which was televised?"

"Yes, it was a good fight and Teddy well beat him."

"But he had a tough time doing it. The champ fought the same guy a little later and beat him easy, an eighth round stoppage as I recall."

"Come off it, Charlie, will you? He stopped him in eight, proving what?"

"You tell me."

"Gladly. You can't name me another fighter who whipped that guy the way Teddy did—by outboxing him completely in every round of the ten."

"I don't get the significance of that."

"The man he fought in Norwich is a southpaw."

"Of course he is."

"So the left hand is his big punch."

"Sure, but when he fought the champ he never landed it."

"Right. All you people are always saying that the way to get to a southpaw is with right hands. Correct?"

"Yep, that way you take his left hand out of action at the same time."

"You know how Teddy fought him?"

"How?"

"He beat him at his own game, with left hands. He beat that fellow standing right in front of him, drawing the left hand, slipping it or taking it high on his head, arms or shoulders and belting the man's brains out and blasting his body apart with short hooks."

"So he made a tougher fight of it."

"Sure, but he and Doc wrote a book for all you others to read. If you're basically a counter puncher, the way to beat a southpaw is with hooks. It's a risk, certainly, because you're inviting him to fire his heavy artillery, but that's the only way to open him up. Teddy gave him a worse beating than that champion did and he wrote something new."

"Even so, he made it tougher for himself."

"So does any explorer. It was Doc made it tougher. You people don't understand Doc."

"I understand him; I've known him for years."

"So do I, and I've watched him all those years. Doc isn't looking for the easiest way of doing things because he tries to build fighters, and there's no easy way of doing that. For nine years he's been building Teddy Baker. He finally found a kid who could learn it all and do it all. He taught it to him in the gym and, most of all, fighting tough fights the tough way--going to the other fella's strength and besting him there. And then, once you've proved it and taken all there was out of it for yourself as a fighter, handling him in any way you want."

"You think he'll try to outbox the other man in this one?"

"No, not in this one. He's arrived now and he'll make the champion fight this one the way Teddy wants it fought."

"He'd better."

Capini motioned towards my glass, but I signalled him nay.

"Look, what you say about Doc may be true. I like Doc."

"He's the last of the real old-timers."

"That's the trouble. Times change and the fight game isn't what it used to be."

"That's the trouble, not Doc."

"With everything you say about Doc, how many times has Teddy fought on TV?"

"Three."

"Ceroni has been shown five times already, and he's been boxing only half as long as Teddy."

"Congratulations."

"The big thing today is to get those TV spots. I'm telling you that, within two years at the most, Joe Ceroni will be Welterweight Champion of the World."

"I wouldn't be surprised."

"As I told you, you'll get a good magazine story out of him."

"How, Charlie? It's a real sacrifice for him to say 'good morning', and that's the last thing he says all day."

"He's just shy. After all, he's only a kid."

"Obviously."

"Listen, it'll make a good story. You should see the mail he gets and they love him on TV. He's a good-looking kid. Why, they've even got bobby-soxers' fan clubs for him. Joe Ceroni clubs and I'm not kidding."

"I know you're not. You probably started the first one."

"What one?"

"The first fan club. Did you stake it?"

"I send them all pictures but that's all. Women are crazy about him; they really are."

"And how's he about women?"

"Ceroni? He's just a kid so what does he know?"

189

"He knows that there are both men and women in this world and that there's a difference."

"He pays no attention to them. He's a fighter. You don't think I'd let him get loused up, do you, all the years I've been managing fighters?"

"No, I'm sure you wouldn't."

I was certain, then, that he knew nothing about it. If he had, he would have known what we all knew and he would have found some way to explain it. This pleased me.

Next morning Ceroni went on the road with Teddy and the others. In the gym he exercised lightly and then, when he went to the dressing-room, Mahoney handled the sparring partners again for Teddy, who was hitting the light bag when Ceroni came out, ready to go to Mahoney's home in Fulham for the night. When he saw Ceroni, Teddy stopped the bag.

"Be lucky, Joe," Teddy said.

"Yeah, thanks," Ceroni responded.

"Hey, silent one," Penny said, walking over with the jump-rope in one hand and sweating. "If the guy gets too awkward in there, just talk him out of it. Give him a little speech, say: 'Look, Mac, let's have a little talk.'"

"Good luck," I said, shaking Ceroni's hand.

"Thanks."

"Can you imagine him talkin' in a fight?" Penny said to Teddy. "Ain't that a laugh?"

"If you watch tomorrow night," Mahoney said to me, "You'll see a good fighter."

"Yes, one good fighter. Yours."

"So?" Mahoney said, winking. "What do you expect from me?"

They walked out of the gym, Ceroni carrying his bags and Mahoney striding ahead of him. I got Teddy's gown off a chair and helped him into it, and Penny followed us into the dressing-room while old Sid went for the hot tea.

"Ceroni look nervous to me," Penny said.

"He'll win it easily," Teddy opined. "I'm not even going to watch it."

"You'll be better off in bed," I said.

After dinner we all went for a stroll for half-an-hour and then went in and watched television. We were watching Michael Parkinson when Doc came in. He had Tim Holland with him and a

190

middleweight named Artie Parkin, and they had driven down in Parkin's car.

"How do you feel?" I said to Doc.

"Shattered."

He looked tired and even the dark-blue suit he was wearing looked too heavy on him.

"Have you eaten?"

"No."

"We'd better have Ivy make you something. Some scrambled eggs and toast and tea?"

"Alright. I'm going upstairs to wash."

"I'll tell Ivy," Teddy said.

"Where do you want us?" Tim Holland said to Capini who was standing in the doorway with his arms crossed, listening.

"There is the room Teddy and Nat Waller had," Capini said, shrugging. "The big room in the back corner."

"I know the room," Parkin said. "I know all the rooms here."

"I'm glad to see you," I said, shaking Artie's hand.

"Gee thanks," he said. "It's been quite a while, no?"

I wasn't glad to see him. Four or five years ago he had been a pretty good middleweight, good enough to fight for a title and almost take it. Then Teddy had taken a decision off him and Parkin had managed to win his next one and had retired. Now he was heavy and even his face looked a little soft and fleshy.

"I'll take the stuff up, eh?" he said to Tim Holland.

"That'll be fine," Artie replied.

"Why don't you move in with me?" I said to Doc. "Let Teddy stay in your room; there's two beds in mine."

"That's what I was going to suggest, I'll be down in a minute."

He went upstairs carrying his bag and following Parkin.

"I'm glad Doc was able to get you," I said to Tim Holland.

Over some thirty years he had worked with nine or ten champions. He was the best trainer in the business and had great hands in the corner. A quiet, immaculate man of medium build, he would have come as a surprise to any stranger who, having heard his name and knowing his business, met him for the first time.

"Listen, I'm glad to be able to do it. Doc and Teddy are nice people and I felt terrible when I heard about Waller."

"We all did."

191

"I was coming down with Artie in a couple of days anyway. The extra time will do him good."

"I didn't even know that he was on the comeback trail."

"What can you do?" he said, rather sadly. "Somebody conned him into putting everything he made fighting for ten years into some roller-skating rink up in Telford. Now they need more money, or they'll lose everything he's got in it."

"That's a shame."

"So they came to me. What else can I do? How else can he make any money? He was good to me when he had it, so I said I'd try to get him into some kind of shape."

"But how much can he make?"

"You tell me. He'll win a few tune-up fights out in the sticks somewhere, and then to get real money he'll have to fight somebody who'll really bash him up. It's terrible, but what's the answer? I've seen something similar happen to a lot of them. They get out of this business and they're easy game for everybody. I feel sorry for him."

"So do I."

When Doc came down, Teddy and I sat with him while he ate his eggs slowly, had one piece of toast and drank his tea.

"So how did it go?" I said.

"It was okay."

"Was there a funeral?" Teddy said.

"Yes, kind of."

"What happened?" Teddy persisted.

"We had a service last night at the funeral parlour. I remembered there was some cleric Nat knew when they were kids. He used to get him tickets to the fights, some Protestant minister who runs a hostel down east, and I managed to get him. He was glad to do it."

"Was anybody there?"

"Yes, just a few. The Board sent a representative and there was Tim Holland plus a few old licence-holders. Nat's brother-in-law was there, an old Jew. My nephew was there and that friend of Nat's managed it."

"Percy?"

"That's him. He had his wife with him and she cried loudly all the time. This morning the cleric and I rode out to the cemetery with the fella from the funeral parlour. We were the only ones to see him lowered down."

192

"Where's he buried?"

"In Camberwell. I got him a small plot--the undertaker from down here arranged it. I'm having a simple stone made for the grave."

"I'd like to be in on that," Teddy said.

"Forget it. It's taken care of."

"But I want to, Doc."

"Alright. Let me have it with the commission after the fight."

XXI

At about eleven o'clock the following morning Doc and Tim Holland had gone into town for tape and gauze. Teddy was lying in his room reading the morning papers when I came up the stairs and saw him there and stopped by the door.

"There's nothing in the fight results about Cassidy's fight," he said.

"Those are early editions we get down here. They come out too early to carry anything other than the prelim results."

"I wish I knew how he made out. He's a nice guy."

"I'll ring the Press Association in Fleet Street."

"It'll be in the evenings, won't it?"

"Probably, but why wait?"

I called the P.A. and got the sports desk. It took the young man who answered a few moments to find what I wanted and then I went back upstairs and told Teddy.

"Cassidy lost," I said, "a decision."

"Did he really? I'm sorry about that. I didn't think that guy he was fighting was much use."

"Let's be honest; neither is Cassidy."

"He's a nice guy, though. Did they say what kind of a fight it was?"

"No. All they were sent was the bare result and it took the kid a couple of minutes to find that."

"Poor old Jakie, too."

"He shouldn't be in the business, either."

"I know, but when you train together you get to like the people around you."

193

"I can understand that."

I went to my room and lay down. I had brought Liebling's 'The Sweet Science' down with me and I was devouring that epic for the umpteenth time when Alf Penny came in. It was something I do every two or three years--get it out and read it one more time. I prize that book the way you prize a great recording that you take out and play again when you feel just right for it and need it.

"Oi!" Penny said, "your two old friends are here."

"Who?"

"Them columnists. Tom Phillips and the little guy, Trevor. He's some writer, huh?"

"Wignall? Yes, they both are. Thanks, Alf."

When I went down they were already in the dining-room, at one of the small tables by the windows, and Capini was bringing them dry martinis.

"Make me one of mine, will you Rene?"

"Yes, Mr. Cutler."

"Doctor Livingstone, I presume?" Tom said, the two of them standing up while we shook hands."

"Absolutely," I said.

"How long you in for?" Trevor said as we sat down.

"Life--until the fight."

"God, you're as loyal as--I can't think--but I'll say Lassie," Trevor said.

"Not likely. She's a better friend than I am. I only hang around because I can't discover a quicker way of putting this kind of a piece together."

"Getting institutionalised?"

"Just about. Thanks for coming."

"Don't thank us," Tom said. "We have to work for a living, too. You don't suppose we could find a couple of columns around here?"

"Any number of them, if you look hard enough."

Capini brought me my drink and left.

"What's the matter with him?" Tom said.

"Nothing He's just permanently sad. Been on the wagon for years."

"You see? That proves it, so let's never get that way."

"No chance at all."

"It's a pleasure to have you aboard, sirs," I said. That was one of our alcoholic gags.

194

"It's a pleasure to be aboard, sir. And what have you been doing down here?"

"Of course, you've heard about Waller?"

"Yes," Wignall said. "I was sorry to hear it; we were chewing it over driving up."

Phillips just sat there, shaking his head slowly.

"And talking about it, got lost?"

"Not then. We got lost later talking about something else. As for Nat, what a nice little person he was I'm sure, but he used to bend my ear something awful."

"Don't say that," Tom said.

"Well, I don't think I'm being unkind. I liked him. He was a nice chap but, half the time, I didn't know what he was talking about, and I don't think he did, either."

"You've already told me that," Tom said, shaking his head.

"Don't pay any attention to him," Wignall said to me. "He's been complaining all morning and he also cries at some of the films on TV.

"I remember at one boxing writers' dinner I needed to go to the gents, and Nat collared me there and started telling me some long story about one of his fights thirty years before. I thought I'd never get back to hear the rest of the speeches."

"If you were wise you wouldn't have," Tom said. "I don't know which boxing writers' dinner you're talking about, but whatever Waller was telling you must have been better than the speeches."

"I quite agree."

"Will you knock it off, then, and finish that drink?"

I signalled to Capini to make three more.

"How are you doing on the story?" Tom said.

"Who knows? I'm walking around and looking and listening and trying to live it as much as I can. How do you know until you've written it?"

"You'll do alright."

"So then Nat dies. If you'll excuse me, Tom, I felt rotten, too, for thinking just what Trevor's been saying. Then, today, I woke up realising I'm even worse. I'm supposed to be writing a piece about a typical, class fighter and how he lives and thinks and feels getting ready to fight a real big one. In the middle of it the trainer dies; what's typical about that? And now I regret Nat dying, firstly because he died and I'll miss him, but also--I'll be

195

honest with you--because I'm going to have to find a way to fit this into the piece. How do you like that?"

"I don't like it at all," Tom said, "but I understand it."

"It's our bread-and-butter," Wignall said. "The piece has to be first."

"I'll tell you something else about this business."

"What?"

"I'm getting tired of becoming emotionally involved with the people I have to write about. I've had far too much of it for too long. I've liked Doc for years and Teddy since before I came down here. Now I'm spending a month with them and, after all the fighters I've known and the fights I've seen--you tend to count them--I've got to go one more and suffer the agony again for two nice guys to whom this one means everything. I like fights where I don't know either man or give a damn about them. Why do I have to get involved in this?"

"Because it's what you're getting paid for."

"But suppose Teddy loses?"

"I don't think he will," Tom said.

"I don't think he will either but, if he does, it's the end for both of them. You know that. It took Doc two years to get this shot and they'll never get another one. How would you like to have everything hanging for you on one hour on a Friday night?"

"I still say he'll win," Tom said.

"I do too, but forgetting what happens to Doc and Teddy--which is most important--what happens to my story if he loses?"

"Well, somebody wins and somebody loses. There's as much of a story in a fighter losing as in a fighter winning, maybe more."

"Sure. You news guys get the best stories in the loser's dressing-room, but that's not the magazine business."

"Whyever not?"

"I had lunch with a nice chap who works on a magazine one day--I won't tell you who--and he was telling me about a piece some writer did for them. He had the idea to do one about a kid's first fight, to be called just that--'The Kid's First Fight.' "

"Sounds like a good idea."

"Yep. He hung around the kid and his family for a few days. On the day of the fight he stayed with him and the mother cooked the boy's last meal and, when he left, she kissed him goodbye. The kid's father went with him to the hall--Bermondsey

Baths, as I recall--and there was the classic dressing-room scene. The boy was in the second bout, just a four-rounder, and when the call came he got up and started for the door. Then he stopped. The trainer said: 'Let's go. Come on!' The kid said: 'No. I'm not going 'cos I'm too scared. I don't want to be a fighter.' He never did. He put his clothes back on and went home with his old man."

"Super job. 'The Kid's First Fight.' "

"Absolutely. But the presiding genius on the magazine says: 'We can't use it.' The bloke telling me said: 'Why not?' The editing genius said: 'He didn't fight. It was supposed to be his first fight but he didn't go through with it. We can't use it.' "

"I don't believe it," Tom said.

"I do," Trevor averred. "It's unspeakable, but maybe the piece was badly done."

"I don't care how badly it was done; put a good writer on it to rewrite it. He'll get the quotes he needs and set the scenes. I'm talking about the scribbling business."

"But Teddy's not going to lose," Tom said.

"I quite agree."

"I haven't seen enough of him to judge," Trevor said. "But in the two or three fights I saw him he looked good."

"Teddy's married, isn't he?" Tom queried.

"Yes."

"You've met his wife?"

"Yes."

"What's she like?"

"So-so."

"You don't like her?" Trevor guessed.

"Not overmuch, But I hope I understand her."

"What's the matter with her? What's she like?"

"She's a good-looking girl with a temperature about two degrees below everyone else's normal who gives the impression that she's very competent and self-sufficient."

"And is she?"

"No."

"Why not?"

"Hell, if you insist I'll give you the run-down."

"Please do." Tom said.

"Well, they're both from the same neighbourhood. I'd guess she was attracted to Teddy because he was the star personage on the block. I think he was attracted to her because of

197

her looks and then because, like most fighters who are so competent in the ring, he's shy and a bit lost elsewhere. Without knowing it, he was seeking outside strength. Now--are you guys still interested, or shall we just drop it?"

"No, Doctor Cutler," Trevor said, "I want to hear this; I'm fascinated."

"Please, let's skip it," I said.

"No, I want to hear it too," Tom said.

"Okay, you asked for it. Now, this poor wench--and I think I feel a bit sorry for her--is also a victim of the modern portrayal of the husband/wife relationship."

"What's that mean translated?" Tom said.

"Togetherness," Trevor offered.

"You know what I mean. The husband comes home and divorces his work and remarries his wife every night. 'And what did you do today, darling?' he says, drawing her down on to his lap."

"I see."

"In this case, it's particularly cruel because there's a triangle--Teddy and his wife and Doc Eastlake."

"Ah, Pythagoras, I see the geometry now," Trevor said.

"Fighting is Teddy's big thing and Doc's his man and she's just outside. This is a wench who needs to be needed."

"Who doesn't?" Tom said.

"Right. As far as I know, she went to three or four of Teddy's pro fights. I'm sure that what he felt in there and what she felt watching it were two entirely different things and I think that's the last try she made."

"This is too bad," Tom said

"Correct again," I said.

I decided not to tell them about the boy, because it was getting me down as it was. I motioned Capini again and he brought us another round and went back to the bar.

"No matter how sad this character is," Trevor said, "he makes a good dry martini."

"So he should. He's an expert."

"He is?"

"Yes. When he had his drinking bouts on he shipped enough of those to fill the pool out there."

"He should never have stopped."

"A doctor scared him. He used to drink them out of milk-bottles."

"Who?" Trevor said. "The doctor?"

"No, Rene."

"Please," Tom said, "drinking martinis out of milk-bottles. You'll spoil these."

"Are you jesting about that?"

"No. Years ago there was a dinner held here one night. The Catenians, or somesuch, were having a special meeting and Capini made up a whole batch of martinis in milk-bottles beforehand. He had them in the refrigerator behind the bar and, when he came down the next morning, he remembered one bottle was left. So, in the course of the day, he got to sneaking nips of that. He told me about it once, when he was still drinking. He got to like them that way and he always had a bottle of them in there-- and swigged them away like nobody's business."

"Now I like him less than ever," Tom said. "What a way to treat a martini!"

"I know what you mean," Trevor said. "The dry martini is meant to be sipped from shell-thin, prefrosted glasses in the quiet dignity of the 'Ritz' men's bar late of a sparkling autumn afternoon."

"Exactly," I said. "It has always seemed to me that the dry martini is the epee sword of alcoholic weapons, to be handled only as such."

"Okay, let's stop drivelling, and don't you folks want to eat?"

"Yes," in chorus.

"Rene!" I said, and he started over.

"He's got some guts, though," Trevor said.

"What?" Tom said. "Out of milk-bottles? It's sacrilegious."

"No. An ex-alcoholic serving at the bar. I admire it."

"Yes?" Capini said.

"They'd like to eat."

"And those were fine martinis, Rene," Trevor said. "This other jerk won't admit it, but they were."

They ordered cold roast-beef sandwiches and coffee, and then Trevor remembered it was Friday and ordered a toasted cheese sandwich instead. They were just starting to eat when Doc and Tim Holland came in and shook hands and sat down. I was glad of all this happening then, too, for Doc.

"We're sorry about Waller," Trevor said.

"Thanks, that's how we all feel. But I'm putting it away now because there's a fight." And Doc sighed, a trifle wearily I thought.

"That's good," Tom said. "How's your tiger?"

"He's just fine. I've been up in town for two days but he'll be ready. This'll be some fight."

"Great. There's a lot of genuine enthusiasm for this one."

"It's about time."

"Yes. It's a pleasure to be writing about a fight the people care about for a change."

"What do you think of the other guy, Doc?"

"He's a very good fighter. He's the champion, isn't he?"

"You've worked against him, haven't you, Tim?"

"Yes," Tim Holland said, "a couple of times. He's got a lot of ability."

"For some reason he doesn't excite me like he should," Trevor said.

"I don't go with all the raving about him," Tom said "I'd rather watch your fighter any day."

"Ta very much."

"How many fighters have you had, Doc?"

"How many fighters have I had? Edward makes a baker's dozen."

"Thirteen fighters in over forty years?"

"That's right, and when I started in the business there were managers who had more than that at the same time. They were commission agents who had somebody fighting for them somewhere almost every night of the week. They used to supply the whole of one side of a bill for promoters and they managed by telephone. Dreadful."

"And often used someone else's phone," Tom said.

"What could they offer a fighter?" Doc demanded. "Two tickets to nowhere, somebody along to carry the pail and a fast count on the finances."

"Did you ever go for a title before, Doc?"

"No."

"You could have captured the big one with Dave McCleave," Tom said.

"I didn't see him fight until he was well over the hill," Trevor said. "But I used to read about him and then, one pre-war

200

night, I was sent to cover a show down in Bournemouth where I watched him box the ears off the young and up-coming Freddie Mills over ten 'threes'. Really, how good was he at his best?"

"The best welterweight in the world for three or four years," I said.

"Very true," Tom said, nodding approval.

"Why didn't you get him the big title, Doc?"

"I offered him a shot at it in America one day. I sat down with him and I said: 'Look, Dave, you've done everything I've asked you to do and I owe you this. If you want the world crown I can get you the match and you and I know you can lick the guy. But they'll only take you on their own patch in Madison Square. Do you want it?' So he said: 'Doc, it's up to you; what do you think?' I said: 'Forget it. You're better off as you are.' He was too."

"Why?"

"I explained it to him. I said: 'If you win the crown and, in any case, it'll be double hard getting a decision in New York so you'd likely need to stop him, do you know who'll be managing you?' He said: 'Why, you will, Doc.' I said: 'No, I'll still be taking my cut, but those politicians at the Board of Control and New York State will be managing you. They'll tell you who you fight and when and where. They'll force you in with every mug whose got an 'in' to a mandatory--all the grabbers and runners who'll make you look bad but who have the right managers--and you'll have one lousy fight after the other. You'll be World Champion, though. On the other hand, if you want to go further along the way we're going, we'll move around the country and make more money fighting men looking to get strong trying to lick you and you'll be a better fighter because of it. It's up to you.'

"He said: 'Doc, I'm for doing it the way we're doing it right now.' He was wise. When he retired, he walked out with one hundred and fifty thou clear and that was money in those days."

"What did Dave do after he retired?"

"He and his wife, Babs, proved great successes in the licensing trade and Dave finished up a senior director of his brewery. I'd bet my boots he'll be at this fight."

"Good, I'd like to see him again," Tom said.

"He'll be there, but only in spirit because he died recently while visiting a boys' boxing club which he set up and patronised. If Teddy wins this title I'll wonder about Dave. He knows he did the right thing but few people know about the kind of fighter he

201

was--the art, the skill, the footwork and the best left hand I've ever seen."

"I'll say," Tom said.

"What do the people know? If he'd held the world title it'd mean something big today."

"Is that why you're going for the championship with Teddy?"

"It's conditions. Television has closed down most of the halls in the country, in fact, only a few promoters with the 'in' with one of the channels can make a financial go of it these days. Where can you take a fighter? I've taken my pro everywhere you can still go. We've fought just about everybody he can fight and he's learned everything I or anybody else can teach him. I'll tell you something else, but don't put it in your stories. Teddy Baker is a better Dave McCleave, and for two reasons. He had it in him-- the gift--even more than Dave, and I've had all these extra years at it. Things I was just getting round to trying with Dave when he started to go over the hill, I picked right up later with this boy. Any good fighter a teacher has grows right out of any that went before him."

"That makes sense."

"So what have I got? I've got a guy who can do everything now. No Board of Control or anybody else can louse him up and, what's most important of all, no other fighter can stay with him."

"I've never seen him in a bad fight."

"That's because he goes to the other fellow's strength. He licks him at that and it's got to be a good fight. Even the clutchers can't grab him because, when they spread their arms to grab, he crouches and unloads two-handedly into their body. And that's the last time they try it that way. With that kind of fighter going for me I'm not afraid of any authority. Besides, what can you make without some kind of title today--and the winner of this will be undisputed world champion."

"Not overmuch."

"When we win that crown I can go to Solomons, Madison Square Garden or anybody else with this kind of fighter and say: 'Listen, tell those advertising people an extra ten thousand.' You can get it with this kind of champion; Robinson got it."

"You're so right."

"You want to talk to him? He's in his room and I'll get him down."

"I'd rather talk to him up there," Tom said.

"Finish your coffee while I go up and see what he's doing."

Doc and Tim Holland went out.

"What a man," Trevor said.

"Now can you see?" Tom said nodding wisely.

"I think I'll write about that, about why you don't go for a title or why you do."

"Good. Then you'll leave your column-picking paws off Teddy."

"There's something he didn't tell you," I said.

"What?"

"He wants that title for himself, too."

"Why not?"

"That's the shame of it. He's getting old but, years ago, he wouldn't have given a damn. You know that, Tom. All this time, over forty or more years, he's had one philosophy--do it right and let the spoils fall where they may, mostly into the hands of leeches and thieves. In the old days there were a few guys around who could appreciate it. Today, in Solomons, the Beckett or Toby's, what do they know? Did you ever have a champion? It's both a crime and a defeat, but Doc wants it for that, too. He's human and I'm complaining."

"Let's hope he gets it."

"He'll get it," Tom said.

"He'll have to," I said. "I told you I'm involved and I am, most horribly. It's a cause. The other man's not a fighter compared with Teddy. He's all show and no meaning but who recognises the difference? Teddy's our standard-bearer. He's just a fighter, but this is a fight against all the rubbish they sell and celebrate today in boxing, on TV, in the bookstores, in our newspapers and magazines and everywhere else. You see that, don't you?"

"I concur," Trevor said.

"Please," Tom pleaded, "two men naked above the waist, carrying no weapons but wearing gloves, are going to fight each other in a square ring over a limited distance under strict rules and regulations, both scaling inside a stipulated weight."

"He's a stubborn so-and-so, isn't he?" Trevor said, nodding at Tom.

"He is. He has no causes to talk about because he's lived them all his life. If there is any such thing, he's a purer Doc."

"Please."

"He can't see himself. For at least twenty-five years he's been writing the purest prose ever to appear in a newspaper, and the purest dialogue to appear anywhere. Do the traffic lights turn red on all sides when he wants to cross the street, though?"

"Are you finished?" Tom said. "Do you mind if we go up and see Teddy?"

Teddy was lying on his bed reading a paperback and, when we came in, he put it aside and got up and shook hands. Then he sat down at the head of the bed with the pillow at his back and Doc came in, bringing a couple of light, straightback chairs.

"How do you feel?" Tom said.

"Fine. I'm in great shape."

"He asked you that," Trevor said, "because we asked Don Cockell in camp once how he felt when he was training for Marciano in San Francisco, and he said: 'Great, but I have to laugh because everyone asks me how I feel. I'm here, getting up early, running on the road, training, eating and sleeping right. How else could I and should I feel?' "

"Don was telling the truth," Teddy said, smiling.

"What were you reading?"

"Just a western. I like to read them once in a while when I'm away in camp. They help me relax and take my mind off things."

"What else to you read?"

"Mostly magazines."

"The articles or the short stories?"

"Both. I like some of the stories but not all of them."

"Does that mean not the fight stories?"

"Quite often. They usually have the fighter, during the fight, thinking about his girl or his mother or some gangster. Believe me, when you're in the ring you don't have a chance to think about anything else. Of course, I never had any gangster threaten me or try to bribe me to lose a fight. Maybe, if I had, I'd think about that, eh?"

"But what do you think about? I mean, specifically what kind of thing?"

"I think of what the other bloke is doing and what he's probably going to do. That I can use. I mean, Doc has always studied the opponents I fight, and we've pretty much got it all worked out, but you actually have to be in with the guy to really find out."

"They all have patterns," Doc said, "and I don't care who they are."

"Then fighters are like writers," Trevor said.

"The good ones have more patterns than the others, that's all."

"So that's what you're thinking about, Teddy?"

"A lot of things, but that's it. The way Doc has taught me-I don't know whether it's okay to say this or not."

He glanced at Doc.

"It's alright. The good fighters you've met knew what you were doing to them, but they couldn't help themselves. What the other fellow discovers in the newspapers isn't going to help him."

"Well, what I mean is that the way Doc has taught me, you give the other guy the impression that he's in charge. That's so he'll box his way and follow his patterns. As Doc says: 'Let him perform.' For example, when I'm pressing an opponent in a certain way, he may jab me a couple of times and then hook off it. He does this a few times in the first couple of rounds and then, when I see it's the pattern, I'm thinking whether I'll try to beat the hook with a straight right hand or if I'll drop down, slip the hook and counter with a hook to the belly. I mean, that's what you're thinking about when you're under fire."

"I rather care for that," Trevor said. "Cite us another one. I don't mean to pry into your secrets, but I've never heard a fighter talk like this before."

"That's alright," Doc concurred.

"I don't know," Teddy said, "there's so many things. Like, suppose I can't get the other fellow to open up. He may throw a few punches, but nothing you can work off. Maybe the only pattern will be a double jab; he'll jab twice and move. So I take those high on the forehead--one, two. He gets confident now because I lean into them a little to make him think he's jabbing hard, whereas actually they've landed off-target. Then, now I'm ready, I take the first one but, on the second, I lean over to my right so I slip it over my left shoulder and I cross a right over the

205

top. It's a good punch because, leaning to the right, I've got my weight on that side and behind it."

"That punch is standard," Doc said. "the big thing is setting the trap. Basically, there's only so many punches and everybody knows what they are--straight ones, hooks and uppercuts from both hands. You've got to con the other man into walking into them. It's thinking, first of all. Then, when he's committed himself, it's timing and placement, that's all."

"That's all?" Teddy said, shaking his head. "I've been at it for nine years and I'm still learning new combinations."

"You'll still be learning the day you pack it all in," Doc said.

"What about the other guy?" Tom said. "Have you seen him fight much?"

"I've seen him a couple of times from ringside and once on TV. Doc and I flew across the pond to see his last fight in Las Vegas."

"What do you think of him?"

"A very good fighter. Lots of natural ability He's got fast hands and he moves beautifully."

"While you're down here," Trevor said, "just how much is he on your mind? You're in camp, working every day towards just one thing. Do you ever dream about the fight?"

"Here we go," I said. "Trevor Wignall's Book of Dreams."

"We're laughing," Tom said to Doc and Teddy, "because, sooner or later, one of us asks this of all of them--Lesnevich, Mills, Cockell, Turpin, Robinson, Woodcock, Boon. You can't escape."

"Amateur psychology," Trevor said. "I wonder, do you ever see the other guy in your mind's eye, like when you're boxing down here?"

"No," Teddy said. "I mean, not when I'm sparring. I've got Lefty 'Satan' Flynn down here..."

"He's here?"

"Sure, and he does a really good imitation of the other man. When you're boxing, though, you're thinking of what's going on, like I said, so I don't see the other guy at all."

"When do you see him, if you do?"

"You see?" Tom said. "You can't get away."

"I know what you mean. I reckon I think about him when I'm doing roadwork in the morning and when I'm hitting the heavy bag. That part of training becomes monotonous and I think of him then."

"Just what do you think and do you visualise the fight?"

"That's about it. You guys must be psychologists. I keep on making up the fight. Sometimes when I'm falling asleep, too, I see him make a move and I make a move. We go through the fight like that."

"How long does the fight last?"

"Oh, I don't see the whole fight, only a part of it. Maybe it's something that happened during the sparring in the gym that day; I see that happening again in the fight."

"Do you see the fight end?"

"Yes, especially at night. No matter what moves I'm thinking over, when I see the two of us I can't stop thinking about it until the fight ends in my mind."

"And how does it end?"

"He's out cold on his back," Teddy said, smiling.

"I like that," Tom said, laughing. "You knock him out."

"Then I drop off to sleep."

"You see?" Trevor said. "Don't knock my Dream Book."

"Teddy," Tom said, "I don't think you've ever been knocked down, have you?"

"Once," Teddy said, looking at Doc, "about four years ago. Doc'll tell you about that."

"Dreadful," Doc said. "He's boxing that Battling Parkin in Stoke. I don't know what he was thinking about. All of a sudden he's got his feet too close together and all his weight on his left foot. That Parkin hit him a hook high on the head that wouldn't topple a coconut and down he goes on his left side. Dreadful."

"I got right up and I knocked the bloke out two rounds later."

"Never mind that. Tell them what I made you do, Edward."

"Oh dear," Teddy said, looking at the floor and clearly embarrassed. "For a week after that Doc made me wear a slipper, one of those bedroom slippers, on my right foot. Everywhere I went I had to wear it for a week, one shoe and one slipper. Was I embarrassed!"

"So you should have been," Doc said, still disgusted. "It was you who embarrassed me. It taught you that you have a right foot, though. It taught you to keep your weight on both feet, on an even keel, didn't it?"

"I'll say. Everywhere I went, in the gym and everywhere else, people asked me: 'What's the matter with your foot?' That went on for a whole week."

"What did you say?"

"I got so fed up with it I started fibbing. I told people that I'd sprained my big toe."

"I go for this," Trevor said.

"Yes, but remember it's mine," Tom insisted.

"I know."

"We should leave him alone now," Trev advised, standing up. "He's got a workout soon."

"Okey-doke."

"You writers amaze me," Teddy said.

"Why?"

"You two. You never take any notes, yet when I read it in the paper it's just what I said."

"That's what you think," Tom said.

"I don't understand how you do it."

"We don't understand how you do what you do either, Teddy." Trevor said.

After they watched Teddy work, Tom and Trevor wrote their copy. The latter phoned his in and then we drove into Guildford where Tom used a free line at the local paper. After dinner we had a few drinks, sitting in the dining-room with Teddy and Doc, swapping stories of the old days for Teddy's benefit until it was ten o'clock.

"I'll see you all tomorrow," Teddy said, rising to his feet.

"Aren't you going to watch Ceroni on TV?" Trevor said.

"No, I need my beauty sleep."

The rest of us watched the fight and it was just about what it had promised to be. For the first six rounds Ceroni moved around, feinting the other man and, when he saw a safe opening, shooting left hands. Ceroni's fans seemed to like it anyway, as could be judged from the screams of encouragement on the TV.

"The little guy has no chance," Trevor said. "He can't reach him and he doesn't know how to make him lead and miss."

"Dreadful," Doc said.

"He'll do a little better from now on," I suggested. "Ceroni will start to tire and slow down."

Ceroni did, and by the ninth round the other guy was getting inside and hitting Joe in the body. When he did this,

Ceroni would clutch him, head back and right out of the way, but, as it was, he won it easily on points.

"After that, I need a drink very badly indeed," Doc said.

XXII

That night Tom and Trevor stayed in a friend's bungalow down the road. They came up next morning for breakfast and then said goodbye to Teddy, Doc and Tim Holland before leaving for 'the big smoke' where they would watch the champion work out in a ring and gym specially set up in a posh night-club in Leicester Square.

"We'll see you when you get sprung," Trevor said when I walked them to his car.

"Don't worry about it," Tom said. "He'll win it well."

"Please God."

"Whatever happens," Trevor said, "you'll get a good story. I never realised the boy was such a good talker."

"He's great on boxing. On everything else he's thin but I don't press him. With a month to give to it I'm trying to let him emerge as if I'm almost not here. It's not the easiest thing to do."

"Stop griping. Do you think the faithful departed have it better?"

"Alright. Take your syndicated papers and your millions of readers and get out of here."

That afternoon Doc sent Teddy eight rounds. Enough had been in the papers and on TV about the coming fight by now, so that there were a great many men, women and children packed into the gym watching while Tim Holland kept on at the sparring partners to pressurise more and Doc leaned on the top rope watching Teddy turn it on.

"Excuse me," one of the male spectators said, walking up to me when Teddy climbed out of the ring and walked over to the heavy bag.

"Yes?"

He was about thirty years old with a mop of blond hair and he needed a shave. He was wearing a red-and-black-checkered woollen shirt, the tails worn outside of his brown corduroy trousers, and a boy of about four was clasping his hand.

"I'm a boxing fan."

"That's good."

"Is the fight going to be on television? Teddy Baker's fight, of course?"

"Only on satellite; you need a satellite dish to be able to see it on Sky."

"How come? We saw it on ITV the last time Teddy Baker fought."

"Not this one. This is for the title."

"So what is a fella supposed to do?"

"You're supposed to go to the fight."

"Them tickets cost a lot of money, don't they?"

"Five hundred pounds special ringside, but the prices range down and you can get up in the gallery bleachers for twenty-five."

"Who's got that much money for a fight? I pay a lot of money for a TV licence and I should be able to watch all the big fights."

"If it'll make you feel any better, you can watch that fella in the ring now box on television on Monday night."

Penny and McCormick were moving around the ring, McCormick stalking Penny.

"Yes? Which one?"

"The white boy."

"What's his name?"

"Alf Penny."

"Is he good?"

"You can see for yourself. He fights the eight-round top-liner over in Chigwell, and transmission begins at nine-thirty on terrestial ITV."

"Really? Thanks a lot."

Teddy was lying face down on the rubbing-table in the dressing-room, naked except for a towel brought up like a loin-cloth, Tim Holland working on him and the air in the small room sharp, but at the same time heavy, with the smell of Wintergreen and Elliman's. Tim had finished with the thighs and calves and was starting on the shoulders.

"This is one of those times I envy fighters," I said.

"I'll give you a rub," Tim responded.

"No, I'd be ashamed, an impostor. A fighter really earns it."

"Phew!" Penny said, coming in and closing the door behind him. "That stinks."

"You don't know what's good," Tim said.

Penny's face, above the while terry-cloth robe and the towel around his neck, was pouring with sweat.

"Our love is forever---" he started to sing, standing there and throwing his arms out. " No---"

"That isn't so good, either," Teddy said, turning his head to look back at Penny. "How about tuning into another station?"

"What's the matter? You getting' edgy?"

"No."

"Listen. If I wasn't such a good fighter, you know what I'd be?"

"I hate to think."

"One of them airline pilots. You go to all them foreign countries and have plenty of skirt in every one."

"Hold it, Penny," I said. "I just met a fan of yours."

"You did? Who?"

"A punter out there in a red-and-black shirt. He thinks you're a great fighter."

"Oh yes? Tell him to be at the Prince Regent in Chigwell Monday night. The old one-two. Bam-bam. Raise me hand, ref. I'm your boy."

"He'll be there."

"Good. I'll give him my autograph. Cheap for a quid."

After breakfast on the morrow, McCormick, old Sid and Penny left in an old Ford banger. A friend of Sid's--a coloured kid about eighteen and an ABA southern Counties winner--had driven it up the night before, and they were going to drop Penny off near Guildford so that he could take a coach or train into London while they went on to Portsmouth to watch the kid in the ABA quarterfinals.

"You just fight your fight, old Sid said to Teddy when they shook hands at the car. "You'll take that other boy."

"Thanks, and good luck to you folks."

"Fight that fight you bin' workin' on. You'll show the people, but good."

"Thanks again."

"Switch on tomorrow night and watch this boy go," Penny said. "I'll see you Friday at the weigh-in, anyway."

"Fine," Teddy said. "Stay lucky, Alf."

"You lads will miss me around here. You'll be sorry I'm gone."

Soon after midday I was lying on my bed reading and Doc was snoozing on his. The window was open and I heard car wheels on the gravel and got up and looked out. It was one of those big black for-hire Daimlers complete with driver, and the newspapermen--six of them--were getting out.

"What is it?" Doc said, sitting up. I hadn't said anything so he must have sensed something.

"The riot squad. That is, the gentlemen of the press."

"It's about time they showed."

"It'll be a riot, too. Dave Caldwell's with them."

"I was afraid of that, but I was hoping he didn't come to watch training any more."

"He doesn't, except for the big ones. I haven't seen him in a year. You're supposed to be honoured."

"A year is too soon. Why does he have to be like that?"

"You know as well as I do. He's getting old."

Doc had put on a tie and was getting into his jacket.

"We all are, but not like that. What's the matter with him?"

"He can't take the competition and his seams are showing."

"Then he should quit."

"Don't get drunk and tell him that."

"I'm not crazy."

Doc went down and I washed and thought about it. When I was just starting in Fleet Street, Caldwell had any number of contracted freelancing jobs with both morning and evening papers. Hand it to him. he was clever. He could cover all the popular sports and he could go, say, to a fight or football match and phone in completely different stories on the same event to several papers. His speciality was running stories which often meant that columnists were released for personal, in-depth analyses in the aftermath. One should never take those years from him because he was the best of his kind, but then it became the second time around for him and the third, and somewhere along the way he got tired of working and resorted to drinking, gaining the nom-de-guerre 'You're a Cad and a Bounder, Caldwell.' He seemed to get the impression that he owned it all, that the football games were played for him and the fights were fought for him. In his cups, I could see him start to resent the new ones among us, and when I read him I could taste all the light ales and martinis turning to vinegar and the whole thing spoiling before the bottom of the barrel and the grave came nigh.

I looked in on Teddy but he was asleep with the white bedspread pulled up over him, so I closed the door again and went down. They were spread along the bar, Doc in the middle with Dave Caldwell, Dave doing the talking and Ernie Jarvis hovering at his side, making certain to be listening and to light Dave's cigarette and to signal Capini for another drink for Dave.

"What the hell are you doing here?" Dave said and we shook hands.

"Hello, Dave. I want to ask the same about you."

He was a striking man, even at nearly seventy and dissipated, and he still dressed like a toff.

"Well, there's a few in the 'Street' and several out-of-town want new slants about this damn fight. I don't think it's going to be so much but, for some reason, there's a lot of interest in it."

"It'll be a good fight."

"It better be, after all those stinkers they've been putting on the television. What are you doing here?"

"I'm doing a magazine piece about Teddy."

"Still with that magazine stuff? Why don't you get back in an honest business, like ours? Those magazine editors don't know what it's all about."

In the time they've been here, I was thinking, he can't have shipped more than one. He really gets off to a flying start these days.

"Magazine editors, what do they know about sports?"

I watched him. He had three at the bar and kept insisting that Doc kept up with him. When we sat down he had another and ordered another one for Doc. He seemed in pretty good humour, talking about the old days and what he once told Ted Broadribb in front of Tommy Farr. But he just picked at his food.

By the time we had finished eating Teddy was going into the gym, so we all went in there. They were too many for the small dressing-room, so they waited for Teddy to come out and then he sat in the first row chair, with Doc sitting next to him. There were four of them in the first row and I sat in the second row with Dave and Ernie Jarvis.

It was so warm in the gym, even with a couple of windows open, that Teddy did not need his robe and he sat there in just his white T-shirt and brief, white-knitted trunks, woollen socks and his ring-shoes. Tim Holland handed him some gauze and he started wrapping his right hand, legs dangling, while they fired questions at him. It was so warm, in fact, that when I looked over at Caldwell his eyelids were heavy and I reckoned that, with the drinks inside him, he might easily fall asleep.

"So what makes you think you can win this fight?" he said, suddenly stirring.

"I just believe I can," Teddy said quietly, still bandaging.

"Sensational! That'll make big news. You ask him something, Ernie."

"Teddy," Ernie complied, "what do you think of the other man technically? I mean, what do you think is his best hand?"

"Who the hell cares about that," Dave said, turning on Ernie.

"His best hand?" Teddy said. "His left."

"What do you want me to ask him?" Ernie said to Dave.

"Get a proper story! What the hell do you think I got you up here for?"

This is going to be great, I was thinking. The only trouble is that I've seen this scene before.

"You say his left hand?" one of them in the front row said. "He's knocked a few of them out with his right."

"I know," Teddy said. "He's got two good hands but I think his left--that jab and hook--is his best."

"The left is the fighter's working hand," Doc said. "The right just comes in for the pay-off."

"Like you," Caldwell said. "You ought to know."

I looked at Doc and saw him stare at Dave and his face set. I wondered if I ought to go out and get Dave another drink. If he didn't knock it out of my hand it would put him to sleep, and that would be a way out of it.

"What about those three fights you lost, Teddy?" one of them in the front asked.

"I lost three, but I won eighty-something."

"I don't mean that."

"I'll answer that," Doc said. "He got two bad decisions, one in Watford and the other in Birmingham."

"That's right," Ernie Jarvis said. "I saw the one in Brum."

"What are you siding with him for?" Caldwell said, turning on Ernie.

214

"The other one he lost," Doc continued, "I got him beaten on purpose."

"I'll bet," Caldwell said, raising his voice.

"Just what do you mean, Doc?" one of them in front said.

"About seven years ago he well beat some guy up in Newcastle. It was a big show, with a couple of heavyweights top-of-the-bill and he started to think he was pretty good."

"I'll bet," Caldwell said again, loudly.

"The next time he fought he looked lousy. He beat the other fellow, but he was trying to make me out a liar and----"

"That's no great feat," Caldwell said.

"He thought he knew it all, so I got him a ten-rounder in Manchester. I put him in with a guy who outscored him, not by much, but he beat him. He needed to be taken down a peg."

"That's true," Teddy said, smoothing the tape on his hand and nodding. "I realise it now."

"You expect us to believe that?" Caldwell said nastily.

"What?" Doc said, and I could see it all over his face now.

"You know what."

"Look, Dave, I don't give a cuss whether you believe it or not."

"Oh, you don't?"

"No."

"You think I'm gonna believe all that stuff, like that line you handed Trev Wignall in that column of his in yesterday's paper?"

So that's it, I thought. It's competition and now he resents Wignall.

"I don't give a twopenny-halfpenny fart what you believe."

"Let's forget it," I said. "Let's have a drink."

"I'm not going to forget it," Dave said. "That crap about why he never had a champion before. Why, you couldn't have won the crown with Lefty Flynn or anybody else, and you won't win it with Teddy Baker, either. You're nothing but a loud mouth."

"If you weren't drunk," Doc said, "I'd chin you."

"Easy, Doc," Teddy said, slowly standing up by Doc's side.

"Who's drunk?" Caldwell said, standing up, Ernie holding him by the right arm. We were all standing now.

"You are," Doc said. "You're a miserable, goddam dirty drunk who stands on corners and abuses people in that column

215

of yours. You don't know the first bloody thing about boxing and you never did. You can't even write well any more because the rot has set in from the inside; you're dead but you don't know it. Don't think you can intimidate me with your lousy prose. Not any more you can't."

"Come on, Doc." I said. "Knock it off"

I knew it was not only the drinks talking, but the fight and Waller and many years and everything.

"Knock it off?" Dave said, sneering at me. "He's going to get knocked off. That fighter of his is going to get flattened and I'm going to say so in the paper tomorrow--that and a few more things."

"I don't give a damn what you say," Doc said.

"Come on away," one of those in front with Doc said.

"You'll see alright; you'll see it in the paper."

"No I won't," Doc said, "because I haven't read any stinking copy of yours for five years and I won't start reading it again tomorrow. And I'll tell you something else. Don't talk like that about my fighter here."

"Forget it, Doc." Teddy said.

"Why not? I'll say and write what I like about him."

"And show your stupidity. He's not only gonna knock that other fella out but, when he does, the guy will go down with his face right in front of yours. Print that if you will."

With that Doc pulled his arm away from Teddy, turned and walked to the back of the gym. Tim Holland followed him and I looked at Teddy, who acknowledged it with a shrug.

"I'm getting out of here," Caldwell said. "I'm going back to town to see the champion and his people. Where's that bloody driver?"

"He's in the bar," Ernie Jarvis said. "What are the rest of us supposed to do?"

"I don't give a f--- what you do. I'm taking him back."

After Dave left, Teddy boxed four rounds and Doc said nothing to him the whole time. Then the rest of them went into the dining-room, found their typewriters and began to write their copy. When I came into the dressing-room, Tim Holland had just brought the tea and Doc was trying to make work for himself, picking things up and putting them down again while the fighters drank their tea.

216

"Well," I said, "now that it's over I'm glad I was present to hear it."

"I'm glad you were too," Doc said.

"I'd have done anything I could to have stopped it, but I couldn't think of anything that would."

"What difference does it make?"

"He'll murder you in his papers tomorrow," Teddy said.

"He'll knock you, too," Doc said; "but what difference does it make? It's about time somebody in this business told him his fortune."

"That's right," I said, "but you really burned that bridge."

"Who needs him? What do I have to worry about him for any more? I've got a fighter that'll stand up for me in there. You knock this one out and you're the champion, and then what have I got to worry about? Dave Caldwell? He only picks on little people."

The next morning, after the work-out, I took Teddy's car and drove into Guildford to get the papers. I read Caldwell's pieces still standing in the confectioner's shop and, when I got back, Doc was in the room and I handed them to him.

"He never even mentions you or Teddy," I said. "He just datelines himself from the All-Stars gym in Paddington and writes about the other bloke and his entourage."

Doc read the pieces quickly, and then chucked the papers on the bed.

"I knew he had no bottle," he said.

"Of course not. He's afraid because he believes Teddy's going to win."

"No bottle," Doc said; "absolutely no guts at all."

XXIII

Then came the quiet days, the quiet days loud with implication.

"Righto," Doc said. "That's enough."

It was Monday afternoon, in the gym.

"How many rounds was that?" Teddy said, when Doc took his gumshield out.

"Seven."

"I feel like working more."

217

"Great. Never mind the bags today. Go in and cool out and we'll weigh after you've showered."

It is one of the most difficult of scientific endeavour, this struggle to bring an athlete up the mountain of his efforts to the peak of his performance at the precise moment when he must perform. That peak place is no bigger than the head of a pin, shrouded in the clouded mysteries of a living being and so, although all try, most fail, for it requires not only the most diligent of climbers but the greatest of guides.

"You have to play the probability," Doc said, explaining it standing by the window and looking out across the parking-space at the fresh greenery beyond and waiting for Teddy. "You ask a fighter how he feels and he says: 'Good' or 'Okay'. But does he know for sure? You got to be able to see your fighter better than he can see himself and play the probability."

"Most of them go wrong trying to bring a fighter up to some fine point the last day. Just reckon the chances of the miss, under or over. Either way you're just as badly off. You can't ask for odds in this life; you've got to make them. I found that out. You reach a level where he's almost where you want him to be four or five days before a fight. It's not as hard to hold that. Then the next step he takes is the step into the ring. He's there and that's where he fights."

The scales were in the room so Teddy slipped out of his shower clogs and Tim Holland took the gown off him. Teddy stood naked and statuesque on the scale while we waited as Doc moved the weights along the bars

"One sixty and a half," he said.

"That's fine," Teddy said.

He stepped down and Tim helped him into the gown again and then Teddy slipped his feet back into the shower clogs. I held the door for him and Tim and Doc followed him out.

"You trust those scales?" I asked Doc.

"I have to. It cost me fifteen nicker for Rene to get the man down here to test them and set everything right. He'll be half-a-pound inside, exactly what I told that Phil Kaplin. So don't you hold any more doors for him."

Tim Holland was following Teddy into the dressing-room.

"What do you mean?" I said.

"He's no invalid. He can open his own doors."

"I was just being polite. What's eating you?"

218

"Nothing. The last few days before a big fight everybody bows and scrapes to a fighter so you'd think he was Lord God Almighty. There's enough pressure building up inside him as it is."

"Sorry."

"Don't be. When I'm not thinking I do it myself. Let's have a drink."

It was that evening and in the sitting-room we sat, all of us--Teddy, Doc and Tim Holland, plus Parkin, Lefty Flynn, Evans and Capini--watching Alf Penny box his eight-rounder. They were two raw kids, all arms and elbows and gloves, trying to knock each other out in a hurry, their heads jolting back with the punches and the crowd yelling themselves hoarse. Then, in the fifth round, Penny was cut above the left eye.

"Oh-law," Teddy said and then: "come on, Alf."

"It's dreadful," Doc said.

They worked feverishly to stem the bleeding in the corner, but in the sixth round it opened again. Now the other boy was going for the eye. The referee was looking at Penny every time he broke them up and after that round, and after the seventh, the doctor got up into the corner to inspect the cut. In the eighth and last round Penny hurt the other kid, the two of them flailing away and the crowd on its' feet, screaming.

"Alf made it some fight," Teddy said, while we waited for the decision. "I think he won it."

"The guts of a burglar," Doc said.

"I still think you've got him wrong," I said.

"Ladies and gentleman," the announcer gave out through his microphone, " the referee's decision is a draw. The referee scores seventy-eight points for both men. A big hand, please, after a wonderful contest."

He needn't have made the request, because the crowd were still standing and applauding.

"I thought Alf won it, cut and all," Teddy said.

"The other fella lost it," Doc said, "going for the eye."

"That's no fighter," Capini said, shaking his head. "Alf Penny is crazy. If he keeps on fighting he'll be hurt and finish with his brains scrambled. Just you watch."

"Come on, bon ami. You know you were on his side."

"On his side? I'm only on your side, nobody else's."

"Thanks a million and good night," Teddy said.

219

It was Tuesday and it rained all day. It was coming down as early-morning mist when Tim Holland and I walked Teddy and the sparring-partners and Artie Parkin across the parking area to the road. The only sound was that of feet on the ashfelt and of the dripping from leaves and branches.

"Let's just walk to the top of the rise," I said to Tim when the fighters set off. "I want to see how it looks today where they're running."

From the top of the rise of the road we could see them making the curve, beyond and below, Teddy in the lead and the three of them matching his pace, but Parkin lagging. Then they disappeared into that grey-blue mist that hung so low.

When it was about time they got back we walked back to the building, and when they came in the mist was on Teddy's wind-jacket in droplets and on his short hair like hoar-frost. His breath hung in front of him like cigarette-smoke until it mingled, lost, with the mist swirling now around us. I wished we were sitting in the sun again, listening to Lefty tell about Australia. I wanted us once more to have all that time.

It was Wednesday and I rang the Press Association in the Street and found out that McCormick had knocked his man out in three rounds and I told Teddy. That afternoon he boxed his last in the silence of the gym, just the squeak of the ring shoes on the canvas, the thud of the big sparring gloves and the sound of the breathing for two rounds, one with Evans and the last with Lefty. In that final session he really turned it on to become the complete fighter.

"Time!" Tim Holland yelled.

"That's all," Doc said, standing close to the ropes and motioning.

"One more," Teddy said. "How about just one more?"

"Come on out of there," Doc said, shaking his head, and then to me: "Now I can breathe again!"

Now it was Thursday, a day of pale sun and cold. After they came off the road and had breakfast, we walked Lefty to the road to meet the 9.25 coach. Flynn, in that same old grey sharkskin suit, carried his kitbag over his shoulder. Evans walked on one side of him, carrying Lefty's cardboard suitbox tied with twine and Teddy walked on the other. We stood across the road again in the sun.

"Here it comes," Evans said.

220

"You're gonna whip that boy," Lefty said, shaking Teddy's hand. "You're gonna be the new champion of the whole wide world."

"That's it. And thanks, Lefty."

"I always know that boy got something missing. He try to be Sugar Ray. I know him since he start. Once I see him punch the big bag in the gym and, when I first come in, I thought it was Robinson, but he ain't. Robinson mean it; this boy don't."

"Thanks Lefty. Thanks for everything."

"I'm glad to do it. Real glad."

"And good luck yourself. You win your own fight."

"Sure," the Satan said, winking.

The coach had stopped and the door was open, waiting for Lefty.

"Is somebody gettin' on or not?" the driver said. "I haven't got all day."

"Sure mister," Lefty said. "I'm sorry."

We watched him get aboard and go down the aisle, looking out at us once and smiling as the bus started, and then we watched it disappear.

"How will you get back?" I said to Evans.

"I won't," he said. "Artie Parkin wants me to work with him. I'm gonna stay on with Parkin."

That evening at dinner Ivy came out of the kitchen and asked Teddy how the steak was. She stood there for a couple of minutes, smiling and nodding and watching him eat, while Doc looked at me and shook his head once. After dinner Tim Holland and I walked with Teddy. We walked for an hour, just taking it easy and talking about the stars and new cars and every boxing story I could remember. When we got back we watched 'Crimewatch' and then a session serial of Z-Cars. Teddy stayed up until eleven o'clock for the first time in camp.

In bed that night I lay for a long while in the darkness listening to Doc turning over and then, finally, hearing his breathing even out. Then I thought of Teddy, lying alone in Doc's old room.

XXIV

When the alarm went off I was floating on my back, suspended half in sleep and half in wakefulness. Now, with its obtrusive ringing, it was as if I were trying to sit up in the water, until suddenly it stopped and I got my feet down to realise that I could stand up in it and that there was no cause for panic.

"You awake?" Doc said.

"Just about."

"How did you sleep?"

"Not very well. You sleep much?"

"No."

"You will after it's over."

"Not right away. It takes me two or three nights to unwind after a fight."

He was up now in his rumpled light blue pyjamas, his white hair shaggy, raising the dark shade at one of the windows.

"It's not a bad day," he said. "It looks nice out."

I waited, half dressed and cold and sitting on the bed, until he came out of the bathroom. Then I went in and, when we had finished dressing, it was 8.15 and I followed him into Teddy's room.

"Doc?" Teddy said, sitting up in the bed, the light from the hall playing across both him and the bed.

"It's a nice day," Doc said, raising first one shade and then the other.

"Is it?"

He was still sitting up in the bed and then he pulled the covers off and swung his legs over the side. He was wearing white pyjamas, with dark red piping edging the collar and down the front and he sat there a moment, the pyjama top failing to hide the bulk of his shoulders. With his right hand he gently massaged the back of that thick neck.

"Close the window, will you please?" he said to Doc.

"I am. You sleep alright?"

"Not wisely but too well. If Artie and Mickey went on the road I never heard them."

"They went and they're back already and having breakfast," Tim Holland said.

He was standing, looking fit and neat, in the doorway. He had on a single-breasted grey suit, white shirt and dark blue tie and he looked like a businessman about to leave for the office.

"Get him a large glass of orange juice, will you?" Doc said to Tim.

"Yep."

Teddy put his gown on then, slid into a pair of slippers and went to the bathroom. When he returned he sat down in the wicker chair and waited, still looking half asleep.

"We'll go down and weigh now," Doc said. "Best get out of those slippers."

"Why?" Teddy said. "I don't want to walk downstairs bare-footed."

"And I don't want you slipping on those stairs. Put those clogs on with heels on them."

Teddy kicked his slippers off, put on his loafers and we went down. We walked through the empty quiet of the gym into the small room and Teddy shed his robe and took the loafers off.

"Shall I take off the pyjamas--they don't weigh much?"

"Take everything off."

Tim Holland took the pyjamas, then the pants and Teddy stepped on the scales, naked and standing straight with just his head bowed, watching Doc slide the weights on the bars.

"Eleven-five and a quarter," Doc read off.

"I hope this scale is right," Teddy said, watching the bar suspended in balance.

"You move your bowels this morning?"

"No. You know I just got up."

"Okay. Put your gown and those shoes on. You're alright; you're just what we aimed at."

Tim Holland helped Teddy back into the gown and then he put his loafers back on. Tim held the door open and Doc and I followed Teddy back upstairs. Then Holland arrived with the orange juice and Teddy sat in the wicker chair and drank it slowly.

"This tastes good," he said.

Doc and I had packed our things the night before and now he started taking Teddy's clothes out of the cupboard, folding them on the bed and packing them into Teddy's bag. By the time he was finished, Teddy was dressed. He had donned the light grey flannel slacks, the light wool maroon sports shirt and the almost cream-coloured sports jacket he had worn when we came down to the country. Though he had shaved the afternoon before, he still looked clean enough

"How are you today, Frank?" he said, seeming really to notice me for the first time.

"I'm fine. I was just thinking you might pose for one of those fashion ads in 'Woman's Own.'

"No chance."

"Never mind that fashion stuff," Doc said. "Anything in the drawers of that cabinet?"

"Just some shirts and underwear in the top drawer. There's that stuff on top of the dressing-table, too. It goes in that bag but I'll do it."

When he had finished putting it in the bag he closed it, handed it to Doc and looked around the room.

"That's all. I'll be glad to get out of here."

"Will you take care of his foot-locker?" Doc said to Holland.

"Already taken care of. When we go down I'll get Artie and Mick to help me move it out."

"Don't forget to leave the cup and the ring-shoes and that stuff out," Teddy said.

"All taken care of. I brought along a zipper bag and it's all in there. Your gown's in there too, and the man from 'Lonsdale' is bringing the trunks to the weigh-in. Don't worry about a thing."

Tim took Teddy's bag from Doc and he and I went into our room and got our own bags. When we came out of our room, Teddy was taking a last look around and we went down to the hall. Capini, in his butcher's apron, was standing there and Tim Holland came out of the dining-room, followed by Artie Parkin and Evans.

"My wife wants to say goodbye, Teddy," Capini said.

"We'll be out by the car," Doc assured him

Teddy held the front door open while we went through with the bags. In the car-park he got out his keys and opened the roomy boot. Tim, Artie and Evans had gone back into the gym for the foot-locker

"Give Frank the keys," Doc said to Teddy.

"Why?"

"He'll drive."

"But I can drive."

"I know you can, but I want you to sit in front with Frank so as to be able to stretch your legs."

"Thirty-odd years without an accident," I said.

"I'm not worried," Teddy said, "I just thought I'd drive."

"So, Teddy," Capini said. His wife was with him, her butcher's apron on over her dark green coat-sweater, a short, grey-haired, red-faced woman, smiling a little too obviously now.

"Right, bon ami," Teddy said, giving it that same faulted pronunciation and shaking Rene's hand.

"Bon, Teddy, you could learn to speak French if you wanted to."

"Thanks for everything, Ivy," Teddy said, holding out his hand to Capini's wife.

"God bless you," she said and, taking Teddy's hand, she pulled him down. With her left arm around his neck she kissed him on the right cheek. "God bless you, Teddy."

"Put that foot-locker in first," Doc said.

Tim Holland was removing the bag he had placed in the luggage boot. One end of the foot-locker rested on the bumper, and Artie held the strap-handle at the other end.

"Some difference, eh Teddy?" he said. "I mean, from the time you and I fought."

"That's true. But you'll do okay, Artie."

"Four or five more fights, that's all for me. It's all getting' too tough."

"All the best, Teddy," Evans said, shaking Teddy's hand. "You'll flatten him."

"Thanks for everything, Mick."

"You'll win it," Artie Parkin said, shaking Teddy's hand.

Teddy showed me how to start the car and I stalled it once, reversing it out. Then we left the four of them there, still standing in the car park. Capini's wife was still holding her smile and waving with just her hand like a small child's ta-ta, as we pulled out.

"It's a good place," Teddy said, "but I'm glad to be getting out of here."

"I understand," I said. "So am I."

"I dare say, but tell me one thing."

"What?"

"Did you really get what you wanted up here? I mean, for the article?"

225

"Yes, thanks to you. It's been fine and I appreciate it."

"How long will it take you to write it?"

"Oh, about two weeks. I'll walk around for about five days, thinking about it. Just about the time when I start getting scared that nothing will come to write, something will happen--I hope. Then it'll take me a week to write it and a couple of days to rewrite it."

"I'm glad I don't have to do it," Teddy said. "Can you just imagine me trying to write something?"

We followed the winding blacktop road through the rolling country down to Guildford, the hills light green and, here and there, the sloping land tilled fresh brown. Once, at such a vista, I had the impulse to stop the car and announce that this would be where we would all get out and live out our years, for it is foolish for a man to have to fight.

"Now we'll make good time," Teddy said as we neared the motorway. We had negotiated teeming Guildford, with its' cinemas, sex shops and ale houses. "They say you can cut half-an-hour off the time it used to take on the old road."

We did, and as the monotony of the M3 set in, Teddy settled down in the 'shotgun-rider's' seat, stretched his legs and put his head back, and when I glanced over at him his eyes were closed. I could hear Doc and Tim Holland talking in the back seat, although I could not actually hear what they were saying, and finally Teddy sat up.

"Were you asleep?"

"No, but that Kew Gardens is some place, isn't it?" I wondered what had made him say that, as we hadn't taken the exit which would have brought us past the place but were now running down the slip-road to Earls Court.

"We'll go straight to the hotel," Doc said as we hit Kensington High Street. The traffic had slowed us right down now and I was constantly trying to measure the engine drag to the distance of the car in front. So solid was the vehicle crush as we passed the Albert Hall and threaded out way towards Knightsbridge that I decided to turn into Sloane Street, cross Vauxhall Bridge and come back over Westminster. As we were midway across the former, Teddy turned and looked up and down the river, with its assorted craft dwarfed against the soaring tower blocks, dignified hotels and the unique Houses of Parliament with their sentry, Big Ben, away in the mid-distance.

226

"Are we in good time?" Teddy said. "We're supposed to be there at half-twelve."

"It's a quarter to now," Doc said. "There's plenty of time. He'll play it late for effect, anyway; the big shot, you know."

I pulled up in the small taxi and clearing-space in front of the Regent Palace, by Piccadilly. Leaving the engine running, I slid out behind Teddy.

"You gentlemen have reservations?" the head doorman said, looking from one to the other of us.

"I've got the reservations," Doc said. "Will you take care of the car?"

"Certainly, sir. We use an underground round the corner for our guests. Who takes the ticket?"

"I'll be taking it," Teddy said.

"Excuse me," the doorman said, handing him the ticket. "You're Teddy Baker, aren't you?"

"Spot on."

"Well, good luck to you," the liveried fellow said, smiling and shaking Teddy's hand. "Be lucky."

"No handshaking," Doc said to Teddy. "You should know better than that with strangers."

"I know," Teddy said, nodding.

"Oh, I'm so sorry, " the doorman said.

We waited in the busy main hall while Doc registered. Then we went up in the lift with several other people and I spotted the pageboy, carrying the hold-all bags, nudge the lift operator, nod back towards Teddy and say some muffled words in his pal's ear.

"How do you feel, Edward?" Doc said when we reached the room.

"Okay."

"You best go to the toilet."

"Yes, I know. I need to."

The two beds, the night table with the lamp on it, the cupboard, writing-table and two easy chairs just about filled the room. Doc opened one of the two windows that looked out on the small, bleak brick quadrangle formed by the other three sides of the hotel, towering, as they did, many floors above us.

"Alright?" he asked, when Teddy returned.

"Of course. Good."

"We may as well go across to the Odeon. It's ten-past-twelve now."

We walked the short distance from the hotel, across the bottom of Shaftesbury Avenue and across the north side of Piccadilly Circus, past the Haymarket, Ward's Irish House, Lyons Corner House, a news theatre and a cinema, then across the street into Leicester Square itself, the grass square centre simmering green, then on the other side we approached the Odeon.

Doc walked with Teddy, and Tim Holland and I followed them; in London, as everywhere, you can always pick out the tourists. As we approached the building scheduled to house the weigh-in, three of them had stopped in the middle of the pavement--a man with the collar of his open-necked sports-shirt worn outside the collar of his jacket, a camera hung over one shoulder, a woman and a girl of about ten. He was pointing to a gigantic fight poster displayed outside the theatre and the woman was nodding. Just as Teddy and Doc tried to get by, the man turned and bumped into Teddy.

"I'm ever so sorry," he was saying as we walked up.

"That's quite alright," Teddy said and we walked on. I should have told him, I was thinking, that he just bumped into Teddy Baker. Then, when he got back to wherever, it would be one of the highlights of the trip and someone would think out loud about the possibility of such a thing happening and someone else would end it all by remarking about it being, really, such a small world.

And now we could see the crowd on the pavement. There must have been at least a hundred there, only a few of them women and a score or more of them teenaged youngsters. One of these spotted Teddy when we were still some thirty yards away and ran towards him with half-a-dozen others following.

"No," Doc said, shaking his head. "No autographs 'til later."

"Aw, cheese," the leading kid said.

One of the photographers came up while others shooed and spread the crowd. Doc and Teddy waited and Tim Holland and I moved to the side. Here and there Teddy's name was being called to him and Teddy was nodding and smiling. He waved a couple of times when he recognised someone.

"Will you wave like that again?" a photographer, on one knee, pleaded.

"Please," another of the photographers remonstrated, pushing back against the ever-growing crowd. "Will you give us a chance to work?"

"Knock him cold, Teddy!" someone shouted. "Flatten him."

Doc led the way then, and Tim Holland followed close behind Teddy. They were still calling to Teddy from the crowd and one of them reached across and slapped him on the back.

"I don't think I even got it," one photographer was saying to another in the foyer. "I'd better send over for yours, if that's okay."

"I don't know what I got myself," the other said.

The foyer was crowded but we pushed and shoved our way through with the help of several hired guards from 'Securicor'. Once we had gained access to the auditorium it was much more orderly and peaceful; down the side aisle and up the steps to backstage without undue difficulty. Inside a square formed by benches on the stage itself only newspapermen, the promoter's people and officials from the Boxing Board were standing.

"Hello,Teddy............."Hiya Teddy?......... Remember me, Teddy?..........Good luck to you, Teddy."

"Good," Doctor Kaplin said. "You're only just on time."

"The other man here yet?" Doc said.

"No, but he'll be here. I'll examine Teddy meanwhile."

"You can weigh him, too. If the other man's not here, never mind the pictures. We're leaving as soon as you're through."

"You come with me, Teddy."

Teddy and Doc started to follow the Board's medical supremo into a little room backstage.

"I'm sorry, Doc," the official said, turning at the door as Teddy walked past him. "Only the fighter."

"Just a minute, Edward," Doc said, "come back out here."

"It's that new rule," Kaplin said. "Only the fighter goes in. I have to examine the fighter alone."

"Not my fighter. Anywhere my fighter goes, I go."

"I can't do anything about it."

229

"Get the top man, Nipper Read. Nobody touches my fighter if I'm not present."

"Oh, come on, Doc, please be reasonable."

"Get him."

The doctor walked over to a desk next to the scale. One of the Board's Stewards was sitting there, talking to a couple of the newspapermen. After a moment the Doctor came back.

"Alright," he said, though shaking his head remorsefully. You can come in, but I was only doing what they told me. I only wish they'd make up their minds."

"You can come in too, Frank," Doc said.

"No thanks. I'll wait here."

"I'm sorry," the doctor said to me, closing the door.

When the three of them finally returned the champion had just arrived, his retinue of half-a-dozen behind him. He had on a chocolate brown sports jacket, cut long, and light tan slacks. Under the jacket he wore a bright yellow shirt, buttoned at the neck, and he walked around the square, loose and brown and smiling and shaking hands here and there.

"There's my man," he said when he saw Teddy, walking up to him smilingly and sticking out his hand.

"Hiya," Teddy acknowledged, taking the hand but limply, as per Doc's instructions.

"You want to come in now?" Doctor Kaplin said.

Doc had Teddy sit down on one of the benches and Ernie Jarvis came across and sat down next to him. One of the other newspapermen was talking to me about that scene between Doc and Dave Caldwell at the Barley Mow, so I could not hear what Ernie was telling Teddy, but Teddy was listening and, now and then, saying something and nodding in agreement.

"Alright," the doctor said, coming out of the little room. "Tell the officials they're ready to weigh."

The champion stood in the doorway, wearing black trunks with white stripes and waistband and his street shoes. One of those with him was putting the brown sports jacket over his impressive shoulders. As Teddy stripped he handed his clothes to Doc and he placed them on the bench. When Teddy was naked, Tim Holland handed him the white trunks with black adorns and he put them on.

"Gentlemen!" the Board's President said, walking cross-stage and nodding around. "Are you both ready?"

230

He shook hands with the champion who gave him the big smile, and then he came over and shook hands with Teddy. The photographers were motioning the others back to the sides and away from the front of the scale.

"Teddy Baker first!" the Board's Chief Inspector shouted.

Teddy walked over barefooted and stepped on the scale. The President moved the balances along the scale arms. Doc, the champion and one of his people stood watching.

"Quiet, please!" someone at the back said loudly. "We won't be able to hear."

"Eleven stone five and three quarters," the Chief Inspector shouted, having received his instruction from the President, "or one-fifty-nine and three-quarters pounds!"

There was a murmur on both the stage and in the auditorium as Teddy stepped down. Then the champion kicked his shoes off and stepped up on to the scale. He said something with a smile to the President who moved the balance back and then, watching it, moved it forward again.

"Eleven stone four and a half or one-fifty-eight and a half pounds," the Chief Inspector relayed to the throng.

"Alright, all you people," one of the photographers said. "How about stepping back now, so we can have a chance to do our work?"

They took pictures of first the champion and then Teddy on the scales, with the other watching and the Board officials behind the scales and beaming. Then they squared them off, the champion looking right at Teddy, with Teddy a little lower and looking at the champion but turned 'southpaw' so that his face would show well.

"That's enough for now," Doc said.

"One more," came the multi-voiced request.

"Come on away," Doc ordered Teddy.

When they were both dressed again, the President had both parties called over to the desk where he gave them the routine about the big crowd and the vast international TV audience and the good, clean fight coupled with the best of luck to both of them. Then he shook hands all round and left. The Chief Inspector brought in the gloves which Teddy tried on. Doc asked him how they felt and then he nodded in agreement and the Chief Inspector took the mitts from Teddy and wrote his name, beside his own signature, on the white lining inside each of them

231

"Now let's get out of here," Doc said.

"Good luck to you, my man," the champion said, nodding to Teddy.

"And the same to you."

We were waiting for a path to be cleared for us in the foyer, the crowd being so thick there, when Doctor Kaplin came out and found me. He wanted to apologise about not letting me in at the examination.

"I quite understand," I said, "Forget it."

"Listen," he said. "People have been telling me about what a story I've got. I mean, all the years I've been involved in the fight business. The fighters I've known and what they were like. We could do a magazine serialisation article."

"I'm sure we could."

"The things fighters say and the way they behave. Nobody else saw them like I did. I mean, like before fights and in the dressing-room afterwards. I've sewed up a lot of fighters, you know. You'd be surprised..."

I could see that Doc was becoming impatient; he signalled to me that he and Teddy were going.

"Yes, doctor, but right now I'm busy and tied up."

"So give me a ring later. Ring me at any time at all." He gave me his suitably embossed card.

"Right you are."

"We might make a lot of money out if it."

I left him standing there.

"Now, I wonder what he wanted?" Doc said, when we finally got away.

"Nothing really. He just wants me to make him famous and wealthy."

We had to push through the crowd on the pavement again, the voices calling to Teddy and wishing him luck. Then we walked up to Lyons Corner House and took the only vacant booth downstairs on the right. I noticed the heads turning, and the three of us had juice and eggs and coffee while Teddy had stewed prunes, two soft-boiled eggs and hot tea and one piece of toast.

Then we strolled back to the hotel and killed a couple of hours. Teddy and Tim chatted and snoozed while Doc and I played gin for a while and then joined the snoozers. Finally we all left to eat a proper last meal. We walked to a small Italian restaurant in Old Compton Street where both Doc and Teddy knew the proprietor. It was one of those places where you descend down some stairs from the pavement, and the boss was looking through the glass of the door when we arrived.

"So," he said, smiling and shaking hands with each of us. "I was afraid you weren't coming."

He was about thirty-five, slim and with a fine head of black hair and dark eyes. He wore an Oxford-grey single-breasted suit and a white shirt with a rather high, small-tabbed collar and a black knitted tie. His nails had been manicured professionally but, with it all, his face was strong.

"This is Vito," Doc said, introducing Tim Holland and me. "He's an old friend."

"Always. Excuse me, gentlemen," Vito said, and he stepped behind us and turned the lock on the door. Then he took a white card from a shelf in the cash counter and hung it against the door.

"That's so we won't be disturbed," he said to me. "We are closed at this time normally, but I keep the chef and the waiter on for Teddy and Doc."

"I'm sorry about that," Doc said.

"For what? They are only too delighted. They love Teddy."

There were about fifteen tables in the room and he led us to one back near the small bar. He pulled out a chair and held it for Teddy.

"We always come here before a fight in London," Doc said to me. "Vito's a good man and he takes good care of us. Picks out the best steaks and the best vegetables. Each morning he goes to the market himself. You'd be surprised what time he gets up."

"Four o'clock," Vito said, nodding. "You have to, if you want to get the best."

"You see?" Doc said. "Every morning, six days a week."

"I know Doc for years," Vito said, smiling on Doc. "Since he managed my brother."

"You managed his brother?" I said.

"Sure. Joey Gaze."

"I knew him; a featherweight. So he was your brother?"

"Gazeliano. Doc changed the name."

"He was a pretty good little fighter," I said.

"Only pretty good," Vito said, "but he liked to fight."

"He wasn't bad," Doc said. "He was a game, honest kid.

233

"He was older than me, so I was young and thought he was great. He would like, though, to have been the fighter that Teddy is."

"Thanks, Vito," Teddy said, smiling.

"I wish he could be here for tonight."

"Where is he?" I said.

"Down living in a place called Christchurch, near Bournemouth. When he quit the ring he found a girl, married her and now, as a hobby, he runs marathons for charity all over the place. Abroad, too. Do all you gentlemen want what Teddy gets, or shall I bring the menu?"

"Frank?"

"Let's have the same as Teddy."

"That's fine with me," Tim Holland said.

"Dino and the waiter want to say hello to Teddy. Then we'll leave you alone."

"That'll be great."

Dino appeared smiling, in his white apron and white chef's hat. He couldn't have been much over five feet tall and I reckoned him to be about sixty years old. The waiter was younger and, of course, taller and he wore a green mess jacket and dark trousers.

"So, tonight you world champion?" Dino said, shaking Teddy's hand and nodding and smiling broadly.

"God willing, Dino. I do hope."

"What, you hope? You know. You eat what Dino prepares and you become champion. Be sure."

"Then we'll all become champions," Tim Holland said.

"That's right," Dino agreed, nodding confidently at Tim. "Teddy to be the new champion tonight."

"Dino's hero as a boy was Carnera," Doc said to me.

"That's right," Dino agreed, nodding. "A good fighter; never mind what they say and the stories they tell about fixed fights."

"Yeah, he wasn't quite the bum they've made him out since," Doc said. "How about Emilio Marconi?"

"Too bad," Dino said. " Could have beaten the world."

"All you have to do to be a good fighter with Dino," Doc joked, "is to get off the plane from Italy."

"Good fighters, " Dino said. "All Italian. Duilio Loi was the best lightweight in the world for years, but they ever let him have a shot at the title. Then there was-----"

234

"So they eat now," Vito said, clapping his hands once. "Do you want something to drink, Doc, or Mr. Cutler, Mr. Holland? Something before you eat, or wine with the meal?"

"Not for me," Doc said. "Frank?"

"No. We'll play it clean, like Teddy."

We had small bowls of Minestrone soup and then went right into the steaks with broccoli and green beans. They were big steaks and Doc and I had given our best about halfway through, but Tim Holland finished his and I watched Teddy eating well until there was just one piece of meat left.

"Don't force yourself," Doc said. "If you feel that's enough, then that's enough."

"It was good," Teddy said, "but that's all I can manage."

They brought Teddy his tea then and the rest of us had coffee. While we were having that, Vito returned with three menus and a ballpoint pen.

"So, how was the steak?"

"Great," Teddy said. "Just as good as ever, Vito."

"Please, then. Would you sign these menus, one for me and one for Dino and one for Costa, the waiter?"

"Course I will."

Teddy inscribed a message and then his name on two of the menus while Vito stood over him, watching him write.

"I'm sorry, but I've forgotten the waiter's name already."

"Costa. Believe me, after the fight tonight I'll be showing this around the bar. Maybe, if you feel like it, you'll drop in."

"I can't, Vito. We're having a party in my old neighbourhood. With my old gang mates."

"I understand. Perhaps next week you'll drop in for dinner, and please bring your wife along also."

"That'd be fine."

Dino, small and plump, was standing by the door to the kitchen. The waiter was with him, smiling also, and Dino called something and Teddy waved back. Vito wished Teddy luck and invited us all to come in again as we climbed the few steps to the pavement.

"How does that little chef ever look into what he's cooking?" I said to Doc.

"You'd be surprised. You should have seen the back there. They've got a long step that runs along in front of the stoves and another one in front of the table. He steps up on that. He's a very good chef."

We walked back to the hotel and the doorman smiled and nodded to Teddy. Doc said that he wanted to get the evening papers and lie down and rest, so Tim Holland and I walked with Teddy. We must have walked almost two miles, over to Green Park and along there, stopping to look at the cars in two showrooms. The streets were in shadow now, but the tops of the tallest buildings, when we headed back, were orange in the late sun and against the blue sky and, when we got back to the room, Doc was lying on the bed, his jacket off, the papers strewn around him.

"Your wife called," he said to Teddy, getting up.

"Did she--what did she say?"

"Nothing."

"Does she want me to ring her back?"

"If it's not too much rouble."

Teddy went to the phone, dialled the number and sat down on the bed. I was trying to think of some conversation to make.

"What are you people going to do now?" I said to Doc and Tim.

"I have to meet a couple of guys in the foyer and give them their tickets." Doc said.

"I've got to meet somebody outside Solomons'," Tim Holland said. "Is that okay with you, Doc?"

"He'll take his snooze now," Doc said, nodding at Teddy who was speaking into the phone. "You don't have to be with him."

"Alright," Teddy was saying into the phone. "Okay."

He put the receiver back in its cradle and turned towards us, still sitting on the bed.

"She wants to be there tonight. She wants two tickets."

"Great," Doc said. "Why didn't she wait until seven o'clock to let you know?"

"I can't help it," Teddy said.

"This is really great," Doc said.

"No matter, Doc," I suggested. "Let's just get the tickets for her."

Doc didn't say anything.

"Does she want them left at one of the windows at Olympia?" I asked Teddy.

"I don't know. I'd be worried about that. With the crowds and all the confusion something might go wrong and she might get shut out. I'd be wondering if she got in or not."

"This beats me," Doc said.

"Look," I said. "I'll flag a cab and take a couple of tickets up to her."

"Don't be silly," Doc said.

"I'm not doing anything for the next couple of hours," I said to him. "Have you got a pair with you?"

"Only those two I've already promised."

"Will you give me those two and go up to Solomons' and get two more off Bobby Broadribb? How about that?"

Doc reached into the inside pocket of his coat which was still lying on the bed and took out his wallet. He handed me two tickets marked 'Staff' and then reached into a trouser pocket and came out with a ten pound note.

"Towards the cab."

"Don't be silly. I can claim the fare with my expenses."

"You try to take your nap," he said to Teddy.

"Alright, but I'd like to look at the papers awhile."

"You're sure you don't want me to stay with him?" Tim Holland said to Doc.

"He'd rather be alone," Doc said.

Doc had his coat on now, and he and Tim were at the door.

"I'll see you down in the bar in about an hour and a half," I said to them.

"Yep, see you there," Doc said and they went out.

"Thanks, Frank," Teddy said.

"Happy to be of service."

"I don't know why she decided to come tonight. She hasn't been to a fight in years, and now she's coming with a girl friend of hers."

"That's good."

"I'll give her a bell and tell her you're bringing the tickets up."

He dialled the number and I went into the bathroom to freshen up. When I came out he had taken his jacket off and had slipped out of his slip-ons. He was trying to straighten out the three afternoon newspapers, the Star, News and Standard, jumbled on the bed and on the floor.

"She has to go out for an hour," he said, "so you can wait awhile."

"Righto."

He was still trying to sort out the papers.

"That Doc," he said. "I like to read a neat paper. When I read it, I keep it neat."

"That has to be the way you're made."

"Doc is so precise about everything to do with boxing, but he throws the papers around and almost destroys them."

"It could be in contempt."

He took one paper, turned to the sports section and lay down on the bed. I took one of the others and sat in the chair to read it.

"It says here the other man is seven to five," Teddy said.

"That's what it says here too."

When he finished the first paper and put it down I took it and put the one I had been reading on the bed beside him.

"Well," he said, "your friend Trev Wignall picks me."

"But not because he's my friend."

"That Dave Caldwell picks the other fellow."

"You had to expect that."

"Ernie Jarvis picks the other bloke, too."

"He works in league with Caldwell."

"I know. He told me that at the weigh-in, but I think he'd have picked the other guy anyway."

There was a knock at the door and Teddy looked up from the paper.

"See who it is, will you?" he said.

I got up and partly opened the door. Alf Penny was standing there, a patch of white bandage and tape bulky over his left eye

"Hello," he said, "can I come in?"

"Of course. Come on in, Alf."

He walked into the room and looked around, then he put his hands in his pockets.

"How are you, Alf?" Teddy said, sitting up. "That was quite a fight."

"Can I see you a minute, Teddy?"

"Sure you can."

"I'll leave you alone," I said.

"No," Teddy said and then to Penny: "You want to see me alone?"

"Yeah, really."

"Then we'll go into the bathroom," Teddy said.

He stood up and led Penny into the bathroom. Penny turned and closed the door behind them. In less than a minute they came out.

"I'll see you," Penny said, and left without looking towards me.

"What's the matter with him?" I said.

"This," Teddy said, and he handed me something. As it dropped into my hand I could see it was a ring. Then I turned it over and saw that it was a man's gold ring with a ruby set in it.

"What's this?" I said, and then it came to me. "Was this Waller's?"

"I'm afraid so."

"How about that? So it was Penny after all."

"That's right. I didn't think he took it, either."

"You know I didn't think so. Whatever made him bring it back now?"

"Who knows?"

I handed the ring back to Teddy and he looked at it.

"What did he say?"

"I don't really know. He said he doesn't know why he did it. He said he was going to take it to a pawnbroker's and then bet the cash on me in the fight. Then he said that today he decided to give it back instead."

"What did you say to all this?"

"Oh, I dunno. I think I said: 'Thanks, Alf.' What else could I say?"

"Nothing. I think I'd better take those tickets up now."

"You know where it is?"

"Sure. I met you there the day we went down to the Barley Mow."

"I forgot that. Thanks a lot, Frank."

"Think nothing of it."

I told the cabbie where I wanted to go and made him feel better by telling him that he could wait for me and bring me back. He cleverly used sideroads to avoid the main evening rush-hour traffic and worked the journey off that, so that we made much better time than I had thought we would.

"Just leave the engine running," I said when I alighted, "because I won't even be going into the house."

There was a light in the living-room, but I had to ring the bell twice before she came to the door. She was wearing grey slacks and a light blue sweater.

"Your tickets, madame," I said, handing them to her.

"Oh hello," she said. "Thanks, thanks a lot."

"Don't thank me. I got them from Doc."

"And broke his heart, I'll bet!"

"Oh, I wouldn't say that. Anyway, you know I'll be rooting hard for all of you tonight. Teddy'll be fine."

"Thanks," she said.

Oh well, I thought when I got back to the cab, I tried anyway. At the hotel I went into the bar and was half-way through a drink when Doc and Tim Holland came in. Doc ordered a Scotch, straight with ice, and Tim asked for a Coke.

"Are you all straightened out?" I asked Doc.

"Ah. Tickets cause more trouble than the opponent. I'm sorry you had to get involved with that."

"You were right about Alf Penny."

"What about him?"

"He came up to see Teddy and he gave him Waller's ring back."

"He did?"

"That's right."

"When?"

"Shortly after you two left. I should apologise to my candidate, Ceroni."

"How about that no-good bum?"

"What happened?" Tim Holland said.

I explained it to him and he kept on shaking his head.

"So what did he give it back for?" Doc demanded. "He'd already put one over."

"God alone knows," I said. "I like to feel that, this day of the big fight, he felt something pulling him for Teddy. Penny's a nutcase and a rogue, but when today dawned he maybe felt something. He found out he's on your side. That's just my theory, of course."

"Who needs him?" Doc said.

240

"That's so," Tim Holland said. "This is some business we're in."

"Yes, but aren't you wrong about this business? If anything, it led him to give the ring back and that gook guts."

"Let's have one more drink," Doc suggested. "I could use another one."

"If we can sit down and you'll take yours with water, I don't want you drinking it straight."

"I could drink a whole bottle tonight and still be sober as a judge," Doc said.

I paid for the drinks at the bar and we went to a small black-topped table in a corner of the dark room. Doc went out once to be sure the phone was cut off in Teddy's room and we nursed that second drink for over half-an-hour. Then we ordered again and we nursed those.

"How do you feel?" I said to Doc, finally.

"How do you think? Forty-five years comes down to one night."

"I know. I don't know what I'm doing getting involved with un-nice people like you and that fighter of yours. Right now I'd like to walk out of here and go to some remote bar and get drunk and not even see the fight. I'd read about it tomorrow."

"Believe me, I'd do just that if I were you."

"I don't believe you."

"For four years I've watched that other guy live or on TV every time I could. I knew they'd move him into that title. If he can find a way to lick Edward tonight it just doesn't add up. Forty-five years don't add up, either. There has got to come a time in that ring tonight when that other feller will know that there's nothing he can do to win. When he knows it he'll show it and everybody everywhere will know it. That will be the moment."

"It'll be what is known as his 'Moment of Truth', I said.

"There's Teddy now," Tim Holland said.

Teddy was standing near the bar. A nicely-dressed young man, with a girl, had turned on his bar-stool and was holding his hand out to Teddy. Teddy avoided the hand by placing his two hands on the other's shoulders and saying something. Then he turned and came over to our table so we made room for him and he sat down.

"What's the matter with you?" Doc said.

"Nothing. I rested and then came looking for you people."

241

"Did you manage to drop off?"

"I don't honestly know but I think so. I feel fine."

Under the slim, subdued lighting in the dark room I could see heads turning at the bar to look at him. Both the bartenders were watching him, too.

"It's about time to leave for Olympia, isn't it?" he said.

"What time is it?" Doc asked.

"Up there," Teddy said, pointing. "It's nearly a quarter past seven."

Where he pointed there was a clock on the wall above and behind the bar. It was set flat into the dark wall, just gilded hands and some rectangular markers for the numbers, that part of the wall serving as the face of the clock.

"In a few minutes," Doc said. "We've got time because you're not expected 'til the first pair are in the ring."

"I got the tickets to Mary," I said to Teddy.

"Oh, thanks. I buzzed her again and she said you were there. She put the boy on the phone."

"How is he?"

"Just fine. Mary promised him I'd buy him something tomorrow."

"He didn't want you to guess the name of his playmate's cousin?"

"No," Teddy said, smiling. "Thank God he forgot that."

The young man came over from the bar with a postcard for Teddy to sign. Then a woman approached with a hotel menu for signature.

"We might as well get out of here," Doc said.

"I'll go up and get the bags," Tim Holland said.

Eddie signed a few more cards and then we moved into the foyer. Teddy stood at the news-stand, scanning the front-page headlines and looking at the magazine covers until Tim came down carrying the two zipper bags.

"Get us a cab, please," Doc said to the doorman outside the main entrance.

"Right away, sir," he replied, whistling for the first cab on the rank to come forward.

"Olympia, Stage Door," Doc instructed the cabbie, and he followed Teddy into the back seat. "Go along the Embankment and move in over the bridge. That'll land you at the side of the building we want."

242

"Thanks and be lucky, Teddy", the doorman said, closing the door.

Tim and I were on the jump seats, back to the driver and divided from him by a glass partition. At a corner the driver had to stop for traffic lights and he pulled the partition back. No sooner had he got going again then he had to halt at a pedestrian crossing.

"You fellas goin' to the fight?" he asked.

"Yes," I answered.

"I only hope it's a good one," he said. "Most of them they've been putting on lately have been real stinkers. Lousy."

XXV

When we stepped out of the cab on to the kerb I could feel the surface tension that held the crowd. Invisible, untouchable, nowhere but everywhere, fragile but all-imprisoning, I have felt it hold paratroopers before a jump, prison inhabitants before an execution, a courtroom before a jury's verdict in a big case, a household before a moment of death. Now it held this crowd, the milling restless bodies on the pavement and the still bodies and turning faces, black and white alike, packed in the rows of seats. It held the mounted police and horses walking the gutters and confined the low murmur, rent only by emergency sirens and car horns, that is distinctive of fight mobs. Inside Olympia and within three hours, perhaps a little more or a little less, something would happen and then this thinnest unseen film of oneness would burst and it would all come out.

"There's Teddy Baker!.........."Hey, Teddy!".........."Teddy Baker!".........."Teddy, you're my boy!"............."Nail him, Teddy!".........."Get Lucky Teddy!".........."Go get him, Teddy!"

We pushed a way through quickly, Doc and Tim leading the way, Teddy with his head down, the crowd parting and calling. Ahead of us, the guard on the 'Stage Door, Artistes only' entrance signalled and his satellite opened the door, at the same time stepping quickly aside to let us by. Then some man shook his finger at Teddy, and called after him.

"Now then, Teddy! I got a lot of cash restin' on you. Just remember that, Teddy."

In the restless movement inside the old building, crowded and excited, there were shouts and waves from unknown faces, jumping and shoving in their effort to see the arrival of the challenger. And then we were out of it, walking the long grey catacomb and into the dressing-room at the Hammersmith end. Behind us the uniformed guard closed the door.

This is the place, I was thinking, the grey walls and the steel lockers, the rubbing-table in the middle of the rectangular cell, the benches against the walls. There it is, the door to the toilet and shower, and that is all.

"They keep it too warm in here," Teddy said, looking around.

"It's good," Doc said. "Take off your coat."

"Here, I'll take it," Tim Holland said.

"Doc!" the uniformed guard said, his head through the partially opened door, "There's somebody out here."

Doc went to the door and looked out. The door opened and Ray came in, wearing a dark blue suit and forcing a smile.

"How are you, son?" he said, walking up to Teddy.

"Fine," Teddy said. He was sitting on one of the benches. "Very good. I thought you'd come up to the hotel."

"I couldn't. My old lady's sick, so when I got away from the place I went over to see her. I'd rather see you here, anyway."

"That's great."

"Very different from the first fight I put you in, eh?" Ray said, looking around and, sort of, saying it to the room and then sitting down next to Teddy.

"True," Teddy agreed. "Remember that night?"

"The whole mob's here. They all send their best wishes."

"Thanks, Ray. Tell them thanks."

"So we'll be in after the fight and we'll all go over together, eh? You're all invited," Ray said to the rest of us. "A real party."

"Cheers, Ray," I said.

"I'd better go," he said, standing up and looking down at Teddy and touching him on the shoulder. "Good luck, champ."

"Many thanks."

"We're all with you and we're not worried, either. You'll lick him."

"I'll see you, Ray," Teddy said, looking up at him. "Don't be anxious."

"Who's anxious?"

244

Ray left then. Doc was hanging his jacket in one of the lockers and Tim Holland was hanging Teddy's gown on a hanger over an open locker door. It was a dark-blue satin robe with white collar and cuffs and the name 'Teddy Baker' in bold white letters on the back. He took two white seconds' jackets out of the other bag and then be began placing his gauze and tape on the rubbing-table.

"Here," Doc said to Teddy, handing him the new white woollen socks, the ring shoes and a pair of long, new yellow laces. "You might as well start on this."

It is a time-killer that some of them use. Teddy took the old laces out of the shoes and then, slowly and carefully, he started threading a new lace into one shoe. He flattened the lace at each turn, always measuring the two ends. He did half-a-dozen turns, and then put the shoe on the bench beside him and started on the other.

The guard opened the door and the Board President came in, followed by the Chief Inspector and Solomons himself. Teddy stood up when the President made formal introductions to both himself and Doc, the smile never leaving the top man's face.

"There's a fine crowd out there, Baker," Nipper Read said. "So the best of luck to you and, please, do us all proud."

"Thank you."

The Chief Inspector, Andy Cunningham, and the promoter gave similar salutations, each smiling all the while. They were still smiling and puffing hefty cigars when they walked out, nodding to the guard, who tipped his cap in salute, as they went.

"Committee men and impresarios," Doc said. "Most everything that's wrong in the business you can blame on them. Self-appointed experts who know nothing."

Teddy sat down again and slipped out of his loafers then took off his socks. Tim Holland took them and put them in the locker and Teddy pulled on the new, white woollen socks. Then he put on the left ring shoe, swung around on the bench and put that foot up on it and carefully and slowly laced it. When he reached the top, he brought the laces around the back to the front again, certain that they were flat, and then knotted them. Tim Holland bent down and cut the laces near the knot with his gauze and tape scissors. Then he cut a length of the tape and handed it to Teddy, who placed it around the shoe near the top so it covered the laces. And, in front of the knot, he smoothed it so that it made a neat white band. Then he put on the right shoe and started on that.

Tim's brother came in, carrying a pail with a bottle in it, the bottle freshly taped around its neck. He couldn't have been more than twenty-five or twenty-six years old and he smiled and nodded around the room.

"Hi," Teddy said, looking up.

"Hiya Teddy, Doc."

"Make some strips of that tape, Joe," Tim said to him.

"Where do you want them?"

"All along the edge of that table. Make some extras, too."

"What are you doing there?" Doc said, looking down at Teddy.

"It's Nat's ring," Teddy said. He had laced the second shoe up to the last pair of eyelets and now he held the ring up to Doc in the palm of his hand. Doc took it, turned it over and looked at it.

"What are you doing with it?"

"I thought I'd just put it on the lace. It won't be in the way and I thought I'd carry it for luck."

"Never mind that luck stuff," Doc said, still holding the ring. "You know better than that."

"I know. I just thought of it this afternoon in the room, that Nat was with me for all those fights."

"Put it on if you want to," Doc said, handing the ring back to Teddy and walking away. "I don't care what you do with it."

Teddy looked at me and smiled and shrugged. He put one end of the lace through the ring, crossed the laces and put the ends through the last two eyelets and finished the shoe. Holland cut the ends and handed him another length of tape.

When he finished with the tape he stood up and walked around, the shoes squeaking a little. Then he did a couple of deep knee-bends, letting his heels come up off the floor, the weight forward on his feet to settle them into the shoes.

"What bout's on now?" he said.

"The second prelim was just starting when I came in," Tim's brother told him."

"That'll be Lefty, won't it?"

"Guess so. I watched him climb in."

"Find out how it goes, I mean when it's over, will you?"

"Course I will."

Now and then we could hear the crowd noise, distant and low. When Tim's brother finished stripping the tape and sticking the ends to the side of the rubbing-table he went out. In about five minutes he came back.

"Lefty won it on points."

"Good," Teddy said, still walking. "Was it a good fight?"

"I don't know. I only saw the last round and a half. Some of the crowd were booing and calling for more action."

"Dreadful," Doc said.

"Put Lefty in your story, will you." Teddy said to me. "He's a great guy."

One of the Board's Area Inspectors came in. He had a clipboard in his hand and, on his face, was the harassed look that all subordinates wear at such times. He nodded around the room in greeting.

"When are you going to tape?" he said to Doc. "It's about time."

"I'll begin now," Doc said. "Tell one of the other man's people to come in."

"I have to stay here with you."

"I'm going down there to watch," Tim Holland said. "I'll tell him."

"And you stay right there with them until they've got the gloves on in the ring," Doc said. "We'll see you down there."

"Right. Joe'll get some ice for you later."

"He doesn't have to stay there," the Area Inspector said. "Once the bandages and tape are on and stamped and initialled he can come back."

"He can stay, as well."

"But why?"

"Because I'm protecting my fighter."

"Have it your way," The Inspector, who was an ex-fighter himself, said, shrugging to me and sitting down on the bench.

Joe moved the tape and gauze to one side and Teddy hoisted himself up on to the rubbing-table, his feet dangling. A couple of minutes after Tim had gone, the champion's man came in, tall and dark, nodding and smiling and big-voiced.

"Mr Teddy Baker, gentlemen, gentlemen, gentlemen."

Since Robinson and George Gainford, I was thinking, they all want to play it the same. They've even got it right down to the voice inflection.

247

Doc started on the right hand, the clean white gauze around the wrist, down and around the hand and back between the fingers and around the hand. One roll of gauze and a small piece of tape to hold it, the narrow strips pinched once in the middle, between the fingers, and then he walked away and opened a locker door and reached for one of the two long strips of tape hanging there.

"Wait a minute," the champion's man said, in that big voice of his.

"Are you in trouble?" Doc said, one hand on one of the strips of tape and turning to look at the champion's man

"Let the gentleman measure it in front of me."

The Inspector took a tape-measure from his pocket, pulled it out and measured the first strip He could see that they were both of the same length.

"Correct," he said. "Exactly."

"Still feeling ill?" Doc said.

"I just go by the Rules, the champion's man said.

"And what do you think I go by?"

"Alright, gents," The Inspector said.

Teddy shrugged to me and Doc finished that hand with the tape, Teddy opening and closing the hand, and then Doc did the other similarly. When he had finished with the second he motioned to Teddy, who held both hands out towards the champion's man and turned them, the white bulks on them beautifully done, palms both up and down.

"Okay with you?" the Inspector said.

"Alright," the champion's man replied.

"That's fine," the Inspector said. He produced a small ink-pad and stamp, and he stamped blue wording across the tape and bandage on the back of each hand. Then he took out a ball-point pen and wrote his initials underneath the imprint on each hand.

"I'll be seeing you gentlemen later," the champion's man said, affecting a bow, and then he left.

"The sob," Doc said. "Dreadful; that's amateur stuff. Get your things off."

Teddy slid off the table and, alternating hands, drove one fist into the palm of the other two or three times. Then he loosened his belt and dropped his slacks. He sat down on the bench and Joe pulled the slacks off and hung them in a locker. Then he helped Teddy out of his shirt and Teddy shed his underwear. Next, walking across the room naked except for the ring-shoes and socks and the bandages on his hands, he hung those up. Then he went into the toilet.

When he emerged he put on the supporter and Doc handed him the white shorts with black adorns and he put those on. With the cup under them they seemed too loose, and he started to move around, first doing deep-knee bends, then rotating arms and shoulders and finally shadow-boxing. In the still of the enclosed place, disturbed only by occasional muffled crowd noise, one could hear the squeak of the ring-shoes and then Teddy's breathing starting to come rhythmically.

Doc stood to one side, never taking his eyes off Teddy, and Tim's brother went out and returned carrying another pail filled with chunks of ice. He waited for Teddy to move by and then carried it into the toilet. I could hear him cracking the ice against the washbowl before he came out for the ice-bag and disappeared back in.

"How are you keeping these days?" the Inspector said, coming over to me.

"I'm fine. And you?"

"I don't know, " he said, dropping his voice. "He's looking good, isn't he?"

"Teddy? Yes, he certainly is."

"You think he'll win?"

"Yes, I do."

"Me, I should be up in the Lake District as of now."

"Why?"

"I got a cottage up there. We like to go there at week-ends, but how can I do it with end-of-the-week fights? These people that come here, they pay big money for ringside and big money right down through the house. I just don't understand it because no fight is worth it. I suppose I've seen too many stumers."

Teddy moved by us now, his face set, head down, hooking and then hooking again. Then he turned smoothly and started back and I could see a little sweat just starting to break out on him. I looked at my watch and it said just after a quarter to ten; I walked over to where Doc stood, arms folded in front of him, watching Teddy like a hawk.

"The sweat looks good," I said. "He looks in peak condition."

"He's never been far off in seven years," Doc said with pride. "When you come to the last step it shouldn't be any steeper than the rest."

"How do you feel yourself?"

"Rotten."

He signalled to Teddy who stopped his warm-up and moved over to him, breathing deeply. Doc took a towel off the rubbing-table and quickly wiped Teddy's face and then he wiped chest, back and arms and, bending down, the legs. He gestured at the rubbing-table, where young Joe had spread two clean white towels. Another was folded at the head end and Teddy hoisted himself up and lay on his back. Doc took yet another clean towel and placed it over Teddy's chest, and then he got the gown and spread it over the fighter.

"I'd like a towel over my eyes," Teddy said.

He was lying directly under the ceiling light, eyes shut, and Doc folded another towel and placed it over Teddy's forehead and eyes. Teddy just lay there, relaxed, the gown moving up and down with his breathing.

"How did the warm-up feel?" Doc said.

"A little stiff in the shoulders and thighs. Not exactly stiff, but not loose, either."

"That's okay," Doc affirmed.

Teddy lay there for over five minutes, his breathing quieting. Doc had come over and was sitting on the bench next to me.

"What the hell can I tell him?" he asked in a low voice, not really as a question, but rather as a statement of fact.

"Absolutely nothing."

"In seven years I've told him everything. He's ready. The last thing I'll remind him of in the corner is not to let the other guy back him up. In the first round he'll find his distance, then he'll either do it or he won't. There's nothing I can do about it now."

"That's right. Just remember that yourself."

We heard the door open and the clang of the timekeeper's bell and the crowd.

"Last round coming up before you're on!" the guard said, sticking his head in and announcing it: "Main event with Teddy Baker next!"

Teddy sat up, the gown sliding to his legs, and Doc got up. Teddy slid off the table and Doc wiped him again with a towel.

250

Then he helped Teddy out of his trunks so that he could visit the toilet.

"You're sure you've got everything?" Doc said to Tim's brother. "All my gear and Tim's?"

"I've got it all."

He had on his white seconds' jacket and Doc went to the locker and put on his. Teddy came back from the loo and Tim's brother helped him step into his cup and pull it up. Then Doc helped him get into his trunks and he moved around, swinging and flexing his head on that fine neck and rotating his shoulders, until he saw Doc holding the gown. Then he put his arms back and Doc lifted the gown up on to him and, walking round him, tied it in the front.

"You're on! Main event! Teddy Baker!" the guard shouted holding the door open, and we could hear the rising, expectant murmuring of the crowd.

"That's us," Inspector Goldberg said. "Let's go."

"All the best, Teddy," I said as he went by.

"Thanks Frank," he said, looking at me quickly, his face very serious.

I followed them out and waited for promoter Solomons to appear with his pocket red-light torch which he used to signal the lighting crew to start the fanfare of trumpets. It came and down the aisle they went behind the police cordon. The crowd noise was near-deafening now, together with the hysterical cries for Teddy and, when they passed my seat, I took one more look at Doc's back and climbed over the back of my seat. Dave Caldwell was sitting on my left.

"Hello," he rasped in an alcoholic voice. "How are things?"

"Fine. And with you?"

"So-so. I suppose you still fancy our boy to win?"

"Indeed I do."

"Well, I don't."

"So I gather. I read your piece today."

"I think he'll get well beaten."

The crowd was still noisy for Teddy when the second fanfare heralded the champion into the ring to our left. He vaulted the ropes with a flourish, his head towel-hooded and his satin robe flying, his arms held up to acknowledge the crowd, the noise swelling then for him. One of the Board's people was bringing the

251

gloves to Teddy's corner to our right and I saw Doc, leaning on the ropes and squinting through his rimless glasses at the other man. Then he was bending over Teddy, who was on the stool before standing up and putting his weight down into one glove, as Doc held it, and then the other. Then he sat down again for the lacing.

"You see that," Dave Caldwell said. "Look what he's got there on his shoe."

"What's that got to do with the fight?"

"A ring. He's got a ring on the lace of his right shoe."

"I know all about that."

"He doesn't even trust that great Doc Eastlake with his jewellery while he's in the ring."

"I was there when he put it on. Do you want to know what it's all about?"

"Don't tell me. You can have your Doc if you want him; I don't have to want him."

It will be enough if you knock him out, Teddy, I was thinking, but it would be more if you could pull if off the way Doc said and drop him face to face with Caldwell. I know it's impossible, but please do it.

""....and a former Middleweight Champion of the World...." Patsy Haygate, the famous Master of Ceremonies, was announcing.

By the time he was through with the introductions the gloves were on. I saw Tim Holland leave the other corner and walk across to Teddy's. Now he was on one knee in front of Teddy, who had first one foot up and then the other, so that Tim could scar the soles of the boots with the points of his scissors. Then the house lights were doused and we stood, and I watched Teddy standing in an eternity while the National Anthems were played. First came 'The Star-Spangled Banner' and then, to a mighty roar of approval, followed 'God Save the Queen.'

"Fifteen rounds for the Middleweight Championship of the World. On my right, wearing black trunks with white stripes, from New York City, scaling eleven stone four and a half pounds, the undefeated champion....

"And, on my left, his challenger, wearing white trunks with black stripes, his record showing only three defeats in ninety bouts, scaling eleven stone five and three quarter pounds, from Lambeth, South East London, your very own Teddy Baker..."

252

The referee was giving his final instructions now, and then they touched gloves and turned and Tim Holland slid the gown off Teddy's shoulders as they walked back to the corner. Doc had one leg outside the ropes and one still inside them when the timekeeper called 'Seconds Out.' Doc slipped the gumshield into Teddy's mouth, saying one last thing, shouting it at Teddy to be heard in the din. Teddy's face was stony, looking across at his opponent and then the bell clanged and Doc slapped Teddy on the back.

Gloves up, elbows in, weight slightly forward and poised for action, Teddy walked out of that corner.

XXVI

It was all over in two minutes forty-eight seconds.

Teddy moved forward slowly, gloves poised and feinting automatically, his head down and eyeing the other out of the tops of his eyes. He was beautiful. He never wasted a motion and the champion met him in mid-ring, high on his toes, head-feinting and hand-feinting, the feints ignored, and then snapping out the jab once, twice.

The first one Teddy took high on his forehead and the second one he slipped over his right shoulder and, in the same move, he brought his own jab up and in. He reached the champion, perfectly placed, between the eyes, but the champion was moving away, jabbing twice more, lithe, still high on his toes. Teddy followed him and then, taking the jabs high as the champion hooked off the next jab, Teddy slipped under it and threw his own hook, hard from the low-hand position, to the body.

The champion dropped his right arm across his body and managed to deflect some of the force of it on to his elbow. Then, in too close, he reached to tie Teddy up, but the challenger got both hands up inside, high on the champion's chest and he pushed his rival off.

With this, the crowd noise rose to a roar and the champion now took his time. He was moving, but occupying the centre of the ring. He jabbed twice and, still head-feinting, faked to move to his left but, instead, circled to his right. Teddy took one step to his own left and he had the champion in front of him again. The champion again faked to move to his left, feinting to jab, but this time he made the move. For that brief part of a moment he had the position on Teddy, but Teddy dropped lower and made the one step to his own right and they were even-steven once more.

I looked at the champion's face and I could see him thinking. Just look at this, all of you, I was thinking. See it. Teddy Baker is building beautifully. He is building slowly, perfectly, the firm foundation. Oh, please see this.

The champion shot out two jabs, still backing off, the first one short but the second one getting home. Teddy stalked him and they exchanged jabs, the champion's whipping out straight, Teddy's coming upwards and in again. Now the champion was almost in a fencing pose, his stance more narrow with the line of the right foot closer to the line of the left but suddenly, as Teddy jabbed, the champion stepped to his right and then, as Teddy led, the champion stepped further to his right leading with the right foot, and threw a right hook over the jab. Teddy twisted underneath it and, as he took the blow back behind the ear, he fired his own right counter into the body. As it carried his weight on to the left foot, he came back with a terrific left hook to the same place.

This was the moment and now it came. Those punches drove the champion back and I saw the hurt, bewildered look on his face that they all carry when faced with the truth, and Teddy threw a follow-up overhand right to the head.

This was the moment indeed and I heard the roar of the crowd and, as suddenly, I realised that all the excitement, all the desire so long controlled, had come out in that right hand but that Teddy was too far out.

The punch missed. Whether it missed by an eighth of an inch or a quarter does not matter. It missed by Teddy's nine years of fighting and by Doc's forty-something years in the game and by all the years all of us have lived. When it missed, it carried all of Teddy's weight to his left foot, off balance because, finally and just once, he tried too soon for too much. He started trying to bring himself back to his right. As he did the champion, bouncing off the ropes, that same look on his face, let his right hand go because this was not the place of his choosing, or the time either, but he knew of nothing else to do.

The punch hit Teddy while his left foot was off the floor. It hit him on the left temple and he went down on his rump, the back of his head hitting the canvas. The crowd was on its feet behind me, screaming, and he fell right in front of me and Dave Caldwell. He rolled over on to his left side brought his legs around behind him and raised himself on to his knees, both gloves pressed to the canvas in front of him. He shook his head. He was alright but he was shaking his head.

Referee Gibbs was on one knee beside him, his right arm tolling off the seconds. Again Teddy shook his head, snapping it violently. He was okay. He was strong.

"....four,....five,....six..."

He was getting up now, reaching for the rope just above us. I saw the champion in the neutral corner across the ring and now Teddy was up and seemingly searching the ring, the whole arena in uproar, then shaking his head again. Now the referee was wiping both Teddy's gloves on his shirt, looking into Teddy's face and then he stepped back to one side and gave the order 'Box On.'

In the bedlam of noise Teddy moved forward but uncertainly, hands low and head tucked behind the left shoulder. As the champion moved out to meet him, right hand cocked, Teddy veered to his own right and started away from him, now quite strongly but strangely, now searching again. When he did, the champion moved around in front of him. Teddy's brains must still have been scrambled when the champion let another right hand go.

This time Teddy fell forward on his face and I and everyone else knew that it was all over. The referee was kneeling, tolling, and I saw that fine body lying there, writhing, trying desperately to get up, just the very first sweat on it, just what should have been the beginning of the quest for the summit. There was so much that body and mind could do together, better than all others. Why couldn't it have been given its chance?

"....nine....out!"

"I told you," Caldwell said, yelling it at me above the cheering and the booing of the crowd. "He's a bum!"

Doc was the first one to him, removing his gum shield, and now the referee was back with him and the doctor was there with Tim Holland. They had him first sitting up and then standing up, holding him under the armpits. He was trying to shake them off but they held him there, the head still searching and, when it turned towards me, I saw the stare of a sleep-walker.

"He doesn't even know where he is," Caldwell said, above the booing that was stronger now than the cheers for the champion, who was now dancing around the ring gloves above his head, his people trying to grab him and hoist him aloft.

They walked Teddy to the corner and he sat there some minutes, his gown over him, the group around him, the boos still coming from upstairs while Patsy Haygate made his announcement and held the champion's hand high for the photographers Then Tim Holland held the bottom ropes down with one foot and the top ropes up with both hands, and Doc and Doctor Kaplin helped Teddy climb gingerly through them. I climbed over the back of my chair and pushed through the crowd at ringside and saw Teddy, his gown loosely draped over him, unable to find the first step down and stumble. They held on to him, though, and I fought my way behind them through the crowd.

"Hey, Carroll!" someone in the mob close to them was screaming. "He's a bum! You're both bums!"

The fight itself had lasted two minutes and forty-eight seconds, including the final count.

XXVII

We stood, almost silently, about two dozen of us outside the dressing-room door. I saw Ray talking to the uniformed guard and that worthy shaking his head, and I saw Freddie and the rest of them from the neighbourhood. I scanned their faces and turned away. As I did, Lefty Flynn saw me and walked over. He had on that grey suit and a clean white T-shirt underneath it and he was carrying his zipper bag.

"Will he be alright?" he said and there seemed to be even fear in his eyes.

"I don't know but I'm sure he will. I can't get in right now."

"He was gonna lick him sure, Mr Cutler."

"I know, but these things happen."

Lefty dropped his head and half turned away.

"Are you okay, son?"

He was crying. He took a clean white handkerchief out of his pocket and blew his nose.

"I'll be fine."

"Good man."

"He was well on top of him, Mr Cutler."

"He was indeed, Lefty."

"He couldn't lose. That was an accident."

"I know"

"Why do the others always get the luck?"

"I can't answer that one."

"But do you think he'll be alright? There was something wrong with him when he got up the first time."

"I think he'll be fine."

"Will you do me a favour?"

"Certainly."

"I can't get in there so I'll have to wait to hear. When you come out, will you tell me truthfully how he is?"

"Surely, Lefty."

"Thank you, Mr. Cutler. I'll wait right over there."

Dave Caldwell walked towards me, then stopped and gave me that authoritative, over-the-shoulder motion with his head. I shifted over to him.

"The ceiling fell in on the plasterer's son," he said. "I warned you."

"Yes."

"They're not letting us in?"

"Not yet awhile."

"I'll get in."

And, with that, he pushed through the crowd around the door. I saw him talking to the guard and then getting excited, but the guard stood shielding the door with his body and shaking his head. Then Caldwell was pushing back out to me.

"A fine goddam thing," he snorted. "I'll fix them. I'll show 'em they don't do that to me."

With that the door opened and the doctor appeared. He stood on the step, the door slightly ajar behind him, the Press Association man, a man from Reuter's, a morning paper man and Ray in the front, all of them trying to look around the doctor and into the room.

"How is he?" someone down front said and the crowd hushed.

"He should be alright," the doctor said. "He's still bothered by what I'll call jarred vision--there isn't any exact term for it."

"Any term for what?"

"Jarred vision."

"His eyes are jarred? How do you know his eyes are jarred?"

"I didn't say his eyes are jarred; I said his vision is jarred, and just temporarily."

"What do you mean by that?"

"We don't get this at all."

"Well, that first punch that hit him, that knocked him down the first time--either that or when his head hit the floor, or maybe both--was the cause. The result is he's experiencing trouble focusing. Probably you noticed that when he got up the first time and couldn't regain his direction."

"Is that what was wrong with him?"

"Yes. You very rarely see this, but that's what happened to him. It may be caused by any one or more of three things; the ocular muscles may be out of kilter, the balancing mechanism in his ear may be disturbed or there may be an injury to the brain, cerebral, through I doubt that here."

"Is there any chance he'll be blind?"

"Definitely none."

"Has he got concussion?"

"Certainly, but hopefully only a slight one. Every fighter who gets knocked out through a blow to the head suffers a concussion. I'm confident he'll be alright."

"But what about his eyes--or his vision?"

"It'll be alright. It'll straighten out."

"How soon?"

"Any time. I expect when he relaxes."

"Is he going to hospital?"

"No. I think he'll be well enough just to go back to his hotel room."

"So let us in then," Dave Caldwell said.

"In a few minutes. Not right now."

"What do you mean, not right now?"

"In a few minutes, all the press will get in if they wish."

"What are you trying to do, giving that Eastlake time to come up with an excuse? Send the manager out here."

258

"He's with the fighter."

"I don't care who he's with. Send him out here."

"Just be patient," the doctor said. "You'll all get in."

He went back into the dressing-room and closed the door and the guard moved back in front if it. The Reuter and Press Association men pushed out and past us and ran down the aisle towards ringside.

"A fine goddam thing," Caldwell said, making an announcement of it. "That phony Eastlake. Before the fight they can't get enough publicity. They want you to write about them. Now he doesn't want to talk, but I'll write about him. I'll write plenty."

"Why don't you shut up?" a voice said.

It was Freddie from Teddy's old neighbourhood and he was looking straight at Caldwell.

"What?"

"You make too much noise. Why don't you shut up?"

"Take it easy, Freddie," I said.

"I don't care about this jerk," Freddie said. "Who does he think he is with that stinking column of his? Just keep your mouth shut round here, mister."

Caldwell turned his back on Freddie. He took out a cigarette and lit it.

"Christ, he's a yella bum," I could hear Freddie saying to someone.

"I'm not going to be stood up out here any longer," Caldwell said to me. "For what?"

He stalked off.

Charlie Hull, of the American agency, Associated Press, came up from ringside, Ernie Jarvis with him. I saw Charlie Mahoney, with Ceroni trailing him, hurrying towards us, calling to Jarvis, but when he saw me he stopped

"Too bad about Teddy," he said.

"Yes, but that's the way it goes in this business."

"I didn't think it would be like that. Something must have happened to him."

"Something did."

"What did you think of Joe last week?"

"He was alright. You were okay, Joe."

"Thanks." Ceroni said, nodding to me.

259

"It's like I told you. He'll be the next welterweight champion. If you want to do that article about him, you let me know. Alright?"

"Agreed."

He took Ceroni by one arm and was trying to get through the crowd to Ernie Jarvis when I saw Mary. She was standing at the edge of the crowd with another woman of about the same age and she was wearing a long, loose red coat, open, and I could see a black dress underneath it. They were both watching the door.

"Mary," I said, having walked up to her "I'm so sorry."

She had just turned to look at me when the door opened and the crowd quieted on seeing the doctor emerge. As a man the crowd pushed forward.

"Only the press," the doctor said. "Just the newspapermen."

" Show your press ticket stubs," the uniformed guard was saying.

"You want to get in, don't you? I asked Mary.

"Yes, but I don't suppose they'll let met."

"Follow me."

"Will you wait for me?" she said to her friend.

"Of course I will," the friend said. "Certainly."

We pushed through the crowd, the guard weeding the others out. A photographer, his camera held high, ahead of me, Mary being pushed against my back. When we reached the door I showed my ticket stub and moved aside to let Mary in ahead of me.

"Press only, lady," the guard said, putting his arm across the door in front of her.

"This is Teddy Baker's wife," I explained.

"I'm sorry," the guard said shaking his head, his arm still in place across the door "Just the press."

"For God's sake. This is Teddy Baker's wife."

"You heard me, mate. I've got my orders. Press only. I'm sorry."

I turned back to say something to Mary but she had turned and was pushing her way back out through the crowd. Another photographer was trying to get by me now, so I turned, almost stumbling over the step, and I was in.

Teddy was sitting on the bench, naked with just a towel across his lap, his head down. Doc was sitting on one side of him and Tim Holland was on the other. When Doc saw me he got up, staggering just a little perhaps through shock and the pulverising heat of that dressing-room.

"How is he?" I said.

"He'll be okay later," But Doc looked far worse than he did the night he came back from Waller's funeral.

"How about you?"

"I'll manage. He tried far too much too early."

"I know," I said.

"If he'd only kept doing what he was doing he was bound to win it."

"Definitely," I said. "He had the other man stopped all along the line. Then he hit him those two punches downstairs and proved it to him."

"Even that punch that toppled him, that was nothing. The guy threw it out of sheer desperation. He shook that off, but why does that have to happen to his eyes? He couldn't focus and, what's more, he still can't."

"It had to happen," I said, "because it's the only way you could lose. Don't ask me why you had to lose, but you did."

"I reckon we did."

"The tragedy is that we all lost, Doc, including that champion who, right now, is being feted and told yet again that he's a great champion. For a second there Teddy made him an honest man, but now he'll believe this bullshit because honest winners are so few. Everybody in this place lost tonight, Doc, but they don't know it."

I have just said it all, I was thinking. I.......

"What's the use of talking about it?" Doc said. "I want to get back to him."

Doc pushed through and sat down next to Teddy again. Reporters were clustered in front of him, the two in front on their knees, the photographers taking turns up on the rubbing-table and shooting their pictures over the heads of the reporters.

"He still can't focus," Doctor Kaplin was saying, standing amid the reporters. "We call it past-pointing, but he should come out of it."

"But he doesn't know where he is," one of the reporters kneeling in front said, looking back over his shoulder at the doctor. It was Ernie Jarvis.

"Let me get in there," the doctor said.

The two in front shifted apart and the doctor knelt down between them and directly in front of Teddy.

"Teddy?" he said. "Look at me."

"Whassat?" Teddy said.

He raised his head and stared with those blank eyes clean through the doctor. His hair was wet and so was his face, a red welt beside the left eye and there was moisture on his body.

"Teddy?" the doctor said. "Who am I?"

It was quiet now in the room, just the flashing of photographers' bulbs

"Huh?"

"We can't hear at the back!" somebody shouted

"Quiet!" somebody else said.

"You know me, Teddy. Who am I?"

"Nat," Teddy said, staring through the doctor. Then he dropped his head again.

"Nat?" Ernie Jarvis said. "Nat who?"

"Look at me, Teddy," the doctor said. "Who am I? I'm a doctor. You saw me today. Doctor who?"

"Eh?"

"He wants to stand up," the doctor said. "Let him stand up. He's alright, except for the eyes."

Teddy stood up slowly, Doc and Tim Holland supporting him. As he did the towel started slipping from his lap but, still staring ahead, he reached down and caught it.

"Teddy?" the doctor persisted.

Teddy turned slowly to his left. Tim Holland backed away and Teddy, staring, placed the towel carefully against he side of the end locker as if he were hanging it up, and then let it go. It dropped to the floor, but he didn't see it and he turned back slowly and they helped him to sit down again.

"You see he can't focus," the doctor said, still kneeling. "This happens sometimes; I've seen it once or twice before. That's why he walked the way he did when he got up the first time.

"Look, Teddy," the doctor went on. "Where are you? Do you know where you are?"

"Got to go," Teddy said, starting to get up.

"No, stay there," the doctor ordered, and Doc and Tim steadied Teddy. "Where are you?"

"Got to go."

262

"Go. Go where? Go where, Teddy?"

"Go? Go to Olympia. Fight."

"You have to go to Olympia, Teddy? Where are you now?"

"Time," Teddy said and then he pointed, staring. He pointed over the heads of those both kneeling and standing. He pointed with his right arm, his hand wavering a little. As he did we all turned in that hot, silent room and looked where he was pointing, high on the opposite wall. There was nothing on the well; it was bare.

I think it was then that I fully realised that, in truth, he was no longer with us. He did not answer when the doctor spoke to him again or show any reaction when they laid him on the rubbing-table with a blanket drawn across his chest. And now his hands were tightly clasped to his forehead and his face had, for me, a deathly pallor about it. Teddy was in a state of collapse.

Somehow there was an air of gloom pervading the whole atmosphere of that dressing-room. The door opened and two ambulance men came in bearing a stretcher. Somehow I couldn't credit what I had just witnessed, though I sensed that there was little hope for poor Teddy Baker.

There was no reason for me to return to ringside but, as I was leaving the arena, I phoned Charing Cross Hospital to which Teddy had been taken, his only companion being Doc, all others like myself being barred 'for the time being'. Naturally, it was far too soon for them to be able to give any information. I should have known that, but I think I hoped that having me enquire after him might in some way aid the stricken boxer.

Next day, with Doc almost out of his mind with worry, two delicate brain operations were performed in an attempt to save Teddy Baker's life, but to no avail. Teddy died thirty-six hours later.

THE END